M000205970

BEYOND
ALL PRICE

Carolyn Poling Schriber

For Nellie, whose life still inspires.

His life was saved by one of those angels of mercy, a volunteer army nurse. He fell into good hands—the blessed hands of a kind-hearted woman! Even here, amid the roar and carnage, was found a woman with the soul to dare danger; the heart to sympathize with the battle-stricken; sense, skill, and experience to make her a treasure beyond all price."

—Frank Moore
Women of the War: Their Heroism and Self-Sacrifice

Roundheads Regimental Headquarters
Beaufort, South Carolina
March, 1862

(left to right): Reverend Robert Audley Brown, Private John Stevenson, Nellie M. Chase (seated), "Uncle Bob," Colonel Daniel Leasure, Doctor Horace Ludington

Photo courtesy of USAMHI

Copyright © 2010 Carolyn Poling Schriber
All Rights Reserved.

Published by Katzenhaus Books
P. O. Box 1629
Cordova, Tennessee 38088

Cover image: Cumberland River at
Fort Donelson, TN
Photo credit: Floyd A. Schriber

ISBN: 0982774508
ISBN-13: 9780982774502

Library of Congress Control Number: 2010929638

I

OLD ACQUAINTANCES

"Colonel Leasure, Sir?"

"Yes, Private, what is it?"

"There's a lady to see you, Sir."

"A lady? Here? To see me? Are you sure you understood correctly?"

"Yes, Sir, I did," Private Stevenson insisted. "She's out at the gate and says she won't talk to anyone but you."

"Good God! It's not my mother, is it, John?" asked Geordy, the colonel's son, who had been laboring diligently over a stack of papers.

"Geordy, you know your mother wouldn't come here," the colonel said.

"No, Sir, it's a young lady. Oh, I didn't mean that your wife isn't young. I mean, ah. . . ." The private blushed and stammered for words.

"It's all right, Private. I understand what you meant. Did she give you any idea of what she wanted? Does she look slatternly? Or is she refined and ladylike?"

"I'm not really sure, Sir. She doesn't look like a lady of the streets, if that's what you mean, but she's awfully forward and determined."

"She asked for me by name, did she?"

"Yes, Sir. And she referred to you as the commander of the Roundheads."

"Humph. That's odd. Secretary Cameron only blessed our regiment with that nickname a couple of days ago. Wonder where she heard of it?"

"Well, Sir, she may have picked it up here. She was asking some of the boys who the best-behaved soldiers were."

"I suppose there's nothing for it but to see her. Tell her I'll be right out. But don't let her into the camp. Right now we don't need extra females wandering through this maze of huts and tents." He glanced with some distaste at another regimental encampment across the dusty road, where whole families were settling into tents. Wives and children had accompanied their newly-enlisted men folk, and the camp was overrun with the clutter of trunks, pots, and all the accouterments of family life. War isn't a game, Daniel Leasure wanted to tell them, and men surrounded by their loved ones will never make the kind of soldiers we need.

Daniel Leasure stood from his makeshift desk, his hands moving automatically to the small of his back as he stretched his cramped muscles. He had spent many an hour drilling with his local militia units and considered himself in good condition. But the paperwork demanded by this new Union Army had kept him confined in his tent all morning, and he was more than ready for a stretch. The heat, too was beginning to bother him. Granted, it was late August, but back home in the hills of western Pennsylvania, even this much heat would have been tempered by breezes and leafy shade. Here in Pittsburgh, the natural vegetation had been leveled, and the dirt and smoke from the city seemed to hover above the ground in a miasmal cloud. It didn't help, either, that this so-called Camp Wilkins had been established on the Allegheny County Fairgrounds, and all the odors and mess of a dozen livestock fairs permeated the wooden structures and the ground on which they camped.

He shook his head at his own sense of discouragement, something he did not want his men to see. At least, I have my own tent, he thought to himself. Those poor farm boys who have followed me here may be used to barns, but I'll bet few of them ever had to bed down in a communal pigsty before this week.

"Geordy, while I deal with this woman, whoever she is, would you take these muster lists around to the various companies of the regiment and make sure they are complete and accurate? Heaven only knows when the army will be paid, but we need to be sure the records are accurate before we go marching off to some God-forsaken Confederate battlefield."

"Yes, Father, . . . uh, Sir." Geordy Leasure was barely out of adolescence and was trying hard to maintain his military demeanor. When his father had first announced he was going to respond to Lincoln's call to arms, Geordy had begged to go along. Despite his mother's tearful protests, his pleas and his father's encouragement had won the day. He had enlisted for a ninety-day term and happily served as a private in the Twelfth Pennsylvania Regiment, although that regiment had never seen any action, nor had they ever fired a shot. This three-year enlistment, however, promised to be a much more dangerous one, and he had been allowed to re-enlist on the understanding he would act as his father's aide-de-camp and would be kept out of harm's way. Geordy correctly assumed he was here only on a probationary basis. This was his testing time—the chance to prove he was a responsible adult. Any lapse on his part would have his father sending him scuttling back to New Castle and the family farm.

The young woman waited for Colonel Leasure outside the hastily-erected picket fence surrounding Camp Wilkins. She was tiny, dressed in a simple dark dress of bombazine and a bonnet that shaded her features. But her erect posture, chin lifted and eyes raised to stare straight at the scene before her, made it clear she was neither demure nor humble. Even as the colonel returned her stare and recognized her obvious youth, he was aware she was a formidable personality.

"Madam, I am Colonel Daniel Leasure of the Roundhead Regiment, at your service, M'am."

"Good morning," she nodded with a miniscule lifting of the corners of her mouth that might have passed for a smile. "I am Nellie Leath. Mrs. Leath," she said. "I have come to serve as your matron."

"Ahhhh, I see. And what, exactly, is a matron?"

"It is my understanding, Sir, that each military regiment is to be accompanied by a skilled woman who can handle the housekeeping chores, so to speak. A matron, as I interpret the term, oversees meals, supplies, and minor medical needs for the soldiers."

"Oh, I see. And you have been sent by the Sanitary Commission, I presume."

"Not exactly." Now the young woman laughed openly. "You really don't remember me, do you?"

"You have me at a disadvantage, M'am. Have we met before?"

"Oh, yes. At York, last June?" She raised an inquiring eyebrow at him, but he still appeared confused. "You were the adjutant with the Twelfth Regiment, and I was a volunteer nurse, assigned to assist Doctor Speer and his small group of surgeons. There wasn't much need for battlefield services. I spent most of my time helping the women of York who had taken in our soldiers as boarders. You came to York one day to visit some of your men who had fallen ill. I was helping care for two of the most serious cases, Corporal Robert Gibson and Sergeant James Miller. You remember them, I assume."

"Yes, of course. I found their eventual deaths most upsetting because I had helped to recruit them. And I do remember a young nurse being particularly helpful. But your name doesn't sound familiar."

"I was using my maiden name then—Nellie Chase."

"Ah, yes, I do remember that name. There was a fuss over you, as I recall. Something about you being related to Lincoln's new Secretary of the Treasury, Salmon P. Chase?"

Nellie winced. "We are only distantly related, if at all. I assure you I have never met the man, and he has never even heard of me. Still, people assumed I had gotten my position with the regiment through some sort of nepotism, while I wanted to be judged on my own merits. That's why I started using my married name, instead. I'm sorry if that confused you."

"I still don't know how you come to be here. Who sent you?"

"No one. I come as a volunteer. I remembered you clearly from York. You impressed me with your kindness, your concern for your men, and your medical knowledge. When I heard you were recruiting a new regiment, to be composed of sincere, God-fearing, and highly moral young men, I sought you out. I want to continue to help in the war effort, and you would seem to be in need of a woman such as I."

Just then, a commotion broke out behind them as two sopping wet young recruits came running for the camp, arms flailing. "Ow, ow, oh, ouch, ow," they yelled. As they neared the colonel, he could see that their faces, red and tear-stained, were covered with angry-looking blotches. Their bare arms, too, were mottled and marked with welts.

"Whoa," said the colonel. "What company are you in? And what in the devil's name have you boys gotten yourselves into?"

"Bees, Sir," said Billy Simpson, the taller of the two. "We're in Company H, from Lawrence County. Zeb here saw some bees leaving that old hay barn down the road. They were a'comin' out from behind a loose board, and he pulled on it, hoping to find him some honeycomb. But there was a whole swarm of them and they attacked. We got away by jumping in the cow pond, but not before they took their revenge."

"We've been stung a hundred times, I know," said Zeb Elliot. "Ow, ow, ow. Sorry, but it burns like fire, Sir."

"How are you going to be a soldier and stand up to battle, if you can't even endure a small dispute with bees?" the colonel asked.

"Well, I would hope the rebels don't come with stingers, Sir."

"Be that as it may, you must learn self-discipline, soldier."

"Excuse me," Nellie interrupted. "Do either of you have some tobacco? If so, may I have it?"

"I had a stogie in my pocket a while back, but I expect it's pretty soggy by now." Billy pulled a dripping cigar from his pocket and held it at arm's length, "Uh, you surely wouldn't want this, M'am."

"Yes, indeed. That's exactly what I need. Hold still, now." She took the cigar from him and began to pull the wet leaves apart, tearing the tobacco into inch-long pieces. Carefully she layered the patches onto the welts left by the bee stings.

"Ouch," the men protested as she worked. "It hurts when you touch them."

"I know. But wait a few minutes. Let me try this." When she finished, she stepped back and allowed a faint smile to move beyond her lips to light up her eyes. "How do you feel now?"

"Ow! Ah—aahhh. It's gone!"

"You're right. They don't sting anymore. How'd you do that?"

"Yes, Mrs. Leath." Colonel Leasure raised an inquiring eyebrow. "How did you know to do that?"

"That's what a matron does, Sir." Nellie suppressed a laugh and resumed her serious demeanor. "To answer your question, Granny Merrill— my grandmother—lived with us when I was growing up. She was known as something of a wise woman and treated the minor ills and injuries of the neighboring families. She taught me some of her secret remedies. Wet tobacco for insect bites was one of them."

"You know, in civilian life, I am a trained doctor," the colonel told her. "I might have prescribed a paste of baking soda, but tobacco would never have entered my mind. I am impressed."

"We all have our little stores of useful knowledge, I suppose. Zeb, Billy, leave those patches on until they dry and fall off. You should be fine. And the next time you want to satisfy your sweet tooth, here's another use for that stogie. Light it and let the smoke penetrate the crack where you think the bees are. It will make the bees sleepy, and you'll be able to help yourself to a chuck of comb without risking another disaster."

"Yes, M'am," they said.

By now a smattering of curiosity-seekers had begun to assemble around the gateway, watching to see what the mutton-chopped colonel was going to do about the young woman who had solved a problem for him. Murmurs and suppressed snickers passed through the crowd. From somewhere near the back, a soft whistle revealed what the onlookers suspected. Reluctant to put on a further show, Colonel Leasure bowed slightly, and offered his arm. "Well, come with me to our headquarters, and we can discuss this further."

The two picked their way through a mass of soldiers, some cooking over an improvised fire. others pounding tent stakes or practicing their drills in the dust. As they passed, every eye watched them. The homesick soldiers saw Mrs. Leath as mother or sister, or neighbor; the more worldly-wise had other notions. But all were struck by the self-assured figure of this lone woman in a campground full of men.

As they walked, the colonel's eyes remained slightly downcast as he picked their way around the inevitable obstacles of a makeshift military camp. This also allowed him to keep his surroundings slightly out of focus, so he did not have to see the curious stares or leering grins of the men who watched their progress. Nellie, however, was openly fascinated. She noted everything as they passed, as if she were keeping a mental inventory. Her eyes twinkled when she noticed a chicken sizzling on a stick over an open fire, while four obviously guilty soldiers pretended to be interested in everything around them except for the purloined fowl. She reacted with a sympathetic smile to a miserable young man who sat staring at a much-creased picture. She noted with interest the men who were reading or writing in their journals. And occasionally she wilted a forward young stud by sneering at his wiggling eyebrows. Nellie recognized and categorized them all as they passed. By the time she and the colonel reached the command tent, she may have known the regiment more intimately than he did.

"Private, I need to interview this lady. Stand by the tent flap and see to it we are not disturbed."

"Yes, Colonel. But what if. . . ?"

"Use your judgment, soldier. Don't interrupt us for an enlistee's petty problems. If a general appears or the war breaks out here in camp, let me know."

"Yes, Sir." Private Stevenson grinned.

"Now, then, Mrs. Leath." Colonel Leasure nodded toward a camp stool. "Please sit down and tell me a bit more about yourself. You are a widow, I presume."

Nellie glanced down at the black bombazine gown she wore and caught her lower lip between her teeth. "Not exactly. My husband and I are separated, and I have found it safer to pass as a widow than to be seen as simply an unattached female. The tenement where I've been living is a bit rough."

"So you deliberately set out to purchase a disguise that would mislead people? I fear these are not the actions of the type of person I want in this regiment." The colonel stood and moved toward the entrance, ready to usher her out of the tent.

"Please, wait. Let me explain." Nellie looked so stricken that despite his best instincts, Colonel Leasure returned to the table.

"First, I didn't go out and purchase the dress. I am a seamstress by trade. I was making this set of widow's weeds for a customer who believed her husband was at death's door. Unfortunately, she died before he did, leaving me with an unpaid-for but perfectly serviceable gown. I could not afford not to put it to good use. As for my marital status, I'm not sure you would want to hear the whole sordid story."

"Oh, but I must. I am not accustomed to making decisions before I am in full possession of the facts. Continue, please."

Nellie sighed and tilted her head back to stare at the ceiling for a moment. She was obviously struggling with her emotions. "I eloped. The young man was a glorious musician who came to my hometown in Maine for a concert series. He could make his horn laugh and cry, and he beguiled every audience. He was handsome and charming, and I was angry with my father and my whole family, for that matter. I have four brothers, two older and two younger. Sometimes it was hard being the only girl. When my handsome musician asked me to run away with him to his home in Bangor, I never hesitated. Certainly I was too young and stupid to think of the consequences. I was imagining a whole new family, wedding vows, and a cottage with a white picket fence.

"That fantasy didn't last long. He took me with him to his home town, but there was no family home there, only a sister who refused him entrance into her residence. He lived in a boarding house, where the landlady had no room for me. He provided for my keep by finding me a position as a seamstress in a wealthy family's home. Otis informed me he didn't believe in church services, but we didn't need a wedding anyway because we were already . . . I think the term he used was 'hand-fasted'. He said I could call myself Mrs. Leath if I chose, but I shouldn't expect him to make a public spectacle of himself or our relationship."

"I've heard of hand-fasting, but I thought the custom died out many years ago," the colonel offered. "You could have returned home, couldn't you?"

"No. My father would never have forgiven me. Oh, he would have taken me back in—good Christian man that he pretends to be. But I would have been a virtual prisoner. I would never have been able to escape from him again. And I needed to be far away from him before he. . . ."

The colonel frowned. It was obvious there was more to the story, but he hesitated to probe more deeply into what was clearly a festering wound. Instead he simply waited for the young woman to regain control and continue.

Nellie swallowed hard and blinked to dispel the unwelcome tears that threatened. "There was more. I soon learned that while my so-called husband made a bit of a living by playing his horn in saloons, his real purpose was to break into the card games that went on there. He was a drunkard and a gambler who cheated every time he could get away with it. When he lost at poker or faro, as he invariably did, he settled his debts by stealing something or passing off a forged deed to a piece of property. We were soon on the run, leaving one town after another, often in the middle of the night and almost always a few steps ahead of the local sheriff."

"Which is how you got to Pittsburgh?"

"Yes, eventually. We arrived last winter. But by then I had pulled myself together and decided to take charge of my life. I didn't want to go hand-in-hand to prison with Otis, even if he did claim we were 'hand-fasted'. I took the advice of a kindly woman who befriended me for a few weeks while we were still in Bangor. She had hired me to work in her tavern in exchange for a small room upstairs. She saw my husband come home drunk night after night and warned me I needed to find a way to support myself."

"And you did that, how?"

Nellie smiled ruefully. "Well, my stint as a seamstress had given me some valuable experience. All I lacked were the tools with which to ply my trade. I began taking small amounts of money out of Otis's pockets when he came home drunk. He never noticed because he never remembered how much he had."

"So, you are a thief, too!"

"No. No. I told myself it was simply a housekeeping allowance, one I was entitled to, even if I was only an ersatz wife. I used the money to put a small down payment on a sewing machine and set myself up as a dressmaker."

"Wait. A payment on a what?"

"Have you not seen the new sewing machine? I suppose not. A gentleman such as yourself would not need such a device. Oh, but they are wonderful time-savers. Not only can I now make a dress in a matter of hours rather than days, the manufacturer allowed me to pay a small amount every week rather than the entire $50.00 at once. I could use the machine to make the money I needed to pay for it."

Nellie's face had brightened with enthusiasm as she spoke, but the smile soon faded. "Besides, my hateful husband didn't care what I was doing, so long as I met his needs and didn't pester him about mine. When he was ready to move on, I made a daring suggestion. I had taken a position as wardrobe mistress for a local theater, and I convinced him it would be better if I stayed here in Pittsburgh and saved some money while he went on to the next town."

"Thus the separation."

"You know, I don't think I would have put it in those terms when he first left. I planned to rejoin him eventually, although the time away from him came as a relief. I did have to move into a small room in a tenement down by the river, and I was often afraid in that neighborhood. But I was also learning to stand on my feet and growing a backbone, perhaps."

Colonel Leasure gave her an appraising look. "A strong one at that," he thought to himself, observing her comfortable but erect posture.

"Then, when Colonel Campbell started to recruit men for the Twelfth Regiment back in April, I saw a chance to escape my past and serve my country at the same time. I asked him to take me on as a nurse for a three-month enlistment, and he agreed. It was a period of learning and renewal for me, and I was sorry to see the regiment disbanded. I returned to Pittsburgh with regret, particularly when Otis immediately learned of my whereabouts and tried to renew our relationship.

"I received a letter from my so-called husband, ordering me to join him at once in Cincinnati. He has purchased some property after a fortuitous winning streak at the gambling tables and is busy turning the house into a brothel. He said it was a sure money-maker because of all the lonely young soldiers who passed through that town. He wanted me there with him to serve as the the madame of the establishment." Nellie blushed and rose to her feet to cover her embarrassment.

"Oh." The colonel had no idea how to respond.

"I didn't even consider going, of course. I wrote him a scathing letter, telling him my position in life had been in decline ever since I met him, but I would not allow him to drag me down any further. I reminded him we were not legally married and told him never to contact me again." She was pacing, now, in her agitation. "I couldn't believe his attitude. In the face of this terrible war, he was so shallow that all he could think of was a way to make money from it!"

She turned and faced the colonel. "That's why I'm here. I would like to be the kind of woman who keeps the home fires burning for her patriot husband. But since he is such a greedy coward, I must assume his responsibilities. Perhaps by accompanying your regiment, I can somehow atone for his failings." It was a noble speech, but one that sounded terribly rehearsed, even to Nellie.

"I still don't know how you found the Roundheads," the colonel said. "My regiment is newly formed and not even christened with an official number."

"A customer mentioned it to me. I delivered a dress I was making to a Miss Witherow and found her all a-twitter over a visit from a distant cousin. His name was Robert something. Moffatt, maybe? In any event, he had arrived in Pittsburgh and had been given a pass to visit his mother's relatives. He told the family all about his new regiment—how it was formed by Scotch-Irish Presbyterians who had settled in western Pennsylvania—and how they were nicknamed 'Roundheads' in honor of their ancestors who fought on the side of Cromwell during the English Civil War.

"Miss Witherow intended to return his visit today to bring him a hymn-book. I begged her to allow me to accompany her, although I didn't tell her why. It seemed to me a group of fighting men who claimed descent from the Covenanters would be decent, God-fearing souls, men with whom I could feel safe."

"Cromwell? Covenanters? Do you really know about such things, or are you trying to impress me?"

"You underestimate me, Sir. I am well-educated, I assure you, even if I have been exposed to the dregs of our society in recent times. I became a teacher after I finished school, although my family made mockery of my employment. My oldest brother, Isaac, used to grumble I would end up as a know-it-all spinster schoolmarm, relying on him and the rest of my family for support all my life. I ran away from home and my teaching position. Now I'm trying to find a new purpose for my life, one that will involve some other type of service to others. I'm hoping this war may offer such opportunities, if you allow me to accompany your troops."

"I can't pay you, you know. The army has no arrangements even to pay our soldiers. A woman volunteer will be unpaid help."

"I need only a place to sleep, a bit to eat, and a useful task that will help me regain my self-respect. I will not demand remuneration beyond that."

Colonel Leasure frowned with hesitation. "We don't know how soon we will be shipped out. Surely you would need time to settle your affairs."

Nellie shook her head. "I pay for my meager room by the night. The theater where I was once employed is closed for the season. The manager there helped me finish paying for my sewing machine, so technically it belongs to him and can be left there. My other belongings will fit into a small hand satchel. I can be ready to *ship out*, as you put it, by morning."

"Ah, but tomorrow is Sunday" Col. Leasure was still hesitant. "Surely you will want to attend your church services. I wouldn't want to think the Roundheads took on a matron who failed in her Christian duties."

"Do you intent to go to church tomorrow, Sir?"

"Certainly. Our boys are marching to the nearby Presbyterian Church for services."

"Then I will be here early to attend those services with them."

Colonel Leasure knew when he was beaten. "Thank you, Mrs. Leath. We will look forward to having you join us. Private Stevenson?" The speed with which the soldier responded left little doubt he had been eavesdropping. "Will you escort Mrs. Leath to wherever Robert Moffatt is entertaining his young cousin, so she can make her way home to fetch her belongings?"

Hardly had Nellie cleared the flap when Geordy burst into the tent. "Father," he exclaimed, forgetting his new military demeanor. "Did you invite that woman to join the regiment? Whatever will Mother say? What is she to do? I can't believe you really hired her."

"I did, Geordy. I am the commander of the regiment, as I recall. I hadn't planned on having a woman accompany us, but I think she'll prove to be invaluable."

"Yes, but where is she to stay?"

"That is your task, young Aide-de-Camp. Go see if you can round up an extra tent, and pitch it somewhere near here, so the staff officers can keep an eye on it. She'll need a cot, a camp stool, a writing desk of some sort, and a chamber pot, I suppose. We'll wait until she returns to determine her other needs. Come. Get on with it, Son."

"But, Father, she's awfully young."

"Yes, she is. But she has the oldest eyes I've ever seen."

2

THE OLD CAMP GROUNDS

Nellie examined the ties that were meant to fasten the flaps of her new tent, and then shook her head as she imagined the neat little bow she would create. Not much of a lock, she thought. But then I'm no longer living in a criminal-infested tenement, either.

She turned slowly and looked around. Lieutenant Geordy Leasure had done a commendable job of procuring her new military lodgings. Her wall tent was shaped much like a little house, with side walls about four feet high and topped with a sloping roof that rose to ten feet in the middle. Its floor dimensions of ten by twelve feet made it by far the largest room she had occupied since running away from her Maine farmhouse two years ago. On the floor, a thick layer of straw protected her skirts from the dirt beneath. Geordy had provided what looked like a sturdy cot, with a clean pillow and blanket. At its foot sat a small empty trunk, presumably for her meager belongings. Along the other wall, he had arranged a couple of packing boxes with boards laid across them to form a rudimentary table. A marvelous folding chair offered both a back and arms for her comfort, along with a camp stool for guests or patients. On the table itself were other items arranged for her use—two tin cups, a metal plate and folding eating utensils, a container with a hinged lid for transporting food from the officer's mess, and most welcome of all, a candlestick with extra candles and a box of matches.

Nellie swallowed hard. *This is home, now, my girl. Buck up and settle in.* She walked to the cot and stared down at it for several seconds, but somehow she could not bring herself to sit down on it. She reacted similarly when she approached the camp chair. Finally she perched on the little stool, feeling herself tensed and poised to flee. Something close to panic seemed to close her throat. *Dear Lord, what have I done? I have no medical training. I'm the only woman in this whole regiment, and I can't possibly deal with the duties expected of me. I should leave now,* she thought, *before anyone comes to depend on me. But I have nowhere else to go.*

She closed her eyes in despair, as images of the day she had spent swirled behind her lids—the officers in their uniforms, staring at her in disapproval; the young recruits with frank curiosity in their glances; the sea of tents that threatened to swamp the old fairgrounds; the smoke of dozens of campfires; the noise and bustle of supply wagons moving through the camp; the bark of someone calling cadence from the distant drill field; the smell of burning coffee mingling with the rancid odor of hundreds of unwashed bodies.

As she had approached Camp Wilkins that morning, she ran straight into Colonel Leasure, leading what appeared to be an entire army of men down the road. "Mrs. Leath. True to your word, I see. Come, we are headed to church."

The church in question was a small whitewashed building, with plain windows but a tall spire pointing to the sky. It was surrounded by a large cemetery and what appeared to be a picnic grounds. The pastor in his severe black suit and clerical collar came out onto the steps of the church to welcome this near invasion. Members of the congregation clustered behind him, craning their necks to see what was happening. Young women jostled each other to reach the front of the crowd and get a good look at this unexpected supply of eligible young men.

"Welcome to our fellowship," said Reverend William Sterling, stepping down to shake the colonel's hand. "I'm afraid we have only a small sanctuary, but we'll hold our service out here so all of your fine young soldiers may participate." Several men carried a sturdy picnic table to the foot of the church steps, and from its top, the pastor led a simple service of

Bible-reading and hymns. He preached a rousing sermon based on the story of the walls of Jericho that came tumbling down when the forces of righteousness approached them. The implications were not lost on the pious young Roundheads, and they cheered his efforts when he finished. Nellie, too, had been buoyed up by the enthusiasm and religious fervor of the crowd and felt herself smiling in a way she had not done for a long time.

Now, sitting alone in her tent, that feeling faded as her recollections drifted on to the meal she had been served in the officers' mess tent. The food had been plentiful but typical of army fare—beef stewed with dried vegetables, beans cooked in molasses, potatoes fried with onions, vats of coffee, and a cracker the soldiers called hardtack. Nellie recognized the hard little squares as the pilot crackers New England fishermen survived on at sea. But when she tried to explain the similarity, she realized no one really expected her to join the conversation. Cowed by their frowning reactions, she had withdrawn, nibbling at the tough beef and keeping her eyes on her plate.

After dinner, Colonel Leasure sent Private Stevenson to usher her around the camp and introduce her to the men. Her reception was less than welcoming. Doctor Ferdinand Gross, the regimental surgeon, was particularly hostile. He greeted her perfunctorily at the entrance to his tent and began to hurl questions at her. What did she know of medicine? Had she any training? No? Any experience? Not much! What did she expect to be able to do? Nellie stammered to answer his questions but could not get the words out before he hit her with another inquiry.

"Have you ever seen a gunshot wound?"

"Y-y-yes. My Uncle Henry shot himself in the foot one time with his hunting rifle, and Granny Merrill had to dig out the shots."

"I'm talking cannonballs, not buckshot! How will you manage on a battlefield?"

"I don't really know yet. When I served with the Twelfth Regiment, the men saw no action, but I hope. . . ."

"Hope! We'll need more than hope when the rebels are firing at us. And what about diseases? We'll have plenty of those to deal with."

"I helped nurse some soldiers who were seriously ill last spring, and I know how my grandmother cared for the members of our family."

"She didn't have to do that in a tent, I presume. And how many of those people she cared for with her home-brewed medicines actually survived?"

"Some did and some didn't."

"None did, I'll wager, if they had anything beyond a common fever or chills. Wait 'til you have to deal with smallpox or diphtheria."

"Granny once sucked the white membrane right out of the throat of a child with diphtheria, and the child survived," Nellie protested.

"Well, don't try that in my hospital! The men will think you are a forward hussy, and if you succeed, you'll only manage to catch the disease yourself. And then what good will you be to us? Can you cook?" he asked.

"Of course I can. I know what to feed invalids, and I can manage the supplies for your hospital, too. I'm not claiming to be an expert on medical care, but I sincerely want to help."

"Well, if I'm stuck with you, try to stay out of my way. If I think of something I need, I'll let you know. Until then, don't bother me. I have enough trouble without being saddled with an ignorant and silly woman." Nellie was mortified by his distain.

Her apprehension increased dramatically shortly after that exchange. As she and the private picked their way from one company to another, a scream from the area of Company F drew them toward the scene. A boy, scarcely old enough to be classified as a soldier, stood with eyes squeezed shut and mouth wide open in a shriek of agony. His companion, paralyzed with shock, was staring at the boy's hand, where it lay on an improvised chopping block next to a small hatchet. He had chopped off part of his left index finger as he held the board he had been cutting. The amputated finger had fallen to the ground. Its stump poured a spreading puddle of blood over the log.

As Nellie stared at the scene, it seemed to her time itself had screeched to a stop. No one moved. Automatically, she grasped the boy's arm and raised it above his head. Ignoring the blood that now ran down her arm as well, she turned to the onlookers. "Give me a clean kerchief," she demanded. When someone complied, she wadded it up to put direct pressure on the wound. Then she looked frantically around for help. "Someone go for Doctor Gross," she said.

While they waited, she spoke softly to the young man. "Don't fret. I know it hurts now, but the doctor will have some quinine to give you for the pain, and it's a clean cut. You're right-handed, aren't you?"

The boy snuffled and nodded.

"Then you'll hardly miss that finger. Be brave now. Here's the doctor coming. He'll have you stitched together in no time. And I'll stay with you as long as you need me."

He nodded again and seemed to relax a bit. Doctor Gross shoved his way through the crowd of onlookers to take charge. "What has happened here?" he asked, but the scene needed little explanation. Only belatedly did he seem to notice Nellie was the one holding the injured arm. "Ah, thank you, Mrs. Leath. I'll take him now."

As the doctor led the victim to a seat and worked at stretching the remaining skin over the stump of a finger, Nellie stayed at the fringe of the crowd. Now the crisis was over, she found she was shaking badly, something she did not want the boy to see. She glanced at her blood-covered hand and clenched it into a fist beneath the folds of her dress. How will I ever get used to this sort of thing? she wondered.

Now, as the sun began to set on her first day as a Roundhead nurse, Nellie found it even harder to swallow her fears. She had never liked evenings. That quiet hour when everything seemed touched with navy blue was a lonely time. She ought to be going home to someone, or something, but nothing awaited her. The fading light meant only another day was over, and chances were that somewhere in that day, she had failed to accomplish her goals. It was a time of regret, of disappointment, and now, of overwhelming fear. She hesitated by the doorway to her tent, reluctant to shut out the fading sounds of camp life, reluctant to lose the light from surrounding campfires.

"Mrs. Leath? Do you have a moment?" The voice out of the growing darkness startled her. Then the shadowy figure moved into the glow of firelight, and she recognized Doctor Gross.

"Oh! Yes, of course. Is something wrong? Is it the boy with the severed finger? Is he worse?" She realized her voice was rising in pitch and she was sounding more and more breathless, but she could not control her panic.

"No, no, nothing's wrong, and I didn't mean to frighten you." The doctor's eyes shifted in discomfort. "I felt I needed to stop by and apologize for my brusque behavior earlier today. I . . . I'm not used to this whole idea of female nurses."

"I understand, really. You don't need to apologize. I'm not used to the idea myself." Nellie grinned a bit despite her pounding heart. "And I seem to frighten easily tonight," she admitted. "How is the boy?"

"He's fine," Gross assured her. "He's feisty, too. Colonel Leasure offered him a free ride home, but he's refusing to leave. Says he's proud to be the first recruit wounded in the regiment. I've given him a warm drink mixed with quinine, and he's sleeping comfortably."

"I'm relieved."

"That's the other thing I came to tell you. You did a fine job this afternoon. Holding that wound above his heart saved him the loss of a great deal of blood."

"He can still be a soldier, then?"

"Yes, of course. As you seem to have reminded him, an injury to his left hand will not hinder him overmuch. All we'll have to do is guard against infection. Unfortunately, I don't have much at hand to accomplish that."

"Honey?"

"What? I beg your pardon!" The doctor stared at her, recoiling in astonishment and distaste.

"No, no. Oh, dear, I didn't mean—surely you didn't think—oh, my!" Nellie was struggling to keep her laughter contained. "I wasn't trying to be forward, Sir. I only meant a thin coat of honey spread over the wound often helps to seal it and keep infection at bay. At least that's what Granny used to tell me." She cocked an eyebrow at him, wondering if he would recognize her small attempt at sarcasm.

"Really? I'll look into that. Probably couldn't hurt."

"I've seen it work, Sir. And a couple of the men found a beehive yesterday. They could get a supply for you."

"Well, then, if we have come to some sort of rapprochement, I had better be getting back to my quarters. There's a lot to be done before we head out tomorrow."

"Tomorrow? So soon?" Nellie gasped. "No one told me. What do I need to do?"

"The word just came in by messenger. Colonel Leasure will announce it in the morning. We are to head for Washington, at the express orders of the Secretary of War. The train will be here tomorrow afternoon."

Nellie sat down abruptly. "No more chance to change my mind, then."

"I hope you weren't considering that." Doctor Gross frowned at her.

She sat for a moment, not even breathing. "I'm afraid." Her voice came out as a whisper.

The words, once spoken, seemed to reverberate around the tent. There was nothing further to be said. The fear was out there now—palpable and irretrievable. Nellie sat unmoving, staring at the floor. If I keep looking at the straw, nothing bad will happen, she told herself. Doctor Gross, too, seemed to be holding his breath as the minutes stretched between them.

"So am I, Mrs. Leath. So am I."

"You, Sir?"

"We are all afraid, Nellie," the doctor answered gently, not even aware he had slipped into a more informal form of address. "This is going to be a terrible war, and I wanted no part of it. If anyone other than Daniel Leasure had tried to recruit me, I would have refused. But I owe him a debt from my own days as a medical student. So here I am, ready to do my duty. But make no mistake, we face years of hardship. Many of the boys you see out there tonight will never come home. And there's no good outcome to be expected from a war within a family."

"A family?"

"Yes, that's what we are. you know, in this young country. Think of it. Less than one hundred years ago, we were united against a common enemy.

We were claiming our share of the land from the native Indian tribes, and we were establishing our independence from the tyranny of the English king. And now, when we have gained all we sought, we are determined to take what we have built together and split it in half. The fabric from which this country was made is being torn asunder, and there's no way to undo that split. Oh, we may stitch it back together in time, but the seam will always show." Doctor Gross stopped pacing, and shook his head. "Forgive me for leaping onto my soapbox. I'm sure you don't need more of a lecture tonight."

"Are you saying we shouldn't be going off to war?"

"No, I'm not saying that. The war is here, whether we like it or not, and we need to see it through. All I really meant to say is you are right to be frightened. We all should be. And we are. But bravery consists, not in the absence of fear, but in doing what you must despite your fears. You're going to make a fine nurse. I saw that kind of bravery in you this afternoon."

Doctor Gross started to leave and then turned back at the doorway. "I was wondering, Mrs. Leath. Do you keep a journal?"

"What? You mean, like a diary?"

"Something like that. There's a trick we picked up in medical studies. You fix up a little notebook that you can carry with you. Then when you come face to face with a new disease or treatment, you jot it down on the spot. It's a great little memory aid. It also provides a place where you can face your fears head-on."

"Does the sutler have something I could use, do you think?"

"I can suggest a better idea. When I get back to my quarters, I'll send an orderly back with a notebook you can use. "My wife gave me a journal when I left to enlist. So did my mother, and an aunt, and a dear little neighbor lady. Each one wanted to make sure I'd write down my experiences. But I'm not much of a writer any more, and I definitely don't need four of them."

"Oh, Sir. Thank you. I'll use it carefully and well."

Nellie watched as the doctor walked toward to the medical tent. "Thank you," she whispered again to his retreating back. Then she drew a deep breath and looked around her tent with a new sense of belonging. In a few minutes, someone cleared his throat outside her tent, and Nellie turned to find an orderly bearing a cloth-wrapped package.

"Doctor Gross said this was for you," he said, thrusting it at her and hurrying away.

"Thank you!" she called after him and then eagerly returned to the makeshift table to unwrap her gift. She found a handsome leather-bound volume of lined pages and a small bundle of sharpened pencils. She caught her breath in surprise. I wasn't expecting anything so elegant, she thought. I will have to choose my words carefully to make them worthy of such a volume. Nellie pulled up her camp chair and settled herself at the table. Slowly and thoughtfully she entered the day's date. and began to write. Almost without realizing it, she filled the first page. Then she blew out her flickering candle, and lay down, surrendering to a deep and untroubled sleep.

3

SEND THEM FORTH

Monday was such a chaotic day that Nellie found she could remember it only in scraps and snippets. She had been in the Officers' Mess, hunting for morning coffee when Colonel Leasure entered.

"Settled in, Mrs. Leath?" he asked.

"I think so. At least I'm catching on to how the camp is organized."

"Well, mustn't get too used to it. We break camp in a matter of hours. Has someone notified you?"

"Doctor Gross mentioned we were headed for Washington, but I don't know the particulars."

"I'll send Private Stevenson to stencil your name on your belongings and see to it your things get stowed. You'll need to pack everything you won't need on the train into your wooden trunk, and make sure your haversack is well-stocked."

"My what? I'm sorry, Sir, but I'm awfully new at this. I don't think I even have a hav . . . haver . . .whatever it is."

Leasure shook his head in evident impatience. "Private Stevenson will straighten you out. I haven't time right now." And he walked off in what appeared to Nellie to be high dander. She had wanted to ask about when they were leaving and how they would travel, but common sense told her this was not the time.

Sometime later, the earnest young private appeared, paint bucket and brush in hand, and began labeling everything in her tent. "After Geordy went to all that trouble to find you nice furnishings, can't have them disappearing on you," he explained.

"Please, Private, can you tell me what's happening? I know everyone in camp is bustling around moving things, but I haven't the faintest idea of what I should be doing."

"Sorry, M'am. We do sometimes forget we need to make special accommodations for you."

"I don't want to be treated as *special*, Private. I want to be clear about my own responsibilities."

"Why don't you start by calling me John," he said. "I'm not used to this military formality myself."

"All right, John. Now, when exactly do we leave, how are we traveling, and what do I need to take with me? Colonel Leasure mentioned something about a well-stocked sack of some sort, but I have no idea what he was talking about."

John crouched comfortably into a seated pose that Nellie associated in her mind with Indians around a fire. He began to tick off items on his fingers. "The Roundhead Regiment has received orders direct from Secretary Stanton, sending us to Washington. We will march out this afternoon to the railroad station, where they are preparing special cars to carry us to Harrisburg. We depart whenever we can get all our men—begging your pardon, M'am—and woman, onto the train, and all our baggage loaded into the supply cars. The trip will take a day or two, depending on the condition of the track and the vagaries of fate."

"Is it dangerous, then?" she asked.

"No more than trains ever are. Have you ridden one before?"

"Oh, no. I've usually traveled by wagon or on foot, with an occasional stage coach ride. I can't even imagine a train."

"Well, visualize a large stage coach, with rows of wooden seats instead of two facing benches. The car has windows, but if you open them, the air fills with smoke and soot from the steam engine. There are lamps, and a small stove for winter heating, and a water barrel, although it's best to carry your own water. The stuff in the barrel usually has a film over it—black if it's nothing but coal dust, green if it's been there a while.

"We'll stop several times, to restock the engine with coal and water, for privy breaks, and maybe, if we're lucky, for a meal or two. We have to change trains in Harrisburg, and then again in Baltimore, because not all railroad tracks are the same width. It's a noisy, dirty, and jostling way to travel, but it'll get us there as fast as humanly possible. There's no need to worry. You'll not be the only one with no experience. Some of these boys had their first ride on a train coming from New Castle to Pittsburgh. You should have seen some of their faces! You'd have thought they were afraid the lines might break, the horses run off, or some other awful strange thing happen to the big wagon with little wheels.

"As for what you'll need, don't carry anything you can do without. Your blanket, pillow, candles and other stuff go in the trunk here. You will need eating utensils, and they go in your haversack."

"That's the word the colonel mentioned, but I certainly don't have one."

"I'll take care of that. You get started packing your trunk, and I'll be back shortly.

True to his word, Private Stevenson returned carrying something Nellie recognized from the farm. At least it looked like the canvas feed bags they had used to feed their horses. "That's a haversack?" she asked. "Do I wear it around my neck?"

"Better over your shoulder, I think. It's really a useful item when we're on the march. It's waterproof and roomy. You can attach your canteen and cup here on the buckle, see? And inside, you put your plate and eating utensils, your food supply, your housewife, your. . . ."

"My housewife?" she interrupted.

John laughed. "It's like a sewing kit, M'am, only more useful, and I picked one up for you at the supply tent. Now let's walk over to the mess, and we'll get your food sorted out."

Nellie looked at the haversack dubiously, still envisioning it as a feed bag from which she would be expected to munch her way through whatever she was given to eat. The supplies the mess sergeant handed her, in fact, did not look much better than the oats she had fed Ole Patch at home. They included the inevitable hardtack, a chunk of salt pork wrapped in greasy paper, some dried vegetables that looked exactly like hay, and linen bags of sugar and coffee. She choked out a "Thank you," because the soldier handing out supplies was surely not responsible for their quality, but she stared into the bag with a stricken expression.

"Don't worry, Mrs. Leath. When we stop for victuals, there'll be kettles and cook fires. You'll put your bits with the others and have a stew cooked up in no time. The great virtue of army cooking is that by the time food is ready, you'll be so hungry it will taste wonderful."

Nellie doubted that, but she nodded gamely.

And so the day went. Tents came down, and heavy wagons trundled by loaded with trunks like Nellie's, each with a company letter and a number on it to identify its owner. Soldiers hustled from supply tent to mess tent, some even making a quick trip into town to mail a letter or have a picture taken. Hastily-rinsed laundry hung from fence posts, drying in the hot August sun. Everywhere there was an air of excitement, hopeful expectation, and nervous apprehension about what lay ahead. A high point in the day came with the arrival of Private Moffatt's father and uncle, driving a wagon loaded with fresh apples. They had come all the way from Beaver County to see the boys off, and to leave with them a final taste of home. Someone passed a couple of apples to Nellie, and she dropped them gratefully into her haversack. Maybe she wouldn't starve after all.

The train trip was every bit as tedious as Private Stevenson had predicted. They departed from Pittsburgh at 4:00 p.m. and spent a long night traveling through the mountains of Pennsylvania. The route wound its way up and down the steeper hills with disorienting switchbacks. One minute the train was headed east; the next, the setting sun blazed into the passengers' eyes. Sometimes the tracks themselves seemed to be perched on the lip of a cliff. After looking out the window once and seeing nothing below her, Nellie kept her gaze resolutely on the interior of the railroad car. But the view there was not particularly edifying, either. The soldiers lolled on the hard seats, trying an amazing variety of postures to make themselves comfortable. Legs dangled into the aisle and arms all akimbo looped themselves around any available support when the train gave a particularly heavy jolt. As darkness fell, heads began to droop, chins planted firmly on chests.

Other heads fell backward, which had the effect of letting their mouths fall open in a disgusting display of bad teeth and worse breath. Snores and snorts echoed through the car.

Nellie was sure she would never sleep under such conditions, but the rhythmic click of the wheels eventually lulled her into an uneasy slumber. Several times she was jolted awake by some rough patch in the tracks that caused the car to sway. Morning found everyone stiff and cranky. The train stopped to take on coal and water around 7 a.m. and the soldiers crawled down from the cars to stretch and brew a quick pot of coffee. The hot drink perked up most of the passengers, although there were those who stomped around swearing they would never again ride one of these iron horses. Nellie sipped her coffee and tried to be optimistic.

The Roundheads arrived in Harrisburg in mid-morning and, as if they were on some leisurely tourist jaunt, were given tours of the State House. Nellie hoped the governor would come out to see them, but she realized that as a group, this new regiment was not much to look at. The three-hour layover also gave those with a bit of money a chance to visit the local eateries, where they were able to purchase a real cooked lunch. The respite was all the more appreciated when the soldiers embarked on the next part of their journey.

The train they boarded in Harrisburg had been cobbled together from whatever railroad stock was empty and available. Unfortunately, this turned out to be a series of boxcars. Some welcomed the chance to sit on the floor and spread out a bit, rather than clinging to a narrow bench. Anyone who took a close look at the floor, however, might have been unwilling to sit upon it. It appeared the boxcars had last been used as pig transport, and they been cleaned only casually. Adding to the discomfort was the accompanying odor. Leaving the doors wide open allowed the breeze to clear out the worst of the fetid air, but it soon began to rain, causing those closest to the open doors to be drenched with back spray from the wheels.

The twelve-hour trip from Harrisburg to Baltimore, was a replay of the previous night. Most slept as soon as darkness fell, and once again the box cars echoed with the assorted sounds of snores, interspersed with groans and muffled exclamations as each tried to find some comfortable spot. Around midnight, Captain David Leckey, commander of Company M, made his way from car to car, waking everyone to more daunting news.

"Men, you need to be prepared for possible unpleasantness once we reach Baltimore," he warned.

"You mean more trouble like the riots that them Michiganders faced?" someone called out.

"Well, we hope it won't be that serious."

"What kind of trouble was that?" someone else asked.

Nellie listened with mounting horror as the story unfolded. "Here's what we know," Captain Leckey began. "Maryland is a border state. They have not seceded, but neither have they supported the Union cause. There are a lot of slave-owners in Baltimore, and they naturally lean toward the side of the South. President Lincoln is worried those who support slavery might try to block the rail lines bringing troops to Washington."

"Well, why didn't we go some other way?" asked another disembodied voice in the darkness.

"I'm afraid there isn't any other rail line. Worse, this track ends on one side of Baltimore, and the line that will take us to Washington is on the other side of town. There's nothing else for it. We will have to disembark and walk through the town."

"What happened to them boys from Michigan?"

"The incident that occurred back in April involved the Sixth Michigan Regiment. Baltimore is pretty much run by renegade firefighter gangs, and one of those gangs, called the 'Plug-Uglies' for reasons you can easily figure out, decided to object when Lincoln sent troops to Baltimore to protect the soldiers who were passing through. Shots were fired on both sides. Before the violence was over, twelve citizens of Baltimore had been killed, along with four members of Michigan's regimental band."

"Damnation!" huffed John Nicklin, who had enlisted as the drum major of the Roundheads. "Why would anyone shoot at a musician? Was their playing that bad?"

"It shouldn't happen again, but there is a rumor a hostile crowd has gathered around the station waiting for our arrival. The engineer is slowing the train, and we'll try to wait them out. We're hoping they'll get tired."

"They couldn't be tired-er than we are," someone grumbled.

As it happened, the weakness of machinery helped to delay their arrival. At one point, a coupler broke, allowing several cars to come loose from the main train. Once the engineer realized the weight of his train had been lessened considerably, he was forced to back up and reattach the cars. More mumblings and grousings surged through the boxcars, and many soldiers took the opportunity to get off the train and stretch their legs while they watched the repairs. As a result, the delay was extended, and they did not arrive in Baltimore until 3 a.m., by which time even the most malicious of trouble-makers had given up and gone home.

The regiment marched across town without incident. Baltimore was a particularly grubby city, its streets lined with ramshackle buildings and lean-tos, rubbish accumulating in gutters and vacant lots. The recent rain had done little to wash away the dirt; instead it had turned it into mud that made footing precarious. Staff officers made sure they surrounded Nellie, so she would not stand out as a target. Still, the fear was palpable until they made it to the safety of the Relay House, where they were to pick up the Washington and Harpers Ferry Railroad. Captain James Cline later described the scene in a letter to his wife: "Streets lit up by the uncertain glare of the streetlamps, with double police at every corner. It looked more like a funeral cortege of some departed spirits than the march of a regiment of soldiers."

Spirits brightened as the first glimmerings of dawn began to show on the horizon. Outside the Relay House, the Roundheads were greeted by the welcome smell of coffee and cooking grease. Trestle tables had been set up under a make-shift pavilion, and there red-faced women bustled back and forth loading those tables with a pick-up breakfast. Platters overflowed with hot biscuits and slivers of country ham. Pitchers of molasses and bowls of fried apples awaited the hungry soldiers.

"Pitch in, boys, there's more where that come from," shouted one plump little woman, her hands still covered with flour.

The men had no hesitation about doing that, but Nellie turned to the cooks. "How wonderful this is," she said. "Who are you, and why are you being so kind?"

"Most of us are wives and mothers of men who have already gone off to war," one explained. "This is what we can do to share in their efforts. It's little enough, in comparison."

"Well, I've never seen anything look so inviting. Thank you, from all of us."

Nellie filled a biscuit with ham and then turned away from the crowd, unwilling to be closed into a shelter when fresh air was available. Needing to stretch, she walked back toward the tracks, where wagons full of their supplies were being loaded onto the next train. She found a spot where a split rail fence bordered the road. She leaned her forearms on it, looking eastward toward the sunrise. She lifted her chin, feeling a soft breeze ruffle the hairs that were coming loose from her hastily pinned bun. The world seemed fresh. Dewdrops still clung to every blade of grass, and the wooded landscape was alight with shades of green.

Suddenly she felt something nudge hard against her left arm and turned in alarm. The intruder was a horse, still hitched to an empty wagon, and the object of its curiosity was the haversack Nellie wore over her shoulder.

"Hello there, you beautiful beast," Nellie murmured as she reached to pat the horse's neck. "You're absolutely right. I think this looks like a feed bag, too. And maybe it is." Nellie rummaged in the haversack and pulled out a slightly bruised but fragrant apple, the last of Mr. Moffatt's farewell offering. She held out the apple in the palm of her hand. "There you go, girl. You've worked hard already this morning." The soft lips that nuzzled her hand reminded Nellie so strongly of home that for a moment she almost forgot where she was and what she was doing.

"Animals always seem to recognize those who love them," a rough voice spoke behind her. "You look positively bucolic standing there with your friend." She turned to see the speaker was Colonel Leasure.

"Good morning, Sir. This is such a peaceful scene, it's hard to believe we're off to war."

"Give it a couple of hours," the colonel said. "Enjoy your new friend. You'll see war soon enough. How are you getting along, Mrs. Leath?"

"I'm well, Sir."

"Good. Good." The briskness was back in his voice. "I've been meaning to check on you and let you know you have indeed started something."

"I've done what?"

"Since you arrived, several soldiers have approached me offering the services of the women in their lives. It seems there are many wives and sisters and mothers who are willing to accompany us to the front. I've arranged for three of the best-qualified to join us after we get to Washington. I'm still not fully convinced you women won't be a handicap on the battlefield, but I can see the need for your services in the camps and hospitals. And if we're going to have women in our regiment, I thought it best to have more than one."

"I see. And what will their role be?"

"Your staff, Mrs. Leath. This is still your idea, and I leave it in your capable hands to transform these ladies into members of the regiment. You can teach them much about self-reliance and confidence. And maybe you can share some of those 'wise-woman' remedies, as well," he added.

"I'll try." There was a pause, but as she sensed the colonel was in no hurry to return to his duties, she ventured another question. "Have you ever been to Washington? I'm really excited to be headed toward our nation's capital."

"Don't expect too much, my dear. Washington, for all its status, is still a small town. A few lovely buildings hold promise. The White House and the Treasury Building demonstrate what this capital may one day become. But right now, it's a hodge-podge. Look one way and you'll see the red brick of the Smithsonian mansion sitting in a field of daisies. Turn another way and you confront the scaffolding around the rising dome of the new Capitol. But in between there are vacant lots, the same sort of rough-and-tumble storefronts we saw in Baltimore, unpaved streets, piles of garbage, and escaped slaves living in tarpaper shanties and lean-tos that defy description.

"But I've read of marble monuments, tree-lined boulevards, lovely rivers, and vast vistas of parkland. Is that all a lie?"

"No, not completely. You'll see the tree-lined boulevards, although there's nothing there but the tree lining. The streets between them are a bit primitive. And the city has taken on something of a double aspect now we're in a time of war. You remember the appearance of Camp Wilkins, with its rows of tents and swarming soldiers? Now imagine creating several Camp Wilkins and dumping them on every park and available vista within that marbled city of your imagination. That's Washington in wartime. It's full of energy and excitement, however. You can make it what you will. Just choose carefully where you look."

"I will, Sir. I'm beginning to understand the world is what I make of it."

4
KALORAMA HEIGHTS

After the long hauls the Roundheads had experienced for the past two nights, the run from Baltimore into Washington was an easy two-hour ride. By 11:00 a.m. they had arrived at the last relay station, where another group of dedicated women had prepared their dinner. This time the tables overflowed with platters of fried chicken and smothered pork chops. Bowls of vegetables offered a welcome change from dried varieties. Boiled new potatoes, green beans cooked with onions, white beans with ham hocks, field peas, and hog jowl with turnip greens shared space with plates of sliced late-season tomatoes, newly-brined pickles, and spicy cole slaw. Cool lemonade promised relief from the rapidly rising heat. And on a side table were cakes and pies of every imaginable variety.

"Welcome to our nation's capital," the women said, and the hungry soldiers responded with cheers.

"We seldom see a meal like this, M'am," said one grizzled sergeant who had been serving in another regiment since Lincoln's initial call.

Nellie was almost too excited to eat, but even she could not resist the lure of fresh food on a real plate. Licking a combination of chicken grease and chocolate frosting from her fingers, she gave a sigh of repletion. Looking around, she noted how the soldiers, almost to a man, had perked up. They were smiling, laughing, relaxing. Mentally Nellie made a note. *I won't be able to see the men fed like this often, but I must try to come up with some sort of treat for them now and then,* she thought. *I've heard an army marches on its stomach, but I never realized how true that is.*

It took several hours for the baggage handlers to unload the train and reload the Roundhead baggage onto wagons. Nellie filled the time by chatting with the women who had provided their meal. One gray-haired lady cheerfully introduced herself as the Widow Barlow. "I don't have anybody to cook for at home anymore," she said, "so I enjoy getting the chance here to put on some really big feeds. Who cooks for all these men when they're in their camps?"

"Well, mostly they do their own cooking, which isn't good, I'm afraid. And at the moment I'm not much help. I can stir up some broth for those who are sickly, but I don't know what to suggest to the men sitting around a campfire with nothing but a great big pot."

"I can help you there. Let me find a scrap of paper and I'll give you a couple of recipes that'll fill their bellies."

By the time the wagons were ready, Nellie had picked up several cooking tips. The Roundheads, however, were not thinking about food as they started on the final leg of their journey, a march through downtown Washington. There was simply too much else to see. Nellie rode on one of the wagons, which gave her a vantage point from which to survey the city as they passed. Her overwhelming impression was one of high energy. Everywhere she looked, crowds of people bustled through the streets, many carrying dispatch cases or bundles of paper. Conveyances of every type moved supplies from one spot to another. As they passed the White House, a steady stream of carriages passed through the gate and unloaded dignified passengers in front of the portico. "Ole Abe holds public visiting hours every afternoon," the wagon driver explained. "About the only way to get a problem solved quick-like around here is to show up and take the request right to the top."

Nellie had noticed several of the gentlemen were accompanied by ladies in wide hoop skirts and parasols. "Can anyone go to one of these audiences?" she asked.

"I s'pose so. Never felt the need myself, but Ole Abe keeps the door open. Says it's not his house—it's the people's White House."

Nellie felt her heart swell with pride at that thought. But right now there were other sights to be taken in. Further down Pennsylvania Avenue, the Willard Hotel competed with the White House for the largest number of carriages being unloaded in front of its doors. Many of the visitors wore full military uniforms, their blue coats and brass buttons giving them an air of power and authority.

All Nellie had read about the vast open areas of the capital seemed true, although many of the open spaces were now filled with military encampments. "Look over there," the driver pointed. "That's the Capitol Building going up. The House of Representatives wing is complete, although most of its offices are now filled with soldiers. And it looks like the Rotunda will have to wait 'til after the war to get finished. It's full of soldiers, too, although that opening where the dome's going to go don't give them much protection."

As they passed the Mall, a barnyard stench overwhelmed them. "That stone stump over there's gonna be Washington's Monument, they say, but nobody's workin' on it, either. This here's the slaughter grounds. The meat purveyors drive whole herds of cattle up here every day to provide food for the troops. I know that kind of thing has to be done somewheres, but it does seem a shame to have it in the heart of the city. Smell gets worse in the heat of the afternoon, seems like."

The Roundheads' destination was a large grassy area in the hills above Rock Creek. As they finished the climb to a bluff overlooking the city, Nellie gasped at the contrasting views in front of her. In one spot, a lovely garden bloomed. Next to it, white tents stretched across the grass as far as she could see. And directly in front of her was a large golden-hued mansion with a two-story entrance arch and smooth stucco walls. "Is this someone's home?" she asked.

"Used to be the home of Joel Barlow," offered one of the officers passing behind her. "He was America's favorite poet during the early years of our Republic."

"Joel Barlow? Oh, I know who he was. He wrote 'The Columbiad.' He was proud of his country and the possibilities it offered to the world. How sad his home has turned into a military camp."

"All of Washington's a military camp now, in case you hadn't noticed, Missy. You don't like that, what are you doing here with us?"

"Oh, I didn't mean that. I just. . . ."

"Don't harass the lady, Josiah," spoke a familiar voice. Doctor Gross approached. "I share her nostalgia for the kind of world Joel Barlow envisioned—as should we all."

"Humph!" The captain was still grumbling as he stomped away.

"Don't mind him, Nellie. Captain Pentecost is angry at the world and everybody in it. That anger makes him a good soldier, though."

Nellie wasn't sure about that statement, but she bit back her comment. Her relationship with Doctor Gross was too new to risk offending him. Instead, she surveyed the area again and asked, "Where are we supposed to camp? Do you know?"

"We'll pitch in that open space over there," he said, pointing. "But it's too late in the day to accomplish much. The colonel just told me the Seventy-Ninth New York regiment has invited us to share their camp tonight. They've had dinner, but their cook fires are still going strong, and they have plenty of rations. I suspect they'll even find a tent for you to stay in tonight. Tomorrow will be soon enough to get us settled."

Night fell swiftly, aided by an encroaching cloud bank. The New York regiment did indeed have room for Nellie. She settled comfortably into a small tent and was soon sound asleep. Most of the soldiers, however, simply stretched out on top of their tents, too tired to force themselves through the struggles of getting the tents erected. Around midnight, Nellie awoke briefly to the sound of rain on the canvas above her head and the grumbling of men who found themselves exposed to the weather.

The next morning, everyone pitched in to get their tents staked quickly, realizing that the rain looked likely to continue for hours. Wet though they were, the men were stirred to action by the sounds of artillery booming in the distance. They had signed up to fight a war, but many seemed agitated to realize they were now near the actual fighting. Yesterday, marching through the capital, they had thought Washington looked impregnably well-fortified. A hundred camps had sprung up around the capital, white tents visible on every hill, in the valleys and fields, and half hidden in the woods. Night had fallen to a continuous drumming of "Retreat", and dawn echoed with the sounds of "Reveille". These were re-assuring and familiar sounds. But those crashing cannons now spoke of the other face of war, a face these innocent farmhands from western Pennsylvania could not envision.

The weekend gave everyone time to settle into a semblance of order. Soldiers drew their rations and rearranged their messes to accommodate the friendships springing up among former strangers. At home, a boy from Beaver County might never have encountered one from Butler County. Here, in this overwhelmingly crowded city, another young man from the rolling hills of Pennsylvania became instant family. The twelve companies of the Roundheads began taking on characteristics of their own. Company H and Company F, both full of recruits from New Castle, contained many of the veterans of Colonel Leasure's first company of three-month volunteers who had seen a bit of service around York as railroad guards. Their prior experience with the Twelfth Pennsylvania was invaluable, as it had produced skilled officers who could lead squad and company drills. On Saturday, the veterans spread themselves out among the other companies, guiding the men to elect staff officers from their own ranks in the understanding that enlisted men would more willingly follow the orders of those they had chosen themselves.

In Company C, James McCaskey and John Wilson were among the newly-christened sergeants appointed to guide their squads through the drills. The two men had been neighbors and friends from childhood. Here, they assumed their positions not because of their military skills but because of their ages. At twenty-two and twenty-four, James and John had just enough seniority over their teen-aged companions to command their respect. Or so they hoped.

"I don't have a clue about what I'm doing," John whispered to James as they tried their hands at organizing a drill.

"No, neither do I. I think the secret is to stand up straight and focus your eyes on the horizon while you shout your orders. That way you'll avoid catching the eye of someone who knows you're lost."

"Look at George Fisher over there. No, don't look. He's laughing himself silly at us, not that he knows any more than we do."

"True, but since he's practically family, he knows how I must be floundering. His brother Simon is married to my sister Sarah Jane, remember." James smiled as he thought of his family. "He probably also remembers the time you and I both fell through the ice on the creek trying to impress that little Hazen girl with our skating skills."

"Don't remind me. He's seen me make a darned fool of myself more than once. How am I going to survive this?"

"Surviving is all that's important, John. You'll learn fast enough in the field."

Colonel Leasure was also busy filling positions on his staff. Some choices were easy. He appointed William H. Powers as another adjutant to assist his son, Samuel G. Leasure. Reverend Robert Audley Browne, pastor of the United Presbyterian Church of New Castle, had immediately signed up as regimental chaplain, although he had to delay his departure until he received an official leave of absence from his congregation. Alva H. Leslie, a merchant and politician from New Castle, brought his business acumen to bear on the quarter master's office. Ferdinand H. Gross, with whose medical talents Leasure was familiar, had initially signed on as surgeon, bringing with him his assistant, Doctor Joseph P. Rossiter. Doctor Gross, however, was so well respected that he was almost immediately promoted to the general staff, U. S. Volunteers. Within a few days Doctor Horace Ludington replaced him on the Roundheads staff. Several young men from the printing office of the New Castle *Chronicle* followed John Nicklin to enlist as regimental musicians. With the exception of Doctor Ludington and Nellie Leath, the members of the Officers Mess who assembled each evening were old friends, a circumstance that enabled them to work easily with one another. Those prior friendships had the additional effect of throwing the newcomers, Nellie and Horace Ludington, together out of their mutual isolation, and they quickly established an easy working relationship.

Reverend Browne was scheduled to take up his duties as chaplain on Saturday, September 14th. Like the Roundheads, he endured an uncomfortable two-day train trip, one made worse by a couple of his traveling companions. Just outside of Harrisburg, a stout older woman plopped herself down next to him on the narrow wooden bench, fished through her port-manteau to extract her knitting, and then pointed toward the Bible Browne was intently reading. "You'd be a religious man, then?" she asked.

Browne looked at her in some surprise. He was not used to strange women trying to engage him in conversation, but he gamely nodded and said, "Yes, M'am. I'm a Presbyterian minister."

"Whatcha doin' on this here train then? Headed for a new church?"

"Ah, in a manner of speaking. I'm traveling to join my hometown regiment in Washington."

"An Army man, then? I thought clergymen was in favor of peace."

"I'm in favor of a righteous cause, M'am."

"Humph! You're givin' up your pulpit to go out and kill people, is it?"

"No, of course not!" Browne was beginning to snort with indignation. He wasn't sure why he was bothering to converse with this busybody, but he felt compelled to explain. "My congregation has given its blessing to this venture. I am to serve as the regiment's chaplain, giving comfort to those in the direst need. My church and family back home will do well without me. It's our nation's sons who stand most in need of my guidance and prayers."

The woman latched onto one key word in that answer. "Your family? You're married? With children? And you're leaving them to get mixed up in this ridiculous war? What does your poor long-suffering wife think of this decision?"

"Mary understands my position, I assure you. And she will have plenty of help when the baby comes."

"Land a' mercy! The woman's pregnant?"

Browne cringed with embarrassment as heads began to turn all around the carriage. "Madam, please. This is not a matter I discuss with strangers. Excuse me." He struggled to his feet, swaying with the motion of the train, and looked about for a safe, masculine area in which to relocate.

He picked a bench occupied by a shabbily-dressed older man who appeared to be asleep. But as he settled himself, the man opened one lazy eye and fixed it upon him. "Got yer goat, did she?" Browne's reply was a simple raised eyebrow.

"Go on with ya," the man continued. "I know how it is with women, believe you me. Jus' let 'em git started and ye cain't shut 'em up."

Browne glared at him.

"She didn't have no business pressin' you like that. What's she care if your wife's unhappy? Personally, I kin seen why you'd leave home if your wife's expectin' another squallin' brat. Every time my wife had a baby she made my life hell."

Fortunately for all concerned, the train squealed to a stop at that moment, and the conductor called out, "Ten-minute rest stop." Browne hurried to the door and jumped onto the siding, grateful to have escaped before he found himself engaged in another war of words. He was more irritated by the man's crude attempts at sympathy than he had been at the old lady's scolding.

If truth be told, he realized, he was delighted to be escaping the domesticity of the family farm and his wife's approaching lying-in. A woman's bodily functions had always been a mystery to him, and he had no desire to learn more than he had to. Mary had never experienced any difficulty giving birth to their children. In fact, Browne felt she enjoyed the process much too much. Unlike the other wives of their acquaintance, who went to great length to conceal their changing bodies, Mary seemed to flaunt hers. She went about patting her abdomen and calling attention to the baby's movements. Browne was sure he was a tolerant man, but he most assuredly did not want to know her navel was beginning to protrude, or her nipples were beginning to darken. Nor did he wish to be drawn into a discussion about his reactions to such matters. Thank goodness for the company of decent, God-fearing Roundheads, he reassured himself. A life without women for a while would be most welcome.

So it was with a mixture of rage and disbelief that the first person he spied when he reached the Roundhead camp on Kalorama Heights displayed a decidedly feminine figure. He sought Col. Leasure in a swirl of indignation, pushing past the sergeant on duty and barging into the command tent. "Daniel! Was that a woman I saw in camp?"

Colonel Leasure looked up from his makeshift desk with a welcoming smile. "Robert, my old friend. How good it is to see you."

"I repeat. Have you allowed a woman to come in among the men? Or didn't you know about her?"

"Robert, Robert, quit sputtering. Of course we have women in the camp. Several wives and mothers have come along to serve as laundresses and cooks, and we had to have at least one matron for our hospital patients."

"This one was no wife or mother! She was a girl with unkempt hair and a flimsy dress. She fled into one of the men's tents when she saw me coming."

"Ah, you must have encountered our Nellie."

"Thunderation, man. What do you mean by 'our Nellie'?"

"Believe it or not, she's. . . ."

"I'll believe it's a good thing I arrived when I did. Who would have thought a Christian man such as yourself could sink so low as to be on first-name terms with a prostitute!"

The colonel had stopped smiling, and he drew himself up as best he could to face off with the tall, lanky minister looming over him. "You are out of line, Sir!"

"No, Colonel, you are the one who has stepped over the line. In the name of God, think about the pernicious effects that woman will have on the innocent souls of our young men."

"Sit down, Robert, or I swear I'll have you thrown out of here and sent packing."

Something about the fire in the colonel's eyes warned Reverend Browne he might do well to take a step back. He sank onto a camp stool. "I'm tired from the trip, Daniel. I'm covered in dust. I haven't eaten anything since morning, not even a sip of water. The whole scene here is more than my exhausted nature can take in. I saw a scruffy-looking girl scurrying among the tents. What am I to think?"

"You could have trusted me, Robert," the colonel answered in clipped tones. "You know me better than to think I have thrown away my moral standards because I have taken up the sword."

"But I know what I saw!"

Leasure strode toward the entrance to the tent. "Private Stevenson, go fetch Nellie and bring her in here. You'll probably find her with Doctor

Ludington, seeing to that young soldier who turned up sick this morning. Tell her I won't keep her from her duties long." He remained standing with his back to Reverend Browne, looking out over his encampment until the private and the girl returned.

"Now then, Robert, I'd like you to meet Mrs. Nellie Chase Leath, from the fine state of Maine. Mrs. Leath serves as our regimental matron and is doing a wonderful job of keeping our men healthy and well-fed. Nellie, this is the good Reverend Robert Audley Browne, of New Castle, Pennsylvania. He will serve as our chaplain, caring for men's souls as you care for their health. I'm counting on the two of you to work together to keep the troops in prime condition."

"Mrs. Leath." The chaplain bowed over her extended hand, which kept his disapproving scowl from being too obvious.

"My pleasure, Reverend Browne." Nellie smiled at him, unaware of the tempest her presence had stirred up.

"How's young Billy Braden doing, Nellie?" Colonel Leasure asked, hoping to demonstrate her skills.

"Doctor thinks he may have measles, Sir. He has funny red spots on the insides of his cheeks, and a blotchy look to his forehead. We have him isolated and resting comfortably for the moment."

"Well, scurry on back to your duties, and tell him I wish him soon recovered. You and the reverend will have further opportunity to get acquainted at dinner."

"Yes, Sir," Nellie nodded. "Nice to have you here, Reverend."

The chaplain nodded back and swallowed a sound that might have been a snort. When she was safely on her way, he looked at the colonel, disapproval still radiating from his every pore. "She's too young, Daniel, and much too attractive."

"If you must judge her, Robert, judge her on what she does, not on her age or appearance."

"I'll be sure to do that."

"Fine. Then welcome to Kalorama Heights. I'll have Private Stevenson show you to your tent. You'll find we are all ready for you. The men will be pleased to have a real church service in the morning. I'll see you at dinner." The dismissal was polite but noticeably cooler than Leasure's original delight at seeing his friend.

As for Nellie, she returned to the tent they were using for sick call with a bemused look on her face. "How's Billy doing, Doctor?"

"Ah, the rash is spreading. It's measles, sure enough, and we can expect a whole outbreak, if we're not careful. When one fellow gets 'em, lots of others will, too. What was so important you were summoned to headquarters?"

"Reverend Browne has arrived, and Colonel Leasure wanted to introduce me, I guess. That's all that happened."

"Well, what sort of fellow is he? To hear these boys talk, you'd think he was a saint walking the earth."

"Uh, he didn't strike me as particularly *saintly*. He's—tall."

"That's it? Tall."

"Well, really tall. The whole time I was there, he seemed to be staring straight ahead at something over my head. I had to strain upward to see his face. And, well, something else was going on, but I don't know what."

"He and the colonel are lifelong friends, are they not?"

"So I've been told. But the tension in the tent was thick as blackstrap molasses."

"Bad news from home?"

"I don't know. Maybe we'll learn more in the mess hall this evening."

The tension Nellie had sensed still hovered over the dinner table. Reverend Browne acknowledged his introduction to Doctor Ludington with a frown. "What happened to Ferdie?" he demanded.

"Doctor Gross has been promoted, Robert, to the general staff."

"Too bad. We need a good doctor."

Nellie was shocked. How rude! she thought to herself. Trying to ease the embarrassment she was sure Doctor Ludington felt, she turned to him. "How's our patient doing?"

"His fever is soaring, I'm afraid, and we haven't received our medical supplies. I've been sponging him with cold water, but I'd feel better if I had a dose of quinine to offer him."

Without stopping to think about the effects her next words would have on the assembled group, Nellie brightened. "I saw some dogwood trees up by the mansion today, and they're full of red berries. One of those crushed into water is as good as quinine, my grandmother always said. Would you like me to fetch some?"

"Do that, Nellie. Your grandmother was absolutely right. I hadn't realized we had dogwoods here."

"You're taking advice from this young woman?" Reverend Browne reared back and sneered at Doctor Ludington. "What kind of doctor are you?"

"Robert!" Colonel Leasure warned.

"I'll do whatever it takes for the good of my patients, Reverend. I hope you'll show the same consideration for their souls!" And on that hostile note, the staff officers began to pack up their mess kits and move toward the door.

Sunday morning dawned bright and comfortably warm. The Roundheads had all learned of Reverend Browne's arrival, and they assembled for worship services with barely concealed eagerness. Nellie, too, was anxious to hear his sermon, hoping that in his official role the pastor would present a more appealing character.

Browne had chosen as his text the 118th Psalm, and his voice boomed over his impromptu congregation.

The Lord is on my side; I will not fear. What can man do unto me?
The Lord taketh my part with them that help me: therefore shall I see my desire upon them that hate me.
It is better to trust in the Lord than to put confidence in man.
It is better to trust in the Lord than to put confidence in princes.

Nellie listened and tried to judge how this message would be received. Of course, the Lord is on our side, she thought, though I doubt anyone here needs to be assured of that. But I wonder. If I were an army officer, I would not be particularly happy about someone telling my soldiers not to trust me. She squinted into the sun to try to catch a glimpse of Colonel Leasure's expression, but his back was to her and his face in shadow.

All nations compasses me about: but in the name of the Lord will I destroy them.
They compassed me about; yea, they compassed me about: but in the name of the Lord I WILL DESTROY THEM.
They compassed me about like bees; they are quenched as the fire of thorns: for in the name of the Lord I WILL DESTROY THEM.

It was a battle cry to end all such cries, and Reverend Browne's voice blasted the rallying phrase over and over again. Nellie had smiled at the reference to swarms of bees. I bet there are a couple of privates here who understand that image, she thought. But as Reverend Browne launched into his sermon, holding up example after example of Confederate generals and politicians who deserved God's wrath, Nellie found her jaw beginning to clench.

The plantation owner who drives his slaves into the dust—I WILL DESTROY HIM!
The smuggler who tries to bring guns through our barricades—I WILL DESTROY HIM!
General Anderson who surrendered Fort Sumter to the rebels—I WILL DESTROY HIM!
Robert E. Lee, abandoning the oath he took at West Point—I WILL DESTROY HIM!
Jefferson Davis, setting himself up as a president to rival our own President Lincoln—I WILL DESTROY HIM!

Like the cannon barrages the Union soldiers could hear in the distance, each shouted imprecation jarred Nellie with its violence. The pressure built up until she could not longer stand to listen as the chaplain re-wrote the Bible to suit his own purposes. As quietly as she could manage, she began to move to the back of the crowd, hoping to slip away without notice. But Reverend Brown had one more denouncement to hurl:

"All who will not hear the word of the Lord in this conflict—I WILL DESTROY HIM!"

Nellie looked back to find the eyes of the chaplain boring straight into her own. I have made an enemy for life, she realized, and I have no idea how I did so.

Supplies came in slowly and in an order whose logic was not readily apparent to the recipients. On Monday, September 9th, the men received their over shirts although the weather was much too hot to wear them. The dress parades held by the officers several days a week revealed a rag-tag regiment, some men sporting the uniforms from prior military service and the raw recruits still outfitted in the clothes in which they had arrived. On Tuesday, September 10th, the men marched to the arsenal, where they were issued old Springfield muskets, not the kind of rifles they had been expecting. That afternoon, the quartermaster handed out new knapsacks and cartridge boxes, although there was no ammunition to be had. Target practice had to be delayed until the following week. Back home, The Lawrence *Journal* reported, "We learn that the Regiment is fully armed, equipped and clothed, except coats, pantaloons and overcoats. Rather an important exception; but it is said they will have all these in a few days." The pants arrived on Friday, September 27th. The rest of the uniforms, including the overcoats, did not arrive until just before the regiment left Washington on October 10th.

Nellie watched all of the preparations for war with amazement. She simply could not get her head around the sheer volume of supplies needed to keep a single regiment equipped. When others complained of their lack of uniforms, Nellie looked at one of the first overcoats to arrive and shook her head over the detailing in its construction. As a seamstress, she understood how much work was involved in making a single coat. She could not fathom what it took to provide those coats for one thousand men. Similarly, she wondered at the amount of food that passed through the Roundhead camp. One day she found the quartermaster in a rare leisure moment and asked him about the numbers.

"We've been here almost a month, Mr. Leslie. Do you have any idea how much food we have consumed?"

"As a matter of fact, Mrs. Leath, I just finished those accounts. Wait here a moment and I'll fetch the numbers for you."

He returned with a scrap of paper. "This is where I did my ciphering. Says here we've used 25 barrels of pork, 11,000 pounds of fresh beef, 7 barrels of preserved beef, 41 pounds of bacon, 172 boxes of hard bread, 162 barrels of flour, 58 bushels of beans, 1600 pounds of rice, 2000 pounds of coffee, 45 pounds of tea, 3500 pounds of sugar, 300 gallons of vinegar, 742 pounds of potatoes, 28 gallons of molasses, 14 bushels of salt, and 740 pounds of hominy."

"And we're just one regiment out of hundreds, maybe thousands," Nellie said. "Where does it all come from?"

"Been downtown to smell the atmosphere around the Mall lately?"

"Oh, I know that's where they slaughter the cattle. But the sugar, the rice, the salt. It's more than I can comprehend."

"We're lucky here in Washington," Alva Leslie explained. "Food and supplies from all over the country arrive here first for distribution. We've been eating well because we're close to the supplies. Things may be different when we ship out. Then we'll have to depend on supply lines remaining open. Or else take what we can get from the countryside."

Nellie smiled, remembering the purloined poultry cooking over campfires back in Camp Wilkins. "I'll wager our young men won't have too much trouble foraging for themselves. But the amounts still astound me."

In late September, a wagon rumbled into camp bringing medical supplies. Doctor Ludington, who was still trying to get himself settled into the regiment, turned to Nellie for help. "Those supplies out there are all for us, but the driver did not have an inventory with him. He unhitched his mule team and left the wagon sitting there. I need to know what we have. Could you and the other women delve into the boxes and chests and make me a list?"

If Nellie had been surprised by the amounts of foodstuffs the regiment required, she was positively overwhelmed by the sight of the medical wagon. One entire crate was filled with rolled bandages torn from used sheeting. They ranged in size from one-half inch wide to four inches wide, and each appeared to be from eight to ten yards long. Other chests held bedding, towels, soap, and bolts of uncut flannel. There were splints of all sizes and shapes, arm slings, and crutches. A large bag held nothing but lint. Cushions, pads, rags, and handkerchiefs were scattered throughout the shipment.

Look here," Nellie pointed out crates that held wine and liquor. "There's enough alcohol here to open a saloon!"

"Humph! I don't know anything about saloons, though I suppose you do," Mrs. White said. "That's for medical uses, I'm sure. Don't you go giving the men ideas about drinking it for pleasure, nor you either, for that matter."

"I'd never do that," Nellie said. She was stunned by the hostility she heard in the older woman's tone. "Surely you don't think. . . ." Then her voice trailed off as she realized that was exactly what Mrs. White did think.

She turned as Mrs. Sample, the sutler's wife, stood up from inventory-ing the medical chest. "Here's a list of everything I can see. I suppose you know what these things are used for. Most of them I've never heard of."

Nellie glanced at the list. Some terms she recognized, of course, but others were a mystery. Even more puzzling were the women's attitudes. Mrs. White seemed to think she was a loose woman, given to drink, while Mrs. Sample assumed she was a font of medical knowledge. Nellie wasn't sure which was worse. But she knew neither opinion was likely to influence its holder to approach her in friendship.

Later that afternoon, she delivered the completed inventory to Doctor Ludington. "We have more supplies than I ever deemed possible, Sir. Whatever are we to do with 240 ground sheets?"

"Just one good battle, Nellie."

"Oh." She clasped a hand over her mouth to hide her dismay. "I'm sorry. I can't seem to get my head around the numbers. And I have no idea what battle will be like."

"I pray you never do, but my head tells me differently. We'll be putting these things to use all too soon."

"Then I'd best be getting busy learning about them. But I've never even heard of some of the medicinal supplies. Oh, I know about some of them. I was happy to see we have quinine at last."

"Yes, although that was a good idea about the dogwood berries the other day. Worked like a charm."

"Well, you could say it *was* a charm, I guess. But I can see it's easier to have a container of quinine at your side rather than having to hunt for a dogwood tree every time someone breaks a fever. And spirits of Nitre. I had a sprightly little aunt who professed to having pains around her heart every few days. She'd pour a teaspoon of aromatic spirits of Nitre into a glass of water, chug it down, and then totter happily off to take a nap. Never seemed to fail."

Doctor Ludington laughed. "Of course. It's a pretty effective narcotic for those with delicate nerves. What didn't you recognize in the medical chest?"

"Blue mass, for one. It sounds like an ugly wart."

"Actually, it's a common druggist's concoction of mercury and chalk, sometimes flavored with licorice root, rose-water, honey, sugar and rose petals. It's said to be good for insomnia, as well as everything from tooth-ache to constipation. I suspect it works mostly by suggestion. If we can't figure out what ails somebody, a few blue mass pills suggest we know what we're doing."

"And basilicon ointment?"

"Lard, pine resin, and beeswax. Good for burns and wounds that won't heal."

"And I've never heard about. . . ."

Doctor Ludington held up his hands. "Look, Nellie, you'll pick these things up as we go. It won't take long, I promise. You're a quick study."

He turned away, seeming to dismiss her concerns, but Nellie continued to worry as she made her way back to her tent. How odd, she thought. The chaplain thinks I'm a floozy, the other nurse thinks I'm a drunk, but the one man who should know I'm a fraud treats me with kindness and more respect for my knowledge than I deserve.

5

CREATURE COMFORTS

The soldiers' work day followed a strict routine, designed to instill discipline as well as military skills. According to the official orders, "Reveille" sounded at sunrise. After company roll call, the men had breakfast and put the company quarters in good order. At eight, the drummers beat the surgeon's call, and those who felt sick mustered at the hospital for medical attention. The rest of the men had squad drill until 9 o'clock. Company drill lasted from ten until twelve. After another roll call, they took a break for dinner. Squad and company drill resumed from two o'clock to half past three. Regimental drill started at half past four and concluded at six with a dress parade. Roll call preceded supper, and the final roll call was at half past eight. The drummers beat "Tattoo" at ten when all lights except in officer's headquarters had to be put out, and all the men not on guard were to retire to bed. Guards had been detailed by the First Sergeants at the morning roll call, and they reported for duty at ten o'clock, the hour for mounting guard.

In practice, not all drills lasted as long as scheduled, particularly as the days passed and the men became more proficient. Soldiers found plenty of time to visit the sutler's tent to purchase small indulgences like peppermint sticks or to replenish their supply of writing paper. A fellow whose feet hurt could steal some time to pare down his corns, while others wrote letters home or read the latest newspapers. They were finding camp life was regulated, but not overly rigorous.

Colonel Leasure had done his best to provide distractions that would ease the tedium of constant drill and target practice. He had brought a troop of eleven musicians with him from his newspaper staff in New Castle, and they were meant to provide entertainment as well as the regulation signals of "Reveille" and "Tattoo". The army did not provide any instruments, however, so the officers of the regiment took up a collection among themselves and sent Private John Emory off to Philadelphia to purchase whatever he could find. With over $400 to spend, he returned with a fine set of instruments—two brass tubas, three brass saxhorns, a rosewood fife, a set of snare drums of varying sizes, and several bugles, some with keys and some without. John Nicklin, the leader of the regimental band, had been thrilled when the instruments arrived, declaring the brasses to be of the finest German manufacture. The snare drums, too, were a matter of pride, each elaborately decorated with scenes that recalled the Union cause.

Around the campfires in the evening, the band members often struck up tunes to lift spirits and sooth away the frustrations of the day. Soon individuals from other companies brought out their personal instruments—guitars, banjos, fiddles and mouth harps—to liven things up. While other regiments made do with bands cobbled together from soldiers who couldn't march straight, the Roundheads had the benefit of trained musicians, and music became a major feature of their camp.

Another of Colonel Leasure's ideas to make camp life more appealing was the regimental newsletter. He returned from the city one day hauling a portable printing press purchased with his own funds. He broached the idea at supper that evening. "Nick, you're already lifting our spirits with your music, but you also know more about the printing trade than anyone here. Do you think you and your mates from the paper back home could produce a small broadsheet now and then to keep up morale?"

"What all would you want in it, Sir?" asked John Nicklin. "Is it to be all official and formal, or can we have some fun with it?"

"By all means, enjoy! There's already enough stuffy paper circulating in this camp. We need some humor, some helpful hints, some rumor-squelching, some human interest stuff."

Nellie somewhat timidly stepped into the discussion. "I could give you some tips on how the men can avoid getting sick. Or maybe, a recipe or two to make the camp rations more palatable."

Reverend Browne snorted, his typical reaction to anything Nellie had to say. "This is an army, Mrs. Leath, not a sewing circle."

"But the men do have to do their own cooking and mending," Nellie persisted, "and most of them are doing so for the first time. I thought I could help."

"Why not start up an 'Agony Auntie' column, while you're at it. I'm sure you could offer a voice of experience to those who are miserably in love."

Nellie felt herself flush to the roots of her hair with anger, but she pressed her lips together and made no response. "Unkind and uncalled for," she heard the colonel murmur to the chaplain. The others pretended not to have heard the acrimonious exchange.

"It can really be a hodge-podge?" asked Danny Cubbison.

"Ah, a veritable stew of things if you like. Just throw everything into the pot and see what you come up with."

"And we could call it the *Kalorama Pot*," suggested Forbes Holton, whose musical talent with the fife often concealed his dry wit.

Leasure grinned. "That may be a bit too suggestive for anyone acquainted with our latrine arrangements. but you're on the right track."

"How about the *Camp Kettle*?" Nicklin offered, and a new Roundhead tradition was born. Nellie was gratified, and not a little smug, when the first issue of the paper carried this introduction:

We have little room to spare, and none to waste in the "Camp Kettle," and shall briefly state that it is our intention to publish it as a daily, or weekly, or occasional paper, just as the exigencies of the service will permit. It is our intention to cook in it a "mess" of short paragraphs replete with useful information on a great many subjects, about which new recruits are supposed to be ignorant. We shall endeavor to make it a welcome visitor beside the campfire and in the quarters, a sort of familiar little friend that whispers kind words and friendly advice to inexperienced men concerning the new position they have assumed, and the new duties that follow. Everything relating to a soldier's duty, and camp life, from mounting guard, to cleaning a musket, will be fit ingredient for the "Kettle." Rules for preserving health and cooking rations will be in place, and all sorts of questions relating to a soldier's duty, and his wants, when respectfully asked in writing, over a responsible name, will find an answer in the next mess that is poured out of the "Kettle."

For her part, Nellie was happy to settle into the relative peacefulness of this waiting period. In the evenings, she often strolled toward the Barlow house, which sat on the top of the hill. There she could look over the city and imagine what life must have been like when Joel Barlow himself lived there, and his circle of literary friends had joined him in dreaming about what this new country had in store. In many ways, it made her sad to realize that dream had deteriorated into civil war. But she could also take pride in the strength of her country as she looked over the masses of soldiers and equipment assembled to defend that dream.

One such evening brought a delightful surprise. As she perched on a low wall, she heard a soft sound at her feet. She peered into the bushes in the gathering dark. She couldn't see much, but the sound became clearer. "Mew, mew," a tiny voice cried. She held out a hand, and slowly a small black and white kitten emerged from the undergrowth. It sniffed tentatively at her fingers, and then the mewing sound turned into a rumbling purr. She picked the kitten up, and it immediately began nuzzling her neck.

"Oh, aren't you sweet! Where on earth did you come from? Do you belong to someone, or are you lost?" She shook her head at the silly notion the kitten might tell her anything. But she held it tightly for a few moments, relishing the warmth of its little body and the love that it seemed to pour out to her.

"I'm sorry. I can't take you home. I don't have a home myself—just a tent in the middle of a dusty army camp. It's no place for a kitten, I'm afraid. But I'm happy to have met you." She put the small animal down, patted it gently on its rear, and turned to go back to camp. She had only taken a few strides when she realized the cat was hard on her trail.

"Shoo. Go home. You can't come with me."

"Meow."

"No, I said." She stamped her foot and the kitten skittered off.

That scene repeated itself all the way back to her tent. Nellie looked around, afraid someone would see her and think she was deliberately bringing the cat into camp. "Please. Go away. Shoo."

"Meoooow."

"Noooooo."

Near the mess tent the kitten seemed to disappear. Nellie hurried to her tent, hoping to get away before he reemerged. But she was not to be so lucky. She had not finished tying her tent flap closed when the little voice once again startled her. This time, it said, "Yowl." Looking out of the flap she saw that the kitten had caught a mouse and was dragging it toward her feet.

"No way, cat. I'm proud of you for catching your own dinner. But you're not eating it in here. Scat!"

Despite Nellie's semi-sincere efforts to drive the cat away, he took up residence behind the mess tent and visited her frequently. And as luck would have it, the first person to discover she was harboring a pet was Reverend Browne. He came around a corner unexpectedly, as she was feeding the kitten a few scraps saved from her own dinner.

"Mrs. Leath! What in the world are you doing?" he demanded. "That's a wild animal. Get away from it!"

"It's not a 'wild animal', Reverend. It's the mess cat, who has been doing us yeoman's service in ridding the area of mice."

"No matter. The army's no place for pets. Get rid of it, or I'll see to it myself." He stomped away.

"What makes you so hateful?" Nellie mumbled to his back. "Don't worry, Oliver. I won't let that bad man hurt you." But she was not sure of that when she was summoned to see Colonel Leasure later that afternoon.

"The chaplain tells me you are keeping pets in the camp, Mrs. Leath."

"Not exactly! There's a young cat that hangs around the mess tent, and I talk to him now and then. That's all."

"Robert says you were feeding it from camp rations."

"Just the scraps from my own plate, Colonel. And Oliver certainly pays his own way around here in rodent control."

"Oliver?" The colonel arched an eyebrow at her.

Nellie realized too late she had just confirmed the pet status she was busily denying. "I call him that," she admitted. "He's a black cat with white feet and neck. He looks all dressed up, like a proper little Puritan, so I thought 'Oliver Cromwell' would be an appropriate name for a Roundhead cat."

Leasure laughed despite himself. "I see no harm in that, so long as you realize the cat will not be able to go with us when we move out. Don't get too attached, Nellie. And keep it out of the way of Reverend Browne."

"I will, Sir. Do you know why the chaplain dislikes me so? I haven't been able to do anything to please him since he got here."

"I don't know, Nellie. Maybe he is uncomfortable around women."

"But he's married, isn't he?"

"Yes, and devotedly so. He writes to Mary every day—sometimes more than once. And he has daughters."

"Then he just hates me in particular?"

"I don't know," the colonel repeated. "Just try not to antagonize him, please—you and the cat both."

Preparations continued throughout the month of September. The Roundheads were becoming a trained military unit in fact as well as name. The changes had started with the arrival of their uniforms. There was something about the act of donning the clothes provided by the army rather than those they had worn from home that transformed a boy into a man. He stood a little taller, took on an air of seriousness, and began to identify those around him as truly his "brothers in arms."

To be sure, the uniforms were not particularly stylish, or even comfortable. The shoes or brogans were known as mudscows. They were made with the rough side of the leather out, with broad soles, low heels, and rawhide laces. Issue stockings were of wool and shirts of flannel. The trousers were made of blue kersey, cut loose and without pleats or cuffs. Some soldiers complained the outfits were not only ugly but totally unsuited for wearing in warm weather.

"I don't see why we can't look more like those Zouaves over there," Henry Campbell complained to his mess mates in Company C. "Just look at them. Red pantaloons with gold braid all the way down the leg, pants bloused into their white gaiters, blue shirts with brass buttons, blue jackets trimmed in red all down the front, and flowing striped sashes. They've got leather leggings to protect their shins and tassels everywhere you look. Really sharp, and I'll bet they're cooler, too."

"Really good targets, you mean. Don't you know anything about hunting, Henry? They get out in the field and somebody'll put a bullet through those fancy duds, easy. I'll keep my dull blue pants and fade right into the shadows. No red for me, thanks," Andrew Leary warned.

"Maybe so, but when we go home on furlough, I'd like to look like a real soldier, not a farm hand."

"Well, you are a farm hand, Henry, but you'll be a soldier, too, and I'll bet folks can tell the difference. At least in these uniforms, you'll have a chance to live long enough to earn a furlough," Sergeant Wilson said.

"I'd still like to have one o' them fez things they wear on their heads," Henry persisted. "They have numbers on theirs."

Henry had hit on a sore point with the Roundheads. The Union forage cap was made of dark blue cloth with a welt around the crown and was supposed to have a yellow metal number in front to designate the regiment. The caps issued to the Roundheads were conspicuously missing that number.

"Yeah, why don't we have our own number?" Archie Slater asked. "I heard it means the state of Pennsylvania don't recognize us."

"And when this war is over, we won't get our pensions 'cause we're not official-like," Sol Smith added.

"Yeah, and we might not ever get paid."

Sergeant Wilson held up his hands for quiet as the mutterings spread across the assembling crowd. "You've only heard part of the story, men. That's the trouble with camp rumors. Things get ugly when folks don't know what's going on. It's true Colonel Leasure got his permission to form a regiment straight from Secretary of War Simon Cameron, not from the governor of Pennsylvania. But Cameron's a Pennsylvanian, like us, and he fully meant for us to be a regular Pennsylvania regiment. It's only paperwork that's holding things up, and the colonel is on his way to Harrisburg right now to sign the papers with Gov. Curtin. You'll get your numbers straight away—and your money, too. Now suppose we all get back to work. It's almost time for company drills."

Routines can have two different effects. For most of the time, the men of the Roundhead Regiment settled comfortably into their days. The workload was light, the food plentiful, and the weather pleasant. Music filled the air, and jokes were encouraged. Friendships blossomed, and life was good. But sometimes creature comforts become almost oppressive. "I didn't sign up for this man's army to sit on a hillside in Washington, D. C., and watch the war getting fought by somebody else!" was a common complaint. The Roundheads began to feel they had been forgotten as the other units came and passed. The *Camp Kettle* mused:

> *Over the river—over the Long Bridge—over into Dixie—over the Chain Bridge—so they go, one steady stream of staunch men in serried columns, bristling with bayonets, rumbling with heavy or light batteries, clanking with sabers; and still they come—the morning sun finds but the debris of the camp of the evening before, and the same sun sets upon the same spot, a busy camp of fresh troops hurrying up and down the streets of their canvas city, like the shadowy figures in some shifting panorama. The Roundhead Regiment has lain four weeks on the heights of the Kalorama, and it is by three weeks the oldest settler to day. Its turn must come, we know not at what hour, but the hour will find us ready to "strike our tents and march away," leaving our "beautiful view" to be enjoyed by some younger brothers of the bayonet and sabre.*

October, however, opened with a series of rapid changes. On Wednesday, Colonel Leasure called the regiment together and read them a letter from Gov. Curtin, recognizing them as the One Hundredth Pennsylvania Volunteer Infantry Regiment. The campground echoed with cheers. And as Sergeant Fisher had predicted, a bag of insignia circulated, each man drawing the brass number that would identify his unit.

"It's about time," somebody mumbled.

"Yeah, but they're nice-looking badges," someone else offered.

"So who are we now, Roundheads or One Hundredth Pennsylvanians?

"Both, I suspect. We have an official designation on our hats and a nickname in our hearts. I'll bet it's the nickname that sticks."

In the days that followed, other supplies flowed into the Roundhead camp, signaling an approaching move. Men who were still missing parts of their uniforms filled out their needs. Ammunition boxes replaced the shells used up in target practice. Although the weather was still warm enough to allow the men to go swimming in Rock Creek, they received their long-awaited overcoats and extra blankets.

"Must mean we're headed somewheres cold."

"Nah, means winter's comin'."

"And we're headed out to meet it, I'll bet."

On Saturday, the arrival of an army major carrying a case full of official-looking papers set the rumor mills into overtime. In the evening Colonel Leasure announced the regiment had received its marching orders, and the men should begin to pack their gear. "I can't tell you more than that right now," he continued, "but you should be ready to march at a moment's notice."

Private James Stevenson, from his vantage point near the colonel's tent, confided in his diary: "Some think we are going to Missouri, some to Kentucky, some to North Carolina—but it is all guesswork. No one, not even the officers, know 'where' or 'when'."

Nellie was so busy organizing the medical wagon that she had little time to think about where they might be headed. On Wednesday evening the colonel announced that the men were to strike their tents at 4 a.m. the next morning. Then, to her surprise, the colonel sent his aide-de-camp to summon Nellie to his tent.

"You sent for me, Sir?" she asked as she hesitated at the edge of the tent flap.

"Yes, Nellie. Come in, please. Have a seat here at the table. I'm clearing up the last of our paper work, and I realized you had never completed your enlistment procedure. We need to take care of that before we move out."

"Enlistment? No, Sir. I told you I was a volunteer. I'm here to help in any way I can, but I'm not going to sign up."

"But you don't get paid if your paperwork is not in order, Mrs. Leath."

Nellie did not miss the change in the way he addressed her, nor did she misinterpret the sudden coolness in the tone of his voice. "I'm not asking to be paid, Colonel. I'm a pure volunteer."

"There's no place in this man's army for a pure volunteer. You will be a member of the regiment or be viewed as a camp-follower, a hanger-on, subject to dismissal at any moment. You'll have no real position, no authority, and no pension." He tossed the pen down with an exasperated sigh.

"I won't sign that paper, Sir. You may dismiss me if you like. Should I leave the camp?"

"No, but this discussion is not over. I don't have time to argue with you any more. You may travel along with us if you choose, but when we are settled, we'll have to revisit this matter." Leasure waved her away.

"I won't change my mind," she countered over her shoulder as she left.

"Well, maybe something will change it for you."

6

ON TO ANNAPOLIS

In the midst of the pre-dawn bustle, Nellie looked around one last time for a glimpse of her little cat, but he was nowhere to be found, perhaps driven into hiding by the commotion all around him. As the regiment finally moved out around 8 a.m., Nellie rode with the driver of the medical wagon. Looking back at the mansion where she had found peace, she whispered a private salute. Good-bye, Oliver. Thank you for being my friend. Good hunting, and stay well. It had begun to drizzle, and Nellie brushed away the moisture on her cheeks, telling herself it was caused by raindrops, not tears.

Despite the rain, the Roundheads moved out at a brisk pace, seemingly eager to get to whatever awaited them. As they passed the White House, President Lincoln himself came out onto the portico and saluted them. The soldiers executed a perfect "Eyes Right" and saluted their president. Then they headed for the train depot with renewed pride and dedication.

"He smiled at us," one soldier declared in admiration.

"Nah, probably got a cold raindrop down his neck. The man's too busy to take time to smile at a bunch of recruits from the hills of Pennsylvania."

"I'm sure he smiled!"

But no one had much to grin about the rest of the day. After a long-delayed breakfast, the men were ready to board a train—any train—and get on with the action. Colonel Leasure moved from company to company, answering questions as best he could and trying to quell the rumors that kept outpacing him.

"Sir, is it true there's fighting on down the track?"

"Yeah, we heard the track's all tore up and we can't get anywhere."

"Why don't we march on?"

"Oh, sure, and get caught up in a fight we didn't start!"

"Better'n sittin' here."

"Quiet!" the colonel said. "As far as I know there's no fighting near by. But those who know this area feel it's safer to transport large units after dark, so we'll delay here until our train arrives this evening. You may, if you like, go out and explore the neighborhood a bit. There's probably even enough time for a jaunt downtown if there's something you need. But be sure to be back here for roll call before dark."

"Where are we headed, Colonel? Have they told you that yet?"

"I know our train is to take us to Annapolis, where we will stage with other regiments for a major expedition. I don't know our final destination."

"Annapolis! Ain't that a Navy base?"

"That's where they train naval cadets, I think. Is that what they're gonna do with us?"

"Hey, I didn't sign up for the Navy. I get sick on boats."

"The Naval Academy is now being used as an Army fort," the colonel explained. "The naval commandant moved the cadets out to a place further north where they'd be safely out of the way of the action. We'll have the advantage of moving into their quarters while we wait for our own deployment. Annapolis is also the state capital of Maryland, so it's a bustling place."

"Probably full of Secesh-folk, if it's anything like Baltimore!"

"All the more reason to maintain a strong Union presence in the area."

"I still don't want to find myself in the Navy!"

"Well, it's a pretty safe bet we're going to be spending some time on the water. But in the meantime, you'll have a chance to relax. They say the harbor there on Chesapeake Bay is one of the most beautiful spots on earth."

"Huh! I don't mind looking at water, as long as there's firm land under my feet. It's them boat decks that bother me."

When Nellie grew tired of listening to the grumbling, she withdrew to the way station, where the women who were cooking for the troops showed her a quiet spot in their cloakroom. She had drifted off into a deep sleep, curled up in a chair whose high back provided a headrest.

Doctor Ludington found her there in the evening and shook her awake. "Nellie! Come on! Wake up!"

It took her a few moments to regain her bearings. "What is it? Are we leaving?"

"No, not yet. We've got a problem in Company B, and I need your help."

Now fully awake, she looked at his serious expression with growing concern. "Someone's hurt?"

"We have a sick soldier—high fever, stomach cramps, and the beginnings of a flat red rash."

"Measles again?"

"Worse. I think he's got typhoid."

"Oh, no," she murmured. They had already lost one soldier to typhoid fever back in camp at Kalorama, so she understood the prognosis. "He'll have to be left behind."

"We can't do that. There are no medical facilities near the station, and if we leave him, he'll die for sure."

"So what do you want me to do?"

"I'm going to put him in the back of the officer's railcar, somewhat isolated from the others. I need you to ride with him. Keep him sponged off with cool water, so the fever stays under control, and see if you can help him drink something. Beyond that, about all you can do is keep him talking, so he doesn't slip away from us. It'll comfort him to have a woman with him."

Annapolis lay only thirty-four miles from Washington, but to the Roundheads, it might as well have been three hundred miles. The tracks were undergoing repair, so the train made frequent stops. Sometimes there was a train coming the other way, and they were forced to back up for miles to find a switch. Even when the way was clear, the engineer had to move slowly, keeping a lookout for damage along the right-of-way. Few of the soldiers got much sleep that night. Some climbed to the top of the cars to get some air, only to be driven back by sudden rain squalls. Others jumped off when they spotted an apple orchard or unharvested corn field, where they could forage for something to eat. And some got off whenever the train backed up.

"Been there before," one man mumbled. "Might as well see what's new waiting for us." He walked ahead, knowing he could pull himself back aboard when the crawling train caught up. It didn't get him there any faster, but it was something to do.

Nellie made her patient, Corporal Billy Sample, as comfortable as she could on the hard wooden benches. To distract him, Nellie cast about for topics of conversation.

"Did you have a pet when you were growing up?" she asked.

"Still do." The soldier made a good effort at smiling. "Big ole' huntin' dog named Charlie. He's a good'un. Smells a 'coon up a tree from a mile off."

"Do you miss him?"

"You bet! Seems like Charlie's always been my best friend. When I was a gangly kid, he was the only one in the whole family who didn't make fun of my pimply face and clumsy feet. Charlie'd just smile that goofy, tongue-dangling smile of his. And if I wanted to read a book instead of going hunting, he'd sit with his head on my knee and wait till I was through."

"So you're a reader! And what did you like to read, Corporal?"

"Anything I could get my hands on. We had a book of Shakespeare I plumb wore out. Charlie didn't understand much of it when I'd read it out to him, but he seemed to like the sound of the words. That's what I mean by him being a good dog. How about you? Did you have pets as a kid?"

"No, not really. We lived on a farm. But Papa made sure there was a firm line between barn and house. Animals were for profit, not for pets."

"What about Oliver?"

"Oliver?" Nellie looked at him in surprise. "How do you know about Oliver?"

"Oh, everybody knew he was your cat. We'd hear you talking to him sometimes out behind the mess tent. And once I saw him sneaking into your tent in the middle of the night."

Nellie struggled with a lump that had suddenly formed in her throat and something that made her eyes water. "I thought. . . ." She couldn't talk.

"It's all right, Miss Nellie. It's natural to love something that loves you back, even if it's a little cat. Do you know what Shakespeare said about love not being love if it changed?"

"Love is not love, which alters when it alteration finds, or bends with the remover to remove," she quoted.

"That's the one. People can change their minds all the time, but not animals like Charlie and Oliver. When this war is over and we can go home again, they'll be waiting for us, the same as always. That's the thought that keeps me going, sometimes. When this here war's over, I'm gonna try to be the kind of man Charlie thinks I am."

"It's a beautiful thought, Billy."

"Yeah," he sighed. "Think I need to rest awhile."

For the rest of the night, Nellie sat with the boy's head propped on her lap and watched him as he slept. Her heart ached—sometimes for him, sometimes for Oliver, and sometimes for that good ole' huntin' dog, waiting for his owner, who might never be coming home.

The week they spent at Annapolis was almost a vacation for most of the Roundheads. As the colonel had promised, they were quartered in two-story houses in the Naval Yard. The buildings were solidly constructed of brick, and the central yard boasted brick walkways, trees of every description, and grassy areas that were beginning to turn brown but were still invitingly soft. The furnishings were utilitarian, but each two-man room had iron bedsteads with real stuffed mattresses. Their meals were cooked on an iron stove and served at long tables. Plates were made of china, and glasses were really glass. For a few days they could forget the flapping of tent canvas and the smell of frying grease and wood smoke.

For Nellie, however, the first days passed in a blur. By Monday, Billy Sample's condition had worsened, and Nellie seldom left his side. He tossed in the throes of delirium, groaning, mumbling, and sometimes shouting out in terror. Once, Nellie was sure she heard him call out to Charlie. There was little anyone could do for him. Sometime late Monday evening, he sank into a stupor whose quietness was as terrifying as his former thrashings had been. Nellie ran to summon the doctor.

"He's not going to make it, is he?"

"We can't say. It's up to the strength of his own constitution, but it doesn't look hopeful."

"It's not fair," she protested. "He's such a fine, simple, good soul. He never hurt anyone. He loved his dog and read Shakespeare. Why should he have to suffer like this?"

Near dawn, Doctor Ludington pulled the blanket over Billy's face. "It's over."

"Shall I go for the chaplain?" she asked. But as she spoke, tears began to course down her cheeks.

"No, I'll do that. You need to get control of yourself, Nellie. You mustn't let Reverend Browne catch you weeping. He'll use it to prove you're not strong enough to go with us into war."

Nellie's chin came up and she glared at the doctor for a moment. Then she realized he was absolutely right. "It's not my first experience with death, and I dare say it won't be my last. I'm fine, Doctor."

"Well, in any event, you need to get some rest. I'll make arrangements for the corporal's body to be shipped home. You've done more here than anyone could have expected of you."

"So he'll go home. At least he'll be spared the horrors of war. But poor Charlie. He didn't want his master coming home this way."

The Roundheads settled into their comfortable surroundings. Colonel Leasure did his best to limit official duties to one short drill period a day, along with only two roll calls, one in the morning and one at nightfall. Company commanders freely distributed passes, so every soldier got at least one chance to go into town and see the sights. Some were content to stroll past the State House, while others nosed about the shops and taverns. Entertainment opportunities lay around every corner, although the strict moral training of the young Roundheads kept most of them from falling victim to the shadiest dealings of saloons, gambling dens, and dance halls. Some of the men took the opportunity to visit one of the bathhouses for the luxury of a long soak in warm water. They got haircuts and shaves and had their likenesses made at a local photographer's shop.

If there was one attraction that outweighed all the others, it was the taste of oysters taken fresh from Chesapeake Bay. Most had never sampled this common seafood, but it took only once to make dedicated oyster connoisseurs out of landlocked farm boys. Shucked oysters were available all over town for six cents a pint, and hungry soldiers could down a quart or two without spoiling their appetites a bit. Once in a while, someone sold them a bad oyster, leading Nellie, who had grown up among oyster-rakers, to encourage the men to go out and gather their own. When she could escape her sick call duties, she walked with her volunteers down to the shoreline and showed the men how and where to gather them.

"Just don't ever eat an oyster whose shell is already opened," she cautioned. "It may look like you're taking the easy way out, but chances are the little creature inside is sick enough—or dead enough—to make you wish you'd never met him." When several of her pupils became skilled enough to rake in a real harvest, Nellie took them all back to the mess kitchen and gave the cooks a lesson in how to make an oyster stew. The respite from the sick room and the appreciation of the diners did much to bolster Nellie's mood.

The Naval Yard itself provided other kinds of distraction for soldiers looking for something different to do. Those who were so inclined could take small boats out onto Dorsey Creek and follow it to where it flowed into the Severn River and the Bay. Fishing was more than a novelty; it provided an excuse to sit still and soak up the fresh air and scenery. There was the Observatory that looked out over the water, and from its decks the men could watch as a fleet of ships began to assemble out in Chesapeake Bay. Even Reverend Browne waxed poetic at the view. He wrote a letter to the newspaper back home, describing how moving he found the sights:

Since I wrote to you a number of steamers have glided into the harbor, and silently tied by the shore or anchored out in deeper water. The latter are ocean Steamers. Four of them have not come in at all, but lie at anchored outside in the deeper waters of the Chesapeake Bay. There is something suggestive of mystery, combined with the conception of wisdom and power in the appearance of these vessels in these waters, and their riding at anchor there so quietly day by day. When I arrived here there were none at all. Now I count seventeen of them from the cupola of the State House. They are beautiful objects, with their clean cut keels, their single chimney stacks, and two masts each; and there they sit like birds upon the water; they resemble to my eye, eagles upon their perch, that seem to be oblivious to every surrounding thing, but whose eyes sweep the horizon, while we know not what moment they may swoop down, and fall like thunderbolts upon their prey.

The chaplain's words gave voice to a underlying tension many of the soldiers were feeling, though they might not have expressed it so eloquently. Oysters roasting over an open fire or frizzing up their edges in a hot stew were all the more wonderful when they remembered the hardtack that filled their knapsacks and promised to be the only meal available on a battlefield. The sounds of fiddles encouraged a hoedown. A banjo plucking out the notes of "Hell Broke Loose in Georgia" helped the men tune out the muffled sounds of gunfire in the distance. And time to write long letters home to friends and family introduced even the wildest carouser to periods of sober introspection.

The men were enjoying their week of liberty, but it took little to touch off a scuffle or an argument. One such incident erupted on Wednesday with the arrival of a runaway slave. An officer from Company K took the man into his own tent and then sought out the colonel for advice.

"He's in a bad way, Colonel—barefoot, clothes hanging in rags, and starving from the looks of him," Captain Van Gorder explained. "Says his name's Jeremiah, but that's all he knows. Can I fix him up and put him to work in the camp?"

"Uh, Captain, we don't keep slaves in this man's army," the colonel said.

"No, of course not, but the Bible says we should take in strangers, clothe the naked, and feed the hungry."

"Reverend Browne would be proud of you, Son, but the Bible doesn't say you then put them to work for you. You may, of course, do what you can to alleviate this man's suffering. See to it he gets a good meal, and while he's eating, your men can poke about and find some civilian shoes and clothing they no longer need. You may even allow him some hours of well-earned sleep. But then, your Christian duty is to take him out of camp and see him safely on his way north."

The men of Company K were more than willing to rally around the runaway. Some of them, to be sure, were mainly curious because they had never seen a black man. One young soldier who came bringing a good used shirt stood slack-jawed when he caught a glimpse of the slave's back crisscrossed with scars. Others, who had been raised in abolitionist families back home, volunteered to go into town and seek out someone who might know the safest route through the slave-holding state.

"There's a community of free blacks in the Uptown area of Annapolis," the colonel advised. "If you can make contact with somebody there, they'll know where he should go."

All might have gone smoothly, if it had not been for the arrival of the slave's owner, pursuing him with the fire of vengeance in his eyes. He strode into the Naval Yard shouting, "Y'all harborin' runaways here? Get outta my way. I want my nigger back!"

"Halt!" ordered the private who was mounting a cursory guard duty at the gate. "You can't come in here."

"The hell I can't! I'm Clyde Pickens, and that there Jeremiah's my nigger, and I mean to have him back. I know he came this way. He was seen."

The commotion brought the Roundheads swarming. A shouting, angry man meant a fight, and they were more than ready for one. While eight of the largest men from Company K surrounded the slave and hustled him out the back door of the barracks, the others ran to join the growing crowd. Captain Van Gorder led the way.

"Damn Yankees! Where is he? I'll have your hides, you miserable bastards."

"Excuse me, Mr. Pickens," said the captain, smiling with a smile that had no touch of humor in it. "Are you saying this man you seek *belongs* to you?"

"Damned right he does, and I'll have him flogged for trying to get away."

"Oh, but first, I think you'll have to prove he *belongs* to you. That's a concept we just don't understand, Sir. Does he have your name on him somewhere?"

"You bet he does —written in the scars on his miserable back."

"Sign your name with an *X*, do you?" shouted someone from the crowd.

"On a slave's hide, I do!" By this time the soldiers had surrounded the man and were closing their circle ever more tightly to prevent his escape.

"Ah, but we'll need something more," the captain continued. "A bill of sale, perhaps."

"Yeah, I got one of them somewheres. He's my nigger, bought and paid for."

"And that bill of sale is signed by whom?"

"I don't know. Some slave trader, I guess."

"Not God himself?"

"What?"

"I'm afraid, Sir, we believe only God can own a man's soul. Without his written word, we can't help you."

"God damn you all to hell! I'll get Gov. Hicks to take this up with your commander. He'll see to it you are all punished for your impudence."

"You do that, Sir. I'm sure the governor will be happy to explain why he's not about to take on several thousand armed soldiers. In the meantime, you're free to go. There are no slaves here, and *your nigger*, as you call him, left here long ago. Go on, now. Scat, before we decide to mark your own miserable hide with our own *peculiar* Union brand."

Slowly the soldiers drew away, opening a gap that pointed the slave owner straight back at the gate. As he backed toward it, they kept pace with him, their voices keeping up a continuous angry murmur of threatening epithets. Their blood was boiling, and it would take some time for them to settle down.

"Show's over, men," announced the colonel as he walked into their midst. "You did a fine job. That fellow will not be able to show a single mark to prove he was treated badly here. But maybe he'll remember Federal soldiers are not to be taken lightly."

"We shoulda strung him up," grumbled one hotheaded soldier.

"No, Sir," Col Leasure replied. "That would have put us on his level. We're better than that. But he'll remember this lesson. Being humbled and ridiculed is often more painful than physical injury. Keep your anger under control until you're in a real fight."

"Is Jeremiah safe?" someone asked.

"Yes, he's in the hands of his own people, who will deliver him to the next way station along their trail to freedom. Now let's get back to work. I think perhaps an extra drill might serve us well. It won't be long before we're given real marching orders."

The Roundheads settled back into their routine, but tensions were even tighter now. When another dispute arose two days later, tempers flared with little provocation. The day started auspiciously enough, with Colonel Leasure and most of his staff being summoned to inspect the transport ship on which their regiment was to travel. That was a signal to everyone it was time to prepare for the next move. All around the quarters of the Hundredth Pennsylvania, other regiments were packing up. From the Naval Yard, the Roundheads watched as the Twenty-First Massachusetts and several other regiments marched past on their way to the steamers. The young Pennsylvanians awaited their turn enthusiastically.

Then a small incident marred the excitement of the day and threatened to sour some of the men on the camaraderie of military life. General Isaac Ingalls Stevens had arrived at the Naval Yard earlier in the week to take command of his brigade, which included the Roundheads, the Fiftieth Pennsylvania, the Eighth Michigan, and the Seventy-Ninth New York Highlanders. Before his promotion to brigadier general, Stevens had been the commander of the Highlanders and was popular with them. But in the assumption of his larger command, he seemed to forget that, for the rest of his brigade, he was still an unknown entity. Stevens had consulted Colonel Leasure about a location for his administrative headquarters, and Leasure had directed him to an empty but spacious brick building. On Friday, Stevens was joined by the man he had selected as the brigade's Quarter Master, a certain William Lilly. But as Lilly was about to move his staff and belongings into the building, an ambulance arrived carrying a smallpox patient.

Stevens and Lilly shrank away in horror at the sight of the man. "Get him away from here," Stevens shouted. "You'll infect us all."

"I'm sorry, Sir," the ambulance attendant replied, "but this is the quarantine house where we house all smallpox patients. Didn't anyone tell you?"

Stevens was a small and tidy man, but capable of flying into a rage that sent brave men cowering before him. "God damn that Leasure," he shouted. "Come with me, Lilly." And the two men stormed into the Roundheads' regimental headquarters. "Where is Colonel Leasure's room?" Stevens demanded.

"Upstairs and to the right," the private on duty replied, "but he's not there."

"Nor will he ever be!" Stevens shouted. He aimed a kick at the door, and gestured to the men who had come to see what the commotion was all about. "Clear out the colonel's things," he ordered. "I want this room."

"I don't think we can do that, Sir, not without the colonel's permission."

"By God, I give the permissions around here."

"Perhaps if you wait a bit, he'll return from his inspection trip and you can discuss the move with him."

"Jesus Christ! Are you all deaf? Move him out," I said.

"But where are we to put his things?"

"You can send them to Hell and the colonel with them, for all I care. Just do what I say. Of all the blasted bloody fools I've met today, you're the worst. Do I have to blow you all up to get your attention? Get your butts in gear, soldiers."

As the men stacked the colonel's things in the hall, Leasure himself mounted the stairs. "What's going on?" he asked curiously.

A clamor of voices shouted at him, so it took a while to sort out the full story. Leasure was surprisingly composed. He turned to Mr. Lilly, who was stomping about impatiently. "I'm sorry about the confusion, Sir. Please convey my apologies to the general. With all due respect, however, you do not want to make your headquarters in this room. You'd be pestered at all hours by men who did not know about the change." He turned to look for his son Geordy.

"My aide-de-camp, Lieutenant Leasure, will show you to another suite of rooms at the end of the hall. I'm sure you'll be more comfortable there."

Reverend Browne had been observing the altercation from the sidelines. "I never heard such profanity, Daniel," he said. "How can you tolerate such behavior?"

"The army is not your typical social gathering, Robert. And I'll wager you've heard worse language in your time. The general has a great deal on his mind, and naturally the stress of being responsible for the lives of 4000 men weighs upon him. Don't judge him too harshly."

"So we tolerate his indignities?"

"Yes, Robert, that's exactly the way of it."

"I'll bow to your command, Daniel, but it's an unhealthy start to our relationship with the man. I suspect many of us will be a long time in forgetting the unpleasantness we've witnessed here today."

Colonel Leasure shook his head. "In the days to come, my friend, you'll look back on this scene as a bastion of serenity."

7

ABOARD THE OCEAN QUEEN

General Stevens' Second Brigade needed two days to load all of its soldiers and staff onto their transports. The general's staff, along with the Eighth Michigan and the Seventy-Ninth New York Highlanders filled the *Vanderbilt*. The Roundheads and half the Fiftieth Pennsylvania boarded the *Ocean Queen*, while the remaining 500 men of the Fiftieth Pennsylvania were assigned to the smaller *Winfield Scott*. The *Ocean Queen* was a two-masted side-wheeler passenger ship. Built in 1857, purchased by Vanderbilt Lines, and rented to the War Department in 1861, it boasted three decks above the water line and two decks below. The ship was originally designed to carry 350 passengers in first- and second-class cabins. The first-class cabins on the upper deck had, for the most part, been left as they were, but the lower decks were crowded with bunks to accommodate up to 1500 passengers. Stacked four high, with as little as two feet between them, the bunks were eighteen inches wide and separated from the next tier by an aisle that could let only one person pass at a time.

Nellie was relieved to learn she and the other women were to be housed in one of the first-class cabins. She was less pleased when she made her way to the cabin and found the other women had taken over the space with all their accouterments. As she opened the cabin door, the women's excited chatter stopped abruptly, and they stared at Nellie with barely concealed hostility.

"Am I in the right cabin?" Nellie asked.

"Prob'ly so," muttered Mrs. White. "There's an empty bunk up on top." She nodded toward the least accessible bunk.

"And my things? I was told they'd been stowed in my cabin." The women looked around with feigned innocence and shrugging shoulders. Finally Nellie spotted her small trunk at the bottom of a stack of boxes.

I won't make a fuss, Nellie told herself. There's not enough room in here to unleash a fight. Instead, she forced herself to smile at her cabinmates. "I'll worry about that later. I just wanted to see where my things were. I'll be back after we get the sick call cabin set up." She backed out of the room as fast as she could. Making her way down the passageway, she spotted Doctor Ludington and hurried to catch up with him.

"Welcome aboard, Doctor. Can I be of help with the medical supplies?"

"You don't need to do that right now, Nellie. We have no patients yet, so we'll have plenty of time to get organized. Have you seen the sick bay? It's nice." He stopped at the door and held it open for Nellie to enter ahead of him.

She looked around with relief. After her own cramped quarters, these wide bunks and ample chairs were a welcome sight. "I'll be happy to stay on duty here," she told the doctor.

"There's no need for you to be on call all the time, Nellie," he began. Then he noted the crestfallen expression on her face. "Your own quarters not up to these standards?" he asked.

"I don't mean to complain, but the other women are unwelcoming. I'm sure they'd be happier if I weren't quartered with them. And it would be disturbing to them if I had to be called out while they were trying to sleep. That's a lame excuse, I suspect, but. . . ."

"Nellie, you're the regimental matron. You should be able to decide where you live and work. I'll be happy to know you are here whenever a sick soldier needs attention. By all means, make yourself comfortable. I'll tell one of the men to move your things from the ladies' cabin. Until then, you might want to take some air on deck. As I came down, I noticed some of the men were looking a bit green in the gills up there. Maybe you can offer them some advice on getting their sea legs."

"I'll try, Sir."

As luck would have it, the first fellow she saw hanging over the rails of the ship in agony was Reverend Browne. "Not feeling well?" she asked solicitously.

"Ah, Mrs. Leath. I'm not one to complain, but I didn't expect the deck to rock this much. I'll adjust, I'm sure. I've been trying to distract myself by reading my Bible, but it's not working."

"Well, that's part of your problem," Nellie said. "Not that there's anything wrong with reading the Bible, mind you, but a pitching deck isn't the best place to do it. If you'll look out at something far away instead of something up close, I think you'll find you'll feel better."

"So I should look back at something on shore and wish that's where I was?"

"No, actually, you need to look out over the water. And don't stare at one spot. Let your eyes move back and forth in rhythm with the waves."

"You speak as if you're familiar with boats," he observed with an arched eyebrow.

"I am, Sir. I grew up near the coast of Maine, and several of my uncles ran fishing boats. I've been on the water as long as I can remember."

"Hmmmm. I'd be interested in hearing all about your past sometime."

I'm sure you would, Nellie thought to herself, but I wouldn't trust you that far! She smiled brightly at him. "Perhaps sometime when you're feeling better. For now, I think you need to concentrate on getting acclimated."

"And what do you recommend?"

"Well, for one thing, you're much too stiff. You're trying to hold yourself rigid to compensate for the moving deck. But when you do that, your body feels one sensation, your eyes tell you something else, and your sense of balance is completely confused. Try moving with the ship. Sway back and forth. Shift your feet. Lean forward and back. Look around. Inhale deeply instead of holding your breath. Just don't look at anything up close."

"Ah, learned advice, I'm sure, spoken by one who is not being assailed by waves of nausea. I, however, must read my Bible to find a topic for tomorrow morning's sermon, regardless of how I may feel."

Nellie shook her head at the stubbornness of the male ego. "Why don't you try something you have memorized, instead? 'He leadeth me beside still waters' might be appropriate." She laughed despite her attempts to look wide-eyed and serious.

"Do you find religion humorous, Mrs. Leath?" the chaplain asked.

"No, Sir, but I don't believe God minds us enjoying ourselves."

"Don't you? A pity. Your attitude reveals much about you." Reverend Browne wheeled away from her and stomped stiff-legged toward the nearest hatch. He almost made it before he had to dash for the rail again and relieve himself of the rest of his lunch.

Yes, Sir. Our attitudes reveal a great deal about ourselves, don't they? Nellie thought. Then she shrugged and turned away.

The *Ocean Queen* was ready to sail out of the harbor at Annapolis and cross Chesapeake Bay on her way to join the rest of the fleet. But the water was rough, and headwinds further delayed her passage. The ship stayed at anchor through Sunday, giving most of the soldiers time to find their sea legs and settle into a new routine. There were so many bodies aboard the vessel it was necessary to limit movements. The cooks served only two meals a day, due to the logistics of getting everyone in and out of the mess cabin.

"You'll get your full ration of food," Colonel Leasure promised, but the more enterprising among the soldiers busied themselves making deals with the cooks to snatch a few extra rations. The sailors on board were more than willing to raid the pantry if it meant a chance to cheat the soldiers. Soon they were doing a brisk business in everything from bread to brandy. One poor fellow was caught sneaking out of the kitchen at night with a plate stacked high with pickles. When the guard shouted at him, he started to run, lost his balance, and scattered the pickles across the deck. Those who witnessed the incident were quicker to gather up the pickles than to help the thief to his feet.

The Sunday sermon was delayed until Sunday evening. When Reverend Browne finally made his way to the deck where the soldiers had been assembled, he looked distinctly pale and shaky. "I have taken as my text today the Twenty-Third Psalm: 'The Lord is my shepherd; I shall not want'."

Nellie took deep breaths to control her amusement. She managed to control herself through the reference to 'still waters', but by the time the chaplain reached the passage about walking 'through the valley of the shadow of death', she had to back her way out of the crowd and flee to the shelter of the sick bay, where she could laugh without disrupting the service. *I should have told him that you don't die from seasickness,* she thought. *You're just afraid you won't.* It took all of her strength to muster a bit of sympathy for the pompous man.

The water was still rough on Monday morning, but fifteen ships set out on their passage to Hampton Roads. This protected area, where the James River and the Elizabeth River flow into Chesapeake Bay, was known as the greatest natural harbor in the world. By the time the *Ocean Queen* and her companions reached Fort Monroe, a six-sided and moated fortress that dominated the southern-most tip of Virginia's peninsula and protected Hampton Roads, the anchorage was already filled by the largest fleet the Union Navy had ever assembled. With the addition of the arrivals from Annapolis, the fleet numbered some eighty vessels, ranging in size from the *Wabash*, the enormous flagship of Admiral Samuel E. DuPont, to a cluster of small tugs and whalers that had been pressed into service to help. Brigadier General Thomas William Sherman was in command of the Army's South Carolina Expeditionary Force of 12,000 men. The expedition was set to enforce the blockade of the southern coast. As the last elements assembled, General Sherman sent a formal message to his men:

The general commanding announces to the expeditionary corps that it is intended to make a descent on the enemy's coast, and probably under circumstances which will demand the utmost vigilance, coolness, and intrepidity on the part of every officer and man of his command. In consideration of the justness and holiness of our cause, of the ardent patriotism which has prompted the virtuous and industrious citizens of our land to fly to their country's standard in the moment of her peril, he most confidently believes that he will be effectually and efficiently supported in his efforts to overthrow a zealous, active, and wily foe, whose cause is unholy and principles untenable.

They were stirring words, and the men of the Hundredth Pennsylvania were ready for action. Unfortunately, naval and military maneuvers were not easy to coordinate. DuPont concentrated on the fleet's preparations to sail. He was looking for good weather and a speedy trip down the coast, hoping to catch the Confederate defenders unaware of their approach and unprepared to defend their harbors from his booming guns. For DuPont, this was a naval mission, one in which the soldiers were unimportant. Sherman, on the other hand, expected the expedition to be an Army assault. To him, the Navy's ships were merely transports. Although the fleet contained a large number of sailing ships loaded with food, equipment, and munitions, Sherman worried his 12,000 men were not adequately supplied, and he did his best to delay the launching of the expedition. As a result, the Expeditionary Force found itself in a self-perpetuating quandary. Food and water had been provided for the journey, but not in sufficient quantities to support a delay in Hampton Roads. The men, of course, consumed those supplies rapidly during the delays, creating a need for restocking and causing further delay.

The men of the Hundredth Pennsylvania tried their best to adapt to life aboard ship, but with nothing to do, they soon became cranky and bored, a sure formula for trouble. Reverend Browne made his rounds to check on behavioral problems, but he could do little more than fulminate. He became especially agitated over the discovery the men of the Fiftieth Pennsylvania were much addicted to playing cards. He became something of a fixture on deck, striding over to the card players and delivering an impromptu sermon on the evils of gambling. For the most part, the men simply ignored him. But in his nightly letter to his wife, he reported in at least one instance the players were so moved they threw their cards overboard on the spot. The chaplain also worried the Roundheads might be unduly influenced by this ungodly behavior and watched them closely for signs of corruption.

But not closely enough. On the second night at anchor, two Roundheads from Company C visited Nellie in the sick bay. Private Hugh Wilson had a blackening eye, a split lip, and a cut over his left eyebrow that bled profusely. His friend Jacob Leary nursed a scratched and swollen left hand. "What on earth happened to the two of you?" Nellie asked as she bustled about finding sticking plasters.

"Do we have to tell?" asked Jacob.

"Well, no, I suppose you don't owe me an explanation, but I'll need to report something to Doctor Ludington."

"We was in a bit of a disagreement—over some money," Hugh offered. Nellie cocked an eyebrow at the men, and somehow the whole story came spilling out. The soldiers had been invited to join a poker game and had been unwilling to admit they knew nothing about the game. They sat down and tried to conceal their ignorance by simply watching what everyone else did. They held their cards and added money to the pot whenever it was their turn. The real players soon caught on and ran the betting up until they had emptied the pockets of the Roundheads. When a member of the Fiftieth raked in his winnings, Hugh and Jacob had gotten up to leave, but the others encouraged them to stay, giving them markers they could use instead of money. Again, the two innocents did as they were told, not realizing they were running up a huge debt. When the game broke up, the winners demanded their money. The frightened and confused Roundheads reacted in panic, and a fistfight had broken out, only to be disrupted by the corporal of the guard, who sent them all packing.

"Whatever possessed you to keep playing?" Nellie demanded. "Did you ever win?"

"I don't know," Hugh answered. "We didn't know how we was supposed to win."

"Oh, my word. You two really need help. This sticking plaster may hold your wounds together, but it's of no use on your ignorance. You'd better stay far away from poker games until somebody teaches you the rules—like the meaning of the word 'fold'."

"Well, nobody in our regiment is going to conduct poker lessons, that's for sure," said Jacob. "Reverend Browne'd have a cow if he caught us!"

"I could."

"What?"

I said I could." Nellie grinned at them. "I was married to a professional gambler in another life. There's not much I don't know about card games."

"Oh, Mrs. Leath! Would you? Could you?"

"That'd be great. I'll bet we could find lots of boys from home who'd like to learn."

"We could have regular classes. I'd really like to get even with those fellows who whomped us."

Nellie held up a hand to stop the flow of words. "Wait a minute. I'll give you two a couple of quick lessons, but I'm not about to start a poker class here in sick bay. Reverend Browne's looking for a chance to get rid of me, and that would do it, sure as anything."

"Fair enough. Can we start now?"

"Well, let me give you a homework assignment. You'll have to know how winning hands are determined. Write the list down and memorize them in order. Then come back tomorrow evening after dinner, and we'll do a bit of practice. Here's the winning list, starting with the lowest: 1 pair; 2 pair; 3 of a kind; a straight (5 cards in a row); a flush (5 cards of the same suit); full house (2 of one value, three of another); 4 of a kind; straight flush (5 in order, all same suit); and royal flush (A-K-Q-J-10 of same suit)."

"Gosh! So that's what they meant by full houses and flushes. No wonder we didn't know what we were doing."

"Oh, and there are a few other terms you need to know. At the beginning of a hand, everyone has to ante up a minimum bet. After the next bet, you have a choice. You can call the bet by matching it, or you can raise the bet, in which case everyone else has to match you. Or you can fold, which means you quit before you lose your socks."

"Which is what we should have done?"

"Exactly. Now go get some rest, and don't get involved in any more card games till you know what you're doing."

"Yes, M'am!"

Nellie should have known better, of course. But she thought the wide-eyed young soldiers from Pennsylvania deserved at least a fighting chance to get their money back. And I really don't see what all the fuss is about, she told herself. When Reverend Browne gets going on how cards are the Devil's playthings, he sounds silly.

When Jacob and Hugh showed up at sick bay the next night, Nellie was ready for their next lesson. She had charmed a lieutenant from the Fiftieth into loaning her a deck of cards she could use for a demonstration. Using a bunk as an improvised table, she soon had the soldiers dealing hands of five-card stud.

"Here's what you need to remember. Always fold when a card on the board beats what you have in your hand. And in general, fold whenever you don't have a pair within the first three cards, unless all three of your cards are the same suit or are in a row. Then you can try one more round to see if you're headed for a flush or a straight."

"But why quit before you've seen all five of your cards?"

"Because each card costs you money, that's why!" Jacob was beginning to catch on.

"One other thing you need to learn. Keep track of all the cards on the table. If you're holding two jacks, and you can see another jack face up on the table, you're pretty much. . . ."

Before she could finish her sentence, the door to the sick bay burst open, and in stomped Reverend Browne. "What in blazes is going on here, Mrs. Leath? Are you . . . gambling?" He was so agitated that drops of spittle flew from his straggly mustache.

"No, no, no, you don't understand," Nellie said, surprised by his unannounced arrival.

"I know what I see!"

"I was trying to explain the game of poker to these young men, so they don't get taken advantage of."

"Poker is a sin! All card-playing is a sin! You'll all go to Hell for this!"

"I doubt that." Nellie had recovered her composure, even as Reverend Browne seemed to be losing his. "I don't remember reading anything about that in my Bible," she went on. "We're not gambling. There's no money being won or lost. We're having a rational discussion about the theory behind the game. Do you have something against rationality?" She glared back at him defiantly. "Being reasonable is a gift from God, is it not?"

"I'll see to it you are fired for this! You're not a fit woman to be associating with this godly regiment. I'm going to the Colonel right this minute."

"You do that, Reverend. But you might wipe your chin first." It was an uncalled-for comment, but Nellie couldn't resist. She was almost relieved the hard feelings between them would be brought out into the open at last.

8

STORMY PASSAGE

The fleet finally lifted anchors on Tuesday, October 29, 1861. The seas were still a bit rough, but the weather was warm and the skies a brilliant blue. For many of the Roundheads, this would be the first time they had sailed out of sight of land, and the experience was as exciting as it was terrifying. Many of the Roundheads had learned Nellie's trick of watching the horizon rather than objects that lay close by, but when the horizon no longer revealed the promise of dry land, they were once again disoriented. The result was a recurrence of sea sickness, so pervasive that later the Camp Kettle recaptured the experience:

> *If any body wants to get to the depth of deepest misery, let him just go to sea, and encounter a small gale the first day out. At first it is all nice, and consummately funny. The ship rises and sinks, and rolls and pitches, and settles away and comes right up again to go through the same gyrations over and over again, and your gait becomes unsteady, and rocky, and your companions laugh at you, and then you laugh at them, and it is all delightful, but by and bye, you begin to experience a sort of goneness all over, some thing not exactly desirable, until at last the vessel rears up at the bow and again goes down and you feel as if the bottom of the briny deep was rushing up through your epigastrium. And you make a rush for any convenient place, and aah! It's disgusting.*

Nellie kept busy, offering advice, honey, ground ginger, and dry crackers to those most afflicted. When all else failed, she sent a couple of the sickest to the prow of the ship, telling them the captain wanted them to keep a sharp lookout for Confederate pirates. It didn't matter that the captain had said no such thing, or that there were no Confederate pirates to be had. The subterfuge worked by forcing them to look out over the water and to shift their feet to keep their balance. Most handled their discomfort with a characteristic touch of humor. Private James C. Stevenson remarked, "I wouldn't care for throwing up the rice and beans, but I hate to lose the crackers after so much hard chewing to get them down."

By the second day, the seas had calmed, and the epidemic of seasickness seemed to have passed. The fleet stretched out as far as the eye could see, the ordered sails and funnels of the ships providing an artificial reassurance that all was well. As the men lounged about the deck, the officers had time to catch up on paperwork and administrative duties. For Nellie, that meant another interview about her behavior. Geordy Leasure sought her out with a message the colonel wanted to see her in his cabin. She didn't have to ask why.

She found Colonel Leasure hard at work at an improvised desk in his quarters. She tapped tentatively at his open doorway. Looking up, he gave her a quick nod and beckoned her to enter.

"If you're busy, Sir, I can come back later," she said.

"No, no, I need to talk to you. Just give me a moment to finish this dispatch. General Sherman does not like to be kept waiting, even when the answer to his question is unimportant."

"I'll wait in the passageway, then."

"Nonsense. Come in and have a seat where you can be comfortable. I won't be long." His attention immediately refocused on the document he was writing. Nellie took a seat, perching gingerly on the edge of a deep armchair that threatened to swallow her if she leaned back. She was uncomfortably aware that from the passageway, anyone walking past the door could see she and the colonel were alone in his cabin. Leasure, however, seemed to have no such qualms, and as he continued to work, she gradually relaxed.

She allowed her gaze to linger over this man whom she barely knew but who had changed her life dramatically.

He's a funny little fellow, she thought. *With that beard and mustache and those muttonchop sideburns, he looks more like a loveable little bear than a military commander. But short as he is, everyone seems to look up to him. I've never heard anyone complain about him, and he does have kind eyes. He's never been anything but gentle with me, though I wouldn't want to cross him. An interesting man. I hope he lets me stay around long enough to get to know him. He's someone I think I could trust.*

Her musings were interrupted by a whistle, which brought an orderly running into the cabin. "Yes, Sir?" the private saluted, and then cast a curious glance at the nurse sitting at the side of the desk.

Nellie cringed, but the colonel seemed not to notice. "See to it this message is delivered to General Sherman's transport as quickly as possible, Soldier."

"Yes, Sir!"

"Now then, Mrs. Leath. I suspect you know why you're here?"

"Reverend Browne has been in to complain again, hasn't he?"

"What were you thinking, Nellie!" The colonel slammed his palm on his desk, and Nellie jumped despite herself. Quick tears sprang to her eyes and she blinked furiously.

"You know how Robert feels about gambling, don't you? You've heard his sermons as he's preached over and over to our boys about the dangers of succumbing to temptation while far from home. Or haven't you been listening?"

"I . . . I . . . I'm sorry, Sir. I've heard him, and I understand what he's been saying, but I thought. . . ."

"No! Don't tell me you're sorry. I want to know what was going on in that pretty little head of yours."

Nellie's mind reeled. She was terrified she was going to be sent home, although how that could be accomplished in the middle of the ocean she had no idea. She worried some of the soldiers she had befriended would witness her disgrace through that open cabin door. And at the same time, a niggling little voice in the back of her mind asked, Did he just call me pretty?

She opened her mouth repeatedly, but no sounds came out. I must look like a goldfish, she thought, and that image brought her close to giggles. And if I'm a goldfish, I'm awfully out of place in the middle of this ocean. If Nellie had been able to move outside herself, she would have been astounded at her own feelings. Here she was, a tough little street urchin who had seldom met a man she didn't secretly despise, all afluster over an encounter with a man old enough—and stern enough—to be her father.

That comparison was enough to conquer the impending fit of giggles. In fact, the thought of her father had made her stomach clench. No, Colonel Leasure, with his warmth and kindness, was as unlike her father as he could be. Pushing unwelcome childhood memories aside, Nellie found she could react to the current reprimand as an adult, not a frightened child. She straightened her back and looked the colonel in the eye.

"If Reverend Browne told you I was gambling, he was in error. I was, however, showing a couple of your Roundheads how a card game works. If that was wrong, I suppose I should apologize."

"In Robert's mind—and perhaps in mine—there's little difference. I repeat, what were you thinking?"

"The two soldiers I was talking to had been cheated badly in a card game with some members of another regiment, Sir. I know they shouldn't have been playing at all, according to Reverend Browne, but the fact remains they were. And because they have been sheltered from the seamier sides of life, they had no idea how to play the game. Their innocence made them easy targets, and as a result they lost all their money and were beaten up in the process. They came to me for sticking plasters. I thought a bit of education might do them more good." Nellie's chin came up in a gesture of defiance. Now that she had a chance to defend her actions, she had exchanged her nervousness for a growing anger.

"Wouldn't it have been better to advise them not to play cards?" the colonel asked.

"No! I try not to tell other people how to lead their lives. I leave that to the likes of Reverend Browne. I was trying to help them understand what had happened in that card game. How can they decide for themselves if something is wrong, if they don't know what that something is all about?"

"Well, it would be wise to tell someone not to drink hemlock without letting them try it for themselves, wouldn't it?"

"That's hardly a fair example, Sir."

"Well, maybe not. But surely you can see how this whole incident looked to Robert, Nellie. He's been waging war against the temptations of the world, and there you were, offering instructions in how to sin with more finesse."

She smiled despite herself, and the tension that had been building in the cabin began to ease. "Yes, of course, I see that. But isn't there something to be said for 'Better the devil you know than the devil you don't'?"

"Well, if there are going to be introductions to devilment, Nellie, it might be better they not come from an attractive young woman whom Robert sees as a temptation in herself."

Nellie let her breath out with a rush. "Is that what he thinks?" A frown wrinkled her forehead. "Why is it men always blame women for their own weaknesses?" she demanded. Another memory flashed past, but she pushed it aside.

"Ah, Nellie, that's an age-old question, isn't it? And not one we're likely to answer. Just remember that Robert Audley Browne is a fervent disciple of St. Paul's version of Christianity. Paul thought women should not speak in public and should defer to men in all affairs. You won't convince Robert that any woman, let alone one as young and pretty as you, can have anything worthwhile to offer. You are Eve. He would prefer you be Mary."

"Is that what you are telling me, too?"

"No. If I felt that way, I would never have allowed you to join the Roundheads. I have a wonderful wife, Nellie—a woman who has taught me men are usually the weaker sex. Isabel is wiser than I in the ways of the world. She is stronger, more talented, and more compassionate than I ever could be. I have witnessed her struggles to be her own person, and I have despaired of the mistreatment she has suffered from the misogynists of our society. I would never place such limitations on a capable woman such as yourself. I'm simply asking you, once again, to be more circumspect in your dealings with the chaplain. You and he are going to be working together, whether either of you like it, and you need to find a way to co-exist."

"So I'm not going to be sent home?"

"Of course not. The regiment needs you."

"But I should keep my mouth shut, right?"

"I'm asking you to curb your tongue, not your thoughts. Can you be generous enough to allow him his erroneous views, even though you know him to be wrong?"

"I'll try. It'll be against my nature, but I'll be as humble as I can."

"You've been doing a fine job for us, Nellie. And we're all learning to rely on your abilities. Thank you for what you do—and for understanding when one of us fails to live up to your expectations of us." Colonel Leasure took Nellie's proffered hand in both of his and gazed at her fondly.

Flustered once again by his kindness, Nellie left the cabin feeling much more humble than she would have believed possible. She stood quietly for a moment, her eyes closed, and breathed deeply to corral her conflicting emotions. Then she squared her shoulders, lifted her chin, and opened her eyes to look straight into the blazing stare of Reverend Browne, who was approaching the colonel's cabin from the other direction. She smiled; he scowled. Their stormy relationship was not easily put to rest.

Nellie had little time to worry about such matters when she returned to sick bay. Robert Moffatt was waiting for her in the corridor. He supported a soldier who appeared decidedly unwell. The young man was small, cadaverously thin, shoulders hunched, angry red blotches marring his otherwise white face, beads of sweat popping out on his brow. He clutched a wadded kerchief to his lips, and periodically his whole body seemed to convulse as he coughed into the cloth.

"Thank God you're here, Miss Nellie! This is Bob Reynolds, my best friend from home, and I think he's terribly ill."

"I'm all right, Robert," the young man gasped. "It's a cold that's settled into my chest."

"No, I think it's more than that. Here, Miss Nellie, feel his forehead. He's burning up."

Nellie gingerly put her hand on the back of the soldier's neck, already knowing what she would find. "You do seem to be running a fever, Bob. Perhaps we'd better find you a bunk here, where you can be more comfortable. May I take your kerchief?"

"No, no, please. I'll be all right." But Private Moffatt tugged at the wad of cloth, and as it came away, splatters of blood told a different story.

Nellie quickly settled Bob into a bunk at the back of the sick bay. "Can you stay with him while I find Doctor Ludington?" she asked.

"Of course. I told you. Me and him are mates—have been since we were tykes. I'll stay as long as he needs me."

Ludington was on the other side of the sick bay, attending to two other new arrivals. Nellie hurried to him. "Excuse me, Sir, but I have a sick soldier I need you to see."

"As do I here," he replied. "Two more cases of measles, I'm afraid. Can you find some makeshift curtains to keep the light from affecting their eyes?"

"Certainly. Right away. But, Sir, I have a patient who's burning up and coughing blood. I really think you need to look at him now."

She now had the doctor's full attention. "Consumption?"

"It could be. I hope not, but. . . ."

Ludington patted the nearer measles case on the shoulder. "Miss Nellie here will take good care of you. You could not be in better hands. I'll look in on you later." With that he hurried off, led unfailingly by the sound of deep coughing.

Nellie bustled through her duties, finding sheets to make up new bunks, brewing pots of catnip tea for the measles patients, and checking on the other soldiers who had only minor ailments to report. She tweezed out a splinter in seconds and treated an ear ache with a quick drop of hot oil. A cold compress on a sprained ankle reduced the swelling. There was a typhoid patient, Private Jasper Vliet, of the Fiftieth Pennsylvania Regiment, but Nellie had little to do with his care. The young man spoke only German, and his sergeant had come in with him, volunteering his services as caregiver as well as translator. She glanced over once in a while to see if help was needed. Most of her attention was drawn to the back of the room, where that white-faced young man struggled to contain his coughs as the doctor examined him.

When he finished his examination, Doctor Ludington's face was grim. He shook the soldier's hand and then helped to ease him back onto the support of several pillows. He spoke quietly to Private Moffatt, and then left the bedside with an ill-concealed sigh.

"Is it consumption?" Nellie asked.

"Of course it is. How could you doubt it?"

"But he'll need to go to hospital! We can't treat him here."

"Really? In case you've forgotten, we're at sea, Mrs. Leath. What would you have me do? Turn the whole fleet of 80 ships and 12,000 men back to Annapolis so one sick soldier could be comfy until he dies?"

"But he'll die here!"

"Yes, he will. And that's not my fault—nor yours. Damn fools sign up for war without a thought of whether they can handle the conditions, and more damn fools let sick men enlist, just to fill up the ranks. Begging your pardon, Mrs. Leath, my language tends to slip when I'm faced with abject stupidity!"

"What about Private Moffatt? Should he be back there with him? Couldn't he catch it?"

"Yes, probably. But he tells me he's been caring for the patient for several days. If he's going to get consumption himself, it's already too late. Might as well let him handle the case rather than expose someone else."

"And if we have two deaths, then?" Nellie couldn't help but be furious at the doctor for his cavalier attitude.

"Then we have two splashes as we bury them at sea. Men are going to die, Nellie. I've warned you of that, and you've seen it already. Herr Vliet over there won't make it through the night. Our own Mathias Crowl, the other typhoid patient, will follow him sooner or later. Moffatt and Reynolds have a while longer to wait. Maybe they'll even make it back to dry land, if any of us do. That's what war is all about. There'll be as many deaths from accident and disease as there are from bullets, but military minds will explain away those deaths as heroic sacrifices. And of course Reverend Browne will inform us all deaths are predestined. In the meantime, I'm supposed to work miracles and save lives! Bah!" He slammed his fist on the table and stomped as far as the door before turning.

"I'm sorry, Nellie. Didn't mean to get on a soapbox and yell at you. You stepped between me and my frustration at the limitations of medicine. We should be looking for cures for diseases, not helping to spread them though military invasions."

"I understand, Sir. And I didn't mean to criticize you. It's hard—harder than I expected. I can handle the physical work, but the emotional demands are a different matter." She stopped as she felt tears begin to brim behind her eyelids.

"We do what we can, Nellie. Come on. It's time for dinner, and you know it's a long time between meals on this ship."

The mess cabin was already crowded by the time they made their way to the lower deck, and Reverend Browne was about to offer a prayer. Nellie slipped into her seat quietly, grateful for a few moments to compose herself before having to make polite conversation with her table mates. Her relief did not last long.

"Let us pray," commanded Reverend Browne in his booming preacher's voice. "Heavenly Father, we come here today humbly ashamed at the corruption that has seeped into our midst. We have forgotten the lessons of our earthly fathers and mothers. We have allowed greed and lasciviousness to enter our hearts. We have openly defied Thy laws and commandments. We are but depraved beasts, indulging our worst instincts and desires. We have strayed ourselves and then lured others to stray with us. We are humbly contrite and beg Thy forgiveness for our manifold sins."

"What on earth is he talking about!" Nellie wondered. "What has happened?"

"Father, we ask Thy forgiveness for allowing a corrupt and evil woman to come into our company. She has lured us with her wiles and tempted us with her blandishments. She has offered to teach us lessons no one should learn. Like Eve, she has taken the apple from the serpent and offered it to us. And we, poor weak creatures that we are, have bitten into its forbidden flesh. Forgive us for not heeding the lesson Adam's fate should have taught us."

No, no, no! Nellie thought. He can't be talking about me. But she knew he was.

"Father, we pray that Thou wilt give wisdom to the young men here, who may be lured into temptation by the promise of secret skills and the prospect of easy money. Let them understand gambling and card playing are tools of the Devil. We pray Thou wilt give strength to the officers of this regiment, that they may stand before their men and witness to the evils of poker and faro and other card games. Give us all the courage to resist when the voice of Jezebel summons us into sin."

Well, which is it? Eve? Or Jezebel, indeed! Nelly could feel the hot waves of anger spreading over her face, leaving it red and blotched.

"Heavenly Father, we confess all men are totally depraved. We know without Thy mercy, no one of us is worthy of salvation. And we know Thy Grace is bestowed upon us unconditionally. If it were not so, not one of us would be saved. We understand Christ's atonement for our sins is limited by Thy will. And we know if we are among the few who have been predestined to join Thee some day in Heaven, we will not be able to resist the bestowing of that great blessing. Therefore, Father, help us to persevere in our faith, believing in all Thou hast taught us. Now grant us the power to go on with our lives, doing Thy will above all others. Bless this food to our use and our bodies to Thy service. In Jesus' name, Amen."

A subdued mumble of "Amens" responded, interspersed with an audible intake of breath as the assembled group struggled to absorb the diatribe to which they had been subjected. Nellie looked up, dreading the sneers she expected to see. Instead, everyone seemed to be busily looking elsewhere. Not a single eye caught hers. They're embarrassed, she realized, although the thought did not help much. As the bowls and platters were passed, she took little to fill her plate, for the accusatory prayer had killed her appetite. Her mouth was so dry that the beans stuck to her palate, and the meat became unchewable. She pushed the food around her plate, trying to make it look as if she were eating something.

As soon as possible, she excused herself and scurried back toward sick bay, which, she was beginning to realize, had become her only hiding place. As she reached the first gangway, a voice behind her called out, "Mrs. Leath.

Please, wait a moment." Nellie turned to see Mrs. Pollock, the youngest of the other women in the regiment. Nellie stared at her, unwilling or unable to say a word.

"Please, I wanted to . . . to say something to . . . to let you know not everybody agrees with Reverend Browne."

"But everyone knows what he thinks of me, don't they?"

"Well, he certainly doesn't hide his feelings, but I think he's being really ridiculous."

"Do you?"

"Of course I do! So do lots of other people."

"I haven't seen many signs of sympathy."

"Perhaps not, but it's there, all the same. My father says. . . ."

"Your father?"

"Yes. Captain Samuel Bentley, of Company E, is my father. Anyway, he says you had a top-notch idea. He told me he wished you had given a few lessons to some of his boys."

"Really! I apologize. I hadn't made the connection. You were introduced as Mrs. Pollock, and I didn't know. . . ."

"Doesn't matter. I'd rather you called me Mary, anyway."

"All right, and I'm Nellie. But your husband is. . . ."

"Dead, at Manassas."

"Oh, I'm sorry!"

Mary drew a deep breath, lifted her chin, and managed a wavering smile. "I can almost say it without breaking down by now. What about yours?"

"A blighter, I'm afraid. The last time I saw him, he was planning to open a brothel for soldiers on leave. When he was trying to talk me into becoming the madame of the house, he kept telling me we ought to make a small fortune from this war. The only thing I could think of to do—to make up for his crassness—was to sign up myself."

Mary swallowed a laugh of surprise. "Has he made a go of it?"

"I don't think so. I recently received another letter telling me he had signed on as a musician with an Ohio regiment. Probably plans to fleece the soldiers with card tricks. But please don't tell Reverend Browne!"

The two women chuckled together, and with that small bond, a friendship was born. "I'm coming back to sick bay with you," Mary said. "I heard you had a pack full of patients, and none of us have been helpful up to this point."

"I could use some help," Nellie agreed. "I can use a friend even more."

With Mary's help, Nellie soon had her patients fed, washed, and settled in for the evening. The two young women smiled at each other as they relaxed for a few moments. "I still don't understand what all that praying was about," Nellie confessed. "Oh, I know the good reverend has a vendetta out against all card players, but there seemed to be much more than that going on. What was I missing?"

"You're not a Presbyterian, are you?"

"No. At home, we attended the Episcopal church, which is pretty intense on ritual and liturgy. But all that stuff about Grace and Predestination was beyond my understanding."

"Well, basically, he was reading all of us a lesson straight out of John Calvin—things we were taught as children in Sunday School. I thought I had heard the last of TULIP long ago."

"Tulip? What on earth is that?"

Mary held up one hand and labeled her fingers T-U-L-I-P. Then she ticked them off, one by one. "These are the basic tenets of Calvinism: Total depravity, Unconditional election, Limited atonement, Irresistible grace, and Perseverance in faith. TULIP. The whole prayer was a Sunday School lecture and a scolding from the preacher because we grown-up children had forgotten our catechism."

"I thought it was directed at me alone."

"In one way, you were the target, but the implication was we are all sinners, complicit in your sin. Everyone was embarrassed, and more than a few were angry at his tone. Reverend Browne may have done you a favor. You'll find a great deal more sympathy now. I'd be willing to bet on it!"

"Please don't!" Nellie laughed. "You'll earn us both another tongue-lashing."

9
HURRICANE

The first of November dawned still and heavy. No wind stirred the few sails the *Ocean Queen* still unfurled. They drooped like wet rags from the rigging, serving only to capture the sooty smoke that issued from the engine stack and then hung in the air. The ocean lay flat, oily and thick. No fish broke the surface to snag a bug, for there were no bugs flying above the still water. The damp air itself pressed down on the shoulders of those few sailors moving about on the deck.

Nellie looked about uneasily. Her eyes tracked the horizon, looking for the ominous line of clouds she was almost certain she would see. Only a faint darkening of the southern horizon warned of trouble to come, but Nellie recognized the signs. "There's a storm brewing, isn't there?" she asked a young captain's mate.

"Could be, M'am. Feels like there's something getting ready to happen, but I don't know what. Never been this far south."

"Nor have I, Mr. Quentin, but if I were at home, I'd be calling this hurricane weather."

"Surely not, Mrs. Leath. Too late in the year for hurricanes. It's November, mind."

"And I take it you've not spent much time in New England!" Nellie replied. "This is exactly the time of year storms come barreling in off the Atlantic and smash the coast of Maine. I've been there all too often."

"But we're off the coast of North Carolina, not Maine," the young sailor explained with exaggerated patience.

"Those New England storms have to come from somewhere," Nellie said. Then she shook her head in exasperation and headed to her duties in the sick bay. We'll know soon enough, she thought.

Her patients, too, seemed to sense something different in the air. "Is it awfully warm out, Miss?" one young soldier asked. "I know yesterday was Halloween, and back home it'd be cold out. But I'm sweating. Does that mean I'm really sick?"

"No, Private Gill, it really is warm out, and there's no breeze to help the air circulate down here below the main deck. I don't think you're running a fever at all," she added, laying her hand on his temple. "In fact, your complaint is a good sign. You're alert enough to be aware of the changes in the weather. Your bout of influenza seems to have about run its course." Nellie smiled at him and moved on.

Other patients were unusually restless, though less articulate about their discomforts. Nellie moved among the injury cases, tarrying over each one long enough to assure herself the wounds were healing and were not displaying signs of infection. The discomforts of the measles cases called for gentle sponge baths, which occupied Nellie for much of the morning. She postponed her visit to her typhoid patient, Mathias Crowl, for as long as she could, knowing he was beyond knowing or caring what was done to him. Like the German patient, Jasper Vliet, he was delirious much of the time now, muttering to himself and twitching in response to invisible annoyances. His hearing had deteriorated, and talking to him had little effect. He had slipped downward toward the foot of his bunk, as if withdrawing from the world—as indeed he was.

"Nurse Leath," called Doctor Ludington.

"Yes, Sir," she answered, hurrying toward the curtained area that shielded Private Reynolds and his case of consumption from the rest of the patients.

"Don't come in here," he warned. "I just need you to set up some equipment. Could you find a small sponge, a shallow cup, and a piece of flexible tubing? I think I have the tubing in my medical case, and any kind of soft spongy material will do. I want to make an inhaler for this patient.

Oh, and while you're looking in my case, see if you can find a small stoppered bottle labeled as 'anti- hemorrhagic' inhalant."

Nellie's face, lined with concern as she had moved from patient to patient, brightened a bit with the possibility something could be done for Bob Reynolds. She watched with fascination as the doctor pressed cotton wool into a metal cup and then dribbled a couple of teaspoonfuls of a darkish liquid into the wool. Tucking one end of the flexible tube into the bottom of the cup, he held the other end to the patient's lips and instructed, "Take deep breaths through your mouth, Robert." The young man choked a bit with his first breath, and then settled into a rhythmic pattern of deep inhalations. The strain on his face eased, and he leaned back on his pillow, eyes closed in relief.

"What's in that?" Nellie asked.

"Witch-hazel, black cohosh, and creosote, among other things. Works wonders when the patient is bleeding from the lungs. It won't cure him, of course, but it dulls the pain and eases the chest."

"Another remedy for my notebook," she commented.

"Still keeping it up?"

"Oh, yes. That was a wonderful suggestion. I want to learn as much as I can. And you're kind to take the time to explain things to me. Some of the other doctors don't like being questioned, I've noticed."

"The more you know, the more help you'll be, I figure. Now, why don't you take a break, go topside, and see if you can find out what's making this old tub of a ship rock. If it gets much rougher, we're going to have to start strapping the patients to their bunks."

Nellie realized for the first time how badly the ship was tossing. The rhythmic rise and fall of the deck had been increasing in intensity for some time, but Nellie had been too busy to notice. Used to the pitching of her uncle's fishing boats, she had simply planted her feet a bit further apart and adjusted unconsciously to the motion.

Now, as she made her way up the gangway ladder to the main deck, she caught her breath with surprise. The wind, nonexistent at breakfast, was now blowing strongly out of the southeast. Looking far southward, Nellie could see a bank of clouds filling the eastern half of the horizon. An unusually straight-sided wall of cloud separated this bank from the wispy clouds that spread westward from it. Nellie's heart plummeted. She was staring straight into the wall of a hurricane, still far out at sea, but judging from the wind direction, likely to be moving directly into the path of the fleet.

The same young mate she had talked to that morning was passing by. "What say you now, Mr. Quentin?" she called to him.

"Oh, it's you again. Still don't think you're gonna get a hurricane, M'am. This is just a bit of a blow. Those of us used to the sea have seen lots worse. Why, I could tell you stories of wave so high that. . . ."

Nellie held up her hands to stop him. "I've probably been to sea more often than you, so don't make light of this situation to me. Look at those swells. Don't you see anything different about them?"

"Naw, they're not threatening. Look how slow they are."

"Exactly! Yesterday, when the weather was calm, the swells were shallow but frequent. Now they have slowed, but they're much deeper. The wave takes longer to travel across the surface because the water is sinking low and rising high. When the swells are as much as fifteen or sixteen seconds apart, it's a sure sign there's a hurricane in the vicinity. Didn't they teach you that during your training?"

The young mate wrinkled his brow in confusion, then shook his head and walked away.

Nellie turned to go back to sick bay, but hesitated when she spotted one of the ship's officers moving toward her. "Lieutenant Blair," she called. "Those clouds look ominous. What does your barometer show?"

"Falling like a stone, M'am," he answered over his shoulder, nodding but unwilling to stop long enough to talk.

Nellie rushed back, eager to report to Doctor Ludington, but the words died in her throat as she saw the stricken look on his face. "Has something happened, Doctor?" she asked.

"Jasper Vliet just died."

"Oh, how sad. I knew he hadn't much of a chance, but I hoped he would hang on for a while longer. Whatever will we do with him in the face of the coming storm?"

"It's really getting ready to blow, then?" he asked, his eyes narrowing in a grimace.

"Yes, Sir. The sailors still are making light of it, thinking we're all land-lubbers, but I can spot a hurricane far off."

"Then we don't want to want to delay his burial at sea. If we get a strong storm, the soldiers don't need to deal with a flying corpse. See if you can find Reverend Browne and some other help, would you?"

"Right away. Knowing his tendency toward sea-sickness, he's probably hanging over a rail at the moment."

While Nellie hurried off to find Reverend Browne and the commander of the Fiftieth Pennsylvania Regiment, Doctor Ludington made his preparations. Gently closing the soldier's eyes, he straightened his clothes and then pulled a blanket around him. He used a needle and stout thread from his medical bag to whip-stitch the blanket closed. When Nellie returned, accompanied by a delegation of wide-eyed young recruits from the Fiftieth, he sent them out to find some sort of weight and a plank. Then he and Jasper's friends lifted the body and carried it up to the main deck.

The deck was alive with activity. The sailors were pulling in every sail, stripping the masts to make them less vulnerable to the ever-increasing gusts of wind. The soldiers had gathered to watch, and a continuing banter passed between the two groups. The Roundheads who had never been out of the sight of land were amazed at the growing waves, and the sailors were taking endless amusement from their wonderment. "You think this is a storm? Just wait!"

A smaller group of passengers assembled near the guardrails to mark the passing of their companion. The soldiers of the Fiftieth looked grim, and the curious ladies of the Roundheads craned their necks to see what such a burial would really be like. Reverend Browne, green with nausea, made short work of the service.

"Jasper Vliet was twenty-three years of age, and he fully expected to return some day to his home in Spruce Grove, Pennsylvania. But God in his wisdom has destined him to end his life here on the high seas. We commend his spirit to Heaven and his body to the ever-sheltering waters." Reverend Browne signaled with a nod of his head to the soldiers supporting the body tied to its plank. They lifted the plank, slipped it over the guard rails, tilted it up, and then let it fall into the roiling waters. Instantly it sank, leaving behind only the finality of a single splash.

The intensity of the weather steadily increased—the waves higher, the winds stronger, the sky black by late afternoon. Still the ship's crew made light of the danger. Lieutenant Blair sought out Reverend Browne and the Roundhead ladies, inviting them to come up from their quarters and witness the power of the storm from the afterdeck. As if this were a show put on merely for their benefit, a crowd gathered on the small deck that jutted out from the stern of the ship. It was surrounded by a guardrail and rope netting that kept objects from dropping off the edge, and the curious held onto it gratefully as they leaned over to look straight down into the water.

Nellie, having finished strapping her patients into their bunks and stowing all objects that might fly around if the ship's motion intensified, emerged again as darkness began to settle around the ship. Seeing her, Mary Pollack waved and beckoned her to join them. Somewhat reluctantly, Nellie climbed the ladder to the afterdeck. "What are you all doing out here?" she asked. "Don't you realize how dangerous this is?"

"Oh, Nellie, must you always be a spoil-sport?" grumbled Mrs. White. "This is an exhilarating experience. Just look how the ship is lifted up by the waves, right out of the water, And then we drop until we are only a few feet above the waves. It's breath-taking!"

"Indeed, Mrs. White—a magnificent seesaw," Reverend Browne agreed. Then, unable to resist the opportunity to preach, he straightened up and gestured around him. "Sick as I am, I cannot resist seeing the grandeur of ocean in one of its most fearful moods. And imagine, dear friends, if we are witnessing the power of one of God's creations, how much greater must be the power of God himself."

Nellie looked over the stern. The *Ocean Queen* was towing the little whaler, *Zeno's Coffin*, because it could not match the pace of the fleet. Now it was pitching wildly in the wake of the larger ship. Its hawser was still tight, so when the *Ocean Queen* rose high with a wave, the little whaler was lifted out of the water. And when the *Ocean Queen* sank into the depths, the bow of the whaler took a full dunking. Nellie could see its crew clinging to the railings as the spray dashed over them and the water flooded the decks.

"Perhaps God is warning you that you should go below," Nellie suggested, but the others ignored her. Concerned for their safety, she looked around to appeal to one of the Roundheads' officers. Major T. J. Hamilton shrugged off her concerns. "I consider that Providence can take care of us on the sea as well as on the land," he told her. "If God intends to bury us in the bottom of the Atlantic, we can not help ourselves much and if not he will deliver us in his own good time and way."

Unable to take comfort in this statement of faith, Nellie turned and started down the ladder. But just as she did so, one of the waves pounding on the port side of the ship rose higher and higher, curling over onto itself and then crashing full onto the deck of the *Ocean Queen*. The force of the water hurled Nellie from her precarious hold on the gangway ladder and smashed her backward onto the deck below. Her head hit the wooden deck and bounced, and for a moment, everything went black. Her mouth and nostrils filled with gritty salt water as she choked her way back to consciousness.

She struggled to sit up or turn onto hands and knees, but a second wave washed over the deck, carrying all loose objects with it. Buckets, tools, and planks of wood battered her. Then the water lifted her, too, and she found herself being carried inexorably toward the starboard railing. She was breathing more water than air, some of it salt from the sea, some fresh from the sheets of rain now lashing the ship from above. Her flailing hands failed to grasp anything to stop her slide as the ship itself rolled from side to side, even as it rose and dipped from bow to stern.

Time seemed to slow, and Nellie realized she might be about to die. She was only slightly surprised to find she was not frightened. Death had never been something she feared. It had been living she had often found unbearably difficult. She saw no visions of her past; her life was not flashing before her eyes. But in her ears echoed one sound she wished she had forgotten—the soft and meaningless splash as Private Vliet's body had disappeared into the angry sea. How awful to disappear, leaving behind no trace of your existence, she thought. If I had known I was about to die, I would have tried harder to give people something to remember me by. Realizing her struggling was gaining her nothing, she tried to make herself go limp, hoping the wave would pass over her.

When strong hands encircled her upper arms and lifted her bodily from the deck, Nellie was almost beyond understanding what was happening. But she knew her precipitous slide had stopped, and she instinctively threw her arms around her rescuer, clinging to him as her last hope. She buried her face in the reassuring shelter of his shoulder and felt the tears start to come. In a moment she was coughing and gasping for air. The terror was late to arrive, but none the less real. Her body trembled and sobs emerged from someplace deep inside, a combination of gratitude for her rescue and grief from a past she had forced herself to forget.

Nellie had still not opened her eyes, as if she feared to look around her. But slowly, her other senses took over. The coat in which she had buried her nose gave off unmistakable odors of wet wool and masculine sweat, accompanied by a touch of bay rum and sweet cherry tobacco smoke. A gruff but gentle voice urged her to "get hold of yourself." And the rough brush of whiskery sideburns scratched her forehead. Suddenly she lifted her head and opened her eyes. "Colonel Leasure!" she gasped.

Embarrassed, she tried to jerk away, but the colonel gently held her and pulled her back into the comforting shelter of his embrace. "It's all right, Nellie. You've had a terrible scare, and you have a nasty bump on your head, but you're safe now. I'll not let you go. When you're feeling a bit calmer, we'll get you safely below deck and have the doctor take a look at your injuries."

She nodded mutely and allowed herself to relax again against that proffered shoulder. She did indeed feel calmer. She had not felt so protected since she was a child and her father had rescued her from a fall in the barn that landed her in the stall of an irritable horse. She remembered her father picking her up and carrying her to safety in a pile of hay. Then inexplicably her memory went black. Only the smell of masculine sweat and tobacco remained, along with a paralyzing fear.

A harsher voice broke through her terror, and another hand gripped her arm and pulled her away. "Here, Daniel, you have more important responsibilities than dealing with a silly female who let herself fall off a ladder. She's not that badly hurt. I'll see to it she gets back to sick bay and her duties there." Reverend Browne tugged again at her arm, urging her toward the gangway to a lower deck.

"Thank you for your help, Robert," the colonel said. "I'll check on you later, Nellie."

"Humph! I'll just bet he will, the poor fool!" Browne grumbled as he shoved Nellie toward the ladder. "Get down there with you and quit throwing yourself at the colonel. He's a married man, in case you hadn't noticed, and he has no need for a foolish hussy making passes at him."

Nellie's mouth came open, but she was speechless with fear and indignation. She was also feeling dizzy and disoriented as she tried to stand on her own, and the chaplain's voice was fading in and out. *Did I misunderstand him?* she wondered. *Surely he couldn't think. . . .*

"Here! What's happened?" cried the doctor as they reached the sick bay door. "Nellie, are you hurt?"

"No, she's just being dramatic," Browne responded for her. "Or maybe she has the vapors. Had a little bump, that's all."

"There's a good deal of blood on the back of your head. More than a 'little bump,' I'd say. Sit down here and let me take a closer look." Ludington parted her hair and gingerly prodded the still-swelling lump. He felt her forehead and cheeks, and then held up two fingers. "What do you see, Nellie?"

"Two fingers? Or three? Things are a little blurry. I've got salt water in my eyes."

"More like a concussion, I'd say, and you're in shock, too. Your skin's abnormally cold. Reverend Browne, please give me a hand here. You need to get her out of these wet clothes and wrapped in some warm blankets, while I get some sticking plasters for her open wounds. Sir?"

But Reverend Browne was backing away, shaking his head and looking almost as pale as Nellie. "No, no, I can't undress a lady. It wouldn't be proper," he mumbled as he turned and dashed out the door, staggering with the roll of the ship.

Mary Pollock observed his departure as she came down the passageway. "Reverend Browne must be sea-sick again," she commented as she entered the sick bay. "He's outside the door on his knees, coughing up his innards. How's Nellie?"

Nellie herself was the first to answer, albeit a bit weakly. "I think he's just sick of me. And I'm all right, Mary. Don't worry about me."

"No. She isn't all right," Doctor Ludington said as he came back carrying his medical bag. "Can you help her get undressed, Mary? There's a flannel night shirt here, and some wool blankets. We need to warm her up quickly."

"I can do it," Nellie protested, but her fingers fumbling at the row of neat little buttons down her bodice proved otherwise. Mary took over with her typical quiet efficiency and soon had Nellie's soggy dress lifted off her head and her undergarments loosened beneath the flannel gown.

Doctor Ludington made quick work of patching her open cuts and then insisted on putting her to bed, wrapped in several blankets. "You need something soothing. The ship is rocking too much for us to risk boiling water for tea or broth, but this may help." He held out a small dosing spoon of an unidentified syrup. "Swallow it quickly," he instructed.

Nellie opened her mouth obediently and then jerked her head away in disgust. "What is that?" she demanded. "It smells like somebody's dirty socks."

"So it does, but it won't taste as bad as it smells. It's a tincture of valerian root. It will quiet you and allow you to get some rest."

"Where's the whiskey when a woman needs it?" Nellie glared at the doctor through tear-filled eyes but then swallowed the vile mixture, which seemed to be the only thing on offer.

"I'll sit with you until you fall asleep," Mary promised. "Here, wipe your eyes."

But try as she might, the tears kept welling up. "I can't quit crying," she said. "I don't hurt all that badly, and I know it's all over. I'm not scared. But the tears won't stop. I feel utterly lost and hopeless."

"Did something else happen tonight, something we don't know about?" Mary smoothed the damp hairs from Nellie's forehead. "Maybe you just needed a good cry," she suggested.

"The fall brought back a few memories and regrets, I guess, but most of all I'm just angry and embarrassed."

"Why embarrassed? The fall certainly wasn't your fault. We were watching from the afterdeck when the wave washed over you. I don't see how you even survived."

"Reverend Browne said . . . he accused me of . . . of staging the whole thing so I could throw myself into the colonel's arms."

"He didn't!"

Nellie shook her head at Mary's shocked denial. "He called me a foolish hussy!"

"And he's an evil old man!" Mary said.

"No, he's not evil, but he hates me for reasons I don't begin to understand, and I'm tired of trying to get along with him. Maybe I just ought to give up and go home—wherever that is." Once again the tears overwhelmed her.

Mary sat quietly, puzzling over the situation while she waited for Nellie's sobs to subside. "Maybe he's the one who is embarrassed," she suggested.

"Embarrassed? Him? Embarrassed about what?"

"About you. Consider for a moment. The chaplain's far from home. He's expected to take the moral high ground in every situation because of his calling. And you're an attractive, unattached woman with an engaging personality and a strong will, one who isn't afraid to stand up to him. What if he is attracted to you?"

"Nonsense. I told you. He hates me."

"Hasn't anyone pointed out to you there's a fine line between love and hatred?"

"Oh, but surely not. No, no, he can't be. Even if you're right, the explanation doesn't help anything. I can't well cozy up to him and take a chance on fanning his ardor, any more than I can avoid being thrown into his company."

"You can try to understand him, Nellie. I'll wager he's not the first difficult man you've had to deal with."

Nellie smiled ruefully. "No, I guess not. I'll try to remember that his outbursts may be coming from his own fears, not my sins." The tears still glistened in her eyes, but a little of the tension drained from her face.

"Sleep now, Nellie. Even a hurricane passes."

As she sank into the first stages of sleep, she was faintly aware of voices near her cot.

"How is Nellie?" Colonel Leasure asked.

"She'll be fine, I think," Doctor Ludington answered. "But I'm a bit concerned about her emotional state."

"Why? What's wrong?"

"I'm not sure. But her usual fighting spirit seems to have disappeared. She's not just frightened or hurt. She's apathetic. She doesn't care about her own condition. It's almost as if she were ready and willing to die. When I checked on her just now, she had folded her hands on her breast and closed her eyes in an eerie imitation of a corpse. If I had told her we were going to fasten her to a plank, I don't think she would have objected a bit."

"That doesn't sound like our Nellie at all. Keep a close eye on her, Doctor. Now you have me worried."

The storm increased in intensity through Saturday night, reaching its peak between midnight and 3:00 a.m. By then, of course, most of the ship's passengers had retired to the relative safety of their quarters, where they could be somewhat protected from the driving rain and roaring wind. They lay bundled on their bunks, holding on or lashing themselves in, and straining in the darkness for warning sounds of rising water or breaking planks.

The ship's captain, Mr. Lee, and his pilot, Captain Godfrey, took pity on Reverend Browne and invited him to share their stateroom for the duration of the storm. It had the advantage of being near the middle of the ship, where the rocking was less noticeable. "You'll be more comfortable here," Lee promised the chaplain, who was still green with seasickness. "Besides, there's little chance either of us will have time to sleep during this storm. You won't be disturbed by our comings and goings."

Reverend Browne found that promise comforting and frightening in equal measure. He knew the captain had meant his words to be reassuring, but beneath them lay another message. This was going to be a long and dangerous night.

Colonel Leasure was also among those who did not sleep. All too aware of the heavy responsibility he held for the lives of a thousand men, and of his utter helplessness in the face of the storm, he spend the night roaming the ship. He moved silently through the dark decks, where his soldiers lay in narrow bunks stacked four high. It was impossible to speak over the roar of the storm, but he did not hesitate to squeeze a few outstretched hands to offer what comfort he could.

In the sick bay once again, he clasped the arm of Doctor Ludington, who returned the gesture—two frightened men overburdened by the knowledge the next few hours might witness the deaths of all aboard. He hesitated at Nellie's bunk to make sure she slept peacefully, and Ludington nodded back in reassurance. The valerian root had done its job of sedating her.

On deck, the seamen gathered in clusters, secretly frightened but at the same time exhilarated by the storm. Like bunches of bragging schoolboys, they competed to tell stories of storms worse than this one. They laughed when the waves threatened to bowl them over and shook the water from their beards with abandon. Some found release in shouting down the crashing waves; others let their laughter escalate to near hysteria. At one point their voices carried below decks so loudly that Colonel Leasure stomped out on deck to give them a tongue-lashing. "Silence! I hope no officer on this boat will make a panic among these men. The consequence would be certain loss of life."

The sailors grinned sheepishly and tempered their conversation, but they also had a laugh at the colonel's expense. "Land-lubber," someone muttered, and the others nodded their heads in agreement.

Throughout the storm, Nellie lay on that cot and saw nothing but blackness ahead of her—no hopes, no better days to come, no purpose in life, no filling up of this emptiness that pervaded her body—and her soul. Doctor Ludington had said he wanted her to rest. That was easy now. She simply could not muster the energy to move. She just wanted to be left alone to adjust to her nothingness.

But remaining alone was next to impossible on a ship crowded with over 1500 people. During the second long night, when the hurricane had blown itself out and the seas had calmed, she became aware of a figure standing next to her cot. A young soldier had come to sick bay seeking a sticking plaster for a minor cut. While there, he asked about her, and Doctor Ludington had pointed to where she lay.

"'Scuse, M'am. I didn't mean to wake you. I jus' wanted to make sure you was all right."

"I'm fine," she said.

"We've all been right worried about you, M'am. I was there. I mean, I saw you fall, and I was scared for you."

"Do I know you?" she asked, wondering why he was there at all.

"Prob'ly not. My name's Jim McCaskey, from Company C. Some of my friends have had dealings with you. You taught a couple of them to play poker. But me? No, I'm just one of the boys. We all know you, though, and we'd be in deep trouble if we'd lost you."

"I doubt that."

"You're important to me, M'am. You remind me of home and my sister, Sarah Jane. She's older'n me by a couple of years, and I always knew I could go to her if I needed somebody to talk to. You seem like the same sort. Not that I need somebody to talk to right now, but it gives me comfort to know you're here if I do. I jus' wanted to make sure you'd be back, cheering us all up and keeping us lively."

He went on his way, and Nellie discovered her head was feeling a bit more normal. She pulled the blankets closer, still not ready to venture beyond her cot. Since it appeared she was going to survive, she would have to reconsider her options.

10

PORT ROYAL SOUND

By Sunday morning the worst of the storm had passed. The seas were still rough, but the wind had died down, and the white caps no longer seemed about to erupt over the sides of the ship. For the soldiers of the Roundhead regiment, however, the most frightening sight was the emptiness of the sea. Their magnificent fleet with its serried ranks of sails was simply gone. From the afterdeck they could see only a tattered hawser where the little *Zeno's Coffin* used to be.

Doctor Ludington found Nellie in the passageway. Gently gripping her arm, he steadied her against the rocking of the ship. "Where are you going, Nellie? You shouldn't even be out of bed."

She shook him off. "My head is healing, Doctor, and I need to go topside. I need to know what is going on."

"We're fine, Nellie. We suffered no major damage or injuries. The ship is at anchor, and we have everything under control."

"No, I need to move. I need to see for myself. Please." Resolutely she turned and headed for the gangway.

The doctor watched her unsteady steps become more assured as she walked. "Do what you must, then."

A beam of sunlight greeted her as she emerged onto the deck. The sky was a brilliant blue, unmarred by clouds. Sailors swarmed over the rigging, rehanging the sails. The soldiers of the Roundhead Regiment lounged on the deck in small groups, chattering among themselves. Nearby, several other ships of the fleet also stood at anchor, their crews similarly busy. Nellie realized she had been holding her breath, taken by surprise that the scene had changed dramatically from her tortured memories of the storm. Now she willed herself to relax.

Once she had regained her sea legs, she moved among the men, inquiring after their well-being. She was astonished to see how welcoming the men were. Apparently it had not only been young Jim McCaskey who had worried about her injuries. As she and her soldiers reassured one another they had indeed survived the battering of a hurricane, Nellie began to piece together the story of what had happened.

The ships of the fleet had separated themselves as much as possible, to ensure they would not be dashed together in the dark. Then they turned their bows directly into the wind and rode out the storm. The fleet commander had opened his sealed orders and signaled clear instructions to every ship in the fleet to head for Port Royal Sound on the coast of South Carolina. The fleet would reassemble offshore there.

To be sure, there were reports of losses. The *Winfield Scott* had her bow caved in and her masts split. The hold had already begun to fill with water when the damage was discovered in the middle of the night. The engine fires went out, and the pumps were too far underwater to work. Soldiers from the Fiftieth Pennsylvania aboard the damaged ship had kept themselves afloat by throwing overboard everything that could be picked up or shoved over the rails. Baggage, guns, tools, food supplies—all were vital but would be useless if they went to the bottom along with the men for whose use they were designated. The soldiers had bailed the ship manually, using barrels rigged with pulleys, even though some of the barrels were half full of crackers or beans.

The *Governor*, carrying a battalion of marines aboard, began to sink during the storm. The marines were rescued by the crew of the *Sabine*, but seven men drowned. Both the *Osceola* and the *Union*, loaded with the Army's artillery, were driven ashore, and ninety-three of their crew members became prisoners of Confederate troops, who must have been amazed to have these spoils of war washed up on their beaches. Still, most of the fleet had survived with only minor damage, and experienced sailors recognized that fact as miraculous, even if they wouldn't admit it to their landlubber companions. They needed little encouragement from Reverend Browne to join the soldiers on the forecastle in a prayer of thanksgiving for their deliverance.

After the service, Nellie remained on the forward deck, looking out toward her first sight of land in several days. She blinked, trying to clear her vision and figure out what she was seeing. At home, when a fishing boat returned home, the shoreline was a narrow outcropping of rocks, closely backed by the dark curtain of a pine forest. Here, the water seemed to lap against a strip of bare land and then a sea of waving grass that stretched far inland. A few bent and twisted trees dotted the far ground, but they were draped in rags, which made no sense at all. And then there were the palm trees, suddenly rising above their gnarled neighbors to wave their fronds in midair. "Palm trees? Here? And what are those rags?" Nelly did not realize her astonishment had been spoken aloud until a voice at her elbow intruded.

"Your first time in the Low Country, M'am?"

"In what?" She turned, puzzled, to find a freckled-faced young sailor grinning at her.

"You're looking at what the natives call 'The Low Country' or 'The Sea Islands,'" he explained. "I used to visit here frequently. My mother's family hailed from Charleston, so we sometimes came to visit my grandparents' rice plantation during the holidays. I grew up paddling around what you're seeing as a sea of grass, which is nothing of the sort. Would you like a quick lesson on South Carolina?"

"Yes, I would, but a geography lesson first, if you please. Where exactly are we? This all looks like it might be some exotic foreign land."

"It's all South Carolina, M'am, although there's some folk who would agree with you it's a foreign land. We're anchored in the roadstead, a protected bit of sea outside the entrance to Port Royal Sound, which is one of the south's great natural harbors. It's anywheres from two to five miles across, and a good ten miles long.

The island to your right is sometimes called Phillip's Island, although it's really part of St. Helena Island. People around here tend to see any creek as a break between two islands, even though it may not separate the two land masses completely. I don't think anybody much lives there; the ground's too marshy. The structure you see at the tip of Phillip's Island is called Bay Point, or Fort Beauregard. If you head about fifty miles further to your right, you come to the city of Charleston. It has a harbor, too, of course, but it's much better protected by narrow channels and a series of forts.

"To your left is Hilton Head Island. There's not much there, either, except for some rice and cotton plantations—and its one fortification, Fort Walker. You can see Fort Walker, almost directly across from Bay Point. Trouble is, the two forts are too far apart to protect the entire channel leading into Port Royal Sound—good for us but bad news for the rebels. Anyhow, if you head further off to your left, the city of Savannah, Georgia, sits at the state border about twenty miles away. In between those two cities lies 'The Low Country'. It's a beautiful swamp filled with islands that change their shape and size with every ebb and flow of the tides."

"A beautiful swamp! What a contradiction of terms!"

"I suppose so, but after you've been here a while, you'll start to see the truth in the phrase."

"You said something about a sea of grass that's nothing of the sort?"

"Ah, yes, and I'm really wondering how many Pennsylvanian backwoodsmen we're going to lose in it. When you look at the coastline, you see a grassy field, right?"

"Yes."

"Except it's not solid ground. It's something called 'pluff mud,' which almost defies description. That grass grows in a sticky, deep mixture of dirt, sand, ground up oyster shells, and rotting plant and animal matter, all diluted with sea water. When the tide comes in, you can paddle a small boat on it. When the tide goes out, it looks like dry land. Sometimes in the summer, it bakes in the heat until it really is solid—at least for a few hours. And it gives off an awful stink, like a rotten egg or a really powerful fart, begging your pardon, M'am.

"Those trees are palmettos, a true palm tree variety. They grow up to sixty feet tall; you can tell a mature palmetto because it will have lost the crisscrossed dead frond stalks around its trunk. The gnarled giants you see are live oak trees. They don't grow terribly tall, but their branches spread out in search of patches of sunlight. They end up looking strangely twisted and distorted, but they are successful survivors, even if they have to bend into torturous shapes to do so."

"There's a good lesson to be learned there, but why are they called 'live' oaks? Aren't all trees live?"

"Ah, that's because their leaves don't turn colors or fall off. They are leathery and stay green all year long. Their acorns are different, too. They are small, long and pointed, and almost black."

"It is like a foreign country, isn't it? And the rags?"

"That's spanish moss. It's not a parasite, but a plant that lives on air and water. It prefers to hang from the branches of trees so it gets as much exposure as possible. In dry weather it's a beautiful silver, but when it rains, you'll see it turn green."

"You're a salesman for the area. It's obvious you love it. It must be painful for you to think of South Carolina as the enemy."

The young ship's mate shrugged his shoulders. "I love their land; I hate their politics. And I believe it's worth fighting to keep this wonderful state a part of the United States. I separate the two. I'll fight them because I believe they are wrong, but I'll welcome them back when they see the errors of their ways."

"I hope that's soon. Thank you, Seaman Scott. I'm looking forward to exploring your islands."

That adventure, however, was still some days away. A series of untoward mishaps and miscalculations combined to postpone the Union attack on Port Royal Harbor. The first order of business was to be sure the fleet reassembled in good order. Through much of Monday and Tuesday the ships straggled in. Sailors in the rigging reversed their usual positions to keep watch, not for land, but for the first glimpse of a sail coming over the horizon. Cries of "Ship ahoy!" replaced the usual shout of "Land ho!" Soldiers and sailors alike hurried to the seaward side of their ships to see who would be the next to arrive. General rejoicing welcomed each arrival, and the cheers continued until each vessel anchored in the roadstead. The ships lined up as close to one another as was safe, and soon the entire mouth of the generous harbor was blocked by several rows of transports and small boats.

And therein lay the first problem. The South Carolina Expeditionary Force had needed over eighty ships to carry all its men and their equipment. But once on site, most of the fleet was unnecessary. So many ships anchored together limited maneuverability and blocked clear sight lines. Of course, everyone wanted to participate in the attack, but Commodore DuPont soon realized he would have to limit his attack squadron to a few ships.

As soon as their surveyor, Captain Charles Boutelle, had marked out the deep channel into Port Royal Sound, Duport began to move the necessary ships into position, the smaller ones first, while they waited for high tide. Even so, Du Pont's flagship, the *Wabash*, passed the bar at the entrance with inches to spare. Then disaster struck again as both the *Wabash* and the *Susquehanna* failed to clear a shoal and found themselves stuck. Much maneuvering and tugging later, they floated free, but they had used up too much time to begin the attack on the scheduled day of November 5th.

The soldiers posed a second problem. The original plan had been to land the army troops somewhere where they could attack the two forts from the side while the gunboats fired at the front. That, too, proved impossible. A small group of scouts reported in confusion that the marshes on either side of the forts provided no solid ground on which to land the troops. Seas of grass rooted in pluff mud were as impassible as a bed of quicksand. The only solid ground lay between the fronts of the forts and the channels from which the gunboats would have to aim at the forts, putting a landing army in the direct line of fire. The 12,000 soldiers aboard the transports would have to become an idle audience for the naval attack on the harbor.

Because they liked and trusted her, many of the soldiers turned to Nellie to voice their frustration, and she tried to be sympathetic.

"We didn't come all this way, sick as dogs, to stand around and watch somebody else fight!"

"Why'd we even bother learning to shoot our guns if nobody's gonna let us use 'em?"

"I got a field back home I cudda been plowin' if this is all I'm gonna do!"

"When do we get our shot?"

"Durn sailors are cocky enough without lettin' them git all the glory!"

"Your turn will come, boys," she assured them. "The Navy's going to soften them up a bit first."

"Don't need 'em softened up," someone said. "Just need to git 'em in my sights."

"Well, personally, I'll be happy to see you all well and uninjured at the end of the day," Nellie said.

DuPont led his fleet of fifteen ships out into the harbor on the morning of November 7th. Staying on the starboard side of the channel, each ship fired upon Fort Beauregard as it passed Bay Point. Then the ships executed a wide turn to port that brought them to an eastern heading in front of Fort Walker. Again each ship fired as she passed and continued toward the mouth of the harbor and another sweeping turn to port that brought her back onto the course, ready for a second pass at each fort. The gunners in Fort Walker had little hope of hitting the moving targets of the Union ships, even if their cannons had been mounted on carriages that allowed rapid swings. The Union guns, however, could remain almost stationary; when one gunship sailed out of range of the fort, the next ship took over.

Despite their protests, few of the Roundheads could resist clustering on the deck of the *Ocean Queen* to watch the action. Nellie and the staff officers had a prime viewing platform on the foredeck, where even the most experienced officers cheered with each bombardment. Before the ships had completed their first lap, however, Nellie gathered her skirts and slipped away to return to the sick bay.

"You didn't have to come back, Nellie," Doctor Ludington said. "Everything is under control here."

"I'm sure it is, but I couldn't stand to watch anymore."

"And why, exactly, was that?" A new voice spoke from the doorway. Reverend Browne stood there, watching her as a cat might stare at a vulnerable mouse. "Because you don't have the stomach for battle?"

"No!" Nellie was furious with herself for reacting automatically to the chaplain's challenging attitude, but she was helpless to control her fury. "I left because it was too beautiful."

"Oh, come, now. I'd believe you if you said it was too loud, or too violent. But beautiful? Hardly."

"It *is* beautiful," she said, struggling to control herself. As if to enlist his support, she half-turned to Doctor Ludington. "You should see it, Doctor. The sky is absolutely clear and the water a deep blue. Our ships move across that water with their white sails billowing, looking almost like ballet dancers skimming across the waves."

She ignored a snort from Reverend Browne and plunged ahead. "Each gun sends up a billow of white smoke and the tracers leave a glowing arc against the sky. It is all graceful and picturesque—so much so that one is tempted to forget about the violence that is being done by those guns. I was enjoying the scene, and I couldn't bring myself to accept the reality of what was going on. That's when I decided to leave. I didn't want to enjoy the spectacle of someone being blown apart by those shells."

"How tender-hearted of you," Reverend Browne threw a patronizing smile at her. "Really, Nellie, aren't you about ready to accept the fact that a war is no place for a lady? I'm sure Captain Lee could arrange for your return passage to Hampton Roads when the extra ships go back."

"I'm not going anywhere, Reverend. I may be 'tender-hearted,' as you put it, but I'm as unafraid of war as any man here. I jus refuse to romanticize it. And I think it's wrong to enjoy it."

"There's nothing wrong with enjoying a victory. How else would an army encourage its soldiers?"

"Ah, but I thought that's what your brand of religion taught." Nellie knew she should drop the issue, but she couldn't resist taking another swipe or two at the pompous man standing over her. "I thought you believed enjoying something was a sin. Didn't you tell me God thought playing cards was the devil's work, Sir?"

"Ah, you mock me, Missy. And you mock your God," Reverend Browne said.

"I do nothing of the sort, Sir." Nellie widened her eyes and fluttered her lashes in her best imitation of surprised innocence. "I don't understand why it is a sin to enjoy playing a game, but not a sin to enjoy seeing people killed."

"That's why war is no place for a woman!" Browne shouted and stomped away. Nellie did not fail to notice he had demoted her from lady to woman.

"Why do you taunt him, Nellie?" Doctor Ludington asked. "You know he wants to get rid of you. Must you keep giving him more excuses to do so?"

Now that he was gone, Nellie felt the anger draining from her, and her shoulders slumped. "I'm sorry. And of course you're right. I shouldn't bait him. But he's unfair in his judgments."

"Yes, he is—and perhaps you are, too."

Nellie flushed with embarrassment. Doctor Ludington had been unfailingly kind to her, and she valued his opinions. "I'm sorry, Sir. You're right, again. I'll make an effort to do better."

Chastened, Nellie spent much of her afternoon bustling about with small chores that really didn't need doing. She straightened pillows, smoothed blankets, and brought dippers of cool water in case a patient had grown thirsty without mentioning it. She alphabetized the medicine shelf, swept the floor, and pressed cool hands on several feverish foreheads. But through it all she listened for, and tried not to hear, the sounds of gunfire bouncing off the water around the ship.

"The battle is over," Mary shouted as she rushed into the sick bay.

"Shhhh." Nellie hushed her automatically and then looked apologetic. "Really? They've stopped shooting at each other?"

"Yes, about half an hour ago. The rebel fort quit returning fire, and Commander DuPont signaled his ships to do the same. Then he led one last foray past Fort Walker, and sent out a landing vessel. We watched as the men disembarked and waded ashore. We were all holding our breath, waiting to see if someone would shoot at them. But there was no response at all. Our boys walked right into the fort through some big holes they had blasted in the wall, and then, after a few minutes, we saw the Confederate flag pulled down and the U.S. flag raised. We've won."

"There wasn't much doubt about that, was there?" Nellie smiled ruefully. "The fort was clearly outgunned."

"Well, true, but the best news came when the landing party reported back to the *Wabash*. The fort didn't just surrender. It's been abandoned. The rebels are gone—those of them who lived long enough to run away, at least."

"Men died trying to defend that fort, then. Don't make light of their sacrifice."

"They were rebels, Nellie! The same as the shooters who killed my husband."

"I know. I'm sorry." Nellie bit her lip to keep from saying anything else that could fuel a disagreement. "What happens now, I wonder?"

"There was a signal from DuPont saying a general landing of all troops would commence in the morning. We'll need to start packing up."

A short time later, Doctor Ludington came back from a meeting with the Roundheads' staff officers. "We're near the front of the anchorage here, so we'll be disembarking early tomorrow," he reported. "Nellie, you and the rest of the ladies will wait aboard ship with the patients still in sick bay until our troops have had time to stake out the camp and pitch the staff tents. We'll send a skiff for you when the hospital area is ready. Until then, you'll have to get the patients ready for transport and keep them quiet. The move will be hard on some of them, so I'm counting on you to see to it they are as well prepared as possible."

"I'm feeling much better, Doc," shouted one measles patient from across the room as he struggled to get out of bed. "I don't need to stay here any more."

"Maybe so, Private," Ludington replied, "but that red rash all over your face and your swollen eyes tell a different story. Back in bed with you now, Son, and close that blackout curtain again. You know light is bad for you." He raised an eyebrow at Nellie. "That's what you can expect to deal with tomorrow. You will see many miraculous cures, but don't believe them. At least not until Reverend Browne confirms the miracle."

"Oh, no, you're not leaving him aboard with us, are you?"

Ludington's grin let Nellie know he was no longer angry with her. "No. Chances are we'll have greater need for him ashore. From what the landing party has reported, it's a grim sight inside the fort—lots of bodies and body parts. Those beautiful shells of ours have left behind all the ugliness of war for us to deal with. It's best Reverend Browne see that for himself. He may come to understand you were right."

II

HILTON HEAD ISLAND

Doctor Ludington's announced schedule proved to be only partially accurate. Each officer seemed to have his own idea about who should land first, and what should be expected once the troops were on solid ground. For most of the men, nothing mattered except getting off the ship where they had been packed tightly for so long. Signal flags and colored lanterns attempted to keep everyone informed but mostly managed to confuse the questions. One set of orders sent the soldiers from the Fiftieth Pennsylvania scurrying to transfer themselves and their belongings to the *Ocean Queen* because the *Winfield Scott* was needed elsewhere. No sooner had they joined the Roundheads on the *Ocean Queen* than orders came for both regiments to transfer to the *Winfield Scott*, which would take them closer to shore.

Similar confusion reigned about the state of occupation of Hilton Head Island itself. Members of the scouting party had reported the Confederate troops gone, but occasional shots and flares from the woods around the abandoned fort suggested not every southerner had high-tailed it for the safety of Charleston. As a result, some soldiers carefully packed their guns and ammunition, while others concentrated on gathering their creature comforts. Reverend Browne was one of those opting for comfort. His haversack contained four big hard crackers, a tin box of sardines, a jar of olives, some chicken and ham, cheese, and pickles. He filled his canteen with a mixture of water and claret. He also packed blankets, a woolen hat, a towel, an extra pair of socks, some stationery, his Bible, and a pen.

Moving nearly 12,000 men from ship to shore with a fleet of surfboats was tedious business. Some of the Roundheads set foot on the island around midnight. Others did not make it until after the sun came up the next morning. They quickly discovered that, while three weeks at sea had given them their sea legs, the voyage had unaccustomed them to walking on dry land. They pelted out of the surfboats one hundred yards from shore and splashed through the water, cheering and shouting with delight. Then they hit the sandy beach, and their legs turned to rubber. Those who arrived in the dark stumbled over unseen obstacles; those who arrived at dawn wished they could not see that those obstacles were dead bodies.

As Doctor Ludington had predicted, the ugliness of war lay spread out for all to see. Artillery shells had struck with enough force to blow the fort's cannons apart. What those shells did to the human body was beyond description. Body parts and piles of unidentifiable gore littered the sand. Other bodies lay partially covered with sand, not because they had been deliberately buried but because the blast had blown them into a hole and then showered them with debris. The soldiers who earlier had cheered each shot now had to deal with the results of the attack. Already unsteady on their feet, many of the soldiers fell to their knees, vomiting the remains of their dinners as they surveyed and smelled the carnage.

Colonel Leasure moved among the men, encouraging them to head inland, where there were fewer bodies to be seen away from the fort walls. But even he hesitated when he found Reverend Browne on his knees near a destroyed cannon. Tears ran down the minister's cheeks as he scrabbled at the sand.

"What are you doing, Robert? Did you lose something?"

"His head. Where is his head? I see his face spread out there on top of that gun breach. He had a lovely crop of whiskers. But where is the rest of his head?"

"Robert, come away now. The soldiers will handle this."

"No. No. I have to find the rest of him. His mother will want to see her son whole before he is buried. I have to find the rest of him. He's here somewhere. We can't just send his face home."

"This soldier won't be going home, Robert. We're sending out a burial detail now. They'll gather up all these pieces and give them a decent burial here on the island. The sun will soon be overhead, and we can't leave them out in the heat."

"But he must have a funeral. See, I have my Testament. And I could wrap him in my blanket."

Colonel Leasure gently lifted his chaplain to his feet. "Have you something stronger than water in your canteen?"

"There's claret, but it's in case the wounded men need it."

"Take a drink, Robert. There aren't any wounded men. They are all past helping. You need to get hold of yourself, not just for your own sake, but for the sake of our soldiers. They'll be looking toward you for guidance. You can't let them see you fall apart."

The minister threw his head back to stare at the sky. "My God, my God. What have we done?" Then he looked around anxiously. "Where's Nellie? I must find her. I must tell her I understand now what she meant. I must apologize. Have you seen her?"

"Nellie? Why, she's still aboard the ship. She and the other women won't be coming ashore until we have the place straightened up. You wouldn't want them to see this."

"But she knew, Daniel. She tried to tell me how awful this would be, and I made fun of her. I told her she didn't belong in the Army. But she . . . she knew . . . and I didn't." Browne's shoulders began to heave again as the sobs broke from his throat.

Looking around in some desperation, the colonel spotted Doctor Ludington and waved him over. "Take care of Robert, will you, Horace? He's had something of a shock."

Got his comeuppance, looks like, Ludington thought, but he dutifully put an arm around the chaplain's shoulders and led him off to the shelter of the large plantation-style house that dominated the interior of the fort. "You'll be more comfortable in here," he explained. "Sit a spell, and take your time coming out. We'll send someone for you if you are needed."

The next several hours passed in a muddle of orders and counter-commands, exultation at being back on land and grief over the horrors of war, exciting discoveries and gruesome remains. As the men came ashore, officers doled out assignments that would allow the Expeditionary Force to settle into an organized camp. The worst task, of course, was the need to bury bodies and body parts as quickly as possible. To the men's relief, yesterday's shells had blasted the ground into sandy hills and deep pits. The burial crews had merely to toss the bodies into the deepest holes and rake the sandy hills flat again. It would be days before the soldiers quit stumbling upon the occasional finger or ear, lying blackened and dry in unexpected spots. But for the most part, the worst of the carnage soon disappeared, and the men's spirits rose in proportion.

Some of the Roundheads were sent on a foraging mission to see what kinds of local foodstuffs they could find to round out their sea rations. Just behind the remains of the fort, they discovered a large field of sweet potatoes and fell to digging them with enthusiasm. They so enjoyed their task that Colonel Leasure shook his head in wry despair, wondering if he would ever make soldiers out of this band of boy-farmers. Others, given the task of exploring the tents and buildings used by the Confederates, were soon happily rummaging through cupboards, chests, and barrels. The order to abandon Fort Walker had come when many of the Confederate officers were at their midday meal, and tables still displayed the remains of that interrupted meal. China plates and silver flatware spoke of the relative luxury these defenders of the coast had experienced, and the variety of dishes and condiments promised that the new inhabitants of Hilton Head would live comfortably on their stores for the foreseeable future.

It was nightfall before Nellie and her charges arrived on shore. When their small landing craft finally reached the shore below the fort, willing hands lifted the stretchers of the patients and carried them into the waiting hospital tent. Doctor Ludington led Nellie around the tent, showing her where items had been stowed.

"This is temporary, you understand," he said. "General Stevens has already staked out the site of a new hospital building, down the road from where our officers are being housed. The engineers have been told to start construction immediately. Plans are to build four wards, joined around a central cloister that will provide exercise grounds, fresh air, and a kitchen garden for the hospital. The outer walls of the wards themselves will be fortified, so the hospital will be safe from attack. Stevens says we'll be here on a permanent basis, and he's planning a base to serve the needs of an army of occupation as well as those of a combat force."

"I'm amazed at how much has already been accomplished," Nellie commented. "We just arrived, but already the men seem much at home and in control."

"That's the general's goal. He's aiming for stability after the turmoil of the voyage. Your own tent is here, by the way, next to this hospital tent. Private Stevenson has it all set up, as it was at Kalorama."

"I'm sure I'll find it when I'm through getting the men settled in," Nellie responded, already looking around for her next task.

"Nonsense. It's late. The orderlies can manage things here. I'm going to walk you to your quarters, and then I'll send over a plate of supper from the mess tent. You've had a busy day out there on the ship. It's time you took a breather."

Nellie sank onto her own camp chair with evident relief. The tin plate delivered by one of the cooks smelled divine. Whipped sweet potatoes, fresh greens, and a succulent roasted pork were such a relief after rice and beans that she was almost reluctant to eat them. Then hunger overwhelmed her, and she cleaned the plate in minutes. Her camp cot, too, was so comfortable after the board bunks of the ship that she wondered for a few minutes if she would be able to sleep. She had only time to hope the men were feeling as much at home as she was before she slipped into oblivion.

The winter sun rose over the Atlantic, streaking the pre-dawn navy sky with ribbons of gold, coral, and rosy pink. The first beams found their way straight through the cracks in the tent flap to urge Nellie awake. She sat up, stretched with delight at how rested she felt, and then made her way to the door of the tent, drawn by those intense colors that now flooded the sky with yellow light and promised a glorious fall day.

This was her first real look at the Hilton Head encampment, and she surveyed it slowly, marveling at the order she saw all around her. When she joined the regiment in Pittsburgh, the camp on the fairgrounds had been a maze of haphazardly pitched tents. On the heights of Kalorama, the regiments had laid out their individual claims in a more orderly fashion, but an overall plan did not exist. Here, groups of eight, ten, or twelve tents stretched out in squared-off rows, each double row separated by a roadway, with cross streets at crisp right angles. The pitch of each tent roof was exactly the same as its neighbor's.

Nellie headed for the hospital tent, where her charges all seemed to be sleeping peacefully. Reassured, she followed the scent of fresh coffee to the mess tent, where the Roundhead staff was beginning to assemble. Nellie tried to appear controlled and serious, but a grin kept trying to force its way through. "What a beautiful place this is," she said as she filled her plate. "And how on earth did you all get this much accomplished in just one day?"

"Well, Nellie, we had 12,000 pairs of willing hands, all as happy to be back on land as you apparently are," said Colonel Leasure. "I take it you approve of your accommodations?"

"Everything's fine, Sir."

"After you finish your breakfast, I'll show you the regimental headquarters and the staff housing." Leasure's offer was motivated only partially by kindness; he also wanted to keep her as far away from the damaged fort as possible. She was not about to let that happen.

"I'd like to visit the fort, Sir. What direction is it from where we are? I arrived so late last night that I couldn't see a thing."

"Not much left to see, I'm afraid," said the colonel. "And we're clearing away the damaged parts as fast as possible. We'll have a new fort soon. There's no need for you to visit the old one."

"Was there a lot of damage?" Nellie asked.

Reverend Browne, who had been sitting quietly at the far end of the table, looked up and spoke for the first time. "Take the colonel's advice, Mrs. Leath. You were completely right about the awfulness of warfare. We all know it now. There's no need to wallow in repercussions or regrets over what had to be done. Leave it alone, for all our sakes."

Nellie might have taken offense at the words, but the tone of the chaplain's voice was so uncharacteristically low and dispirited that she could only stare at him. This was not the fiery voice of God with whom she had often argued. This was the voice of a broken man who had aged overnight.

He sat slumped on the bench. His eyes seemed to sink into the dark circles around them. He was pale, unshaven, and rumpled. And unless she had completely misunderstood him, he had just attempted an apology for his diatribe of two days earlier. She looked toward the other officers for guidance, but their gazes were averted, as if they, too, could not bear to look at Reverend Browne in his grief. Because she could not find the right words for a response, Nellie simply nodded and bowed her head. In a moment conversations resumed, and the breakfast gathering broke up.

By the time Nellie and the colonel left the mess, soldiers were swarming everywhere, all seemingly intent on the jobs to be done. Nellie shook her head in amazement. "I can't even begin to absorb all of this, Sir. Can you give me some landmarks to cling to? Right now I'm not sure I could find my way back to the hospital tent."

"Well, you are standing in the Roundhead section of the encampment, facing due north, at the corner of Wright Avenue and Sherman Avenue." Leasure chuckled as Nellie's eyes widened in disbelief. "Yes, my dear, the command staff has already named many of the streets after themselves."

"But how did they know where the streets would be? Was this whole area part of the fort?"

"No. No. Look straight ahead of you. That bit of masonry wall you see is Fort Walker. And no, again. This is as close as I intend to allow you to get. It was really a small defensive fortification, holding maybe two hundred men. We have over twelve thousand. Our camp, which, by the way, will be named Fort Welles, will be a huge base of operations. Most of the area you see filled with tents was cleared farmland. Yesterday General Stevens had only to lay out the plan and put the men to work."

"I'm astonished," Nellie said. "Do you mean he planned this whole lay-out in one day?"

"General Stevens is a remarkable little man," Leasure replied. "I'm sure it's no secret I have had my quarrels with him, but I have never questioned the depth of his knowledge and military skill. When we made camp in Washington, we erected the tents first and then let the men trample out the paths that wound between them. The result, you will remember, was not pretty—or efficient. Yesterday, General Stevens held up all construction until the street layout was marked out. Then the tents, as you see, went up in orderly rows, just as he had intended."

"So he had a plan for the whole thing in his head before we even arrived?"

"Probably so. He was firm in designating the areas for each facility. As the horses were unloaded, he pointed them at the stable area, which will lie well north of the old fort. The ordnance crews were sent straight to the remains of the old arsenals, where their weaponry and ammunition could be protected. He's even designated a separate street for the sutlers and the washerwomen. It's off to your left there, and the venders are already at work erecting their own little shops."

"It's a perfect location—close to the men's tents, but not scattered higgly-piggly among them."

"Yes, although I'm afraid the soldiers have already discarded Stevens' name for the street. They're calling it 'Robber's Row', which is probably more accurate than anything the general could have come up with."

Nellie shared his amusement. "The name will stick, too. I'm sure of it."

"Now turn around and look down Wright Avenue behind you. On your left is the guard house and the provost's quarters, followed by your tent and the regimental hospital. You'll be conveniently located for sick call, but separated enough from the men's activities that your patients will not be disturbed. Those two-story clapboard buildings you see between your facility and the beach are officer's quarters. The houses are pretty utilitarian, but they are solidly built, and positioned to catch the coastal breezes. They were apparently used as summer homes by the local plantation owners. We've inherited their furnishings and their stores of provisions. The one closest at this end is our regimental headquarters. That's where the staff and I will be living as long as we are here."

"And are we here for the duration of the war, Sir?"

"No, I think not. There's a great deal of work to be done here at the moment, and every hand is needed. The general has ordered that our entire encampment, which extends over a mile on every side, is to be surrounded by a fifteen-foot ditch and a twenty-foot embankment. Our men will be shoveling dirt for weeks. But once that fortification is in place, most of us will be taking control of the other islands along the coast. I don't know where we will be going, but I'm sure Hilton Head is only a stop-over on our journey."

"Then I'd better do whatever exploring I want to do right away. I'm fascinated by the strange vegetation, and I'll bet there are some interesting animals lurking in the undergrowth, too."

Colonel Leasure shook his head at her, but smiled at the same time. "You and your love of animals! But be careful, my dear. At least keep a lookout for alligators in the swampy areas. They are not to be toyed with. You might want to take one of the orderlies with you if you are determined to go nosing around."

"Yes, Sir. I'd better be getting back." She stopped as she caught sight of Reverend Browne making his way slowly down the road toward his tent. His back was bent like that of a much older man. His feet shuffled, and his eyes remained fixed on the ground. Nellie glanced at the colonel and saw that he, too, was watching the chaplain.

"Is he going to be all right, do you think?" she asked.

"All right? I hope so. No, I'm sure he will. But it's going to take a while."

"Was whatever he saw so terrible?" Nellie asked.

"No, it's not that it was all that horrible. Our soldiers saw the same sights, and they've not been so badly afflicted. But for Robert. . . ." Colonel Leasure seemed to pull his next sigh from the bottoms of his boots, but he clearly wanted to talk. He perched on a nearby barrel and gestured for Nellie to join him on a nearby crate.

"I've been trying to work this out for myself, and I can understand why you are worried about him. For some men—like Robert—religion provides a buffer between their emotions and the realities of the world around them. Their faith makes it possible to deal with matters that otherwise might overwhelm them. Robert deals with death every day, but he has always done so with his hand on his Testament and the standard words of consolation on his lips. He performs funerals with the deceased laid out in the family parlor wearing good clothes, eyes carefully closed as if in sleep, the unpleasant odors held at bay by flowers and burning candles. The message of Scriptures is that death is a new beginning, the goal of a Christian life accomplished.

The deceased is in heaven—at peace—with his Heavenly Father. You've heard it all. And Robert takes as much comfort in that message as do his hearers.

"Yesterday he saw and smelled death undisguised. He saw body parts, smashed heads, gory piles of intestines, and there was no way to hide the ugliness. He had his Testament out, but there was no one to hear his comfort, no body to bury with his rituals. For perhaps the first time, his religion failed to protect him. It was of no use, and therefore neither was he."

"So he's doing what? Mourning the loss of himself?"

"Yes, perhaps that's exactly it. He's having a real crisis of faith, although he probably does not recognize it as such. This is going to sound cruel, but I think he'll begin to recover as soon as someone dies a natural death. Then he can once again take refuge in the sacraments that have always shielded him."

"What should I hope for? That someone dies, so Reverend Browne can feel useful again? Or that no one dies, and he continues to despair?"

"Well, that's a decision you'll not have to make. Someone is sure to die. This is an inherently unhealthy climate, do whatever you will to keep your men in good physical condition."

Nellie stared at the colonel for a moment, recognizing the truth in what he was saying but still haunted by the fact Reverend Browne would be helped only when someone else died. "I'm glad I've not been taught to use religion that way." She grimaced. "Although I probably use medicine to do much the same thing. I'm trying to hold illness at bay with my salves and tinctures. And maybe if they all fail me, I'll be as broken and disheartened as the chaplain."

"We all have faith in something, Nellie, even if it's in the necessity of doing our jobs, which, by the way, we had better be about."

12

LIFE AND DEATH IN THE LOW COUNTRY

In the days that followed, Nellie had many occasions to remember Colonel Leasure's predictions about Reverend Browne. Diseases spread through the camp at Hilton Head. The men had brought measles and mumps with them when they landed, and the dampness and unaccustomed heat of the sea islands seemed to exacerbate the spread of infection. No one had expected mosquitoes to still be a problem at this time of year, but they swarmed through the camp, accompanied by colonies of fleas and clouds of other tiny stinging and biting midges. The men called them "no-see-ums," which was an accurate description. Within days, previously healthy soldiers came down with high fevers and chills that ran in cycles of three or four days.

Doctor Ludington diagnosed malarial fevers, and he and Nellie passed out doses of quinine until supplies ran dangerously low. Cases of sniffles turned into the deep, wracking coughs of pneumonia, and typhoid reappeared. Adding to the crowds in the hospital tents were the injured, whose unfamiliarity with chores such as digging a fifteen-foot ditch and piling up a twenty-foot earthwork led to sprains, broken bones, wrenched backs, and nasty cuts from shovel edges. Nellie's plans to explore the island never materialized. By the end of each day, she wanted only to fall into an exhausted sleep.

Malarial fevers caused by the miasmal climate frequently led to complications and deaths. Soon the question was not whether someone was going to die, but how many would succumb. In the first two weeks of the occupation of Hilton Head, nine soldiers died. The makeshift Pinewood Cemetery at the edge of the camp began to fill almost before it was ready. Nellie and her nurses grieved over their failures, becoming more and more discouraged as the days passed.

For each burial, Reverend Browne emerged from his private reveries to perform the services, and his voice grew stronger with each death, as Colonel Leasure had predicted. Browne described the problems in a letter to his father.

> It has been a week to try our faith, bravery and patience. Death has been busy in our ranks. The process of acclimation goes hard with our Northern constitution; and many are sick. We brought the measles ashore with us, and it has spread till there are many cases, but in general they are progressing favorably. There are some cases of dysentery, pneumonia, and remittent fever. The latter is of a severer type than is common in our climate. Since we landed as many as nine more have died, two of whom were last week and seven this week; and these sudden strokes of death among us have filled the Colonel, physicians, nurses and others including myself who feel care and responsibility, with sadness.

The medical staff, of course, came in daily contact with the diseases that were ravaging the camp. Several of the women accompanying the regiment grew alarmed at the possibility of their own deaths and found a variety of excuses to keep themselves away from the patients who were suffering the most. Even Mary Pollack's father demanded she stay away from the hospital tents. Nellie struggled to cover the shortage of nursing staff by working double shifts herself. Doctor Ludington was not unaware of her efforts, but he himself was so busy he failed to notice the early signs Nellie was faltering under her workload. It was, in fact, a patient who first drew his attention to the problem.

"Doctor? Have you noticed how pale and thin our Nurse Nellie is lately?" asked a private who was well on his way to recovery from a case of scarlet fever. "I think she may be working too hard. She's in here day and night, and I never see her take a break, even for meals."

Doctor Ludington started at the question. "Come to think of it, she hasn't been eating in the mess tent lately. I guess I assumed she was taking her meals here in the hospital."

"I don't think she's eating or sleeping," the young soldier went on. "I'm no medical man, but I'd feel better if you took a look at her."

"I'll do that. Thank you."

Ludington found Nellie at a makeshift desk, making notes on the day's patients and treatments. When she looked up at him, he was shocked at her pallor. Her eyes were dull, and when her lips smiled, the rest of her face remained blank. "Nellie," he said, "Are you feeling all right?"

She stared at him for a moment and then gingerly shook her head. "Just a bit of a headache. Nothing to worry about."

"I'm not so sure about that. May I feel your pulse?" He took her slender wrist and noted the rapid heartbeats that felt like little bubbles bursting under the skin. Her skin was clammy with cold, and when he pushed up her sleeve, her arm immediately puckered into goose-bumps.

"You're cold."

"It's chilly in here," she said. "It's November, after all."

"It's actually warm in here, Nellie. How long have you been feeling ill?"

"I'm not ill," she insisted. "I'm tired."

"I don't think so. Can you stand up for me?"

"Of course. But why?" She pushed the chair back and stood, grasping the edge of the desk to steady herself. She squeezed her eyes shut for a moment, trying to stop the room from spinning around her. Then she staggered and sat down abruptly, refusing to meet the doctor's eyes.

"Orderly!" Doctor Ludington called. "Mrs. Leath is not feeling well. Please help her to her tent and then summon Mary Pollack to stay with her. I'll be there in a couple of minutes, Nellie."

For the next three days, Nellie lay on her cot, almost insensible to her surroundings. She alternated rapidly from shivering with cold to flushing with fever. She refused food, and drank only sparingly. She jerked her head away when someone tried to administer medicine of any kind. Finally Doctor Ludington lost his patience with her. "You're a terrible patient, Nellie! What would you do if one of your soldiers refused all your efforts to help?"

"I'd realize he was ready to die," she mumbled. "Leave me alone."

Now seriously concerned, Ludington sought help from Colonel Leasure. "I can't get through to her, Daniel. It's as if she is willing herself to die. I don't think she has one of the more serious malarial fevers. Her symptoms aren't all that severe, but she's given up. There's not a spark of life in her. She's lying there waiting for her body to shut down."

Daniel Leasure did not need to hear more. He strode directly to her tent, dismissing the nurse and orderly who were attending her. He clasped her hand and shook her shoulder. "Nellie? What's all this I hear about you?"

Her eyes cleared a little as she gazed up at him. "I'm dying, Colonel. I'm not going to survive this illness, whatever Doctor Ludington chooses to call it."

"Nellie, no, I can't accept that."

"It's all right. I'm ready to die. Life has been a burden to me. If I can die here, at my post, in the service of my country, I am more than willing to do so."

"Well, I'm not willing to let you do it," Colonel Leasure replied. "And you're not 'dying at your post'. Your post is out there in the hospital, taking care of our patients. You're not serving your country by lying here feeling sorry for yourself and tying up the time of our medical staff who are needed elsewhere."

Now Nellie was glaring at him, and he was delighted to see the spark return to her eyes. "I'm not faking my illness, Colonel," she answered.

"No, you've been ill, I admit. I'm a doctor, remember? You're weak from lack of food and water, and you've had a bit of a bout with this coastal fever that's been going around. But it's not going to kill you, any more than that fall on board the Ocean Queen was going to kill you. You seem to enjoy the drama that surrounds the possibility you might die, but we don't have time for it at the moment."

"What would you have me do?" she asked, tears beginning to brim under her lashes. "When I tried to work my way though the illness, Doctor Ludington sent me to my bed. Now that I'm here, you're chastising me for not being at work."

"Just don't die, Nellie. We need you back, as soon as you feel able. You need to work at getting well. Right now you're letting the weakness of your body dictate to your flagging spirit. But your spirit has always been strong. Give it the upper hand over this illness."

Nellie didn't answer. Her eyes closed and her lips pressed together in a tight line. She struggled to pull herself together. Two days later, she was back at work, a bit shaky but cheerful as ever. The two doctors watched her covertly as she moved among her patients.

"You were right, Daniel," Doctor Ludington admitted. "Her malady was more in her mind than in her body. I wonder what it is that makes her so ready to welcome death."

"We may never know, Horace. She's a troubled soul, obviously. Whatever happened to her in her former life has scarred her. She's afraid of something, and she's holding it at bay by devoting herself to a righteous cause. As long as she's helping others, the threat of her past can't reach her. When her work disappears, the fears return."

For the soldiers of the Roundhead Regiment, homesickness glorified and exaggerated their memories of autumns filled with brilliant red and gold trees, rolling hills of amber grain, and the rich smells of burning bonfires. Like other Union soldiers, they could find little to like in the scenery of their current surroundings. Stephen Walkley, who originally came from Connecticut, complained:

If I walk outside to see the beauties of nature, there are none to see. The Palmettoes are interesting; the live oaks with their silvery moss are beautiful, but all else is a flat waste of dreary, dirty sand. The matted vines trail down into the dank edges of the swamps and the hot sun by day decays them enough to exhale malarious gases by night. Aside

*from the fort I have not seen a hill a foot high nor a rock big enough
to throw at a robin.*

Insects continued to be a problem. Mosquitoes, fleas, chinch bugs, and
deer flies do not die off easily in the warm, wet South Carolina climate.
Pennsylvanians, used to killing frosts in early autumn, did not expect to
be assaulted by squads of tiny nuisances in November. Nellie had several
ideas that might help the sufferers, but she could hardly keep up with the
demand. She suggested solutions of chloride of lime, arsenic, or soap, but
few had the time to brush the substances on all the surfaces of their living
quarters. Closing off an area and fuming it with camphor, burning brown
sugar, or plantains dipped in milk would work only if the rooms could be
sealed off. She sent some soldiers on a hunt for wild garlic to hang around
their necks, and for bites, she recommended vinegar. The cures sometimes
worked, but the soldiers complained the awful smells were almost as irritat-
ing as the bites.

For Nellie herself, the worst insect invasion came from palmetto bugs.
These looked like giant cockroaches, some of them an inch or more in
length. They made a creepy clicking noise, and Nellie swore she could hear
their toes scrabbling in the dirt. On one occasion, challenged by an unusually large specimen in the ward, she upended a bucket over it until she could
find some brave soul to squash it. She was horrified a moment later to see
the bucket sliding across the floor as the palmetto bug pushed it along. It
sometimes seemed to Nellie she was stranded on a deserted island inhabited
only by God's nastiest creatures.

Nellie was correct in seeing Hilton Head as a deserted island, and it
was not only a result of the recent exodus when the Union forces attacked
Port Royal Sound. Hilton Head provided an excellent port as well as a thin
but fertile soil, both of which made it a desirable location for invasion and
occupation. Early island plantations raising indigo and tea were targeted
by the British during the American Revolution. Many were attacked, their
crops and slaves carried off on British ships. Again during the War of 1812,
the British burned Hilton Head plantations along the navigable waterways.
Some planters simply gave up and moved inland early in the nineteenth

century, while others hung on until the shallow soil became depleted of nutrients. As the market for tea and indigo declined, long-staple cotton became the crop of choice, and, as it did so, planters needed fresh soil, uncontaminated by salt marshes. Long before the Expeditionary Force landed at Fort Walker, a number of plantations on Hilton Head had been abandoned and left to the ravages of time and weather.

Colonel Leasure, Doctor Luddington, and several other officers set out one day to refresh themselves by exploring the island, but what they found left them feeling sadder than when they left the fort. After hacking their way through heavy underbrush, they began to discern the remains of old roads, which in turn led them to abandoned plantations. Further along the path, they came to an old burial ground, again in the midst of tangled underbrush, the fences broken down, and the tombstones broken to pieces. They spotted one huge marble mausoleum and identified some family names—Kirk, Grimes, McCabe, and Baynard—sad reminders of the fleeting nature of human prosperity.

All were disturbed by their contacts with the Negroes who were living in the interior of the island. The Roundheads, many of whom came from staunchly abolitionist families, had set out in the assumption they were fighting to free the slaves. They believed in equality and freedom for all men. Their own ancestors had fled from Ireland to escape oppression. Their hometown churches taught that slavery was a sin. Innocently the men had believed that, when the rebels were defeated, the slaves would become free and equal citizens. They were ill-prepared for the realities of Hilton Head Island.

When the Confederate troops of Fort Walker fled, the civilians living on the island headed for the safety of Charleston or points further inland. But the slaves had neither joined the flight nor left their everyday tasks on the plantations. Without supervision from overseers, they went about the job of harvesting the crops, taking care of abandoned animals, and raising their families in the same little cabins where they had lived all of their lives. Occasionally one would wander into the Union camp looking for help with a sick child or hoping for employment. But for the most part, they kept to themselves, seeming to be almost as angry about the invasion as had been their owners.

The commanding officers were confounded by the existence of abandoned slaves. General Sherman estimated there were at least nine thousand blacks on Hilton Head. With increasing frequency, he wrote to headquarters and to Lincoln himself, begging for help, or at least instructions, on how to handle the problem:

> *Hordes of totally uneducated, ignorant, and improvident blacks have been abandoned by their constitutional guardians, not only to all the future chances of anarchy and starvation, but in such a state of abject ignorance and mental stolidity as to preclude all possibility of self-government and self-maintenance in their present condition.*

He exaggerated the helplessness of the slaves but not the frustrations of the soldiers.

"Why don't they leave?" was a common point of discussion among the men. "Don't they understand they are free? What's stopping them?"

"I feel like I brought somebody a birthday present and they said, 'No, thanks'," Jim McCaskey complained. "We've handed them their freedom, and they don't want it."

"Yeah. I thought that was what we were fighting about," Jacob Leary agreed. "If we're wasting our time, I'd rather be home at my chores. It'd sure be easier than digging this confounded ditch."

"Did you hear Reverend Browne has taken one of the slaves into his tent as his own personal servant?" The speaker was John Wilson, a cocky Pennsylvanian who often thought the worst of his friends and comrades. "Calls him Tony and says he's teaching him to read the Bible. Needs somebody to wash his socks more likely."

"The Reverend wouldn't do that," someone protested. "Colonel Leasure already said, back in Annapolis, we couldn't keep the blacks as servants."

"Yeah, but that was before he was surrounded by them," John replied. "Maybe we should follow Browne's example and get our own crew of slaves to dig for a while."

Jim McCaskey shook his head in exasperation. "I still believe in our cause. We're here to put an end to slavery. The slaves around here don't understand that yet. Once the war's over, and there's no threat of the plantation owners coming back, they'll see what good we've done. Give them time."

Nellie, too, had much to learn about the slaves she thought they had come to rescue. One morning at breakfast, she was trying to make pleasant conversation with the chaplain. "How do you think the morale of the troops is holding up?" she asked him. "You talk to them when they are at their most discouraged. Are they sorry they came, do you think?"

"Ah, no, Mrs. Leath. They're tired and sore and dirty, but they still believe in the cause for which they enlisted. They're having some contact out in the woods with the slaves whose owners abandoned them here on this island when we landed. They're learning at first hand what life has been like under conditions of slavery, and many of them have been visibly upset by the stories they have been told."

"There are slaves living in the woods? I had no idea! I haven't seen any Negroes here in camp, so I assumed they had all left."

"No indeed. When the planters saw Fort Walker was about to fall, they skedaddled with only what they could carry in their arms. They ordered their slaves to follow, but no one seems to have enforced that order. For the most part, the slaves simply hunkered down and hid until their masters left."

"But what are they doing out there? We've taken over the plantation houses and eaten their food supplies. Are they really living in the woods, like primitives?"

"I'm sure they are God's creatures, and He is watching over them. You needn't worry your pretty little head over them."

Nellie felt herself being to bristle with indignation at his patronizing remark. Swallowing hard, she tried to keep smiling. "Are they looking for our help? Should we be doing something positive for them?"

"Mrs. Leath, be realistic. There are hundreds of slaves out there, and they don't belong to us. They haven't been freed because a northern army arrived on their shores. They're not our responsibility." The chaplain looked as if he were growing more and more exasperated with her.

"But. . . ."

Nellie's next protest was interrupted by a shout and cry for help from outside the tent. "Someone come quick! It's a bomb!"

Every officer in the mess tent leaped to respond to the call, Nellie and Reverend Browne along with them. Just outside, a frantic young private, white with fear, pointed to another soldier standing a few feet away. Sergeant Benjamin Scott Stuart was holding a large unexploded artillery shell, turning it over in his hands and examining its workings.

"Ben, stop!" shouted Captain Armstrong, the commander of Company A. "It'll blow!"

"No, Sir," Scott said. "If I can get this fuse out, it won't be able to explode."

"You can't get that fuse out."

"Stop!"

"Somebody run and find help from the ordnance crew."

Shouts came from all around, but the observers seemed rooted to their spots. All realized they were watching a disaster unfold, but no one knew what to do. As if in slow motion, Sergeant Scott began to twist the fuse. Not a soul took a breath. The fuse seemed to come loose, and then, as Scott looked up with a grin of triumph on his freckled face, the shell exploded.

The concussion echoed across the dirt field, driving the onlookers backward. The sound was first unbelievably loud and then abnormally silent as eardrums reacted to unbearable noise. Most stood frozen. Then, out of the crowd burst Reverend Browne, Nellie close on his heels. The two of them knelt by the supine form of the sergeant who had tried to prevent the accident he had caused.

"He's still alive," Nellie said, unable to tear her eyes from the horror of what lay before her. The shell had blown a hole in the sergeant's abdomen, his intestines a bloody mess, his liver and heart visible within his chest cavity. But above the hideous wound, his chest still moved. Both his legs had been broken by the blast and lay twisted at improbable angles. His arms flailed helplessly, and Nellie saw in disbelief he had lost both hands.

Reverend Browne sat on the ground, cradling the man's head on his lap as the soldier tried to speak through the blood clogging his mouth. "Mrs. Leath, for God's sake. Get him some water."

"But he can't drink, Sir. He has no. . . ."

"Nellie!" the chaplain's voice boomed at her. "He needs to clear his throat. Get him water!"

Someone was already passing a tin cup to her. Carefully she held the cup to his lips, and to her amazement, he gulped the water down. She could not look to see where it went.

"Reverend," the young man gasped. "Will you pray with me?"

"Certainly, my Son. I'll speak the words and you follow along. Our Father, who art in heaven, hallowed be Thy name. Thy kingdom . . . ."

Nellie found herself murmuring the familiar words along with them. The soldier was trying to fold his missing hands in a gesture of prayer. She reached over and took hold of the stumps of his arms, enclosing them in her own folded hands. It seemed to her the soldier's voice became a bit stronger as the three of them reached the end, ". . . Thine be the power and the glory, forever and ever, Amen."

Nellie felt a vast emptiness expanding inside her, but the dying young soldier was not through twisting her heart. "Reverend, will you tell my mother I was not afraid to die? And send my love to my dear wife Lizzie. She thought I'd be coming home soon to raise our family. Tell her . . . tell her I wanted to."

"Rest easy, Son. I'll personally see to it all your loved ones receive your final thoughts. And I'm sure they are sending you their blessings. They do not want you to worry about them. All will be well, I promise, and you'll see them again one day soon."

Sergeant Scott breathed a huge sigh, and Nellie waited for his next breath. It never came. Reverend Browne drew his hand gently over his eyes, closing them for the last time.

"Is there a blanket to cover him?" he asked.

Other hands took over now, and when Nellie looked around, Reverend Browne was already gone. Colonel Leasure was still there, however, and he helped Nellie to her feet, handling her as if she, too, had received a mortal blow. He accompanied her to her tent and sat with her silently for a while, seeming to understand no words were capable of easing the horror of the last few minutes.

At last she looked up at him. "All those things the chaplain said about seeing his loved ones — do you think he really believes that?"

"Of course he does, Nellie. That's what makes it possible for him to offer consolation to those *in extremis*. And you must take consolation yourself in the fact Sergeant Stuart had a good death."

"A 'good death'? That's another contradiction. How can any death be good?"

"It's what every soldier hopes for. A 'good death' demonstrates the soldier's courage, his concern for others, and his own acceptance of his fate. Sergeant Stuart was beyond feeling the pain of his wounds. He died trying to keep his comrades from being injured by that shell. He had time to make his peace with God and to leave encouraging words for his loved ones. He would not have asked for more."

Nellie kept shaking her head. "But it was all so senseless."

"When we mourn, Nellie, we mourn not for the dying but for the living." Reverend Browne spoke as he stood in the doorway to her tent. "Is she going to be all right, Colonel?"

"Yes," they spoke in unison. Then Nellie added, "Thank you, Reverend Browne. You were wonderful out there. You were much more useful than I was. I'm beginning to understand that." A faint smile touched her trembling lips. The chaplain repaid her with a scowl as he turned to leave. Colonel Leasure's eyes moved from one to the other. "Just maybe," he thought. "Just maybe these two can find some common ground between them."

13
ON TO BEAUFORT

There were no solutions to the problems of Hilton Head, of course, but a promise of relief arrived on Dec. 5th. Colonel Leasure and some of the other regimental commanders had been absent for several days. They returned late that evening, and Leasure immediately summoned his company commanders to a briefing in the mess tent.

"We're moving out," he announced.

A clamor of voices broke out: "Who?" "When?" "How soon?" "Where are we going?" "Are we headed into battle?" "Are we abandoning Hilton Head?"

Leasure held up his hands for silence. "It's General Stephens' brigade—that's us, along with the Eighth Michigan, the Highlanders of the Seventy-Ninth New York, and the Dirty Dutch of the Fiftieth Pennsylvania. We're headed up river to occupy Port Royal Island, which the Confederacy has already abandoned. We've drawn the lucky straw, because we're assigned to hold Beaufort against all comers."

"What's Beaufort?"

"It's one of the prettiest cities you'll ever see. It sits on the bank of the Beaufort River, which flows into Port Royal Harbor. It's where the plantation owners from all over the low country maintained their summer residences. The climate is said to be especially healthy. The houses are mansions with huge back lots for the staffs of slaves who run the residences. It has several stores, churches, meeting halls, a post office, government offices, a courthouse, even a library. And for you, John Nicklin," he said, pointing at the director of the regimental band, "a real bandstand in a park right across the street from our house."

"Our house! Are you saying we're moving out of these musty tents?"

"Right you are. We've been exploring the city the past few days, picking out the places that will be most comfortable."

"I'm dreaming!"

"No, it's real enough, but make no mistake. We'll have a lot of work to do, and most of our men will still be in camp tents on the outskirts of town. General Wright will have his command post on the town square, in the former John Mark Verdier House. He's coming with us so he can establish a more central command over the entire coastal area. We represent the first wave of Union occupation of South Carolina. The other troops will eventually move north and south to take Charleston and Savannah. Our job is to hold Beaufort, so the rebels can't use the Charleston and Savannah Railroad, which runs above Port Royal Island."

"But we'll be in town?" asked James Cornelius, captain of Company C.

"Our headquarters will be right in the center of the city," Leasure said. "Each company will have its own plantation house, along the outskirts of town, to guard all access. You, Jim, will take your men to the Barnwell plantation north of town. The house there is well-furnished. It even has a piano, and an old Negro mammy who has offered to stay on as your cook. There will be room for your officers to stay in the house, and there's a shady clearing where the men can pitch their tents nearby. The rest of you will have similar accommodations."

"And regimental headquarters?"

"The Roundheads headquarters will be in the Leverett House. It belonged to an Episcopalian minister who raised a family of eleven children in it, so it's good-sized. It sits on a slight hill overlooking the river. Across the street on one side will be General Stevens' brigade headquarters, and on the other side will be a huge hospital for the Roundheads."

He looked around to spot Doctor Ludington and Mrs. Leath. "Your hospital will be the Fuller House, which used to belong to a medical doctor. The doctor's office and equipment are still in place. It's an odd structure, build out of oyster shell concrete, but they say it keeps wonderfully cool in summer and warm in winter. It has a total of four wings of two stories each, so you will have a surgery and seven wards."

"How soon do we leave?" asked Alva Leslie, the quartermaster.

"Immediately. I'm afraid you'll have to work through most of the night, Alva. We must begin to load the ship at daybreak. We'll be traveling in the *Winfield Scott*, and most of you are already familiar with her layout. You company commanders should have your men prepare rations for twenty-four hours, pack their things, and break camp first thing in the morning. We will assemble at the wharf and load as quickly as possible. We have to sail with the incoming tide to get that ship though the shallows of the river, and there will be no time to lose."

As it happened, of course, things did not go as quickly as hoped, and the ship's crew missed both the morning and the evening tides. The soldiers spent all of Friday and Friday night tied up at the dock; the ship finally sailed at 6:00 a.m. on Saturday. The trip was only a matter of some twenty miles, but sailing was slow on the river, and they did not arrive at Beaufort until late afternoon. As had happened before, Colonel Leasure asked Nellie to stay aboard with her hospital patients until all unloading was finished. She managed to cajole the ship's mess crew into cooking up some soup to feed her patients Saturday evening.

It was midnight before the ambulance wagons pulled up at the dock and the sick and injured disembarked. Colonel Leasure was there to supervise, and he touched Nellie's arm gently. "Come with me. You'll ride back to headquarters in our carriage."

"But the men will need me," she protested.

"Nonsense. The hospital is all set up and ready for them. The rest of the medical staff can manage fine. You've been on constant duty for eighteen hours. You need a good night's rest, and I've arranged quarters for you at the Leverett House."

A few gaslights illuminated the central main street, but once the road bent to the right to follow the line of the shore, Nellie could see little until the carriage came to a stop in a brick-paved yard surrounded by tall buildings. Despite the lateness of the hour, the yard swarmed with figures unloading wagons and unhitching horses. Among them were dark faces, including those of several small children who deftly avoided being stepped upon as they tried to see what was going on.

Private Stevenson was there to help her down from the carriage. "Come inside, Miss Nellie," he said. "The slaves have your room all ready for you." He led her up a broad flight of stairs and through a doorway into a dark hall. He stopped at the first doorway on the right, stepping back to let her precede him into the room. She took in little of what she was seeing. A banked fire glowed in the fireplace, and a candle shaded by a glass lamp threw shadows across vague outlines of furniture.

"There's a chaise here," he pointed out, and she sank onto it gratefully. "Your trunks and supplies are in the corner. I'm sure there will be someone to help you unpack and get settled in the morning."

"Thank you, John. You always seem to find perfect lodgings for me. You needn't bother further. I'll be fine here. I'll rest a few moments longer and then retire for the night."

She awoke hours later, stiff and cramped from the awkward half-reclining position in which she had slept. Sunlight was creeping through the curtains, and a slight noise told her she was not alone. Sitting up, she saw a young slave girl, who had just placed a steaming pitcher and basin on the marble-topped dresser near the door. "Mornin', M'am. This be you water and towel."

"Thank you, uh . . . I'm sorry. What is your name?"

"I's Maudy, M'am," the girl said as she backed out the door, shutting it firmly between them.

Well, that didn't last long, Nellie observed to herself. She had been ready to ask several questions, but perhaps one didn't hold conversations with slaves. How would I know? she asked herself. I've never talked to a slave at all, let alone had one waiting on me and bringing me things. How odd it feels!

She began to look around the room, needing to answer her questions for herself. With a sigh of relief, she spotted a screen in the left back corner. It sheltered an empty iron tub and a chamber stool of carved dark wood. The seat lifted to reveal a chamber pot painted with lively roses and daisies.

Nellie smiled in delight. "This surely was a girl's room. It goes way beyond anything Private Stevenson could have come up with."

Her immediate needs dealt with, she was ready to survey her new quarters. The floor was covered with a woven woolen rug and the windows draped with heavy brocade curtains. The bed, small and narrow though it was, looked deep and comfortable. Its coverlet was a hand-worked quilt of flowered gingham patches in a daisy petal design. The chaise on which she had slept was upholstered in dark green velvet, with tucks and buttons all along its back. Two smaller armchairs flanked the fireplace. A low table held a couple of books and a vase of fresh flowers. And there were her boxes of belongings, stacked neatly next to a tall wardrobe with a mirror set into one of its doors.

All of this for me! she thought in disbelief. If the Colonel really means for me to be housed here, I'll be living in luxury. Her curiosity now fully aroused, she splashed a bit of water on her face, smoothed the unruly tendrils of hair curling around her forehead, shook out her skirts, and declared herself ready to explore the rest of the house. Her courage lasted long enough for her to open the door and step into the hall. Straight across the way stood a closed door, and a staircase that led to the third floor. To her left the door she had come through last night now stood open to a small porch and the yard beyond. To her right, the hall led past two facing rooms with doors ajar, toward a massive front entrance with sidelights and fanlight now filled with the rosy tints of the rising sun.

Nellie hesitated, curiosity competing with trepidation as she tried to take in the layout of the house. Tentatively she ventured down the hall toward the two rooms that seemed to be standing open. Neither showed any sign of human occupancy, but the furnishings suggested both might have originally been used as parlors. Settees and armchairs arranged in pairs flanked ornate fireplaces. Small carved and gilded tables were scattered about the rooms, while mirrors and chandeliers reflected the available light. The walls were covered in what looked like silk, setting off what must have been family portraits. In contrast to its original design, the parlor on her right was crammed with trunks, cots, and boxes she recognized from the medical tent. Across the hall, several official looking trunks stenciled with Colonel Leasure's name cluttered the other front room.

Thinking the front door was probably locked, Nellie walked back down the hall and stepped out the back door onto the porch. What had seemed only a scene of mass confusion when she had arrived now resolved itself into a working yard that stretched far back to the next street. On the east side, a long stucco building was a scene of bustling activity as slaves went about their tasks. The carriage in which she had arrived still stood on the paving bricks outside what was obviously a carriage house. Further along, multiple arched doors opened into stables, from which restless horses whinnied their request for breakfast. And near the end of the building stood what appeared to be workshops. One, already issuing smoke and a fiery glow, suggested a blacksmith at work.

Across the yard to the west was a matching building, but this one seemed to be spewing small black children. Several of them were lined up on the edge of a makeshift porch, swinging their bare legs and feet as they ate from wooden bowls, some with spoons, some with nimble little fingers. Slave women made their way in and out of the kitchen, which was giving off fragrant wood smoke and the smells of coffee and frying meat. Just past the porch, steam drifted from another door as women carrying bundles of cloth passed through into what must have been a laundry room.

Looking upward, Nellie noted the second level of these building had small open windows with flapping shutters as their only closure. Beyond the buildings, a grassy yard extended to a back wall with a firmly closed gateway. Huge live oak and pecan trees overhung the grassy areas, but there, too, was evidence of hard work going on. A chicken coop, a vegetable plot with something newly green sprouting up in rows, a couple of peach trees, a pigpen, a woodpile, and several small storage sheds filled the yard.

The porch on which Nellie stood was too shallow to let her get a good look back at the main house without venturing into the yard. She glanced to the foot of the stairs, wondering if she dared go down and do some exploring. As if he had read her thoughts, a elderly but dignified black man approached and came up the stairs toward her. "Begging pardon, M'am, but dis here's de slave quarters. It be best if you goes back inside."

"I didn't mean to snoop," Nellie said, "but there didn't seem to be anyone around in the house, and I smelled coffee."

"The gen'mens is all still sleepin', I reckon," the man replied. "You come back inside now, M'am, and I do sumwhat 'bout you breakfus'."

"You are . . .?"

"You kin calls me Uncle Bob," he offered. "When de Rev'nd and his family lived here, I runned de house. Mrs. Leverett liked to call me her butler. Now I jes' try to keep everythin' goin' smooth wit' us black folk." He opened the back door for Nellie, then followed her inside and opened the door nearest the stairs. "Dis here be de dinin' room. You kin sit a spell and I's gonna get Maybelle stirrin' y'all up some breakfus'."

"I don't want to be a bother. Is there somewhere I could fix my own? We brought provisions with us."

"No, M'am. Dat's not hows we do it. Cookhouse be out in de yard, so as not to set de house on fire. Cook bring de food over to de warming room below here, and Maybelle bring it up de back stairs fo' you."

"Just coffee will do."

"Yes'm. I'se gonna git dat right now, but de gen'mens be gonna want somethin' to stick to dere ribs. I'se gonna take care of it. You jes' rest a spell."

Nellie sank onto one of the cane chairs arranged around the heavy dining table. She felt terribly awkward and out of place after so many months in the primitive eating arrangements of mess tents and shipboard mess halls. I've fallen off the edge of the earth, she mused to herself.

In a few minutes Uncle Bob returned with a steaming cup of coffee, and a heavy pot, which he placed on the serving buffet against the far wall. Nellie took the cup gratefully and inhaled its fragrant steam, realizing she was indeed hungry.

"Should I speak with Maybelle about what we might have for breakfast?" she asked.

"No, M'am. You wants somethin,' you tell me, and I be de one to tell Cook. Maybelle jes' bring de dishes in. For now, I'se 'fraid y'all be settlin' for what's already cookin."

"Of course. I didn't mean to seem ungrateful."

"No, M'am. You 'n' me—we'll work together jes fine to keep dis ol' house runnin' de way you like it."

"Well, but I'm not the one in charge, Uncle Bob. You'll probably have to work with the Colonel on things like that."

"No, M'am. I ain't workin' wit' no kernel. Dis be de way it be. White menfolk be in charge of what be outside. Womenfolk be in charge inside de house. I done see'd but one white woman 'round here, so you be in charge." He nodded vigorously and stomped out of the room.

The edge of the world, indeed, Nellie sighed.

Not long after Uncle Bob's dramatic exit, the colonel himself appeared in the doorway to the dining room. "Do I smell coffee?" he asked.

Nellie turned to greet him. She realized she was absurdly relieved to see someone else from the regiment, to make sure she was not dreaming this whole encounter with the plantation house and its slave staff. "Good morning, Colonel Leasure. Yes, it's good coffee, too, and there's a whole pot of it on the sideboard. May I pour you a cup?"

"Yes, please. And then you can tell me how you managed to find it."

But before Nellie could move to the sideboard, a slave woman scurried into the room from a doorway concealed in the wall paneling. She made a dash for the coffee pot, murmuring, "S'cuse," and poured the colonel's coffee herself.

"Are you Maybelle?" Nellie asked.

The woman nodded, ducked her head, and disappeared back through the wall passage.

Leasure stood gaping at the little scene he had just witnessed. "Nellie? What's going on?"

Nellie chuckled at his bemused expression. "We are caught in the middle of a pecking order. That was Maybelle, I think. Her job is to bring us food, which she gets from somebody called Cook. And Cook takes orders from Uncle Bob, who is a formidable black butler. I have nothing to do with any of this. Uncle Bob sat me down in here and informed me of the process by which we will get breakfast—eventually."

"And where is this 'Uncle Bob' getting his orders?"

"From himself, apparently. He has been at pains to explain to me how things are done around here. But you'll have to talk to him yourself. I'm hesitant to try to explain his point of view."

As if on cue, the door panel slipped open again and Uncle Bob himself appeared, leading Maybelle and Maudy, the young woman Nellie had encountered in her bedroom. The two women carried trays of dishes, which they arranged on the sideboard. Uncle Bob stood by, watching the procedure critically. He reached over to adjust an item or two, and then came to Nellie, pulling out her chair. "M'am, you breakfus' be ready.' Only then did he turn and acknowledge the presence of the colonel with a curt, "Sir."

"Good morning. Are you the 'Uncle Bob' Nellie was telling me about?" the colonel asked.

"Yessir. I'se Uncle Bob and I'se in charge here."

"Oh." Leasure seemed a bit taken aback by the finality of that statement. "You are responsible for this meal?"

"I'se responsible for de whole house. I'se here to do whatever Miss Nellie tell me to do, and she agree dat you gen'mens prob'ly be hungry dis mornin'."

Leasure was not sure how to respond to that explanation. Instead he turned his attention to the sideboard, where the slave women were waiting to help him fill his plate. "What have we here? Eggs, I see, and country ham and biscuits, and . . . ." His voice trailed off as he uncovered two more bowls, both containing viscous white substances. "Which is the oatmeal?"

"Dat not oatmeal, Sir. Ain't you never see'd grits before? Nor sassige gravy?"

"Well, as a matter of fact, no," Leasure said. "I've never heard of grits, and I've certainly not eaten white gravy. Does it go over the ham?"

Uncle Bob signed in exasperation at the backwardness of these northerners. "Southern folk eat dese all de time," he said. Then he delivered a lecture, as if to backward children. "Grits is ground up hominy. We eats 'em for ever' meal. Dey's starchy and fillin', and you can flavor 'em however you likes. Fo' breakfast you kin pour some of dat sorghum over 'em. Fo' dinner dey's good wit' fishes or shrimps. As for de sassige gravy, dat go on de biscuits, of course. What does you folks eat on you biscuits?"

Nelly tucked her chin into her collar to control her giggles at Uncle Bob's explanation and the colonel's look of bemusement. She knew he had never heard of sorghum, either, but this time he was clever enough not to reveal his ignorance.

"Well, thank you, Uncle Bob," he said. "I'm sure we will all enjoy this wonderful spread. I'll want to talk to you later about arrangements for the day-to-day operation of our headquarters here."

"Miss Nellie be lettin' me know whatever you need," Uncle Bob answered as he left the room.

"Did I miss something?" the colonel asked.

Nellie flushed. "That was not my idea. I tried to tell Uncle Bob he needed to talk to you, but he would only explain that as far as the slaves are concerned, white men rule outside, and white women are in control inside the house. He sees me as the woman in charge, just as Mrs. Leverett was when they were living here. I'm sorry, Sir. Maybe you'll be able to dissuade him of his notions."

"Actually, Nellie, it might be a pretty workable plan. Have you had time to explore the house?"

"Not really. I've only peered into the front parlors and looked out the back door. Then Uncle Bob caught me, and I've been doing as he says ever since."

"Well, my plan is to use one parlor as my office, and Doctor Ludington will have his surgery in the other. We'll hold the officer mess in here, and you will have your small sitting bedroom across the hall. Upstairs there are two bedrooms, one for my son and me and the other for Reverend Browne. Then there is a huge sleeping porch that stretches all across the back of the house. There's room for a dozen beds or hammocks there, and it should serve well as a convalescent ward for those officers who are not ill but are recuperating or hobbled by injury. The rest of the medical staff and the regular patients will be next door in the Tabby Manse."

"What's that?"

"That's what folks here call the Fuller House next door. It's going to hold our main hospital wards. As our regimental matron, you should be able to handle supplies and provisions for both houses from here. I'm sure

Uncle Bob will help you coordinate that." Colonel Leasure allowed himself to laugh at last. "I'll wager you'll be a tougher boss than I would have been."

"But, Sir, I don't know how to handle slaves. I don't even know if it is right for us to be using them at all. We came here to abolish slavery, I thought."

"Ah, Nellie, there's your good heart speaking again. But think for a moment. What would happen if I said we would not use slaves here? What if I told them they were free and they should go on their way? Where would they go? What would they do?"

"But. . . ."

"We're not going to be slave owners, Nellie. We're not going to beat them, or sell them, or keep them in chains. I plan to pay the blacks as civilian workers. But you must remember. Those quarters you saw out in the yard are their homes. Their families, their jobs, their tools and possessions are all here, and we have no right to take those things away from them. In a few months or years, this war will be over, and we will be the ones to leave. The slaves belong here, and we'll help them remain."

As Nellie and the colonel filled their plates, the other officers began to filter into the dining room. As each man sniffed at the contents of the sideboard, Nellie and the colonel tried to explain the unfamiliar dishes. But now their explanations were accompanied by the first-hand experience of the others.

"Try some of that sausage gravy over a biscuit. It's real good."

"Don't much care for that sorghum."

"Yes, but the grits ain't bad with butter and salt and pepper. Try mixing 'em with your eggs."

"Coffee's especially good, although it has a bitter aftertaste, like there's something in it besides coffee."

"Here's Uncle Bob. Maybe he can tell us what's different about the coffee."

"Oh, dem's de acorns you be tasting." Bob explained with a shrug.

"Acorns!" Several men spluttered and set their mugs down in haste. But one look at the colonel's face warned them not to make a fuss.

Hoping to change the subject, Colonel Leasure looked around and asked, "Where's Robert Browne? It's not like him to miss a meal."

"The door to his room was still closed when I came down, Papa," Geordy replied. "But you're right. He should have been down long ago. Furthermore, it's Sunday, when he'll be wanting to preach to somebody. Shall I go up and see what's keeping him?"

"Please do that, Geordy."

The officers returned to the remains of their meal with gusto. Then came a voice from the top of the stairs. "Pa! Doctor Ludington! Come quick! Reverend Browne's taken ill."

Nellie followed the Colonel and Doctor Ludington up the stairs but stopped to talk to Tony, Browne's adopted slave boy who now served as his personal servant. He was hovering outside the door to the guest bedroom, eyes wide with fright and wringing his hands in distress. When he saw Nellie, his emotions boiled over.

"I doesn't . . . don't . . . know what be happenin', Miss Nellie. Las' night, de Revern', he cold. Had me stoke de fire right up, but dat didn't help. I brought extra quilts down from de attic, an' he bundled up in dem when he went to bed."

"Did he complain of feeling sick, Tony?"

"No, M'am, jes' cold. But dis mornin' when I goes in to wake him, all de quilts in a pile on de floor, an' he be red in de face and thrashin' 'round. I put my hand on his shoulder to wake him, and he be jes' burnin' up and talkin' foolish. Den he start shoutin' and askin' for Mary somebody. An' he call me 'Willie' when he knowed my name be Tony. I was jes' comin' fo' to git some help when young Massa Leasure come up de stairs. I'se sorry."

It was an ominous description. She had watched enough soldiers suffer and die from malaria since they arrived in South Carolina to recognize the symptoms. A disease that killed the young and healthy was even more dangerous for a middle-aged man. Still, panic would not help. She patted Tony on the back and assured him he had done everything correctly. "He's in good hands, Tony. The doctors will take care of him from here on. But they will probably need you to run errands, so you stay close by, all right?"

"Yes, M'am. I surely will do dat." He still looked terribly frightened.

When Nellie entered the room, she could see why. Reverend Browne was in the throes of delirium, rolling his head from side to side and mumbling incoherently. His lips were dry and cracked; his breathing labored and interrupted by dry coughing.

Doctor Ludington glanced up and nodded at her. "Nellie, do you know where we packed our supply of quinine?"

"Yes, Sir. I can find it. All the boxes of medical supplies are labeled, although I'm not sure we have much real quinine left."

"Get me whatever you can find. And Nellie, if you see any slaves along the way, send them for cool water and towels."

That was a job for Tony. She caught his arm and dragged him with her as she hurried downstairs. He scurried one way in the downstairs hall, heading for the cistern located outside the back door, while Nellie went in search of the medical supplies.

That was the start of two long weeks. Reverend Browne's illness followed the expected four-day cycle. After the fever reached its peak, he broke into a heavy sweat that cooled him down and relieved most of his symptoms. He experienced one day during which he felt weak but was sure he had recovered. Then the chills returned, followed by another bout of fever. His demeanor fluctuated with the various stages. Each time the chills returned, he plunged into a black depression, angry he could not achieve any control over whatever was ravaging his body. Then the fevers and delirium took over, making him irrational and difficult to control. When the sweat broke, he experienced a state of euphoria, sure each time he was cured. By each fourth day, he demanded to be allowed to get up and go back to work. At best, he kept himself occupied by asking Tony and Nellie to rearrange his room for greater comfort. And then once again, came the plunge into blackness.

Tony and Nellie spelled one another in offering as much care as possible. Tony bore the heaviest part of the burden, since Nellie had other duties as well. Doctor Ludington still expected her to do rounds with him at the hospital next door, and Colonel Leasure had decided to leave the day-to-day running of the household in her hands. There were medical supplies to be unpacked, inventoried, and re-ordered. The slave women needed instruction on how to adjust their duties to include cooking and laundry for the hospital patients.

Routinely, visitors from Hilton Head arrived at the door, curious to see the inside of the house and expecting a meal and perhaps a bed for the night. Nellie had never been one to pay much attention to military ranks, but she soon found she could survive only by distinguishing in some way who mattered and who did not. A visiting general demanded their best hospitality. A young lieutenant accompanied by one of the nursing staff found himself shuffled off to the hospital mess.

At one point, when Nellie was nearly prostrate with exhaustion, she complained loudly to Uncle Bob about his household staff. "I don't have time to tell these women what to do every day! I explain our needs, and they nod and do what they are asked. But the next day, they wait again until I give them the same set of instructions. Why can't they show a bit of initiative? Surely they can see when it is time for breakfast? Or when the laundry needs to be carried out to the washhouse?"

Uncle Bob shook his head and smiled his knowing smile at her minor tantrum. "Initiative, Miss Nellie? You want slaves to show initiative? You doesn't know much 'bout slavery, does you?"

"I know when people are not doing the job I expect them to do!"

"But initiative? You teach a slave to initiate his own actions, and he be gonna initiate hisself right out dat door. Dat be what he be gonna do!"

"But I thought you all were happy here. This is your home."

"We loves our families and our friends. We maybe even loves our jobs. Dis house is all de home most of us has ever know'd. But you don't want to test our loyalty too far, Missy. We all be playin' our roles, and you best be playin' yours by de rules, too."

She wasn't sure what he meant by his references to role-playing, but she was learning more as time passed. She was mistress of a plantation house run by slaves, and she needed to behave that way, even if it was out of character for her.

She was also learning more about Reverend Browne. On his good days, he felt compelled to write his customary letters to his family. The malaria in his system, however, had left him with a distinct tremor that affected his handwriting. Because he did not want to worry anyone, he asked Nellie to write the letters while he dictated them, explaining to his wife that the doctors would not let him out of bed to write at the desk. Every three or four days, she spend an hour transcribing his thoughts—a most curious experience.

He composed his words as if he were speaking directly to his wife, and there were many times when he seemed to forget Nellie was in the room at all. Certainly he didn't seem to realize how revealing his outpourings were. There were intimate messages—often soul-searchings—and he never mentioned them in any other context. Nellie was moved by his obvious affection for all the members of his family, not just his wife, but his father and his children, too.

She was more confused by his musings on the meaning of his illness. If someone had asked her a month earlier, she would have said the chaplain used his religion as a weapon against the bad behavior of others. Now she saw he turned that weapon even more harshly against himself. He believed all illness was the result of God's wrath, and he spent much time ruminating over his own misdeeds. He believed God was punishing him for his sins, and he knew those sins to be grievous and numerous because of the severity of his disease. He searched his conscience, trying to decide what he had done that had angered his God.

He described his prayers and his better impulses, but he spent more time enumerating those thoughts and deeds that might be construed as sins. He frequently called himself a misanthrope, hating men and women alike who infringed on his privacy. Nellie cringed at that one a bit. Certainly her medical interventions had been part of that infringement. He catalogued his impatience with the weaknesses of others, his outbursts of temper, and his lack of compassion. He had not had many opportunities to commit overt sins, but he found no limit to his sins of omission. He mourned and regretted each one of them in his musings.

He was a tormented man, consumed not so much by his hatred of others as by his hatred of himself. Nellie found herself feeling sorry for him, even though she could not always forgive him for how he turned that self-hatred against others. These letter-writing sessions left her drained and exhausted. She nursed him as diligently as she could, but she always left his sickroom with a sense of relief. And no one prayed harder for his swift recovery than Nellie Chase.

14

SETTLING IN

Just when Nellie began to feel at ease with her new role as a plantation mistress and to believe Reverend Browne was truly on the way to a full recovery, a new crisis erupted. She entered the dining room one morning to find it shuttered and empty. She stepped back into the hall to look for Uncle Bob, but no one was around.

As she approached the back porch, she saw the yard was similarly quiet and deserted. What's going on? she wondered. She had never ventured through the dining room door used by the slaves, nor had she ever seen the warming kitchen below the dining room. Uncle Bob had made it clear her presence would be unwelcome there, and she had respected his instructions. But now, knowing the men would soon be coming downstairs for breakfast, she pushed the pocket door aside gingerly and bent down to listen to what was going on below stairs.

A grief-stricken wail echoed up the stairwell. Niceties cast aside, Nellie dashed down the stairs to find Maybelle collapsed on the floor, fists raised above her head, face raised to an unseen ceiling, cries shaking her entire body. Maudy stood by, wringing her hands but unable to help. Nellie fell to her knees, gripping the trembling shoulders. "Maybelle? Maybelle! What has happened?"

The slave woman looked at her without recognition, so caught up in her own grief she was unable to make the transition to ordinary speech, She shook her head, although she did not draw away. Nellie turned to Maudy with the same question.

"It's her little girl, Glory. She have de smallpox, an' Unca' Bob, he say he be gonna take her out in de swamp and leave her, so's de rest of us don't git it."

"What? We haven't had any smallpox here. Has one of our doctors seen her?"

"No, M'am. Jist Unca' Bob. He take one look and chase ever' body outta de room."

Anger washed over Nellie in a flood. She was willing to let Uncle Bob run the household, but this was going too far. "Uncle Bob does not make medical decisions, and certainly not life-ending ones," she said. "Maybelle, get up. I want to see Glory right now."

"But. . . ."

"No arguments. Take me to her."

Maybelle stood, reaching out to the rough stone walls of the passageway to steady herself. Then she led the way through the warming kitchen and out the door into the yard. Nellie followed and Maudy brought up the rear, still wringing her hands. The morning was cold and damp, and now a thick fog was settling in. It blurred the lines of the outbuildings and muffled their footsteps across the herringbone pattern of the brick forecourt. The little procession made its way onto the porch of the cookhouse, past the laundry room, and into a dark hallway. Maybelle hesitated for a moment at the foot of a rickety staircase set against the wall.

"Go!" Nellie ordered.

"You be careful, M'am," Maudy warned. "Des steps is solidest near de wall, but you gots to watch for holes."

As she picked her way up the steps, leaning as best she could on the solid wall for extra support, Nellie wondered at the lives of these slaves, who must pass up and down this way several times a day. We need to make some changes around here, she told herself. But a sick child comes first.

The stairs emerged into a hallway that was slightly brighter, thanks to the row of unprotected windows looking out over the yard below. On the other side of the hall, darker rooms, built without windows or ventilation, cadged what light they could by leaving their doors open. Maybelle pushed open the only closed door with a soft call. "Glory? Honeychile? How you feeling?"

"I'se itchy, Mama," came a small voice from the dark.

"Get me a lamp. Candles. Something." Nellie pointed to Maudy. Then, as her eyes adjusted to the gloom, she made her way to the small pallet laid out near the fireplace. "I'm a nurse, Glory. May I look at your itches?"

The child stared back at her, her eyes bright more in fear than with fever. Gently, Nellie pulled up the tiny shirt to check her chest. Then she turned to the mother.

"Maybelle, I need you to think carefully. How long has she been sick? Where did the first rash appear? Was it on her face or on her chest?"

"It be on her tummy, I 'members. She not be sick, an'I didn't see no sores, but she be scratchin' at her tummy day 'fore yestiday. An' dis mornin, I sees all des bumps on her. Dat's when Unca Bob come in and say she have de smallpox." Maybelle was close to breaking down again.

Nellie reached out to steady her. "She doesn't have smallpox, I promise you. She has a case of chickenpox, that's all. If it were smallpox, she would have been sick days before the rash broke out. The smallpox would have started on her face and hands, and you would have seen it right away. Chickenpox starts on the chest and moves up to the face later. Also, smallpox sores are hard to the touch, while these are squishy. She's going to be uncomfortable for a few days, but she'll soon be up and playing again."

Maybelle began to wail again, but it was a happy wail, "Praise be! Thank'e, Lord."

"Now then, Glory. You must try not to scratch your itches. That only makes them hurt worse, and it will spoil your pretty little face. Right after breakfast I'm going to bring your mama some lotion to put on the itchy places to make them better. Will you try not to scratch for me?"

"Yes'm. I promises. But M'am?"

"Yes?"

"Is I gonna be better by Slave Ule? Dat be de bestes' part of de year and I doesn't want to miss it."

Nellie looked toward the women in confusion. "We'll see, Glory. We'll try to get you better by then. You can help by trying to get some sleep now, all right?"

"Yes'm."

At the door, Nellie put out a hand to stop the two slave women. "Maybelle, you stay here with Glory. Don't let anyone take her anywhere, do you hear? If anybody tries, even Uncle Bob, send him to me—if I haven't found him first. And while you're here, cut Glory's fingernails real short, so she can't scratch. You might even try putting some socks on her hands. Tell her they're puppets. And Maudy, you get yourself down to the kitchen and get breakfast set up. You've helped enough that you know what to do. The colonel will be down soon, if he's not already, and he and his men will want to be fed. Scurry now."

Nellie crossed the yard, peering around to see if she could spot Uncle Bob, but in the thick fog, no one seemed to be moving. She headed up the stairs to the back porch and entered the main hall of the house, where she met an irritated Colonel Leasure. "Nellie! Where in blazes have you been? And where is everyone else? It's past breakfast time, and the table is empty!"

Nellie held up both hands in front of her. "We need to talk. Come into the dining room." The colonel, sensing the anger fueling his head nurse, followed meekly, sitting down at the table and watching in bemusement as Nellie stomped to the serving door and shouted, "Maudy! Get a move on!"

"I'se a' comin', M'am." The younger woman came in bearing a coffee-pot. Nellie took it from her at the doorway and sent her hustling back for food. Then she poured a cup of coffee for herself and for the colonel before sitting down across from him.

"Now, then!" Quickly she described the drama of the morning.

"You're sure it's chickenpox?"

"Yes, Sir. No doubt." Quickly she reviewed the case for him, and he nodded his agreement. "But Uncle Bob needs to be told not to go around making medical diagnoses. And then I have some other questions for him, too. Can you get him in here?"

The colonel nodded again. He strode to the door and bellowed, "Bob!"

Tony appeared at the foot of the steps, his eyes wide at the tone of the colonel's voice. "He be upstairs, Sir. I be gonna fetch him." But the colonel was already bounding up to shout again. "Bob! I want you in the dining room. Now!"

The second shout did the trick. Bob appeared in the doorway, looking affronted at having been summoned so rudely. "No need to shout, Sir."

"Oh, yes, there is," the colonel responded. "You've been scaring the servants half to death with your amateur medical pronouncements. That little girl has chickenpox, not smallpox, and you had no business frightening her mother with threats of abandoning her in a swamp. You have a house full of doctors here. Come to us with medical problems, understand?"

"Well, it looked like smallpox to me, Sir. I'se jist tryin' to keep everybody safe."

"You do that by not overstepping your bounds. Understand? Now, Miss Nellie has something else to talk to you about."

With an exaggerated sigh that stopped short of becoming an insult, Uncle Bob turned to her. "M'am?"

"Little Glory was worried about something called 'Slave Ule'. What in the world is that?"

"Dat be a Christmas celebration Massa Leverett used to let us black folks have."

"Ule? Oh, Yule! Christmas! I'd nearly forgotten." Nellie caught her breath as she realized it was indeed December. "And what happens in this Slave Yule celebration?"

"Well, we all gonna be busy on Christmas Day servin' de white folk, so we gets several days afore Christmas for ourselfs. Slave Yule usually start on a Sattiday, after we does half-day chores. De men go out an' gather up some greenery fo' de decorations, and de women and chilluns go oysterin'. Mos' ever' night we roasts sweet 'taters an' oysters in de coals of de fire and has ourselfs a feast. When it be dark, Old Letitia call all de chilluns roun' and tell 'em de story o' how de baby Jesus come. Den we sings Christmas songs an' spirituals til de chilluns go to sleep, and den we has a 'Stomp' in de back of de yard." He finished his description and looked from Nellie to the colonel with raised eyebrows, waiting to gauge their reactions.

"No wonder Glory doesn't want to miss it. It sounds like a good time." Nellie was smiling despite her former anger.

Leasure nodded his agreement. "By all means. We wouldn't want to interfere with such a delightful tradition. Let's see. Tomorrow is Saturday, the 14th. Will the next Saturday, the 21st, be suitable for starting your Yuletide celebration?"

"Yes, Sir." Now Uncle Bob was smiling, too. "Thank you, Sir."

"Now," the colonel demanded, "Where in blazes is my breakfast?"

Later that day, Nellie finished her hospital rounds and made her way back to the slave quarters. Apparently the word about her intervention with little Glory had spread. The slaves met her with broad grins and greetings instead of wary looks and downcast eyes. "Hello, Miss Nellie!" "Thank you." "Can I gits you sumpin?" Even Cook stuck her head out the door of the kitchen to ask if Nellie had any special requests for dinner. "I has some nice fried chicken for y'all tonight. Hope dat's all right?"

Nellie grinned back. She hadn't realized how tentative she had felt around the slaves until they began treating her as one of their own. Now the yard felt like she was coming home, and she basked in the warmth of their acceptance. Her footsteps were light as she hurried up the stairs to visit her littlest patient. She hesitated at the door to Maybelle's room.

"Hello, Glory. May I come in?"

"Oh, Miss Nellie! I's glad to see you."

"How are you feeling, honey?"

"Pretty good. Look! Mama made me some mittens for my hands, and she be gonna sew buttons on dem tonight so dey has eyes. Den I kin talk to 'em when nobody be 'round."

Nellie's heart broke at the sound of loneliness in the child's voice. "I know it's hard, being up here all alone, but you'll be better soon, I promise. Did Mama tell you? Slave Yule won't happen for ten days yet. You're not going to miss it after all."

"Goody! It be lots of fun, even if dere won't be no presents dis year."

"No presents? Why is that? You've been good, haven't you?"

"Yes'm, but it's Massa Lev'rett who be givin' us our presents, an' he done skedaddled, 'long with all de other white folk."

"Oh!" Nellie was at a loss as to what to say. This child had the power to move her to tears with her combination of childish longing and bravery.

The little voice went on, filling the silent void that threatened to swallow Nellie on the spot. "But we can dig our own sweet 'taters and get our own oysters, so it still be a party. Be you gonna come?"

"Ah, we'll see. For now, let's put some of this nice lotion I brought on the itchiest of your sores. It'll help them heal." Nellie had stirred up a thin paste of boiled oatmeal, soda, and watered vinegar. She dabbed it cautiously on the most inflamed areas of the rash, not wanting to overwhelm the child by the vinegary smell. Glory, however, did not seem to mind. She lay back, visibly soothed by the coolness of the treatment. "I'll leave the bottle over here on the table so your mama can put more on when you need it. But don't you use it," Nellie cautioned. Wait for a grownup to help, OK?"

"Yes'm." Glory was already drifting off to sleep as Nellie left.

As she picked her way down the rickety staircase, Nellie spotted Colonel Leasure walking through the yard. On an impulse, she shouted for him to wait a moment. Going only as far as the door, she beckoned for him to come inside.

"What is it, Nellie? I can hardly see in here."

"Well, that's part of my point. I want you to see how dangerous this staircase is. Our house servants all live in rooms upstairs, and they have to go up and down here because it's their only access to their quarters. Can we get a couple of our soldiers who are handy with tools to come in and reinforce the treads? And maybe put a railing on the outer edge, too? I'm terrified every time I go up to see little Glory."

"I understand why! We'll get somebody to fix it right away, and we'll call it a Christmas present from us to the servants. Speaking of which, may I see you in my office in an hour or so? We need to talk about Christmas."

With that pronouncement, he hurried out again into the yard, off to deal with one of his never-ending responsibilities. Nellie followed, but almost stumbled as she saw Reverend Brown standing on the back porch of the residence, watching them both with one of his disapproving frowns on his face. He shouldn't even be out of bed, she grumbled to herself. But look at him. Spying and passing judgments as usual. Shaking her head, she headed toward the house. If he saw the colonel and me coming out of somewhere we don't belong, I'm sure we'll hear about it. Might as well get it over with.

Shoulders thrust back in fighting posture, she climbed the stairs. "Good afternoon, Reverend. Are you feeling well? Do you need help in returning to your bed?"

"Humph! Don't patronize me, Missy! What lies beyond that doorway you came out of?"

"The slaves' rooms." She smiled brightly.

"And I suppose you had business in there?"

"Yes." No sense in giving him more information than he asked for.

"And the colonel, too, I suppose?" Browne's eyebrows were raised almost high enough to meet his hairline.

"As a matter of fact, yes."

"And that would be. . . ?"

"You'll have to ask him," Nellie replied, giving him a rude toss of her head as she shouldered past him and headed for her room. Closing the door behind her, she leaned for a moment on the doorframe. Her temporary anger flowed from her, leaving her limp and somewhat ashamed. I don't know why I let him provoke me so, she realized. It only makes matters worse, somehow.

As the late afternoon shadows began to spread over the front yard, Nellie made her way to the colonel's office. She loved the view from the front windows that looked over the bay, where the water was now still and glassy. "How do you ever get any work done in here?" she asked as the colonel ushered her to an armchair in front of the window. "I'm afraid I'd sit and gawk at the beauty of this place."

"Sometimes I do," Leasure answered with a grin. He stood at the window for a moment and then turned away deliberately. "Christmas," he pronounced.

"Yes. We definitely need to do something." Nellie said, and then stopped as the colonel held up his hand.

"I've been doing some checking. It seems the tradition down here is that the slave owners give their slaves gifts at Christmas—new clothes, a pocket knife, a pipe, a head kerchief, shoes, a bit of cash, extra food rations—that sort of thing. And the children get candy, nuts, maybe a ball. These people are working for us now, and the least we can do is fill their owners' shoes in this regard."

Nellie breathed a sigh of relief. "Yes indeed. Little Glory told me earlier today there wouldn't be any Christmas presents this year because 'Massa Leverett done skedaddled.' She broke my heart."

"Well, we'll do our best to fix that. I'll add the cost into our expenses for labor. How would you like to go shopping?"

"Shopping? But where?"

"I've learned some of the free blacks in town are opening up the stores again. Why don't you take Mary Pollack with you, and a couple of the young blades around here to carry the packages, and make a day of it?"

"I'd love to. But I'll need a list of the slaves. I've seen many of them in the yard, but I don't know all their names."

"Uncle Bob can take care of that for you."

"All right! I'll get started planning right away." Nellie began to rise from her chair, but the colonel motioned her to wait.

"I'm not through, I'm afraid. I have more chores for you. We need to throw a party."

"A party." Nellie let her breathe out in a swoosh as she sat down again. "For?"

"We're going to have lots of homesick soldiers around here, come Christmas. They'll have a day off and a good meal—maybe some games in their companies. But I'd like to invite the staff, the officers and the non-commissioned officers, along with the band, to come here on Christmas afternoon. I thought we could serve some punch, eggnog, cookies, that sort of thing. The band can play some music. Just try to make the day a bit more festive for them."

"Of course we can do that. I'll talk to Cook and see what ideas she may have."

15

A SOUTHERN CHRISTMAS

Slave Yule was a resounding success. Colonel Leasure invited the slaves to gather in the forecourt on the Saturday morning before Christmas and distributed their Christmas gifts. "It's early," he explained, "but this way you will get to enjoy your gifts as part of your celebration for the next few days."

Nellie had done a wonderful job of Christmas shopping. Her trip to the ransacked stores in downtown Beaufort was disappointing, but she had found many great ideas when she talked to the camp sutler. Each of the men received a pipe and a plug of tobacco. The teenaged boys got pocketknives, while the younger boys received slingshots and balls. The women had new headscarves and the army 'housewives,' or sewing kits. Teenaged girls received mirrors and ribbons, and there were rag dolls for the littlest girls. All adults were given a small amount of money to spend on whatever they chose, and the children had enough peppermint sticks and oranges to last for days.

While the slaves had been busy at their tasks, a couple of the regimental carpenters had slipped into the stairwells that led to the slave quarters. They patched the stairs and installed handrails, both for the family rooms above the kitchen and the stable hands' quarters above the carriage house. And when Cook opened the door to her cookhouse on Saturday morning, she found hams, barrels of flour and cornmeal, prized sugar and coffee, and bags of beans and rice.

"All of dis fo' us? We'uns gonna has oursel's a feast." When Nellie stopped by later in the morning to see if Cook had everything she needed, the bustling slave woman hugged her.

"Thank you. You be doin' so much for us black folk." She hesitated, and then added, "You can calls me Bessie if you wants." Nellie felt as if she had been given a gift all her own.

The officers and staff of the regiment watched the activities in the yard with a mixture of amazement and puzzlement. "What's that huge pile of brush for?" Private Stevenson asked Uncle Bob. "There's enough of it, but it doesn't look like it would make a good bonfire."

"No, we not be gonna burn dat. Dat's wild grape vine, wisteria, an' greenery fo' makin' de wreaths. You come out back later dis afternoon an' we' be showin' you how we puts 'em t'gether."

"Wreaths? Oh, as in decorations!"

"Yessir. We be doin' some big 'uns for de front of de big house, and some little 'uns for oursel's. De women be makin' swags, too, for all de mantels in de main house."

"No Christmas tree?"

"Ain't no good Christmas trees growin' round here, 'lessin you wants to hang some paper chains on a palmetto bush. And dem things so sharp, you doesn't want 'em in de house. But der gonna be candles, once we gits through dippin' 'em and dryin' 'em tonight."

The festive mood was contagious, and the Union soldiers soon found themselves humming Christmas carols as they went about their business. Some even pitched in to help the slaves dig their fire pit in the back yard. The only soul who seemed less than jovial was the recovering Reverend Browne, who wandered downstairs from his sickroom to find out what all the racket was about. "Do these people realize Christmas is a holy day?" he asked Colonel Leasure. "Are they planning to go to their church? Or should I be making arrangements to preach to them?"

"I think they'll hold their own kind of worship, Robert. Let them be."

"Humph! Looks like heathen stuff out there to me," he grumbled. "What are we doing about our own Christian men, Daniel? Is there a place here where we can hold services?"

"There's a Presbyterian Church in town, and our men have already been holding regular prayer services. If you'd like, we can have a Christmas service there. Would you sketch out a worship program? I can have John Nicklin and his boys provide the music."

"And a proper Christmas dinner?"

"All taken care of, Robert. Nellie is a superb manager, and she and Cook have been working on menus for days. We'll serve our own resident staff here just after noon on Christmas Day, and then we're opening the house for visits from all the company staffs. We'll have syllabub and desserts, along with some good camaraderie. I want to help our men feel a bit less lost here in the deep south at Christmas."

"Syllabub? What's that?"

"Well, Nellie says it's Cook's special holiday drink. Contains whipped milk, fruit juice, and other flavorings. I thought it best not to inquire too closely about that."

"And who will serve all this, since you seem to have given the slaves a vacation?"

Colonel Leasure was rapidly losing patience with his cantankerous old friend. "Robert! Give me credit for being in control of this regiment. The slaves are doing their celebrating now, and we're letting them enjoy themselves to the fullest. By Christmas morning, they'll be back at work, and we'll have our holiday, as nice as I can make it for Pennsylvanians stranded in South Carolina. You don't need to worry about it, nor supervise it, for that matter. Oh, and by the way. You may want to keep to your room at the front of the house for the next few evenings, with the door closed. There'll be some singing and dancing in the yard, with my full approval!"

The slaves' celebration was every bit as much fun as little Glory had predicted it would be. It lasted from Saturday afternoon to Tuesday evening, which was also Christmas Eve. For Nellie, the days ran seamlessly into each other. She had wandered out with Private Stevenson on Saturday afternoon to learn how the slaves made their wreaths. Uncle Bob was eager to teach them, but Nellie soon found her hands were not strong enough to control the thick grape vines that formed the foundation of each wreath. Bob took the thick end of a vine, twisted it into a symmetrical loop, and then began to wind the rest of the vine in and out of the first loop. Soon he had a circle of four or five intertwined vines that held its own shape. Then he picked a second strand of wisteria vine, keeping up the same braiding motion, but weaving the thinner vine more closely. It formed a network over the sturdy frame, one that could be used to hold the various pieces of greenery in place.

At that point Nellie stepped in again, trying her hand at adding individual pine needle clusters, sprigs of boxwood, sprays of leathery magnolia leaves, and holly branches. "Don't be puttin' too much holly dere," Uncle Bob warned. "Dose leaves be prickly and you be havin' trouble holding de wreath if de holly branches be too close together."

"How do you fasten the pine cones to the wreath?" Nelly asked.

"Jist use a piece of wisteria like a string. I ties mine right under de top row of spines and then ties de whole thing to de form."

"But the one I did just hangs there," she said.

"If'n you tie de cones on first and then fill around 'em wit' de pine, dey stays put," Bob said. "You does the same wit' des here Japonica blossoms."

"Oh, those are beautiful. I've never seen them before."

"Dey's de flowers from a tea bush, so I hears. De're common around old plantation houses."

Nellie had to admit her efforts were producing a lopsided and straggly wreath. "Better hide this one on the warming kitchen door so no one sees it." She laughed at her efforts. Still, she enjoyed the experience tremendously, and the smell of pine sap and fresh flowers made Christmas seem more real. The slaves already had an impressive array of decorations, and Bob hurried off to supervise the hanging of wreaths on doors and windows all over the property.

Feeling a bit self-conscious about intruding on the slaves' celebration, Nellie returned to the house. But on Christmas Eve, the sounds coming from the yard tempted her to watch the festivities. She had finished laying out the cold supper of biscuits, ham, and salad Maybelle had left for the officers, when a cry of "Hear me!" drew her back to the door. An incredibly old black woman stood in the doorway to the slave quarters. Dusk was settling over the yard, and firelight reflected off light surfaces and drew attention to those who moved. Bent almost double, leaning heavily on a walking stick as gnarled as she was, she summoned the children. "Come, an' I be gonna tell you 'bout how de baby Jesus done come."

Old Letitia slowly made her way toward a stool near the huge bonfire in the yard. She launched into her tale as she walked, speaking the Gullah language Nellie had come to recognize as the slaves' private means of communication. The children flocked behind to hear her words.

Een dat time, Caesar Augustus been de big leada, de emperor ob de Roman people. E make a law een all de town een de wol weh e habe tority, say ebrybody haffa go ta town faa count by de hed and write down e nyame.

Nellie found herself translating in her head:

And it came to pass in those days, that there went out a decree from Caesar Augustus, that all the world should be taxed . . . And all went to be taxed, every one into his own city.

The simplicity and beauty of Letitia's version took nothing away from the story, while making it immediate and understandable to the children.

They clustered close to her, eyes wide, mouths open in wonder, as she recited the story of Jesus' birth. As she reached the part where the animals of the stable knelt down to the baby, one of the horses whinnied from its stall and everyone—Nellie included—gasped. It was a magical moment, one Nellie would remember for years whenever she heard the verses from the Gospel of Luke. A bit later, it was the sound of singing that moved her, as the crowd marked the end of Letitia's recital with several spirituals.

Nellie was still standing in the shadows of the porch, unwilling to turn her back on this demonstration of simple faith, when out of the darkness came a shaky little voice. "Miss Nellie? Kin I talks to you?"

"Glory! You startled me, Child. Of course, come up here and sit with me."

"I'se not 'llowed to go up des steps, Miss Nellie. Dat's de big house. Kin you lean over here?"

Nellie hurried down the steps to join the child on her level. "What is it, honey? Are you still feeling puny?"

"No, M'am. I'se fine. But dis little kitty's sick. Her mama won't take care of her, and I's 'fraid she be gonna die. And I can't lets her die on Christmas!"

In the light from the fire, Nellie saw the child was holding a small basket with some rags in it. And huddled among the rags was the tiniest kitten Nellie had ever seen. She was pure white, and she looked up at Nellie with two huge eyes that did not match. One was blue, the other green.

Gently Nellie picked her up, noting that the tiny ears were limp and the body under the fur had little substance to it. "Poor thing, I think she's hungry."

"Yes'm. De moma cat won't let her nurse no more."

"Well, come with me, both of you. We'll find some milk in the warming kitchen." Once there, Nellie twisted a scrap of cloth to a point, dipped it into some warm cream, and pushed it into the kitten's mouth. After an initial splutter or two, the kitten latched onto the cloth and began to suck.

"Why don't her mama like her, Miss Nellie?"

"I don't know, Glory. Maybe she has too many kittens to feed?"

"No, M'am. Dere only be three in de litter."

"Hmmmm. There's an old wives' tale about cats. Let me try something." Nellie reached behind her and pushed an iron pot lid to the stone floor. Glory screeched and jumped at the sudden clatter. The kitten never stopped sucking. "I think she's deaf," Nellie said. "White cats with mismatched eyes often are."

"But why don't her mama feel sorry fo' her, den?" Glory demanded.

"Maybe she thinks she's too weak to survive. But I'll tell you what. I think we can make her strong again. Will it be all right if I keep her for a little while?"

"Oh, yes, M'am. I was hopin' you would. She could be your cat, an' I could visit her all de time."

Nellie smiled at the child's earnestness. "Thank you for bringing me a cat, Glory. She makes a nice Christmas present. What shall we name her?

"She look like a little cotton ball."

"Then Cotton she will be! Now you best get back before your mama misses you. Come visit her tomorrow."

"Oh I will. G'night, Miss Nellie. G'night, Cotton."

After the joyous celebrations of the slaves, Christmas Day at Roundheads Headquarters moved from somber to dismal as the day progressed. The staff officers started the morning by traipsing out to the Presbyterian church, where they expected Reverend Browne to rejoice in his recovery and in the true meaning of the holiday. Instead, he treated them to a grim picture of the Holy Family, driven out of Bethlehem by the evil actions of Herod and into exile in the barren land of Egypt. With the help of Browne's clever rhetoric, Herod appeared as Jefferson Davis, ordering the slaying of young black children. The angel's voice became that of Lincoln, calling on all good Christian men to travel to a distant land to save their country. Egypt's shore took on the characteristics of the Atlantic coast, complete with sea grass to replace the bullrushes. Sand was sand, and the message was clear. This was an exile, one to be suffered willingly until the good Lord chose to send the Roundheads home. Instead of Christmas carols, Browne called the men to sing "Onward Christian Soldiers," a hymn rousing enough, but certainly not designed to put the regiment in a holiday mood. They left the church gloomily reminded of their own exile.

Back at the Leverett House, Bessie the cook had outdone herself to prepare a Christmas feast. First, she sent out oysters on the half shell, followed by a fish soup brimming with clams, shrimp, and chunks of snapper. Then the slave girls brought the main feast while the startled Roundheads watched in amazement. At one end of the side board, a fat turkey spilled forth his chestnut and cornbread stuffing. At the other end sat a roasted boar's head, apple in mouth, ready for carving should anyone be brave enough to tackle the chore. In between were bowls of sweet potatoes, green beans, field peas, rice, gravy, turnip greens, and tiny broiled quail. The finishing touch—blackberry and pecan pies, sugar cookies and gingerbread men, and a formidable fruitcake—awaited the diners on the back buffet server.

The staff took their places at what had become a banquet table, draped in fine linen to set off the decorated china service and the sparkling silver.

All were still dressed in their church-going finery, so they presented a handsome picture. Nellie lingered until last, making sure all was in order. Then she slipped into her accustomed place at the foot of the table, facing Colonel Leasure, who commanded the attention of the table.

"Reverend Browne, will you lead us in the. . . ."

"Mrs. Leath!" the chaplain's voice interrupted. "You are too presumptuous. The occasion of a holiday meal does not give you permission to take a position that does not belong to you. Please join the rest of the servants for your dinner."

Nellie caught her breath and fumbled with her napkin as she tried to push the chair back from the table. She knew tears were brimming beneath her lids, and instead of a blessing on this food, her only prayer was that she could escape the room without crying.

But Colonel Leasure was as quick to shout, "No, Nellie! Don't you dare move."

The others were frozen witnesses. Most of the officers were staring at their laps because they did not want to watch the coming clash. The slaves visibly shrank into themselves, as if they feared the boiling anger in the room would eventually find its way onto their own shoulders and backs. No one seemed to breathe.

Colonel Leasure stood, stretching his small stature as best he could, to take a position of command over the table. "Robert, my friend," he began, the coldness of his voice belying the word *friend*. "You are still unwell. I apologize for asking you to join us this day before you have gained complete control of your faculties. Obviously, you need to return to your room to rest."

"I need no such thing. And there's nothing wrong with my faculties." Now the chaplain stood, his tall skinny figure towering over the stocky little man who had confronted him. "That woman," he shouted, pointing his finger at Nellie, "is not your wife and not the mistress of this house. She is a common doxie, dragged in off the street, and she has made a complete fool of you. If you want to imperil your immortal soul through your sinful acts, I suppose there is nothing I can do to stop you. But I will not sit at this table and watch her flaunt herself as your mistress before men who are required to respect you in battle. This situation is intolerable, and I will not be a part of it." He threw his napkin to the seat of the chair and crashed out of the room, slamming the door behind him.

If there had been a contest to determine who was whiter—Nellie or the colonel—the judges would have had an impossible task. The silence lasted too long, and the players on this impromptu stage could not bring themselves to move. The slaves were rolling their eyes as they tried to glimpse each other's reactions. Nellie sat with head bowed, tears dripping unnoticed into her lap.

At last, Colonel Leasure spoke. "Do the rest of you feel the same way as Reverend Browne?" he asked.

"Father, how can you even ask such a question?" Geordy was the first to answer, and he thus released the others to join him in a chorus of indignation at the chaplain's remarks.

"Mrs. Leath has done nothing but good for this regiment."

"She's the heart of the regiment, if you ask me."

"Surely, the Reverend didn't mean to imply that you. . . ."

"No! No one thinks that."

"What kind of a sick mind comes up with that sort of idea?"

"Look at what she's done for us this Christmas Day, and he's gone and ruined it!"

"No, he hasn't," Geordy said. "We don't need to let his distorted ideas upset us. Let's show him what we think by enjoying this feast. Nellie, ask the servants to pass the potatoes."

Even Nellie was forced to smile as she watched the young men devour the Christmas feast Bessie had planned for them. It would take more than a few moments of unpleasantness to kill their appetites. She also wanted to smile at their affirmation of her part in the regiment. Still, there was a hot lump in her throat that let her swallow only a few morsels of the meal. And she could not bring herself to look at the colonel. The words of the attack kept echoing in her ears: "doxie," "off the street," "sinful," "flaunt herself."

Colonel Leasure ate his dinner in silence, waiting until all were finished before he spoke again. "A fine meal. You serve us well, Nellie, as matron of the regiment and as mistress in this house. I propose we postpone our desserts until we are joined by the rest of our guests. In little over half an hour, we will open the house to all Union officers who care to join us in our holiday celebrations. The women have prepared an interesting syllabub, along with a non-alcoholic punch and an assortment of Christmas cakes and other delicacies. The regimental band will be playing carols in the front yard, and there will be games in the park across the street. I expect each man of you to be present to help our guests feel welcome. And Nellie, you will assume your rightful place at the front door to welcome every one of them. The chaplain will be kept to his room, if I have to lock him in." With that pronouncement, the colonel stood and strode out of the dining room, his exit accompanied by more than one chuckle.

The crisis passed, at least temporarily. The next hours were filled with the demands of hospitality. The house quickly filled, and not only with the staff of the Roundhead Regiment. General Stevens showed up early, accompanied by his brigade officers. That was no surprise, of course. General Stevens was famous for his ability to scent out any affair at which alcohol might be playing a part. The other regiments, too, began to arrive—the Pennsylvanians from the Fiftieth, followed by the New York Highlanders, and the Michiganders. No other regimental commander had thought to throw a reception for his own men, so the Roundheads played host to the entire brigade.

It was not a terribly merry celebration, but it was loud. The syllabub, whose ingredients Colonel Leasure professed not to know, was a tremendous hit. Nellie knew, because she had helped whip it, that it contained a bottle of brandy and a bottle of port in addition to the usual ingredients. As the afternoon progressed, however, she noticed the level of the punch bowl never seemed to decrease, although many cups were being filled from it. Doubting this was evidence of one of Reverend Browne's miracles, she watched closely and had only to wait a few minutes to catch an officer surreptitiously emptying the contents of a pocket flask into the bowl. Some gentlemen, well-schooled in their manners, brought a Christmas gift of wine with them, and those bottles, too, were finding their way to the punch bowl. Nellie hurried out to find Bessie, to see if she could dilute the alcohol with a bit more whipped milk.

As usual, the cook was already prepared. "Don' you worry, Miss Nellie. I's pourin' in more milk ever' time dey adds more likker. At least it be gonna coat dere stomachs."

The party drew to a close at nightfall, and at last Nellie could retire to her own room. She needed more than anything to be alone, to have some time to sort out the emotional upheavals that had ripped through the center of her day. No sooner had she sat down than little Cotton scrambled up into her lap, where she used Nellie's arm as a support for a kitten bath. You're right, little one, Nellie thought. I need to lick my wounds, too. She held her tight and let the hot tears flow at last.

16

New Year, New Beginnings

Nellie awakened on the day after Christmas with a new sense of determination, fueled by righteous anger. *I am not going to stay in a place where my virtue and competence are forever being challenged,* she told herself. This was exactly the situation she had imagined when she refused to sign up as an official member of the regiment, back at Kalorama. She would inform Colonel Leasure she was leaving, pack her satchel with the few belongings she had brought with her, catch a ride with the first person to pass through Beaufort on their way to Hilton Head, and then book passage on the next steamer leaving for the North. It didn't matter to her where it might be going. She wanted to be gone.

That storm of indignation carried her resolutely out into the hall and then diminished to a whimper as she discovered the door to Colonel Leasure's office standing ajar and the office empty. *Well, he must be here somewhere,* she told herself, re-squaring her shoulders and stomping down to the dining room. It was also empty, although it showed signs of some early breakfast activity. Mugs of lukewarm coffee, scattered crumbs on the table, and chairs hastily pushed back suggested a stand-up snack.

"What in the world is going on?" she asked out loud, not really expecting an answer from the empty walls.

"If you be lookin fo' de kernel, dey all be long gone," Uncle Bob responded from the doorway.

Nellie whirled around, more startled than she cared to admit. "Gone? Where would they all have gone so early on Boxing Day?"

"I's sure I doesn't know what Boxing Day be, M'am, but we was woken up before daylight by dat dere Gen' Stevens a bangin' on de fron' door. He shouted dey was all to meet at General Wright's headquarters in a half hour. De kernel an' all de other staff went barrellin' outta here as soon as dey was dressed."

"Were they armed? I mean, were they in full uniform? Did they look like they were headed into a battle?"

"Nah, Miss Nellie, dey was jus' a ragged bunch, slappin' saddles on whatever nags dey could get to in de stables and gallopin' out o' here like de house was on fire."

Her determination to leave was now thoroughly deflated. "Is there anyone else here?"

"No, M'am. Jist you. Guess you be in change of all of us 'til somebody gits back."

"Wonderful. Then send Maybelle in here with some hot breakfast for me, and tell her to straighten up this mess."

Nellie lingered over her breakfast, enjoying the unusual peace and quiet. Life around here would be pretty good if it weren't for the men, she thought with a half smile.

Then, as if a stray thought could break a spell, Doctor Ludington entered the dining room. He looked a bit flushed and windblown, as if he had returned from a brisk ride. "Doctor Ludington! Uncle Bob told me everyone had gone. Have you been here all along? Do you know what's happening? Are we under attack?"

"No, Nellie, nothing as dramatic as all that. The staff was summoned to the Vernier House this morning because General Wright wanted to plan a campaign. The others are still there, plotting away. I came back because my only duty, and yours, will be to keep the hospital and home fires burning."

"I still don't understand."

"Patience, Nellie. You need to learn that. Let me get my breakfast organized, and then I'll tell you as much as I know. But not in here. We can't trust the slaves not to reveal what's going on. Meet me in my surgery after breakfast, and I'll fill you in."

Nellie subsided into a frustrated silence. The morning was not going at all the way she had planned. She pushed her plate away and stood. "I'll be in my room. Tap on the door, or send a slave, when you have time for me," she said.

That was distinctly ungracious of me, she thought as she retired to her room. But maybe it doesn't matter anymore. I'll be leaving here soon, and they can all think as they like.

The summons from Doctor Ludington came shortly. Nellie entered his surgery without speaking, waiting to hear what the regiment had in store for her now. She seldom came into the surgery. The doctor held his private consultations with patients there, and he usually had no need for the services of a nurse. Nellie and the doctor interacted only as they did hospital rounds together or consulted on matters of patient care or meals. Her eyes surveyed the tables of unfamiliar instruments and stacks of medical books. This was a side of the medical profession that Nellie did not know, but this was not the time to ask questions.

"All right, " Doctor Ludington began. "Here's what I know. The general has ordered a massive attack on Coosaw Ferry. Do you know where that is?"

"No idea." Nellie shrugged.

"Well, at the northernmost tip of this island, there is a rope ferry across the Coosaw River. The Confederates protect it with a fort and some embankments on the far side of the river. That's how their spies have been able to get on and off the island without our catching them. Our attack will be designed to capture the ferry and take control of the fort."

"Wait. What's a rope ferry?"

"It's just a sturdy rope strung from one side of the river to the other. The river current is strong at that location, which makes it difficult to pole or row a boat straight across. The ferryman grabs the rope and pulls the ferry across, hand over hand."

"So why not cut the rope? Surely it doesn't take a whole battalion to do that."

"Because we want the ferry for our own use, Nellie." The doctor smiled a bit indulgently at her evident weak understanding of military matters. "And we want the fort. It also guards the route from Beaufort to Pocotaligo."

"Where?"

"Pocotaligo. It's a whistle stop town on the main line of the Charleston and Savannah Railway. If we had access to Pocotaligo, we'd be able to disrupt rebel supply and troop movements between the two largest cities along the south Atlantic coast. It's a tiny spot with critical importance."

"And this is going to happen—today?"

"No, the attack is scheduled for the early morning hours of New Years' Day."

"What?" Nellie shook her head in exasperation. "That's a holiday for the men. What are they thinking?"

By now, the doctor was beginning to lose patience with Nellie. "They are thinking like soldiers, Nellie. That's something you seem totally incapable of doing!"

"But. . . ."

"But what?" He stood now, looming over her. "You want another ersatz holiday celebration like the one we all plodded through yesterday? You think New Year's would be better? We'd all drink on the stroke of midnight and cheer the promise of a bright new year? Then on New Year's Day we'd hold another Commander's Reception, where we'd all drag ourselves through the formalities and survive the experience only by spiking the punch until it was absolutely poisonous? And that would make these homesick soldiers happy, right?"

"Well. . . ."

"No. What's going to make them happy is a little honest-to-God fighting—a chance to take a shot at the enemy—a small skirmish where they can try out their equipment without too much danger of being blown to bits—a minor victory they can inflate to a major bragging right—something they can write home about—something that gives this expedition some meaning."

"Of course. I understand. I just thought. . . ."

"You just thought like a woman. And if Reverend Browne had heard you, he'd be pointing a finger at you and thundering, "That's why a war is no place for a lady!"

"That would be better than being called a doxie someone dragged in off the street," she replied.

"Nellie, you've got to get over that incident. It was an aberration. We don't think of you that way. But you need to be careful in what you say. It is not your job to question military decisions. It's not even your job to understand those decisions. You do have an important role in this regiment, and you need to keep it firmly in mind. We don't need an elegant hostess or an entertainment director. We need a firm hand on the household staff, one that makes sure we have the clothes, the food, the equipment we need—when we need it. You make this regiment function, Nellie. But don't try to play house with your position. You are the matron of the regiment, not the mistress of the plantation. There's a huge difference. If you are clear on what that difference is, you'll not leave yourself wide open to the kind of attack that occurred yesterday."

Nellie could think of no adequate response to that argument. She simply stood, bowed her head in agreement, and left the office. Once back in her own room, however, the fury overtook her again. "What happened was not my fault!" She threw her hands in the air and snarled at the little white kitten who was sleeping in the exact middle of her bed. "Get off of there," she demanded, completely forgetting the cat was deaf and had no idea she was shouting. Awakened by the movement in the room, the kitten opened her mismatched eyes widely and then blinked them slowly in the universal cat language that said, "I love you."

"Don't try to soften me up," Nellie said. "I'm not in the mood to share a cuddle session. I want to kill something." Her movements still jerky and harsh, Nellie headed across the room, only to bump into the small table by the settee. A fragile figurine landed on the floor with a satisfying crash, and Nellie glared at it for falling. "I don't care what wonderful things the General has planned," she told the kitten. "I'm out of place here. Doctor Ludington made that clear again, although he probably didn't intend to. I'm leaving as soon as I can pack my things and find transportation."

"Mew."

"You? What about you? You're just a cat. Glory will take care of you."

"M'am?" Another voice interrupted. "Did I hear something break?"

"Oh, Maudy. Uh, yes, that figurine fell from the table. Sweep it up, please, before the kitten cuts a paw and bleeds all over the room. And then find my travel valise for me."

"Yes'm. What dat be?"

"The valise? It's my hand satchel. I had my personal belongings in it when I arrived. Now I need to pack them up again. I'm leaving immediately."

Maudy was shaking her head. "It prob'ly be in de storage room in de lower floor. I'se not 'llowed in dere."

"Then find someone who is, Maudy." The slave girl scurried off, and Nellie resigned herself to something of a wait. To keep busy, she turned to the mundane chores of her day, checking the house slaves to be sure they had straightened the rooms and then heading out to the cookhouse to discuss the meals of the day with Bessie.

After the events of Slave Yule, Nellie expected a bit of warmth and comfort from her new-found friend, but the kitchen atmosphere was distinctly chilly. Nellie didn't need to see Maudy slipping out the back door to know that word of her intention to leave had spread ahead of her. Bessie stared at her, lips clamped shut in a harsh, disapproving line. She shook her head slowly, as she was wont to do over the misbehavior of a slave child. Then she pointed at the makeshift table in the corner. "Sit you'self down over dere. I has some sassy-fras tea abrewin' an' we needs to have a little talk."

"I came to talk about today's menus, Bessie," Nellie replied, matching the coldness in the cook's voice, "not for a social visit."

"Dis not a social visit! Wha's dis Maudy tell me about you packin' up and leavin'?"

"I'm quitting my job here, Bessie. Some of the officers have made it clear they don't approve of my presence, and I'm obliging them by leaving."

"Not 'some' officers, girl. Jist dat mean ol' preacherman, an' who care what he think."

"Well, I care. I'm tired of being accused of things I've never done, tired of trying to please a whole houseful of strong-willed men the way I had to do at home, tired of having all the responsibility and no respect."

"So, what's you gonna do? Run away, like some little black-assed slave girl?" Nellie recoiled in shock at the older woman's language, but Bessie's glare never wavered. "You so stoopid, you think you jis gonna get out on'na road an hitch a ride to de promised land?"

"I'm leaving as soon as I can arrange proper transportation, Bessie. I'm not 'running away'."

"Yes, you is, sho' 'nuf. I knows when a body be runnin' away from what she cain't face. But I didn't 'spect to see a white woman doin' it."

"What's color got to do with it? Stop throwing that in my face." Nellie was once again primed for a fight.

"Runnin' away be somethin' a black woman do when she cain't take no more 'buse. But she run away 'cause she don' have no other choice. And even when she be a' runnin' fo' all she be worth, she know deep in her heart she ain't got a chance to make her life different. She jis' runnin' from one bad choice to another. You be a white woman. You free. You gots choices. You kin choose the life you wants to live. But you doesn't reach dat life by runnin' away like some little black-assed slave girl." Bessie finished her argument with a defiant toss of her head that dared Nellie to contradict what she had said.

Of course, Nellie did exactly that. "I'm not running away."

"Yeah, you is. You skered, an' mad, an' hurt. If you ain't runnin' away, tell me where you thinks you be goin'."

"I'm going back to Hilton Head. From there I'll take passage on a northbound steamer to—well, to New York, or Boston, or wherever it's heading."

"Yeah? Den what?"

"Then I'll look for work."

"What kind o' work?"

"I don't know—whatever someone needs."

"See dere? You not runnin' to anythin', not even a town. And you don't know what you be gonna do when you gets dere. Dat's called runnin' away in my eye."

Suddenly, helplessly, Nellie dissolved into tears. Deep sobs racked her body. She was making wailing noises she hadn't known she could make.

Bessie sat down beside her, not touching but letting her comforting presence make itself felt. Eventually the storm subsided, and Nellie lifted her streaked face. Dashing the last tears away and scrubbing at her dripping nose, she spoke in a soft, shocked voice.

"I think I've been running away from things all my life. I've just never faced it. I ran away from home without knowing the man who offered to take care of me. I joined him in running from sheriffs when his gambling debts got out of hand. I fled from him when he started to take out his own frustrations on my battered face. I hid from him in a dirty tenement, and then ran away from it when the drugs and outlawry threatened to swamp me. I was still running away when I joined the Roundheads. I don't know how to do anything *except* run away."

"So stop. Quit runnin'."

"I don't think I can. The lives I've led have made me what I am, and no matter how hard I try to hide the past, someone like Reverend Browne manages to see through the disguise."

"Like I says before. You be a white woman. You's got choices. Start by not acting like a black-assed slave woman."

"But I can't. . . ."

"'Course you can. Choose to stay here and do de job we'uns all needs you to do." When Nellie stared back at her with doubt in her eyes, Bessie smiled and added, "At leas' fo' a little while. Stay an' find out if things don' git themselfs better. If dat don' work, if you cain't be a strong white woman, I be gonna teach you how to be a good runaway black woman. If you wants to be successful, you has to know de way to use dat fear to make you strong."

The next few days were too busy for Nellie to think about anything other than work. Most of the staff officers came home by late afternoon, but Colonel Leasure had ridden off with General Stevens to survey the terrain over which the regiments would have to pass. He returned on Saturday, and like the other officers, immediately threw himself into the logistics of the coming attack. Nellie's days were filled with shouted orders, demands for more ammunition, more food supplies, more individualized orders going out to the various Roundhead companies. She became adept at allocating the foodstuffs and medical supplies, as she filled the men's haversacks with everything they might need to survive this short battle. She even found time to smile at herself a bit as she remembered the days, not all that long ago, when she had not even known what a haversack was.

Deployment began on the night of December 30th. General Stevens took his main force of the Eighth Michigan, the Seventy-Ninth New York, and the Fiftieth Pennsylvania out first, marching them in a long loop, carrying them across the river on gunboats, and then ordering them to crawl though the tangled woods to take their positions behind the fort. Flatbeds moved the rest of the men into place. Two companies of Roundheads and two companies of New York Highlanders followed a similar loop on the other side of the island to take up their positions at Seabrook Plantation. The Navy steamed its gunboats toward the ferry, staying out of a direct line of sight from the fort.

Three companies of Roundheads spread out to guard the approaches to the city of Beaufort. The rest, along with Colonel Leasure, marched directly to the island terminus of the ferry, ready to attack the fort from the front, once the rear assault had been launched. All they had to do was wait until it was time to light up the sky with their own version of a New Year's celebration.

The Second Brigade began its move at 1:00 a.m. on New Year's Day. By dawn they had the Confederate posts in their gunsights. The troops swarmed into the fort and over the batteries that defended it, overwhelming the small force of defenders, who had no choice but to flee into the woods. The landing parties joined the main force at the fort, and all was secured by 11:00 a.m. The army took time to repair the damage that had been done to the ferry and leveled the fort and its outlying batteries. Then triumphant after their first engagement, they marched back to Beaufort on January 3rd.

As Nellie watched their return, she was relieved, of course, but also amused at the way the soldiers seemed to be rubbing their hands in glee. The brigade as a whole had suffered only one death and fourteen wounded, none of them among the Roundheads. It had been a glorious way to celebrate, and Doctor Ludington's predictions had been right. No holiday would ever mean more to these men than the one on which they got their first taste of enemy fire and the even sweeter taste of victory.

17

CHANGES IN THE WEATHER

The first two weeks of January defied the usual definition of winter. Temperatures in the 70s, deep blue skies, and flowers bursting forth from bushes all over the island suggested May rather than January to Pennsylvania natives. Spirits were still high over the battle at the Coosaw River ferry, and, for perhaps the first time since arriving in South Carolina, the soldiers moved about their duties with broad smiles on their faces.

One bright morning, Nellie recognized the young sergeant who arrived with a set of papers for the colonel. "You're Jim McCaskey, aren't you?" she asked. "I remember you from the night of the hurricane."

"Yes, M'am." Young McCaskey caught himself as he was about to snap into a salute. "I didn't expect you to remember me."

"You were kind at a moment when I much needed kindness. I wouldn't forget that. How have you been? Were you involved in the action at the ferry?"

"Oh, you bet I was, and it was wonderful."

Nellie smiled at his enthusiasm. "Well, tell me about it."

"Me and my company was stationed at that plantation—Seabrook, they call it. Our job was to capture the guns and soldiers in the battery after the Navy got through firing at 'em. We waited, all hid-like, and finally two boats came down the river from the direction of Beaufort and started hurling shells into the battery. By the time they was done, there warn't nothin' left of that there battery for us to capture.

"The boat captains come up to the pier at the plantation and loaded us all aboard. We sailed on down to the ferry, but we had to git in line behind the boats carrying Colonel Leasure and his four companies across the river. And by the time we got there, that fight was over, too, and we didn't even get off the boat. I had a first-class seat, though, for all of the show. Best New Year's Eve I ever spent."

"The best news for me was none of our soldiers were hurt," Nellie said.

"Yes, M'am, but we got bragging rights, too. The Roundheads was the first ones into the fort, and one of the Navy officers said we was the coolest bunch under fire he had ever seen." James beamed from ear to ear as he went on about his mission.

Another account of the battle appeared in the *Camp Kettle* on January 7th:

> *The enemy had become insolent and taunted us in many ways, besides erecting batteries and fortifications along the shore at various points, and it became necessary to give them a slight rebuke, and besides our fellows up here in front were "spilin' for a fite" and it was thought best to give them a "New Years frolic" and an opportunity of getting accustomed to stand fire at the same time. We had the frolic, and we stood fire, which is more than can be said by some other people we saw that day.*

Nellie absorbed all the reports with mixed emotions. One part of her wanted to rejoice with the soldiers; the other nagged at her about her future with the regiment. Several times after the soldiers returned, Nellie thought about talking to Colonel Leasure. He was rumored to be somewhat unwell, however, and was not spending as much time in his office as usual. When she asked Doctor Ludington about his well-being, the doctor invited her into his surgery. "He has a touch of dysentery, Nellie. Not serious, but he's had it since before the battle. I tried to tell him he shouldn't be up and about, but he couldn't let his men march into action without him. One of the surgeons stayed with him, making sure he rested whenever possible, and giving him opium and camphor pills to relieve his pain. He doesn't want anyone to know, however—finds it all a bit embarrassing, I suppose. Just give him some time to recover before you try to talk to him, if that's what you had in mind."

The next Saturday afternoon, once most of her duties had shut down for the weekend, Nellie took her kitten and a cup of tea out onto the piazza to enjoy the weather. She eyed the sky with a bit of concern. Little clouds were sailing in, forming a pattern her fisherman uncle would have called 'a mackerel sky'. It usually meant a change in the weather was coming, she knew. And because she also knew herself pretty well, she realized a rainy period might send her spirits plunging, too. Oh, come on, Nellie. It's January 11th. What did you expect? Good weather can't last forever. Nor good moods, either, for that matter, she scolded herself.

She was surprised when Uncle Bob interrupted her musings. "That Miz Mary Pollock be here to see you. Come up with her father while he be here on biz'ness. Should I sends her out here?"

"Oh, yes, by all means. And ask Maudy to bring another cup and some more tea." Nellie rose from her rocker and greeted her friend with open arms. "How nice to see you, Mary. I hope you are well."

"I'm well, thank you, but I've been somewhat concerned about you. At your Christmas Day festivities, you seemed to be deliberately avoiding me, so I never got the change to wish you a happy New Year. I've wanted to come back, but I had to wait until Father was coming. In the aftermath of the battle, he doesn't want me traveling about the island on my own."

"Does he think you'd be in danger? From what?"

"Oh, snipers and such. I don't know, but I try to please him when he gets one of his ideas."

"Well, I'm glad you're here now. I can really use some company. I've been talking to little Cotton, but since she's a kitten, and deaf to boot, it doesn't get me far."

"Oh, she's beautiful. May I hold her?"

Nellie handed her the kitten, but Cotton refused to settle in Mary's lap. She wiggled and twisted and ducked her head. As soon as she got the chance, she jumped down and scampered back to Nellie, clambering up her skirts to settle in her accustomed spot.

"She's really devoted to you, isn't she?"

"I'm all she knows," Nellie explained. "I still have to feed her with a bit of twisted rag dipped in cream. I suspect she thinks I'm her mother."

Mary drew a deep breath. "And we are avoiding the issue that brought me here. What was wrong on Christmas Day? Had I done something to offend you?"

"No, no, Mary. It had nothing to do with you. We had had a flair-up over Christmas dinner. The delightful Reverend Browne demanded I leave the table and accused the Colonel and me of having some sort of illicit relationship. It was all nasty and shocking, coming in that setting. But I suppose I should have expected nothing less of the good chaplain. It was his first full day out of his sickroom, and he did not approve of the family atmosphere he found downstairs."

"That miserable man!" Mary shook her head. "So that's why he moved out of here and over to the Fuller House to complete his recuperation? I heard about that, but there has been no explanation of what brought it on."

"I don't know whether he left in anger or whether Colonel Leasure suggested he leave. It was an intolerable situation, as you can imagine, and I was relieved to have him gone."

"For your sake, I'm glad. Hope the doctors keep him penned up over there for a good long time."

Nellie shrugged. "It won't be an issue much longer."

"What do you mean?"

"I'm getting ready to leave, Mary."

"Oh, no. Why? None of this is your fault. You can't let Reverend Browne drive you away. You have a job to do here."

"So Bessie tells me," Nellie said.

"Bessie?"

"Our cook. I was looking for my valise the day after Christmas, planning to take the first chance I found to get out of here. Bessie heard about it, since the slaves always know what's going on, and she scolded me. You should have heard her go on. Or maybe you shouldn't. Her language was a bit coarse for civilized company."

Nellie smiled despite herself, and Mary joined in her laughter. "But what did she say? Obviously you took it to heart. You're still here."

"She started by telling me the difference between black folks and white folks. She said black women run away because they don't have any other choice. But a white woman, in her view, has choices and should only run to something, not away from something."

Mary sat quietly for a moment. "Run to something, not away from something. It's good advice, isn't it?"

"Of course it is. She's a wise woman. And I've been thinking about it a lot. She's certainly right about my life. I've been running away from things for as long as I can remember. I've never known where I was going or what I wanted. I just fled—from an abusive father, a vicious husband, a dangerous living environment. And I've landed in some pretty unexpected and nasty spots—barrooms, gambling dens, jail cells, theater basements, dirty tenements, and now an army camp. I admit this is not what I planned to do with my life. But then, I never planned to do anything. I don't even know how to find somewhere to run to, which is why I'm still here. You can tell me not to run away and I'll agree, but I don't know how to do anything else."

Mary spoke softly. "I know, Nellie, I know. I felt the same way after Robert died. I simply couldn't see a way ahead."

"But you did take control of your life."

"Eventually. My father gave me some good advice, too. It's a little different than the wisdom Bessie offered you, but I think both ideas lead us in the same direction."

"And that was?"

"He said we can't live in the past because it's already gone. And we can't live for the future because we don't know whether we even have a future. All we can do is live in the present. It's all we have, and all we may ever have. We need to make each day important and valuable. All we can do is learn as much as we can from the present and enjoy it to the fullest, so that we can be ready for whatever the future may hold."

Nellie thought about it for a few moments. "So we can be ready if someday we find something to run to."

"Exactly. You can't force your future into some kind of mold. You can only be ready to accept it."

Once the holidays were over, the soldiers of General Stevens' Second Brigade settled into a period of watchful waiting but comfortable living. The Confederates, after their embarrassing defeat at the Battle of Coosaw Ferry, were more careful about sending spies or sharpshooters on forays into Union territory. With one victory, the Yankees had declared their military superiority, and the lesson was taken. There were a few scattered incidents, but they were mostly unpleasant rather than dangerous.

One wealthy widow who had been forced to flee her plantation on Port Royal Island began sending the Union officers packages of silver coffin nails. It was her version of a death threat, they guessed, but no one was ever sure exactly what motivated the gifts. Other soldiers reported finding human skulls lying about. These had been carefully labeled as "Yankee skull" and had handles attached so they could be used as drinking cups. Macabre, perhaps, but more the workings of a slightly deranged mind than a serious military challenge. The Roundheads could afford to relax and enjoy their South Carolina stay.

Daniel Leasure, too, had had time to recover from his recent illness, and he was newly determined to put the ongoing feud within his staff to rest. He began by calling Nellie into his office one late afternoon. She was, for the most part, the victim of Reverend Browne's attacks, but he knew he could not placate the chaplain without her active assistance.

"Mrs. Leath," he began, and the formal address warned Nellie this was to be no ordinary conversation. "When you came to me to sign on as our matron, you seemed forthright in telling your story. But as I look back upon that interview, I've come to realize you actually told me little. You named your home state, but not the town. You talked about your parents but without giving them names. The same was true of your description of your husband—colorful, sometimes brutally honest descriptions, but no real identifying facts. You bought a sewing machine from a sales man who gave you a new way to pay it off—again, no name of company or salesman.

You were hired by the nameless manager of a nameless theater. You lived in a dangerous tenement, but you made it clear there was no record of its residents. Surely you must see such omissions might someday raise questions about your true identity?"

Nellie's gaze did not waver. Only a close look at her hands would have revealed their slight tremor. "So, you want to check my story now. Do I understand you correctly?"

"I'm not through! I have to consider this lack of precise information in the light of another event—one in which you refused to sign formal enlistment papers with the regiment, even though it would have meant you would receive a small salary. What are you hiding, Mrs. Leath?"

Nellie bowed her head for a few long moments. When she lifted her eyes to the colonel's again, the lashes sparkled with unshed tears. "I suppose I'm hiding myself, Sir."

"I beg your pardon?"

"I'm hiding from my past. I don't want anyone to find me and drag me back into a life I've worked hard to escape. That was why I didn't want to sign the government's papers. As for the story I told you, it was all painfully true. I just didn't want anyone prying into my past. If that's wrong, if I've betrayed your trust somehow, I'm sorry."

"No, you haven't betrayed me in any way. You've done everything you promised, and much more. But you know Reverend Browne is determined to run you out of this regiment. He keeps demanding information from me, and he won't accept the fact I don't have it."

"He's investigating me?"

"Yes, he is. He has many friends in Pittsburgh, as do I, and I hear rumors he is circulating questions about you. He seems particularly concerned about your association with a theater, an institution he regards as only a bit less sinful than the pits of Hell themselves, apparently."

"How awful of him!"

"Nellie, Robert is not an evil man. He's too zealous sometimes, and he's terribly stubborn when he gets an idea in his head. But he's not evil. In fact, I believe if he knew you were in any sort of danger, he would be the first to step in."

"If you say so."

"You're going to have to trust me on this matter, Nellie. I suspect you could safely reveal to him exactly who you are and all the identifying bits you've left out of your original story. If he understood why you didn't want that information spread around, he would keep it to himself. He is, after all a man of the cloth."

"All right. What do you want me to tell you?"

"Well, start by giving me a few facts I should have checked while we were still in Pittsburgh. What was the name of the theater where you served as wardrobe mistress, and who was your employer? Can I send someone to talk to him?"

"It was the New Pittsburgh Theatre, and the manager was a Mr. William Henderson. He was in many ways a frustrated actor, who was better at staging a theater production than at performing in one. He had made his peace with his own failed ambitions but had little tolerance for the ambitions of others. He was impatient, snappish, and generally bored with women. He may not even remember me. You're welcome to try, however. Will that satisfy you?"

"It's not for me. Nellie. It's to help me be in a position to defend you. With your permission, I'm going to send this information to my wife. She is in Pittsburgh frequently on business. She can make a discreet inquiry about your job at the theater, and if she confirms your story, the chaplain will accept her word."

"And that will be the end of this?"

"Well, Robert's going to want to hear the rest of your story from your own lips. Will you do that, if I can arrange an audience with the three of us? Can you bring us some kind of proof of someone who knows you, something easily verifiable, to convince him you are not a 'devil's spawn'?"

"I'll try. But if I sense he's going to use the information against me, I'll be forced to flee—again."

Inwardly, Nellie was shaking her head at her own fickle emotions. Just days before, she had been ready to quit her job. Now here she was, trying her best to save it. Do I always want what I can't have? she wondered. If that's so, I'm doomed to be forever unhappy.

18

THE PAST REVISITED

A few weeks later, Nellie was seated across the room from the two men who held control over her life. "My name is Ellen Merrill Chase," she began, "although everyone has always called me Nellie. That part's not a lie." The small attempt at humor made Leasure's cheek twitch, although Browne seemed unmoved.

"I was born on March 1, 1838, in Windham, Maine. My parents are Jane Steele Merrill and Jacob E. Chase. I grew up on a prosperous 4,000 acre farm, although my father was also a carriage-maker by trade. My family was well-known in the town. We were members of the Episcopal Church, and my father often served on one city commission or another. I have four brothers. Edwin and Isaac are slightly older than I, while Jacob and Eastman are younger.

"Wait!" Reverend Browne interrupted. "You were born in 1838? You're only twenty-three? Daniel, how can that be? You hired a mere child."

Daniel Leasure was also somewhat surprised. "I didn't realize you were that young. Since you had been working with the Twelfth Pennsylvania when we first met, I assumed you were older. You always seemed self-possessed and mature."

Once again, Reverend Browne lifted a hand to stop the flow of the story. "So, Daniel, you admit you knew this young woman before she joined our regiment? I find that disturbing."

"I knew her only as a nurse attached to Colonel Campbell's regimental headquarters, Robert. But that's part of the reason I readily agreed to take her on as our matron. There's nothing 'disturbing' about that. Go on with your story, Nellie."

"At home I had been the top scholar at Miss Hutchin's Academy for Women, the finest school in Windham. When I graduated, I wanted more than anything to go on to the nearby Normal School and prepare to be a teacher. However, my father had different ideas. He refused to pay for any more education—said women didn't need it. Miss Hutchins offered me a job anyway, teaching the youngest children. That gave me something to do, but it paid next to nothing, and my brothers constantly made fun of their spinster schoolmarm of a sister.

"My father wanted me to marry our fifty-year-old neighbor, so the two farms might someday be joined. Old Man Jones, as I called him, was willing to take me without a dowry, which appealed to my father's miserly nature. I had to choose between living at home as the family spinster, or moving next door to marry an old man who made me cringe.

"Neither choice was as attractive as the charming musician who passed through town about then. He was a little short, stocky in a way that suggested muscular strength, with black curly hair that was usually in need of a cut. His Irish blue eyes could change from sparkle to icy coldness without warning. He was a superb musician, playing French horn, trumpet, and almost any other brass instrument. Of course, I later found out that while he was a charmer, he was also a drunkard, a gambler, a liar, a forger, and a thief. His name, if you want to look him up, is Otis Henry Leath, and he's from Bangor, Maine, where he was once apprenticed to a shoemaker.

"He flattered me, pursued me, was charming to my mother and polite to my father, and he promised me the moon and the stars. Once he had me thoroughly smitten, he dropped a bombshell, telling me he must leave town for a job in Bangor. 'Come with me,' he offered, and I could not resist. He promised to arrange our marriage with a minister he knew in an adjoining town. And so we eloped. The ceremony was not the kind of wedding I had always wanted. We met the so-called friend in a dirty hotel room. He pulled a ragged Bible out of the bedside table to bolster his authority, had us clasp hands, and declared us wed. As we traveled on toward Bangor, Otis told me of his big plan—we would save our money and buy a hotel. Then he would run the saloon while I did the cooking and cleaning."

"And you believed that cock-and-bull story?"

"I was nineteen, Reverend Browne. I'd never even had a beau. I had no idea what I was getting into. I kept dreaming of a small cottage with a white picket fence. When we reached Bangor, I was expecting to meet his family. Instead, I learned he had only a sister, and she refused to have anything to do with him. We took a room in a seedy hotel above the saloon where he was to work. He suggested I could help pay off the room by taking a job. He even found me a position as a seamstress for a prominent family, but I didn't last long. I had no experience at fancy needlework. Then he ordered me to start working in the tavern kitchen.

"One day Mrs. McMurphey, the tavern keeper's wife, found me weeping on the back porch. She was a motherly little woman, and she soon had me pouring my heart out. I thought I was a failure as a wife, that I knew nothing about how to keep my husband happy, that I had no friends to talk to. As she comforted me, her cat approached, and I reached down absently to pet it. When the cat skittered away, my tears came even harder. 'See, I don't even know how to befriend a cat,' I wailed.

"When I had cried myself out, Mrs. McMurphey showed me how to hold out a hand without moving, and soon that big old striped tiger cat was purring and weaving around my ankles. Seeing how happy that made me, she gave me one of the kittens from the stables for my own. I named him Pythagoras, and did my best to hide him from Otis. Pythagorus might have only been a kitten, but he was my best friend, and I adored him.

"Mrs. McMurphey taught me many lessons in the weeks we were there—about how to learn by watching those around me and about trying to give people what they need. I watched her handle her own husband when he was too far gone in his cups, and I saw how she made those around her feel more comfortable. I tried to become a good wife. I really tried. But I knew Otis was not a lovable man.

"He used his job as a saloon musician to study the customers and watch the local gamblers. He encouraged strangers to buy drinks for him, and he appeared to handle his drinking well, at least for a while. He was in his own element surrounded by card games, flowing liquor, and loose women. He kept me out of sight so I wouldn't cramp his style. Once he got paid, he used part of his wages to join the poker games. He played on the weaknesses of the other gamblers, and was not above cheating when he could get away with it. But he was also arrogant and took too many risks because of his overconfidence.

"Soon he was losing large sums of money and had to find other ways to pay his gambling debts. He was a dexterous pickpocket and a sneak thief. If that didn't work, he tried forging deeds to none-existent pieces of property. When things started going really badly for him, a mean streak appeared. He would comes home drunk and berate me for spending money on food. Eventually he started hitting me.

"When the sheriff got wind of Otis's illegal activities, we had to leave town in the middle of the night. We traveled from place to place, always heading west, where law enforcement was less organized. I held on to Pythagoras as my only friend and my emotional shield, although I kept the cat well out of Otis's way. We moved through New York and Pennsylvania, stopped for a while in Elyria, Ohio, and then moved on toward Pittsburgh. That last leg, however, was dramatically more frightening.

"One night, when we were fleeing the local sheriff in a stolen wagon, Pythagoras scratched Otis by accident. He grabbed him by the scruff of his neck, spun him around over his head, and hurled him against a tree-trunk. I knew then how dangerous he was. If he could be a cat-killer, he could also kill me."

"And how did you escape from this dangerous cat-killer?" Browne asked.

"Well, I began by convincing a local dry goods merchant to sell me a sewing machine I could pay for a bit at a time. When Otis came home drunk and passed out, I filched money from his pockets. When I had enough for a down payment, I purchased my sewing machine on time and posted an ad at the general store offering to do sewing for people. It was not a terribly bad plan, but lower Pittsburgh was not the best place to try it. People who lived in the Pointe didn't have much money to spare on a personal seamstress. Eventually Mr. Henderson of the local theater saw my placard and offered me a position as wardrobe mistress. I hesitated at first, knowing theaters had a bad reputation. But then Otis announced we were about to move again. He told me the country was soon going to be consumed by a great civil war, and he intended, not to fight in that war, but to make a profit from it. He wanted to try his luck in Cincinnati because of the high number of troop movements on that part of the Ohio River.

"I made up my mind. I was too afraid of him to tell him I was leaving him, but in my own mind I knew that was what I was doing. I told him about the new job, manipulating him to see it as money coming in. Money always appealed to him. Then I suggested I could stay in Pittsburgh and work through the end of the theater season, while he went on to Cincinnati and found a place for us there. I would join him, I promised, with a tidy little nest egg. He bought the whole story.

"Once he was gone, I could breathe again. I found a cheap room with kitchen privileges in the Guardhouse and began my new job. I didn't have much contact with the actors, except when they came downstairs with an occasional fitting problem, but I slowly befriended one of the minor actresses who seemed especially shy and lonely."

"Is she still there? Could she speak up on your behalf?" the colonel asked.

"No. I don't know where she is."

"Did you have any other friends in Pittsburgh, anyone else who would give you a good character recommendation?" Nellie only shook her head.

Reverend Browne spoke up. "Yours is a horrific story, Mrs. Leath, and I'm truly sorry you have had to face this sort of experience. But I don't see it goes far in justifying your own behaviors. And it certainly does not carry much of a recommendation for your position in this regiment."

"Reverend Browne, I want to speak to you privately. Nellie, would you excuse us for a few moments?"

"Of course." Nellie slipped quietly from the room, grateful for the respite. She wandered out onto the piazza and stood looking out over the Beaufort River. Even though it was January, the huge live oak trees that surrounded the Leverett House retained their leathery green leaves. The park that extended from the road down to the shoreline where the sea oats took over was also filled with unseasonably green vegetation. The late afternoon sun turned the river beyond the park into a bronzed mirror. The water lay absolutely still, unmarked by the passage of small boats or the intrusions of fishermen. Above, the sky was a deep azure blue, with not a cloud in sight. Nellie breathed in, as if she could somehow absorb the whole scene into her own being.

This world can be beautiful and peaceful, she thought. Why is it we humans have to keep stirring up trouble? I could stand here forever, content to enjoy this view and appreciate its wonders.

Then she caught her breath as she realized the direction of her thoughts. What am I thinking? Stay here forever? A few hours ago, I was intent on shaking the sands of Beaufort from my feet once and for all. I thought I wanted nothing more than a chance to escape. Now here I am, on the verge of getting myself fired on moral grounds, and I'm scared to death I will have to leave. I'm perverse! I apparently have no idea what I really want. I manage never to want what I have until someone threatens to take it away.

Irritated now with her own indecision, she began to pace back and forth on the veranda. I could go back in there and tell the colonel I'm leaving. Refuse to answer any more questions. Refuse to defend myself. Just quit, and be done with it. I'm sure Reverend Browne would be happy to help me pack. But then I'd be running away again. And if I give up on this chance to make a new life for myself, I might never have another. On the other hand, I suppose I'm not going to get a choice. The decision will be made for me. Maybe they're in there now, trying to decide how to tell me I'm through. Mary said we should live for today. All right. Let's see what happens next. If I'm going to lose the chance to smell the magnolias and camellias, I'd better enjoy the few moments I have left.

Inside Colonel Leasure's office, another sort of discussion was ongoing, as the colonel led the self-righteous chaplain to a position from which he could be persuaded to extend some Christian charity to the young woman pacing outside.

"Robert, you've asked me why I didn't know more about Nellie before I let her join the regiment. Did you assume I was somehow so smitten by her youthful appearance I lost all good sense?"

"No, Daniel, I didn't think that—at least not at first. But you have to admit she does not fit the image one usually has of a nurse provided from the Sanitary Commission."

"No, she doesn't. But I could see she was kind, and caring, and she has a good head on her shoulders. I did check, too. Before we left Pittsburgh, I contacted Colonel Campbell of the Twelfth Regiment. I also sent a letter to Isabel, asking her to look into the young woman's background. Isabel contacted Robert Moffatt's relatives there in Pittsburgh, and the Witherows spoke highly of Nellie. They knew nothing of her early background, but they knew she was an honest and reliable employee. More recently, Nellie gave me the name of the man who employed her as a wardrobe mistress in Pittsburgh."

"In the theater?" The chaplain was still skeptical.

"Oh, Robert, you are such a Puritan. Yes, she worked in a theater. It was the New Pittsburgh Theater, an establishment I myself have patronized in the past to see such great performers as Edwin Booth and Charlotte Cushman. Isabel was able to track down Mr. William Henderson, who has since moved up in the world to become manager of the New Opera House. He confirmed Nellie took care of the costumes for the acting company, but he also said she never set foot on the stage. Never even watched a performance. Just did her job and went off home, he reported. Isabel said he was entirely complimentary.

"Nellie is not an evil woman, Robert. She's young, and she sometimes makes mistakes in judgment, as the young are wont to do. But in a crisis, she is superb. I would trust her with my life. And I did trust her with your life, I might remind you. It was Nellie who managed your care while you were prostrate with malaria. If it had not been for her constant ministrations, we might not have you with us today."

The chaplain was at last taken aback, and he had the grace to show it. Still, he was not ready to accept Nellie with open arms. "I had my friends checking in Pittsburgh, too, Daniel. I'm not waging an unreasonable vendetta against the woman. But I am still concerned. My friends tell me before she joined the regiment, she was living in a deplorable slum that had grown up around the old Arsenal, at the spot where the Allegheny and the

Monongahela join to form the Ohio River. I've been told some of the tenants remember Nellie as a willful and forward young woman. What's worse, however, everyone who knew her also remembers she shared her room with an actress, even if she was not one herself. And said actress caused an upheaval by taking an overdose of opium and nearly dying right there in their room. If one is known by the company one keeps, your Nellie has made some pretty poor choices among her friends."

"I've heard part of that story, Robert, and there's more to it than you've learned. But let's ask Nellie."

Seated once again in what she had come to think of as her "grilling seat," Nellie launched into the story of her only real friend in Pittsburgh. She pulled out a small photograph showing a fragile-looking blonde girl with elfin features and a tight-lipped small smile. "That's Belle Morgan," she explained. "We exchanged pictures shortly before she left Pittsburgh. We promised to keep in touch, but I've never heard from her again.

"Like me, Belle came from a comfortable home situation, but her fortunes deteriorated when her parents died in an accident with a runaway carriage. Belle went to live with a maiden aunt in Cleveland, and there fell in love with a young lawyer. Her maiden aunt would not hear of a romance, claiming Belle was far too young. Secretly the lovers pledged their engagement, but the old aunt thwarted every attempt of the two of them to spend time together. Then the lawyer was offered a new job teaching in a law school some miles from Cleveland. When he moved away, the old aunt made life so miserable for Belle that she ran away. When she could not locate her lover, she went back to Pittsburgh and became a walking lady."

"In other words, a prostitute," Browne sneered.

"No, not at all. A *walking lady* in theater terms is a bit player. She walked on and off the stage, for instance during a street scene, to give the audience the impression there were other people around the main characters. But she was never required to say a word. That was a good thing, too, because Belle was so petrified on stage she couldn't have made a sound. She only took the job when she could find no other way to support herself. And she knew she had cut herself off from the rest of her family, who hated anything to do with the stage. People will do almost anything to save themselves when they are hungry enough, Reverend Browne.

"Belle's troubles did not end there. She made only a pittance when she worked, and, because not every play had a need of a walking lady, she often went penniless. Eventually she agreed to marry a stage-door Johnny who promised her the world. After only a few weeks of marriage, Johnny left her and went off to California to make his fortune, leaving her on the streets once more.

"That's when I offered to share my room with her. I didn't have much, but she had nothing. We did have some experiences in common, as I'm sure you can realize. One day Belle's husband sent word he had divorced her to marry a wealthy widow who held claim to a gold mine. Her marriage was officially over, just like that. The next week, it was my turn. That's when I received my own letter from Otis. The letter demanded I join him in Cincinnati, where he had bought an old house and was turning it into a brothel catering to military customers. I was to be his madame, supervising the prostitutes and running the house.

"What saved Belle and me both for the moment was being able to share our anger. We assured each other we would be better off without our respective men. We did pretty well, for a time. But at the end of the performance season, my work was cut, and it was obvious Belle would not be rehired. She fell into a great despondence. She was too fragile to do heavy work, too pretty to be trusted, too weak to stand up for herself. One horrible greasy man offered her a position as his mistress, but the prospect actually made her gag.

"One day I came home from work to find Belle unconscious, lying dressed all in white on her bed. I detected a heartbeat and shallow breaths and ran for help. I was finally able to summon a local doctor, who spotted the evidence Belle had taken an overdose of opium. He shrugged her off, suggesting I put her feet in some hot water to revive her.

"Another boarder in the house, a more practical Irishman, sprang to the rescue by forcing her to drink something that caused vomiting. When she recovered, Belle decided she might as well become what everyone thought she was. With the last bit of her savings she bought passage to New York

City, hoping to pass herself off as an actress, but willing to become a prostitute if that was what it took. And, as I said, I never heard from her again."

"It's a tragic story, no doubt," Reverend Browne commented. "And it soundly condemns our society, which has no means of protecting such a young girl. I sincerely regret what happened to Miss Morgan. But what has all this to do with you?"

"We saved her life, but for me, her near-death was a life-changing experience."

"What do you mean?" Colonel Leasure asked. This was a part of the story he had not heard.

"Well, for a moment, when I saw Belle all laid out on the bed, I envied her. I even wished I could lie down beside her and join her in death. That shocks you, I suppose."

"No, actually it doesn't. I've seen your willingness to die before, both on board the *Ocean Queen* and when you were ill in Hilton Head."

"My willingness to die? Yes, I suppose that's where it began. My life was hard back then, and, living where we did in Pittsburgh, the possibility of death was never far removed. We were surrounded by poverty, disease, and a culture of drug use. Our neighbors were rats, starving children, and villainous thugs. Even the air we breathed was poisonous with coal smoke and the stench of garbage. Belle's white dress was a symbol of a better life to come, and its promise was enticing."

"So, what stopped you?" Reverend Browne asked, wrinkling his nose in distaste at the whole episode.

"Her death would have been pointless." Nellie stopped, turning her eyes to look far away at something neither man could see. "I don't expect to live a long life, nor do I fear death. But I do fear leaving nothing behind to show I was here—or that my life mattered."

"A pretty sentiment. But you have glossed over the rest of your own story, haven't you? What have you done about your own marriage?"

"If it ever was a marriage," Nellie said. "I immediately wrote to Otis, reminding him I came from a genteel and highly-respected family. I was raised to have high standards and even higher morals. But ever since I met Otis, I had been sinking deeper and deeper into his own shady underworld, and I hated it. I told him plainly I no longer considered myself married to him, and he should never try to contact me again. I even kept a copy of the letter to protect myself. I'll show it to you, if you wish."

"And you haven't heard from him again?"

"Only once. He wrote to tell me he had joined the Second Ohio Cavalry as a musician in the regimental band. Whether he is still with them or not, I could not say. I really doubt he will last long as a soldier. You can check if you like, as long as you don't let him know where I am. He has a long memory when it comes to revenge."

"And you?" Colonel Leasure asked. "Have you been able to put your experiences behind you?"

"That's why I joined the Twelfth Regiment and then the Roundheads, Sir. I saw what had happened to Belle, and I feared for my own end. When she finally gave in to the temptation to use her . . . uh, her assets . . . to support herself, I realized I could easily do the same thing. But I did not want to continue down that dangerous path. Coming to work for the regiment was not only safe. It offered a way to make myself into the kind of person I wanted to become. I'm helping people, I'm supporting a cause I believe in strongly, and I'm taking an active role in determining my own fate. If I die as an army nurse, it will mean I gave my life in service to my country. I would like to leave that small mark on history, and I don't want to give up that possibility."

"No one will ever ask you to, Nellie. Not under my watch." The colonel stood, indicating the end of the discussion. Reverend Browne had nothing further to add.

19
FAMILY VISITS

Nellie had little time in February to contemplate what had transpired during her interview with Colonel Leasure and Reverend Browne. Slightly warmer weather seemed to bring out the travel lust in the northern troops stationed in and around Hilton Head. Beaufort was a prime destination, thanks at least in part to members of the Roundheads Regiment, who were not above bragging about the comfortable situation in which they found themselves. Their letters described luxurious plantation houses used as their quarters and a bounty of foodstuffs that far surpassed the usual Army fare. Even the *Camp Kettle* bragged about their surroundings:

> *We are sitting before our open windows, in one of the deserted palaces, surrounded by shrubbery green as the leaves of June and the air filled with the perfume of roses that bloom in beauty all around us. As we write, two vases filled with flowers of every color, gorgeous as the dreams of fairy land, stand before us, and their graceful and brilliant hues seduce our eyes. Ah! 'land of the sunny South,' where summer lingers in the lap of winter, and impatient spring, with hurrying steps resumes her reign of roses. Eden was scarce more fair.*

Such descriptions were irresistible to men who had been in Army camps too long. A steady stream of visitors turned up in Beaufort, knocking on doors at mealtimes in hopes of being invited to share in the bounty. One such group from the Forty-Eighth New York Regiment arrived at the

Leverett House one day at the beginning of the month. There were six of them, two nurses, two lieutenants, and two captains, one of whom happened to be the son of Chaplain Strickland, who served the Hilton Head troops. They brought with them a letter of introduction from the chaplain and arrived around 9:00 a.m., all of them starved because they had come up on the morning mail packet without having had breakfast.

Nellie invited them in and set the slave women to preparing breakfast for them. She also invited them to return for dinner. That impromptu meal caused her to be late making her usual rounds of the hospital next door, and set Reverend Browne off into another fit of temper. He wrote to his wife:

> *I don't enjoy what some people call social life. If that means to have your time invaded, the sacred quiet of all you have for a home turned into the din and bustle of a caravanserai, and your table surrounded and your provisions eaten by uninvited and unwelcome, because intensely selfish, intruders, who don the hallowed name of guests, then do I hate social life with a most hearty hatred."*

If that visit had upset Reverend Browne, however, he had a more interesting one to look forward to. Colonel Leasure announced on February 3rd that the Roundheads were expecting some important Northern visitors. General Stevens' wife, Margaret, had organized a party of family members who were on their way to cheer up their menfolk. In the traveling party were Isabel Leasure and her three younger children, two wives of company commanders in the Hundredth Pennsylvania, and Willie Browne, Robert's eleven-year-old son.

"Is that kind of travel safe?" Nellie asked.

"General Stevens assures us there will be no military actions in the Sea Islands until we are ready to attack Fort Pulaski and Savannah, Georgia, sometime in late April or May. Weather at sea is good this time of year, so there should be no hindrance to their passage. Nellie, we'll need to talk about arrangements this afternoon."

"Of course, Sir. I'll be eager to get started."

Reverend Browne cocked a doubtful eyebrow at her statement, but he made no comment.

Later that day, Nellie and the colonel met in his office. "What can I do to help?" she asked.

"You don't need to do anything special for my family. They'll be so overjoyed to be here they won't notice if the walls fall in."

"But sleeping arrangements?"

"That, yes. I'm asking Reverend Browne to move back in here permanently. Having him camped out at the hospital is an unnecessary demonstration of his disapproval, and it should have ended weeks ago. He and Willie will share the west bedroom upstairs. We'll move a couple of trundle beds into my room for my two youngest children. Jimmy is old enough that he and Geordy can move out onto the sleeping porch. We'll sling a couple more hammocks for them out there. Jimmy adores his older brother, and he'll be delighted with the arrangement. And that should about do it for here. The other travelers will be staying with their own family members."

"Should we plan a bit of a welcoming party for everyone? I'm sure the staff will want to meet Mrs. Leasure, and it might be easier for her to get that sort of thing over all at once. Then you and she can have some private time without other folks barging in."

"As usual, you have good ideas, Nellie. They are scheduled to arrive next Saturday, so perhaps we could have Open House on Sunday afternoon—even invite the Stevens' party and the other women who traveled with her. Or am I letting this get out of hand?"

"No, Sir. It's no trouble. We'll serve a genteel fruit punch rather than that lethal syllabub that brewed itself during the Christmas party."

Colonel Leasure laughed. "You seem in good spirits, Nellie. How are you, really? Here, sit down for a moment. Have you fully recovered from that grilling we gave you over your past?"

"You know? I think it may have been the best thing you could have done. I'd been hiding my past for a long time, and the more I tried to hide it, the more guilty it made me feel. Once I said all those things out loud,

I discovered the ground was not going to open up and swallow me after all. It's been a tremendous relief."

"I'm glad. Once he was confronted by the facts, even Robert quit being suspicious of you. We all have done things we're not proud of. The trick, I think, is to get over feeling ashamed of the past so we can move forward."

"And I'm trying to do exactly that. You may not have realized it, but right after the Christmas disaster, I was ready to pack my bag and run as far away from here as I could. Bessie the cook and Mary Pollack talked me out of headlong flight, but it took a while to completely suppress the urge to run away. Your belief in me gave me a reason to stay." Nellie stopped to take a deep breath and straighten her shoulders. "I have a job to do here. I'd better get to it."

"Wait. One more thing. I've been thinking about your situation. Have you considered starting to use your maiden name again?"

"Oh! No, I hadn't. What makes you suggest it?"

"Well, every time somebody calls you 'Mrs. Leath', you are reminded of the past you are trying to escape. Besides that, both Reverend Browne and I have, as you know, been trying to follow up on the details of the story you've told us. I can assure you, now, no record exists of a marriage between you and Otis Leath in the state of Maine. And because you moved frequently from state to state, it would be impossible to make a case for a common law marriage. You are free, Nellie. You always have been."

"But how can I do that? A woman can't just go around changing her name when it suits her, can she?"

"You did when you eloped with Otis, even though you had no proof of a marriage that would have made the change legal."

"But everyone knows me as Mrs. Leath."

"Stop 'but-ing,' Miss Chase. We'll announce your name change to the people with whom you come in contact every day. We'll tell them your marriage has ended, and you are re-taking your maiden name. That's all they need to know. Others will pick up on the change as they hear it. It won't take long, I promise."

After a long pause, Nellie took a deep breath and nodded. "Let's do it. Now."

The family reunions that took place in the middle of February were a great success, as was the little reception Nellie planned for them. Old friends stopped by for a few minutes to welcome the visitors, but no one stayed long. Everyone seemed to realize the importance of giving their commander some free time to enjoy his family. The only unfortunate incident involved General Stevens, who arrived already well on his way to falling-down drunk. He came barreling into the Leverett House shouting, "Where's my favorite regimental commander?" Behind him, his wife tugged ineffectually at his coat sleeve. "I want Colonel Leasure!"

The colonel hurried to the front hall, well aware of how difficult the general could be after a few drinks. "General Stevens!" he greeted him. "Is this the lovely Margaret, whose brilliant idea has brought us all together?" He reached out to take her proffered hand, but the general interrupted him by draping an arm around his shoulder.

"This is Daniel, Margaret. He's the finest, most capala . . . capable . . . of all my regimental officers. I love him like a brother. And his is the finest regiment under my command. You should have seen his men at the battle we had at Coo-Coo Landing—cool, brave, ready to give no quarter."

"Coo-Coo Landing? Oh, you mean Coosaw Ferry. Thank you, Sir, but we were just doing our duty."

"Nonsense, Daniel. You were extra . . . extra-ordinan . . . uh. . . ."

"You're trying to say extraordinary, dear," Mrs. Stevens whispered to him. She looked to Colonel Leasure in a silent apology, but he was busy trying to extricate himself from the general's bear hug.

"General, please come down to the dining room. Nellie is serving tea, and she also has some fine finger sandwiches."

"Tea? Finger san'iches? Can't a man get a decent drink around here?"

"Not right now, General. It's a bit early for most of us. Oh, careful. Watch your step. We can't have you tripping over a rug."

Despite his bluster, the general's knees were beginning to turn to rubber, and he fell heavily over one of the dining chairs as he attempted to enter the room. There was nothing to do but to summon his aides and have them help the general home. Mrs. Stevens, following the stumbling procession, stopped to clasp Mrs. Leasure's hand. "I'm sorry to have disrupted your party, my dear. Isaac can usually hold his liquor better than this. Unfortunately he drinks most heavily when he is happy, so our happiest celebrations often end this way."

"It was not a problem, Margaret. Please don't worry about it. I hope he'll be feeling better soon."

"Oh, he'll sleep this off and wake up with a horrendous head on his shoulders. Then I'll nurse him and pamper him, and he'll soon be happy as a clam and ready for another round." With a smile and a wave, Margaret hurried after her husband.

Nellie had been watching the scene from the hall. "Poor woman," she murmured.

"Don't you believe it." Mrs. Leasure laughed, taking Nellie's arm in her own. "Daniel has told me something of your experience with a hard-drinking man, and I can understand how you might misconstrue what you have just seen. I'm not making light of a drunken and abusive husband. But this is not one of those situations. The Stevenses have lived their entire married life this way. He drinks, she gets a chance to take care of him for a while, and they are both happy. Not every marriage founders on a husband's weakness. Sometimes it is only a husband's weakness that allows a woman to develop her own strengths."

For the rest of the visit, husbands and wives, parents and children, all reveled in their reunion, and their joy was so palpable that it spread to those around them. Daniel and Isabel were so obviously a couple that Nellie could only watch them in wonder. In ordinary conversation, they finished each other's sentences and sometimes chimed in with exactly the same word. They were never demonstrative in their affection, but it showed in their gestures— the way they sat facing each other, even when side by side—the silent messages that passed between their eyes without need for verbal communication.

If I had seen a marriage like theirs when I was growing up, I would have known what I had with Otis was a sham, Nellie told herself. She realized she had never really seen other couples as they worked out the intricacies of their marriages. Certainly she had not been aware of any real interaction between her own parents. She couldn't even remember hearing them talk about anything except the mundane details of daily life.

The Leasures spent long hours with the children from whom they had been separated. Daniel could often be found on the floor of his office with the little ones, helping them play with their toy soldiers or reading them a story. It was obvious Isabel had feared for the safety of Geordy, her first-born son. She could hardly keep her hands from him, wanting to brush the hair out of his eyes, admiring his new military posture, and marveling at how grown-up he looked and sounded.

"I promised you he would be all right, Isabel," Nellie heard the colonel telling his wife one day.

"I know, dear, and I believed you, as I always do. But it hurt to be separated from him. I knew you had enough experience to keep yourself safe for me, but I wasn't sure Geordy was ready to leave the nest. Obviously he was. You've done a wonderful job with him, Daniel."

The Browne reunion was a bit more restrained, but no less sincere. Willie was an energetic child, never able to sit still long. The chaplain's efforts to learn from him what was going on at home usually ended with Willie wriggling in his seat until his father gave up in exasperation and let him run on to his latest explorations. Willie had become quick friends with a couple of the slave children, and he spent long hours with them, learning how to gather oysters (and eat them raw!), how to extract the seeds from cotton, and how to pole a skiff across a sea of pluff mud. He ended each day scratched, muscle-sore, and exhausted. But his childish eyes glowed as he told his father of his adventures.

For his part, Robert soon learned to step back and watch his son blossom before his eyes. Willie had brought with him a set of family portraits, so his father could see the youngest children, including the newborn baby who had kept Mary Browne from making this trip. Nellie did not miss the sadness when Robert looked them over time and time again. Gently, she offered to put the photographs on display. When she noticed the chaplain was being left out of discussions about family members, she frequently pointed out the pictures or commented on what a handsome family the Brownes were.

At the first of their nightly dinners in the staff dining room, Nellie quietly ceded her seat at the end of the table to Mrs. Leasure. But when she attempted to leave the room as soon as the meal preparations were complete, the colonel intervened. "Nellie, you are as much a part of this military staff as any man here," he told her quietly. "If you want to let Isabel sit at the foot of the table, that's fine and gracious of you. But you will join us for meals. Sit on her right side, so you can still keep an eye on things. Please."

And so it was that Nellie also witnessed her first intellectual debate between husband and wife. Nellie had never seen a wife disagree with her husband in public, but the occasion arose almost immediately.

"Daniel? Do these Negroes wait on your table all the time? Or is this a show for my benefit?" Isabel waited until the soup course had been served and the slaves had withdrawn to the kitchen. But now there was no mistaking the disapproval in her voice.

"These are the house slaves the Leveretts left behind when they fled from our November invasion," Daniel explained, watching his wife warily. "They are doing the jobs they have always had."

"Then they are slaves. And you are using them as slaves." Her voice was cold. "I thought you were coming down here to free the slaves, not appropriate them."

"And what does that mean, Isabel? To free the slaves. It's a lovely-sounding phrase, but how would you go about that?"

"It means turning them loose. Letting them go where they will and become whatever they want to become."

"Just exactly how would they do that, pray tell? With what resources? Where would they go? What skills would they have to market?"

"Whatever—wherever—they wanted."

Daniel was shaking his head. "No. They would have to do whatever they knew. And what they know is what they do here. You have to understand, Isabel, this house and yard is all many of these people have ever known. There is a cemetery at the back of the yard. Some of their grandparents and great-grandparents are buried there. This is home. To drive them away would be more cruel than keeping them as slaves. Besides, we don't think of them as slaves. They are servants. We pay them a small amount, feed them, clothe them, put food on their tables. I would not stop them from leaving if they so chose, but they don't so choose."

"But they must be freed."

"The law of the land says they are still slaves, Isabel. President Lincoln is in no hurry for emancipation because he recognizes the problems I'm trying to show you. You can't send an army in and tell these people to go away and be free. They have to be taught what freedom means. And we're not at that point yet. It's going to take a massive government effort to put an end to slavery, and it will probably have to wait until we win the war first."

"I can't accept that."

"You will. Take some time this week to talk to Uncle Bob, who runs this house with the efficiency of an English butler. Talk to Maybelle, our table servant, who is related in some way to almost every Negro on this property. Talk to Bessie, the cook who dishes out wisdom with every dish. Ask them what they want. They'll tell you they want dignity, respect, protection from hostile attacks, security—the list could go on and on. But freedom will not be high on their list."

"I want to believe you, Daniel, but it goes against everything I've ever heard about the evils of slavery."

"Yes, and the people you've been listening to have never lived the reality. It's easy to paint a picture of Simon Legree with his whip, slaves in chains and manacles, babies being torn from their mothers' breasts, families being broken up and sold to different owners. Maybe that happens some places, but I've never seen it. What's real is exactly what you will see here. Have Nellie show you around the yard tomorrow. She is loved and welcomed in the slave quarters. She moves among them easily and does whatever she can to make their lives better. Spend some time with her, and then see how you feel."

"All right. I'll do as you say. Perhaps I have rushed to judgment, but I must make that determination on my own."

"I would expect no less from you, my dear. Now could we please summon the 'servants' and get on with our meal?"

The next day, Isabel asked Nellie to show her around the slave quarters. The two women moved down the east side of the yard, stopping to pat some horse muzzles and meet the stable hands.

"This is Samuel, Mrs. Leasure. He is married to Maybelle, who served us our dinner last night. Oh, and that bouncing little five-year-old doing somersaults on the grass is his delightful daughter, Glory."

"It's nice to meet you, Samuel. What exactly is your job here?" Mrs. Leasure inquired.

"I'se in charge of all des stables here. I sees to it dat de animals is fed right an' brushed down, an' has der pens cleaned out. De stable slaves all reports to me an' I gives dem der orders."

"And you are happy with your job?"

"Yes'm. I'se been workin' over here ever since I been a litl'un like Glory."

"Can you read and write, Samuel?"

"No'm. Never did see de need for book larnin'. De horses, dey don' needs me to reads to 'em."

"But what if you could leave here? Go out in the world and make a better life for yourself? Wouldn't you need to read and write, then?"

"What fo' I be wantin' to do dat? I be happy here. My fam'ly be here. No need for me to go traipsin' off."

"Oh." Mrs. Leasure was at a loss for words, and she would experience that same feeling over and over as they walked the length of the yard. They stopped to visit the blacksmith, busy shoeing a horse. They got some help from a slave woman in identifying the various herbs still growing in the garden. They saw the pig pen, the chicken coop, and peered into the laundry room, where billowing steam almost obscured the women working there. Each time Mrs. Leasure asked a version of her same questions, she received the same answers. Most of the slaves looked at her, puzzled as to why she was asking about such foolishness. Not a single slave seemed interested in the idea of freedom.

Isabel had specifically asked to visit the oldest woman in the compound. She had heard the story of the Gullah Christmas story that the children heard during Slave Yule, and she was anxious to meet the story-teller. They found Old Letitia sitting a spell in the kitchen with Bessie the cook.

"I've been told you did a beautiful job of telling the children the Christmas story," Isabel ventured.

"Yes'm. Dat be my job fo' as long as I lives."

"I'd be interested to know who taught you to read the Bible."

Letitia shook her head and chuckled until the blackened stubs of her teeth showed. "I'se never see'd dat dere Bible, and I sure as shootin' cain't read it."

"But you knew the whole story from the Book of Luke, my husband told me."

"I don' know no Luke. I jis' tells de story de way I's been hearin' it since I be a wee girl."

"From memory!"

"Yes'm. I knows most o' de Bible stories—all 'bout dat Noah an' his boat, Adam and dat big ole' snake, Moses in de sea oats, de walls dat came tumblin' down. I ain't never read em, mind. I jis' has 'em up here and in here." She pounded herself on her forehead and then on the chest. "I'se de place dey is stored. An' when I passes, den de oldest woman here be gonna take over and recite the same stories 'cause she's hear'd 'em from me for so long. 'Scuse me now. It be time for my nap."

Isabel turned to Nellie as the old woman made her teetering way out the side door. "I am overwhelmed. I've heard those stories, too. But I couldn't recite them. I've never memorized them."

"Perhaps because you have the privilege of relying on the written word," Nellie suggested. "These women must rely on their memories, so that's what they do."

"But if they could read. . . ."

"Then their oral culture would disappear. And I'm not sure that would be a change for the better."

"Yes, I'm beginning to see that. There's much I don't understand about the Negroes, isn't there?"

"Why you be askin' so many questions 'bout us, den?" Bessie asked.

"Because I want to understand. I thought you slaves wanted to be freed. Now I can't find anyone here who feels that way."

"I'se not sure I knows what freedom be," Bessie replied. "It sure not be freedom if somebody make us leave de place we calls home. It not be freedom if we all gets sent to school to larn readin' an' writin' if'n we doesn't want to go. De only freedom I knows is when peoples leave us be an' don't try to change us."

"But you could have a better life."

"I believes de bes' life is jist stayin' where you be planted and doin' you' best right here. Now why don't you white ladies git outta my kitchen an' let me git back to what I does best."

"So much for the stereotypical brow-beaten slave," Isabel observed as they made their way back to the main house. "Do you think she's ever heard of Voltaire's *Candide*?"

"Nellie laughed. "I doubt it, but she's pretty good evidence Voltaire's wisdom transcends generations—and classes—and races."

It was a subdued Isabel who joined the staff at the dinner table that evening. She smiled at the slaves as they served her, but made no comments. Finally Daniel could stand it no longer. "Did you and Nellie have an interesting day, my dear?"

"Yes. And I must apologize for judging you harshly last evening. But I still need to know. What are you going to do about these people? You can't become a slave owner like the southerners you drove out of here. What is being done to preserve their culture while you try to integrate them into our society?"

"You're talking about the tasks of generations, I'm afraid. But now that you are more open to hearing about them, I'll be happy to point out some changes that are coming. As a matter of fact, all of you need to know what's going to be happening," Daniel said as he looked around the table.

"Changes, Sir?" The staff officers looked apprehensive at the word.

"Yes, indeed. Or more precisely, new arrivals who are coming as the instruments of change."

"Now I am curious," Isabel said as she leaned forward toward her husband.

"Well, a mail ship has arrived in Hilton Head, and aboard was a gentleman by the name of Lieutenant Colonel William H. Reynolds. He's been sent by Lincoln's Secretary of the Treasury to take charge of the cotton plantations here on the islands. When we arrived last November, we disrupted the cotton harvest. And as you know, the white population of the low country fled in panic when our ships appeared in Port Royal Sound. Most of them left behind their slaves and all the possessions they could not carry.

"Some cotton fields had been picked but not taken to market; others were still waiting for the slave crews to move through. There's a valuable crop out there, and it's still viable. On several plantations, the black overseers have kept the slaves at work in the fields, and I hear reports they work better when they are bossed by their own rather than by the white masters. But the sad truth is, not even the overseers know the first thing about getting the crops to market. Even if they could transport it, most southern cotton was shipped overseas to England, and those markets have been disrupted by our blockade of the southern coastline.

"Colonel Reynolds and his staff will be moving onto these plantations in the next weeks to set up shop as cotton agents. Where necessary, they will organize work details to get the harvest picked. And they will take charge of shipping the cotton crop north to be used in our own United States cotton mills. Reynolds also has the authority to confiscate whatever he needs to get the job done. That means he well may appear here in Beaufort and take over some of the plantations we have been using for our own convenience. Once the crops are in, he is to organize the slaves to replant."

"Take over our plantations? That's unfair."

"He can't do that, can he?"

"That's not right."

Colonel Leasure shook his head. "That's how important that cotton crop is to the financial stability of the United States government, gentlemen. I don't think you want to challenge the methods by which it gets into our hands."

"But how is that a change for the better, Daniel? Isn't it just exchanging one slave driver for another?" Isabel was back on the attack.

"I hope not, my dear. Lincoln's intention, I believe, is to turn the slaves into independent farmers. But that will take training, as you yourself have pointed out. The cotton agents will act quickly to salvage the current crop. Then they can make plans, along with the Negro overseers, to turn the plantations into self-governing smaller farms. The slaves will be given their own land, and the agents will be there to guide them as they make the transition. It could be a good thing."

"I'll wait to hear how it works out," Isabel said doubtfully.

"You may be more excited about the other new arrivals."

"And they are. . .?"

"Teachers."

"Really?" Isabel and Nellie both leaned forward in anticipation. "Where from?"

"As I understand it, there are two groups. Some of them are members of the Boston Educational Commission for Freedmen, and others are missionaries sponsored by the American Missionary Society in New York. Nellie, you might remember a visit we had from a gentleman by the name of Edward L. Pierce back in January."

"Vaguely, Sir. Was he the one who kept talking about the need for humanitarian aid without ever defining what that might be?"

"That's the one, and we laughed about his innocence at the time. But he returned home and recruited some fifty-three men and women who are due here in early March. From what I've been able to learn, there are all sorts of folks in his group—clerks, doctors, divinity students, teachers, abolitionists. Their intention is to prepare the slaves for full independence and citizenship."

"Won't their goals interfere with those of the cotton agents?" Doctor Ludington asked.

"Perhaps. But both Reynolds and Pierce have been sent here by Secretary Chase and at Lincoln's order. If all goes well, Reynolds' people will concentrate on the immediate employment needs of the Negroes, and Pierce and his sincere little band will work on more long-range efforts to spread education among them."

"What if the two groups don't co-operate with your proposed division of labor, Daniel?"

"Then we do our best to stay out of the way."

20

JAMES ISLAND AND
SECESSIONVILLE

The change, when it came, created massive upheaval. Generals Hunter and Benham had agreed it was time to move on the city of Charleston. No one doubted the importance of such an assault. Charleston was the birthplace of the Confederacy, the site of the first shots fired, the symbol of everything the South believed in. No major military installation stood there, although a series of small forts protected the main channels leading into Charleston Harbor. And even though much of Charleston had been destroyed in an accidental fire the preceding December, the city was still a bastion of Southern sympathies and southern traditions. If it fell, the Union leaders believed, the rest of the South would collapse inward on itself.

General Benham planned a two-pronged attack. One division, led by General Wright, would cross the Edisto River, march across Johns Island, and take possession of the abandoned town of Legareville on the Stono River. That would put them within a short boat ride of James Island, where the most dangerous of the protecting forts were located. The other division, led by General Stevens, would travel by steamer, first to Hilton Head, where they would pick up additional regiments and then sail for the mouth of the Stono River itself. Naval gunboats would precede the army steamers up the Stono, blasting any challenges to their movements.

For Nellie, the plans were only a familiar variation of the other troop movements in which she had participated, except this one was larger, and better armed, and was being taken more seriously than any other she had witnessed. Colonel Leasure once again gave her her orders, which involved making alternate care arrangements for those patients who could not leave the hospital and sorting out which of the patients were really strong enough and mobile enough to accompany the main army. The supply lists for Doctor Ludington were also longer and more comprehensive. This time she did not question the need for so many ground cloths. She knew all too well why they would be needed.

Just as before, the colonel warned her she and her ambulatory patients would be the last to load aboard the steamers. They would not disembark during the brief stop at Hilton Head, and they would remain aboard ship until suitable quarters could be arranged on James Island.

"Yes, Sir. I understand. Please don't worry about me."

"Well, but I do worry, Nellie. I must ask you to keep out of the way but at the same time to make yourself instantly available if we go into battle and nurses are needed. That sounds contradictory and confusing, even to me."

"I'll be there if you need me, Sir." Nellie was touched by his concern. She was still smiling when his next instruction came.

"And get rid of that confounded cat!" Her heart plummeted, although she should have known she would not be able to take a cat into battle. The thought of losing that warm bundle of fluff reminded her of all the other pets she had lost—Pythagorus, Oliver, and now Cotton.

"I'll leave her with the slaves, Sir. They'll take care of her for me, and I can always come back for her." Nellie wished she could believe her own words.

The move to James Island was torturous. The rain came down in a steady deluge. Nellie and the troops aboard their steamer had shelter, but those marching across Johns Island bogged down. Men bearing heavy packs found the mud sucked the boots right off their feet.

Colonel Edwin Metcalf of the Rhode Island regiment later described the misery of their march:

A short victorious march to Charleston, and the whole sea coast is ours! How simple, easy, natural—how well contrived, how impossible

*to fail! Alas! No; success was certain—if it should not rain, and it did
rain. In June, rains will come in South Carolina and when they come,
men's plans always fail if they won't stand drowning . . . . How the
water did pour! How the road deepened and lengthened . . . Our little
army was floundered. I saw the hardiest in my command, proud, self-
reliant officers and men, sit down and cry like children while they cut
off their shoes, and then dragged themselves along to shelter."*

Nellie's own low point came when the Second Division made its way
onto James Island and set up camp on whatever bits of solid ground they
could find. Try as she might, she could not fully disguise her distaste at being housed in a tent once again. The canvas had been stored for a long time
in damp conditions, and the musty smell permeated everything in the tent.
Out came the tin plates and cups, a come-down from the English porcelain
on which the Roundhead staff had been taking their meals. No slaves stood
ready to do her bidding. Once again she had to fetch whatever she needed
for herself. There was not even a beautiful landscape to soothe her sinking
spirits.

James Island was a swamp, and a particularly nasty one at that. More
than half of the "land" was accessible only at low tide, and then only when
the sun dried out the pluff mud. A few high ridges offered crude roadways,
and some plantation owners had taken advantage of the sogginess of the
soil to create vast rice fields. Cotton crops grew only on the highest ground.
Rough wooden causeways stretched here and there across the watery channels, testimony to the dangers of trying to march an army across the island.
And then there were the bugs. Fleas and mosquitoes swarmed, and it was
impossible to keep them out of the tents.

Nellie tried not to complain, but one night in the mess tent she confronted the colonel. "Why in the world is the army interested in holding
this miserable swamp? There's no place big enough to hold a battle, as far as
I can see, and even if we won a battle, what would we do with the place?"

"It's a fair question, Nellie. Obviously our target is the city of Charleston. Look, I'll draw you a map," he said, picking up a stick and drawing
some lines in the dirt floor. "Charleston sits on a peninsula at the far end

of Charleston Harbor here. Fort Sumter, the place that started this whole mess, is on an island in the middle of the harbor. Now, precisely because of the land conditions you have so vividly described, it's going to take a naval attack to bring the city to its knees. But a naval attack, as we have already discovered, faces almost insurmountable dangers from two other forts that guard the entrance to the harbor: Fort Moultrie on the east side of the harbor (and we can't get there!) and Fort Johnson, here on James Island. If we can take Fort Johnson from the rear, the Navy will be able to sail right into the harbor through the main shipping channel. The only thing stopping us, besides the pluff mud, of course, is a small Confederate line between us and the rest of the island. If we can breach that line, we go right on to Fort Johnson and clear the way for the Navy.

"Well, I haven't seen any Confederates around here, unless they've taken to enlisting mosquitoes."

"They are out there, I promise you. That's why I've given orders you and the other women will not leave this camp."

"But. . . ."

"I'm not in the mood for arguments, Nellie. There are little picket outposts all over this island. We're sending well-armed squads of men to flush them out, but they know the footpaths better than we do. We're getting organized for an attack, but those preparations take time. This is not a little two-day exercise like Coosaw Ferry. We're here to get a job done, and we'll be staying until it's completed."

"Of course, Sir. I didn't mean to sound critical."

If Nellie had doubted the colonel's words, she soon saw evidence of the Confederate presence for herself. One afternoon, a scouting squad of Roundheads came back to camp fairly dancing with glee and dragging two cannons behind them. They had stumbled across a band of rebel soldiers who were trying to establish a firing position on a ridge within sight of the Union camp. When the Confederates spotted blue uniforms, they abandoned the attempt. One cannon slipped off the causeway and become bogged down in the mud. After several futile attempts to free it, they fled, leaving all three of the 8-inch Howitzers behind.

The Union soldiers seized the cannons and brought them back to camp. Along the way, they were spotted by a crew of soldiers from the Confederate Eutaw Battalion, but the rebels assumed these were retreating Yankees, dragging their own cannons behind them. A few shots sailed over their heads, but the "retreating" Yankees came home without a scratch. It was a great morale boost for the entire camp.

Another incident served to balance those high spirits with a dose of grim reality. Captain James Cline led a squadron out to explore the grounds of the abandoned Legare Plantation in hopes of moving part of the camp to a more forward position. Other Union soldiers from the Twenty-Eighth Massachusetts and the Seventy-Ninth New York moved toward the surrounding woods, where they ran into more soldiers from the Eutaw Battalion. As the rebels came pouring out of the woods, Captain Cline and twenty-two members of the Roundhead regiment found themselves cut off and surrounded. The Confederates forced them to lay down their swords, and then marched them off in the direction of earthworks being erected near a small settlement known as Secessionville. Within a couple of days, official word came: the men were being held as prisoners of war and had been transported to Charleston.

Skirmishes near Grimball's Plantation brought more casualties. In a gunfight between the Eutaw Battalion and the Forty-Sixth New York, two men died and five were wounded. Two days later, Union regiments faced a Georgia regiment in a more serious conflict. This time there were three Unions soldiers dead and nineteen wounded. Nellie was too busy in the hospital tent to reflect on what was happening, but it was clear the casualty list was mounting: twenty-two prisoners, five dead, and twenty-four wounded soldiers before the battle lines had even been drawn.

The ordinary soldiers felt they had come a long way to do absolutely nothing once again. As they waited, and grumbled, the war still seemed far removed. For Nellie, on the other hand, the first realities of treating battle injuries were shock enough. These are bullet wounds, she kept telling herself. What if they had been hit with cannon balls instead of bullets? She realized the coming days would put her own courage to a test, and she tried to steel herself against the revulsion she felt at torn flesh and suppurating wounds. Doctor Ludington watched her quietly, knowing this was a struggle she had to face on her own. No platitudes would serve her as well as a few more harsh realities.

The commanders were busy with plans for the coming attack, although they were having trouble coming to an agreement. General Hunter was nearing retirement and wanted to do nothing that might ruin his career at this late stage. His second in command, General Benham, was younger and brash to the point of insubordination. His philosophy was to take the riskiest route, hoping for a victory that would surprise and delight the Army high command. As for the two brigade commanders, they, too were ill-matched. Gen Wright was cautious to a fault. He would not agree to a plan that put those same men in danger of their lives. General Stevens was probably the most competent officer of all, but he deeply resented having to answer to a commander he felt was unfit for duty. He wrote to his wife to take out his frustrations, calling Benham "an ass and an imbecile—vascillatory, and utterly unfit to command—a dreadful man of no earthly use except as a nuisance and obstruction."

Such obvious differences meant days passed without a resolution. On June 15th, General Hunter made a quick trip back to Hilton Head to placate his wife by taking her to dinner with Admiral DuPont. As soon as he was gone, Benham made his move, issuing orders for an attack on the earthwork at Secessionville.

Benham's fellow officers did not question the importance of that earthwork. It blocked the only dry access to the causeway that led straight to Fort Johnson. If they could take possession of that position, they could not only open the way to Charleston Harbor but also protect their troops from any attack from the rear. But what made the site appealing was precisely what made it a difficult target. Just outside of Secessionville, the dry land narrowed to a width of about thirty yards. On either side, swamps and hedge rows would effectively prevent the soldiers from spreading out in front of the fortification. Instead, the men would be marching down a funnel that pointed them straight into the guns surmounting the earthwork. If they were fired upon, there would be no place to run. That meant this must be a surprise attack, carried out silently, under the cover of darkness, if it had any hope of succeeding.

Nellie and the other nurses watched the men form their lines. The plan was to get underway at midnight, but one delay piled upon another. It was almost 4:00 a.m. before the men left camp. The sun was brightening the horizon, and although it was a cloudy morning, even the women knew visibility was improving. Instead of fading into the night shadows, the ranks of armed men were silhouetted against the sky. Benham gave one more order that shocked everyone. "Unload your rifles and attach bayonets," he ordered. "We will not fire at the enemy. We are going to sneak up on him and kill him in his sleep."

Nellie looked at the other women with worried eyes. "But what if they see us coming and shoot first?" No one had an answer.

The first reports filtering back to the camp were contradictory, some telling of a great victory and others, a great defeat. What Nellie saw—and what frightened her—was that by 9:00 a.m. the men returning to camp came not in their usual brisk marching formation but in clumps of running men and limping stragglers. There was fear in their eyes, and their breathe came in ragged gasps. Seeing Lieutenant Morton of Company C, she hurried to waylay him. "Please, Philo, tell me what has happened."

He simply shook his head, his eyes brimming with tears as he pushed past her and headed for his tent. "You don't want to know," he said as he passed her.

Oh, God! Nellie whispered to herself. Then, seeing George Fisher making his way to the hospital tent, she hurried to see if he needed help. "Private Fisher, are you looking for something?"

"The colonel wants his surgical instruments."

"But we're all set up here. Why would he move them?" Nellie realized she was interfering, but could not seem to stop herself.

"They're setting up a field hospital down at the Rivers Plantation. Not enough room for the wounded in here," he mumbled, as he gathered up what instruments he could.

"Then I'm going out there with you. What can I carry?"

"No, Miss Nellie," he answered. "The colonel ain't gonna want you to see what's going on out there. You should stay here to care for those with only minor wounds."

"Nonsense! Any woman here can wield a sticking plaster for a scratch. I'm the matron of the regiment, and I will go with you. The colonel will need me, and I promised to be there."

"Suit yourself, then. I don't have time to argue. Just don't slow me down." George Fisher set off back down the road with a determined stride, and Nellie fairly ran to keep up with him. I'll not get in anyone's way, she promised herself. But if men need surgeons, they also need nurses.

Before they reached the Rivers House, Nellie could see a line of stretcher-bearers moving toward it from the direction of the battle. By the time they reached the front portico, she could hear the screams and moans of wounded soldiers. There was an odor in the air, too, a stomach-churning mixture of gunpowder, chloroform, blood, and excrement. Swallowing hard, she pushed her way through the ever-growing crowds, looking for only one man, the colonel who needed her.

She found him in the front parlor working over a makeshift table that had been set up by an open window. The colonel had stripped out of his battle uniform down to an undershirt with sleeves rolled back. The patient on the table was unconscious. At his head stood a soldier who apparently had been dragooned into service. He held an chloroform-soaked cloth over the patient's mouth and nose, but his own eyes were tightly squeezed shut, and he appeared to be swaying on his feet.

Nellie moved to him, gently taking the cloth from him and nodding in the direction of the door. He fled in gratitude. Colonel Leasure had not looked up, so Nellie spoke quietly. "I'm here, Sir. Just tell me what you need me to do."

"Thank you," he said. "Just keep that cloth lightly over his nostrils. If he starts to twitch, you may need to add another drop or two."

Nellie forced herself to look at what was happening on the table. The colonel, now reverting to his former life as a doctor, was using a nasty-looking saw to cut through the man's thighbone. Below the knee, only tatters of flesh and bone remained of what had been a strong young leg. She now noticed the patient had a strip of leather—possibly someone's belt—clenched between his teeth. And on either side, young, white-faced soldiers stood holding his arms in case he should begin to regain consciousness. Nellie felt her gorge rising, but she swallowed hard, determined not to let the horror of what she was witnessing overwhelm her.

The colonel finished. He lifted the remains of the leg and threw it out the window before turning to the job of suturing the veins and sewing a flap of skin over the remaining stump. Nellie could not completely suppress a cry at the idea of disposing of body parts so casually. The colonel raised an eyebrow in her direction. "Don't look out the window. The pile of limbs must be accumulating on the ground by now."

"That many, Sir?"

"More than I want to contemplate, Nellie. It has been a horrendous disaster, the kind of slaughter you never imagine could occur. They mowed us down as if we were in a shooting gallery. But there's not time to talk about that now. Every minute we delay, a wounded man loses more blood."

They worked, side by side, without further extraneous comment. Orderlies shifted this patient to a rough pallet on the floor, while another pair delivered the next one and dumped him on the table. There was not time to assess the case fully. Was he breathing? Did he have a relatively strong heartbeat? If so, it was time to remove mangled limbs and try to staunch the bleeding from body wounds. If the answers to the first two questions were negative, the colonel shook his head and signaled for the next case.

For Nellie, some of the worst cases were those whose stomachs had been blown open. Often the soldier was still conscious, clutching his own intestines as they spilled from his abdomen. And the look in his eyes spoke clearly of his terror. For these men, as for the amputees, the whiffs of chloroform came as a welcome respite. One was bleeding profusely from the head, and the streaming blood had obscured his features until Nellie wiped it away. Then she recognized Private Hugh Wilson from Company C, and another "Oh no!" escaped her lips.

The colonel took a moment to teach Nellie a lesson. "Look closely," he instructed. "Head wounds bleed like the devil, even when they are shallow. Don't let them scare you. However, in this case we do have a serious problem. It looks like a bullet fragment hit his eye, although I don't think it penetrated the socket. We'll have to enucleate it."

"Enucleate? I don't even know what that means," Nellie confessed.

"It means taking the eyeball out."

"But he'll be blind!"

"Better that than letting the eye fester and having the infection spread to his brain. Then he'd be dead," Leasure said. "Go out to the kitchen and see if you can find me a spoon or a small scoop of some sort—eyeball-sized."

This time Nellie could not control her heaving stomach. She ran from the room and headed for the door before she vomited on her own shoes. But when the spasms were over, she did as she was told. She grabbed a spoon and a small gravy ladle and went back to her duties. At least now I'll be working on an empty stomach, she told herself ruefully.

The parade of patients continued without respite. Nellie later remembered Reverend Browne had been there, moving from pallet to pallet as he offered prayers and words of comfort. When a patient died, it was Browne who covered the man's face with sheeting and said a few sad words over his body before it was carried off. She also remembered a poignant moment when General Stevens entered the makeshift hospital.

"I was told Colonel Leasure was here. He's not injured, is he?" he demanded of the first upright soldier he saw.

"He's over there, Sir," came the answer. "He was a doctor before all this happened. I think he's one again."

Stevens waited a few moments until Leasure finished what he was doing. Then he strode over and clasped his hand. Tears poured down his cheeks as he said, "God bless you, you brave soldier and good man."

Leasure nodded and pressed his hand in acknowledgement. Then he returned to what was his only job at the moment—trying to save the next life that passed through his hands.

Nellie worked without looking up. A part of her that was exhausted by their labors hoped each patient would be the last. At the same time, she realized if the patients quit arriving, it would mean the rest were dead.

At last, the steady stream did come to an end. Leasure looked at her for the first time in hours. "You look like hell, Nellie," he commented.

"So do you, Sir."

"I'm not ready to close the operating theater," he said. "There might still be someone out there who will need us. Let's go out on the portico for a few minutes. We could both stand to get the smell of chloroform out of our noses."

It was almost 9:00 p.m., and the sky was darkening rapidly, lit only here and there by lingering streaks of an orange sunset. Without seeming to consult one another, they sat side by side on the steps. Fresh air was exactly what they both needed.

At last Nellie spoke softly. "I've been terrified all day I would recognize someone I knew. Not that I would wish these horrors on anyone, but there are a few soldiers, particularly from Company C, who remind me of my younger brothers. I've been listening so long to their problems and nursing their minor illnesses that I feel a real kinship with some of them. Hugh Wilson is one of them, but he's going to be all right, isn't he? His eye will heal?"

"Company C, you say?" The colonel winced and then reached over to take her hand. "They lost four men, I'm afraid, and I know of at least seven others who were wounded. They were right in the front line when the rebels opened fire upon us. I'm sorry, Nellie."

"Who? Please tell me."

"Well, Hugh and Johnny Moore were the only ones who were wounded seriously. You haven't seen the others because their injuries were superficial and they went back to camp for treatment."

"Who? Who's dead?" she demanded.

"John Watson and Billy Anderson both died on the field." Two others were mortally wounded in the battle. The stretcher-bearers went to get them but couldn't get back to that part of the battlefield. Jim McCaskey and Jacob Leary almost certainly died of their wounds out there. They were hit by cannonballs and would have bled out in a matter of minutes."

"No, no! Not Jim and Jacob! Jacob was one of the young men I taught to play poker. And Jim McCaskey. He was such a fine young man, innocent and open. He once told me I reminded him of his older sister. He missed her terribly." Nellie was now crying uncontrollably.

The colonel put a comforting arm around her shoulders and pulled her close. His eyes continued to stare at the horizon, and he began to speak of the battle for the first time.

"I should have taken that fort. It would have been mine if Benham had not ordered a retreat. My men were fresh. They would not give ground till I gave the word, and they rallied like heroes under a most terrible fire. They marched into hell and survived. Then that victory was stripped from them, making all the sacrifices of their fellows meaningless. How can I face them?"

Now Leasure was crying, too, and the grizzled colonel and the young nurse gave full release to the emotions they had been holding back for so long. There was comfort for both of them, and they clung to each other desperately. The day had come to an end, but neither would ever be the same.

From the doorway, Reverend Browne watched them silently. He had seen his worst suspicions confirmed, but not even he could have the temerity to intrude on their shared grief. Accusations could wait.

21

EMOTIONS IN TURMOIL

Nothing was accomplished by the battle at Secessionville. Neither side lost or gained any territory. The Union Army was no nearer its objectives, nor was Charleston any safer from the threat of attack. When the dust of battle cleared, all that remained were abandoned cotton fields littered with spent ammunition, newly dug graves, and individual lives that were forever altered.

The effects of the Battle of Secessionville, however, remained with the Roundheads for a long time. Colonel Daniel Leasure reported to his wife, "The whole nature of the men seems changed, and they have the look and bearing of veterans. The regiment now shows its blood and its intellectual superiority in all critical and dangerous positions." But not all was well in the Roundhead camp.

A flurry of departures gave silent testimony to the discouragement many men felt. Adjutant William Powers resigned on July 3rd, and Lieutenant Colonel James Armstrong followed him, pleading feeble health on July 12th. Two privates deserted, taking the easiest way out by simply walking away. Three young lieutenants also resigned during the next weeks, one of whom was Lieutenant Philo Morton, who had had the difficult task of writing condolence letters to the parents of those who had died in Company C. He did his duty, and then resigned, so he would never have to do that again.

The regimental band might have continued to be an integral part of the Roundhead experience, but the expense of maintaining individual musicians' units in each regiment was too high. On July 17, 1862, Congress issued Public Law 165, which abolished the regimental bands and gave the musicians thirty days to enlist as regular soldiers or accept a discharge. John Nicklin came to Colonel Leasure to discuss their prospects.

"I will not leave this regiment," he said, "but most of the band members do not agree with me. They signed on as musicians and did not do much training as foot soldiers. To ask them to pick up a rifle instead of a horn is too much. Especially after they saw what happened in Secessionville."

"Anyone in particular who might be swayed by a word from me?"

"I doubt it, Sir. Captain Cubbison was not even with us on James Island, but he heard the stories that traveled back to Beaufort. He no longer believes the war is going to be over soon. Many of the men like him signed on with clear expectations they would be home within a year. Now it seems like we are stuck forever."

In the end Nicklin and William Gordon, the two primary musicians, transferred to Company K, but the other nine members accepted their discharges. The loss of the band, of course, also meant the end of the regimental newspaper, for the musicians were the writers and printers of the *Camp Kettle*. The regiment might have been behaving more like professional soldiers after their first battlefield experience, but much of the music and humor had gone out of their lives.

Nellie fought every day to keep from sinking into a black pit of depression. She had come into the war hoping to do something worthwhile. She had been willing to lay down her own life for her country. But now the deaths, the devastating wounds, the discouragement of the soldiers all seemed to suggest her best efforts were wasted. Oh, she kept up with her duties, but the bounce had gone out of her step. The sparkle in her eyes and the smile on her face were missing. The soldiers who knew her best watched her with increasing concern.

The Union forces stayed on James Island until the beginning of July. The men kept busy fortifying the camp and erecting batteries against the earthworks they had failed to capture. They were never to get a chance to use them. When General Hunter ordered the troops to abandon James Island, the Roundheads boarded a steamer, sailed to Hilton Head, and then returned to Beaufort, where they camped outside of town while their officers cleared out the necessary paperwork and returned the confiscated buildings to their previous occupants.

For Nellie, knowing this would be her last trip back to the Leverett House made the homecoming bittersweet. She had learned to love many of the slaves who had served the regiment well. Then, too, she had had many plans for making their lives better. She had hoped to persuade one of the missionaries to set up a school for the Leverett, Smith, and Fuller slaves, so those who wanted an education could learn to read, cipher, and expand their knowledge of the world around them. Now, however, it appeared they would simply be thrown back on their own resources. Whether they would remain disciplined enough to assure their own survival was still much in doubt.

She was so dismayed at the thought of abandoning these people that she approached Colonel Leverett about staying behind. "I could do it, Sir. You left me in charge when you marched the regiment off to Coosaw Ferry, and when you took them out on that camping adventure while Fort Pulaski was being attacked. Why couldn't you trust me to stay here and manage things? The missionary women would help, I know."

"And what would that accomplish?"

"I would be doing something good for them. They need me much more than the Army does."

"You're being ridiculous, Nellie! Of course you can't stay here. I'm responsible for bringing you to South Carolina, and I'll be responsible for taking you back north. "

"I'm not an official part of this regiment, let me remind you. You don't pay me, which means you have no control over me. I'm strictly a volunteer. So now I quit volunteering for your regiment. I'm volunteering to work with these poor abandoned slaves, instead."

"No, I need you. When we reach Virginia, our sick and wounded men will be sent off to a convalescent hospital to finish their recoveries. I'm sending you with them. The rest of the regiment will be headed straight into another battle, and there will be other nurses attached to our new brigade. You will be the only familiar thing our casualties will have to hold onto."

"What? What are you saying? That I'm to be sent off to a convalescent hospital while the rest of the Roundheads move on?"

"Yes. That's the plan." Colonel Leasure looked decidedly uncomfortable, but he tried to keep his voice calm.

"So I'm being fired?"

"No. You're not being fired," the colonel said, "just assigned to a new set of duties."

"You can't do that! This regiment is my life."

"Excuse me," the colonel said. "Didn't you quit a moment ago?"

Nellie was growing angrier, and the volume of her voice rose until she could be heard through the door and windows. "You're not being fair."

"Don't make this personal, Nellie."

"But it is personal. This is my life we're talking about. You don't own me. Quit behaving as if you do."

"I will, when you quit behaving like some wronged woman."

Outside, an audience was gathering. The soldiers were fascinated and had already begun to read their own interpretations into the quarrel. "Told ya they was sleepin' together," one leering private commented. "I always knew sumpthin' was up between those two."

"Nah. I still don't believe it. But I didn't know nobody pays her."

"That don't seem right! No wonder she wants to leave us."

"Well, sounds like she'll be leavin' us one way or t'other."

"Maybe we could do something for her," Christian Lobingier suggested. "Take up a collection or something."

"Would she accept it? Nurse Nellie has always seemed pretty standoffish to me."

"She prob'ly would if we said it was a thank you gift for all she's done for us. Why don't you start it up, Chris?"

"I will, and I'm the first to kick in my dollar."

"I still don't know. If she and the colonel are involved with each other, we don't want to let her know we overheard all this."

Reverend Browne came around the corner of the house to see what the ruckus was about. He was in time to hear the argument rise to a new level.

"Nellie, dear Nellie, please be reasonable," he heard the colonel say. "There's nothing more you can do for these people. When we leave, their owners may come filtering back, and they won't be coming to welcome a northern nurse into the family."

"But what if they don't come back? Uncle Bob runs the house well when he has someone to order his supplies and pay for them. But he can't keep this whole staff alive on the produce of that pitiful little garden out in the yard. You might as well be sentencing them to death."

"I'm doing no such thing. And you are being melodramatic. Maybe Reverend Browne was right about you being an actress at heart."

"That was a low blow. I thought you were fonder of me than that."

"It doesn't matter how fond of you I am. I'm doing what is best for all concerned."

Outside, eyes rolled and heads nodded. "Who would have thought the colonel. . . ." one soldier said, as Reverend Browne caught at his arm.

"Who would have thought—what? It's a sin to bear false witness, Son. Don't you go accusing the colonel of things unless you know they are true. And even then, it would be none of your business."

"Hey, Reverend, it sure sounds like a lovers' quarrel in there."

"And you have too much time on your hands. Be off with you and find something useful to do." The chaplain managed to embarrass most of the listeners into moving away, but that did not keep him from remembering his own accusations. He stayed as the argument inside took off on a new tack.

"If I have to leave, can I at least take little Glory with me? She is a sweet child and she really wants to start going to school. I could teach her during my time off, and she could help around our camp."

"Nellie, Nellie. You sound like one of the worst of the slave owners. Would you break up her family, take Maybelle's daughter away from her, just because you want her? You have no claim on that child, and I don't want you to mention it again. We're departing in two days. You will be packed and ready to board the transport ship, and you had better be alone. And don't plan on taking that damned cat with you, either!"

Nellie gasped in fury. "You're no better than Otis Leath, dictating my every move and taking me away from everything I love."

"I won't hear another word on this subject. Talk to me again when you have stopped being a silly woman." The colonel slammed his way out of the office and out the front door.

Reverend Browne barely managed to duck around the corner so as not to be caught eavesdropping. He watched speculatively as Leasure made his way across the street and stood staring at the water's edge. He's cooling off, Browne told himself, but I still have to wonder why he lets that foolish woman bother him so.

The quarrel had been heated, but both Leasure and Nellie soon regretted their disagreement. Leasure, for his part, was sorry he had called Nellie a "silly woman," and murmured an apology the next time he saw her. And Nellie? She was learning that emotional reactions usually netted her the exact opposite of whatever she had been trying to accomplish. She, too, was ready to apologize. With a warm smile, she acknowledged the colonel's effort and reassured him she carried no grudges.

The word to move out came quickly. On July 9th, General Stevens received orders calling for the entire brigade to depart for Newport News, Virginia, by 10:00 a.m. the next morning. Some of the men from the Roundheads, along with the Forty-Sixth New York and the Seventy-Ninth New York were still pitching their tents at Smith's Plantation when they were told to pack what they needed and report to the harbor at Beaufort.

"What about all this camp?" asked one private. "I just now pounded in the last peg of this rickety tent."

"We're leaving the tents behind. They're ragged and they'll take up too much room. Take only your personal belongings and your weapons, ammunition, and food supplies," his sergeant said. "These old canvas rags are too worn out to do us any good in Virginia. Leave 'em where they stand."

The men worked far into the night, ferrying their supplies from shore out to the transports. Then they boarded the steamer *Cosmopolitan,* which would carry them to Hilton Head. Waiting for them there was their ocean transport, the newly-christened *Merrimac* on her maiden voyage.

Nellie and the staff officers watched the boarding from the railing of the ship as the morning sun lit up the shoreline of the island. "South Carolina can be so beautiful," Nellie said. "I almost wish it had been rainy and muggy this morning so I would not be reluctant to turn away from the view."

"You did like it here, didn't you?" Doctor Ludington smiled at her pensive expression.

"Yes, despite the pluff mud and the bugs and the sand, I found it warm and welcoming. Life seems to move more slowly here than it does in the north. And the birds and fish and wildlife are strange and wonderful. The sky is bluer, the water more inviting, the sea grass—oh, I do sound silly. But I'm regretting much more than leaving the scenery."

"Still worried about the slaves?" asked Colonel Leasure as he joined the group.

"Yes, Sir, I am. I feel as if we are leaving a huge job undone here. We came to free the slaves, but all we've really done is disrupt the way of life they knew. The invasion chased away their masters, but we didn't know how to help the slaves they left behind. We've been floundering, falling into a pattern of master and slave because that's all they understood. And we had no alternatives to offer them."

"I understand," Leasure said. "We could have done much, and we've done little. Trouble is, I feel the same way about our military efforts." He shook his head.

"So we've wasted our time?" asked young Geordy. "I can't accept that. We've lost too many good men, suffered too much, worked too hard. . . ."

"I didn't say we had wasted our time, Son. Of course what we've done was important. Our presence stopped the Confederate forces from turning this vast harbor into the center of a naval initiative that might have destroyed the Union blockade. We've disrupted communications and transportation between two of the most important cities of the Confederacy. But there is always more that could have been done. And it is not wrong to regret those failures and omissions. Awareness of them is what helps us do a better job the next time."

"You may be right, Sir, " Nellie responded. "I wish I could believe I will have another chance some day to right the wrongs I have seen here."

"Well, you may not be here. But somewhere else? Surely that's possible. The key to loving what you do is the continuing belief there is hope for a better future. Soldiers keep fighting because they believe in their country and because they have a vision of a better world than the one in which they are living."

"So you think we'll have another chance to redeem the defeat we suffered at Secessionville?" Geordy asked, looking at his father doubtfully.

"I do. There's a major offensive developing in Virginia, and we get to be a part of that. Put the South Carolina experience behind you, enjoy your sea voyage, and get ready for your next challenge. That goes for you, too, Nellie. This ship has its own medical facility, so you can relax completely for a change. You deserve a few days off."

"Thank you, Sir. I'll probably be sticking close to my own quarters during the trip," she replied as she moved off, clutching her hand satchel possessively.

Nellie had good reason to hold her bag close. Once she reached her cabin, she opened it and pulled out a bedraggled and irritated young cat. Cotton glared at her for a moment before she began pointedly to wash her face and paws. Then, shaking herself, she began to pace the cabin, looking for a convenient box and something to eat. Nellie rushed to put down some sheets of newspaper and two feeding bowls, hiding them as best she could underneath her berth. The young cat was not easily mollified. She gave Nellie a flick of her tail and scooted away each time Nellie tried to pet her.

"All right, then, be mad at me if you want. But at least I didn't leave you behind!"

Cotton couldn't hear her, but she mimicked Nellie's open mouth and gave a tiny squeak, the best she could do, since she had never heard a real meow.

For the first couple of days at sea, Nellie managed to hide her secret, and she took great delight in sharing her berth with that soft bit of fur. But then the ship steamed into a patch of rough water, and the movement of the deck startled the cat. She shook her head and stumbled on her usually nimble paws.

"You'll get used to it," Nellie tried to tell her.

The cat's response was a hoarse hack Nellie recognized as the preamble to the appearance of a hair ball. "No, please don't get sea-sick," Nellie begged. But it was too late. The cat gagged and disgorged her recently-eaten breakfast. Then in a panic, she scampered toward the door, just as it opened.

"I'm sorry," Mary Pollock said. "I've gotten the wrong door. Oh! What was that?"

"That was Cotton. Quick! You've got to help me catch her before anyone else sees her."

"Nellie! You didn't bring that cat after the colonel told you not to?"

"Of course, I did. Come on!" Gathering their skirts above their ankles, the two women ran pell-mell through the passageway.

"Call her," Mary suggested.

"She's deaf!"

"Maybe a piece of yarn?"

"Don't happen to have one."

The cat hesitated at the foot of the gangway, not knowing which direction to turn. And from above descended the dapper little General Stevens. "Look out! A rat!" he shouted.

Mary began to giggle, but Nellie's face blanched.

"I'm sorry, Sir. It's just a cat."

"I hate cats!"

"I'll take care of her." Nellie scooped the kitten into her arms and cuddled her protectively.

"Miss Chase! Is that the famous animal you and Colonel Leasure fought about?

"Yes, Sir."

"You've disobeyed a direct order of a superior officer! I'll see you court-martialed for this," he said.

"Well, technically, Sir, I'm a volunteer. I never signed the papers to join the Army in any capacity, so he couldn't have given me a military order. But I promise. I'll take care of this. She'll never bother you again."

"Humph! We'll see about that." The general snorted as he walked away.

"Oh, Nellie. You're going to be in such trouble," Mary said. "What are you going to do?"

"I'm going back to my quarters, and I'll thank you to knock before you barge in the next time."

"Please don't be angry. I didn't realize the cat would get out. I'm sorry."

"I'll keep the door on the latch from now on," Nellie said. "It wasn't all your fault."

"If there's anything I can do. . . ."

"No. Now I wait for the sword to fall on my neck, I suppose."

The blow was not long in coming. If Nellie had been above deck, she would have seen a livid Colonel Stevens shouting at the Roundheads' commander. "Colonel, I have lost patience with you and that little lady-friend of yours!"

"General? What in the world are you talking about? *Who* are you talking about?"

"Nellie Chase, of course. She's gone too far this time, and it's your fault she thinks she can get away with doing anything she wants."

"Nellie? She's not my lady-friend, and I don't like the implication she is," the colonel said.

"She certainly seems to think she has you wrapped around her finger. Why else would she have had the temerity to bring that animal aboard this ship?"

"That animal? What animal?" Then the colonel's eyes narrowed with understanding. "She brought the cat with her."

"Yes, indeed. And I almost fell over it in the passageway just now."

"I can't believe it." Leasure shook his head. "I'll take care of the cat, Sir."

"You'd better take care of the lady, instead," Stevens said. "Get rid of her, Leasure. This is no place for someone like her. She's impertinent and pushy, undisciplined, and arrogant.

Thinking the general was somehow now making fun of the situation, the colonel smiled. "Well, I could throw the cat overboard for you, Sir, but I can hardly throw the lady overboard with her." It was the wrong thing to say, since the general was not joking.

"So I understand. You must have a special relationship with 'the lady'. She herself told me she never signed the papers to become an official member of the regiment. She has come along as . . . as what, Colonel? Is she your mistress? Your personal white slave? Perhaps a daughter whose existence you have never admitted?"

"General Stevens! That is uncalled for, and an insult to both me and Miss Chase. She has her own reasons for not wanting to leave behind a paper record of her whereabouts, and I sympathize with her circumstances. She is not, and never has been, anything to me other than a efficient matron, one who has helped to keep my regiment running smoothly. I resent the slur on her character and on mine."

"Resent anything you like, Daniel. The fact remains the entire regiment is talking about the two of you. Something in your behavior, or hers, must have given the men that impression," the general said.

"It's nothing but gossip, Sir, and I will put an end to it."

"Start by getting rid of the cat now! That's an order. And when we reach Newport News, you will send Miss Chase packing. I do not want to lay eyes upon her again. Do you understand?"

"Yes, Sir."

Leasure was still shaking with rage as he returned to his stateroom. His son, Geordy, soon joined him there, latching the door behind him. "What's going on, Father? Half the crew witnessed that confrontation between you and the general."

Daniel buried his face in his hands for a moment. "What are they saying, Geordy?"

"Well, most of the men are snickering about General Stevens being scared by a huge rat that turned out to be Nellie's kitten. They say he was hopping around, screeching and pointing his finger at the threatening beast, when Nellie and Mary came racing down the passageway, their skirts hiked up to their knees. They were chasing the cat, apparently, and didn't expect to run into anyone else. That part has become a joke."

"That part. What else?"

"Then he and Nellie got into a shouting match, and you know how she can get when she is really angry. She sounded the way she did talking to you the other day—uh, so I've been told." Geordy was floundering, realizing he had said too much.

The father knew his son too well to misunderstand the truth. "So you heard that, too. Were there others? Why didn't you tell me then?"

"I didn't want to embarrass you, Father. And I didn't realize the rumors about the two of you were going to spread all through the regiment."

"All through the regiment, Geordy? Does everyone now believe Miss Chase and I are somehow involved with each other?"

"I'm afraid they do now, since they heard the general accuse you of it."

"And they believed him? When he was practically frothing at the mouth?"

"Oh, Father. You have to understand it's not one instance. Reverend Browne accused the two of you back at Christmas, and he pointedly moved out of the Leverett House, telling people he didn't approve of what was going on there. You can deny it all you want, but as far as the men are concerned, it makes a good story."

"What about you, Geordy? Do you believe it?"

"Of course not! But you're going to have to find a way to put a stop to the rumors."

"I know that, Geordy. Nellie will be leaving us as soon as we make port."

Geordy sighed and shook his head. "It'll be a real shame to lose her. I've always liked her, and I think half the soldiers in the regiment have been in love with her at one point or another. Maybe they've been assuming you'd feel the same way they do."

"Whatever their reasons, the matter is becoming disruptive, and I can't afford to let it continue. I'll see to it she gets home safely, and I'll take care of the cat, too."

Geordy hesitated at the door. "You wouldn't really throw that cat overboard, would you?"

"Geordy, you must know me better than that! I'm not the kind of man who is ever unfaithful to his wife, nor have I ever treated an animal cruelly." Colonel Leasure was a bit irritated with his son. " I have an idea for the cat. I have to work out a few details first. I'd appreciate it if you demonstrated a bit of faith in me."

It took several hours for Colonel Leasure to put all the pieces together, but by late afternoon, he was ready for his meeting with Nellie. He sent Private Stevenson to her cabin to summon her. Nellie had evidently been waiting, for they returned promptly. "Thank you, Private. Please wait in the passageway and see to it we are not disturbed. And no, don't close the door! I have nothing to hide in here." He motioned Nellie to a seat across the desk from him.

For a few minutes, he said nothing, nor did Nellie. Both seemed willing to let the other set the tone of the meeting. At last, Daniel spoke. "I'm disappointed in you, Nellie."

"I'm sorry," she said. "I had no idea bringing Cotton aboard the ship would set off this storm. I thought she would be quiet, and she doesn't eat much. No one would have to know."

"All of that is irrelevant," the colonel said. "The point is, I asked you to do something, and you completely ignored me."

"But I thought. . . ."

"It was not your place to have an opinion. I gave you a direct order, and I expected you to obey it."

"I . . . I apologize. It was juvenile and silly of me, and I should have known better."

"Yes, you should have. But it's too late for you to apologize and expect me to pat you on your head and send you back to work."

"You're firing me." It was a statement, not a question.

"Yes, I am. But first, I want to be sure you understand the damage you have caused."

"I'm afraid I don't understand. The kitten was in the passageway for only a couple of minutes. Mary and I would have caught her at the foot of the gangway, and no one would have been the wiser if General Stevens had not happened along at that moment. It was unfortunate timing, but I still don't see the great harm it caused."

"Don't you? Well, let me enlighten you. On a ship this size, there are always observers. General Stevens has become a laughingstock among the men because he was frightened of a kitten. The story is being passed around even now, and every time it is repeated and embellished, he looks weaker and sillier. There's the first piece of damage. Your actions have managed to destroy the respect a general deserves from his troops."

"But it was hardly my fault he mistook. . . ."

"I don't want to hear it. The second piece of damage occurred when the general confronted me on deck in front of who knows how many men. He called you my 'lady friend' and blamed me for letting you wrap me around your little finger. Among the terms he used to describe you were 'impertinent,' 'pushy,' and 'undisciplined'. By the time he was through, he had confirmed every rumor, every accusation Robert Browne made against us. Now, my son tells me even the Roundhead soldiers believe we are somehow carrying on an affair under their noses. I have lost their respect and every bit of moral control I might have once held over them."

"But you know that's not so! Can't you tell them. . . ?" Nellie's voice was rising to near hysteria.

"Please keep your voice down. Everybody aboard this ship is going to want to know what's going on in here. We don't need to add a third act to this little drama."

"So I'll leave. Is that what you want?" she said.

"I wish the solution were that simple, Nellie. The harsh truth is this is going to haunt all of us for a long time. In a few short weeks, General Stevens and I will be leading these men into another battle, one potentially more dangerous than the debacle at Secessonville. And I don't know what will happen. At Secessionville, I asked the men to come to me and regroup in the face of overwhelming odds, and they did so because they trusted me. Now they believe I've lied to them. Will they trust me again? I don't know. Will they obey an order from General Stevens? That's even more doubtful. It may sound ridiculous, but the lives of good men may be lost because of a half-grown deaf cat running down a passageway."

Nellie could only shake her head in despair as tears flowed down her cheeks.

"Here's what is going to happen, Nellie, and it is not open to discussion. Private Stevenson will see you safely back to your cabin, where a soldier will be standing guard at your door. Then he will take the cat from you and deal with it as I have instructed."

"You're going to kill her!"

"You lost your right to determine the cat's fate when you failed to leave her with the slaves who would have taken care of her. You may think whatever you will of me. You will spend the next few days under house arrest. Your meals will be delivered, but you will neither see nor talk to anyone except your guard until we reach port. You will be the last person to disembark from the ship. You will be provided a ride to the depot, and someone will put you on a train back to Pittsburgh. Where you go from there, I really don't care, as long as you never try to contact a member of the Roundhead Regiment again. Do you understand me?"

Nellie could only nod as she stood and made her way to the door. Her back was straight, her face was resolute, but her heart felt as if it had been ripped from her chest. She had known the terror of running away from a bad situation. She had been doing that most of her life. But never before had she been driven away, and the pit of despair that loomed before her seemed bottomless.

Nellie didn't remember much about the rest of the voyage. She might have been able to accept the firing without falling apart. But when Colonel Leasure suggested her actions might have contributed to his own future inability to lead his men into battle, she was devastated. A small part of her argued that he was exaggerating. Her sin was too small to have such widespread results. But then came the other voices, led by that of Reverend Browne, all saying, "You're the sinner. Their blood is on your hands."

She crawled into her berth and lay there shivering for a long time. Days? Perhaps. Gradually she became aware of a piercing pain in her right side. It felt like a sharp dagger inserted between her ribs. When she tried to stand, she could only mange to stay erect at all by clutching that side and bending over. She was feverish, too, but she could not bring herself to call for help. She pulled the covers tighter under her chin and hoped she was going to die there. The guard delivered her meals on schedule, but she always pretended to be asleep. Once in a while she tried to manage a few bites, but everything tasted like sawdust. The guard made no comment when he took the untouched meals away.

She knew they would be saying Nellie was being melodramatic again, but she didn't really care what anyone thought. She could not bear to think of the same people who had condemned her offering false sympathy if she did indeed prove to be ill. She simply waited for time to pass. She could not think about the future, because she could not imagine how horrible it would be. They were sending her back to Pittsburgh, that filthy, evil city she had worked so hard to escape. The boarding house loomed, more offers of prostitution, more gossipy folks ready to carry the word of her return to Otis Leath. Fear and revulsion fought for top place on her list of emotions.

When the ship docked in Newport News, the colonel sent Private Stevenson to be sure Nellie was ready to depart. He found her still lying in her berth, unable to make herself move.

"Nellie, are you ill?"

"I don't know."

"Can you stand up?"

"I suppose so." But when she tried to stand, the pain in her side was so severe she had to grasp the side of the berth to keep from falling over. She clutched it while sweat beaded on her forehead.

"I'm going to get Colonel Leasure," he said in a panic.

"No," she managed to gasp. "Get Ludington." While he was gone she lowered herself gingerly into a sitting position, and it was there the kindly doctor found her.

"My God," she heard him say. "Nellie, how long have you been like this? You look ghastly."

She simply shook my head. "I don't know." Ever since the colonel locked me in here, she wanted to say, but the room started to spin and go dark.

The next thing she remembered was waking up on a cot in a military tent. Mary Pollock was there with her, waiting to take orders from the doctors who stood around her.

"It seems like appendicitis," one young orderly suggested. "But the pain is on the wrong side."

"Her temperature is not all that elevated. I think she has fretted and stewed herself into this state. The guard reports she hasn't eaten in three days. That alone could cause her to faint and suffer cramps."

"I don't think so," she heard Colonel Leasure argue. "Mary, get her undressed and into this overlarge gown. I'm going to want to see that portion of her side where she keeps touching and then wincing."

Mary had a struggle getting her clothes removed, because Nellie was unable to be of any help. All she could do was cry out whenever someone touched her too firmly. But at last the task was finished. The doctors returned, and with a great show of preserving her modesty, they gradually managed to uncover a portion of her right ribcage below the breast. There was a collective intake of breath.

"What is that?" someone asked.

Nellie wanted to ask the same question, but she was too woozy to formulate the words—or to understand what she heard them saying next: "inflammation, pustules, oozing liquid, scabs forming in layers, like shingles."

In her confused state of consciousness, she remembered thinking, *They've mistaken me for a roof!* Or did she say it out loud? She wasn't really sure. Then they rolled her onto her side and uncovered her back.

"See how the lesions cover her whole right side while the left side remains unaffected? She definitely has a bad case of shingles."

If she hadn't hurt so badly, she might have giggled. Instead, she passed out again. She regained consciousness once or twice, each time hearing disembodied voices discussing her condition as if she were not in the room.

"She's too young to have shingles."

"Not if she had recently had an emotional experience."

"I still think she's faking it."

"Not with a rash like that!"

"What can be done for her?"

"Nothing. Shingles is not usually a fatal disease; it just makes you wish you were dead."

"We can't leave her in this condition."

"No, but we can't take her with us, either. She's not fit to travel, even if General Stevens would allow it, which he won't."

"Keep giving her morphine—enough to keep her under without killing her—while we find a place to send her."

At some point, Reverend Browne arrived. There was no mistaking his booming baritone when he was in full preacher mode. After speculating on the likelihood of her demise, he launched into his own analysis: "Poor woman! Six years of the morning of life spent as the wife of a bad man have laden her so heavily for the future, that one sees with less regret the doors of that home opening to her 'where the wicked cease from troubling and the weary are at rest'."

If Nellie had had the strength to be furious, she would have been. She couldn't be sure whether he thought she was one of the wicked or one of the weary, but it was clear he would not be sorry to hear of her death.

Then someone was lifting her onto a litter, and two men carried her out of the tent. They had trouble holding the litter steady, and the jostling movement sent such searing pain through her side that she passed out again.

22

HEALING INTERLUDE

Nellie awoke in a small room with whitewashed walls and a scrubbed pine floor partially covered by a woven rag rug. The furniture was also pine, plain but sturdy. The bed was draped in crisp white sheets, and on the table next to it stood a glass, a basin, and a pitcher of water. At the foot of the bed hung a small crucifix, with a withered palm branch tucked behind it. She was more comfortable than she had been in days, but she was also mystified. *Have I died?* she asked herself. *Is this heaven or the foyer to hell? And whatever it is, how in the world did I get here?*

As if in answer to her unspoken questions, a soft voice responded, "Ah, you are awake. How are you feeling?" From a hidden corner of the room came the rustling of skirts as a diminutive woman enshrouded in black came to stand by the bed. Her hair was tucked under a white wimple, then draped in a black veil. From her waist dangled a string of beads and a silver cross. A high white collar and cuffs set off the blackness of her habit. She laid a cool hand on Nellie's brow.

"You're a nun."

"Yes, my child. I am Sister Mary Xavier. I've been sitting with you, waiting for you to wake up."

"Where am I? Is this a hospital? A convent? I don't understand."

"It's a bit of both, actually. This is the hospital wing of the Sisters of Charity of Our Lady Of Mercy Convent in Newport News. You don't remember arriving here?"

"No, no. There has been some kind of dreadful mistake," Nellie said. "I'm not a Catholic."

"It doesn't matter. You are ill and were brought to our doorstep. We take in anyone who needs our care, as Our Lord would have us do."

"But I'm not even religious. And I'm a terrible sinner. Reverend Browne, our Presbyterian chaplain, said I would rot in Hell for my sins. He didn't want anyone to help me. I can't ask help of you, a good Catholic."

"A Presbyterian minister told you that? Well, pooh! What does he know? Those Presbyterians can be a hard-nosed bunch. They're good at preaching guilt, but they've not learned much about forgiveness."

Nellie smiled despite herself. "But . . . but . . . ."

"Hush, child. I don't believe for a moment you are a terrible sinner. But it doesn't matter. An army colonel delivered you to us and asked if we could nurse you back to health. We agreed to do so, and that is the end of the matter."

"An army colonel? Colonel Leasure?"

"Yes, I believe that was his name. Again, it doesn't matter. We are here to nurse you back to health. When was the last time you had something to eat? You're rail-thin."

"I don't remember. I don't even know what day it is. I know I had a terrible pain, and then the doctors started giving me morphine every time I woke. I'd hear them talking about me. They kept saying I was a roof. I didn't understand." Nellie realized she was not making much sense, and hot tears threatened.

"They said you were a roof?" The sister looked at her in complete bafflement and then began to laugh. "Oh, Miss Nellie, you really were out of it, weren't you? You have a disease called shingles, my dear. But they're not the kind you put on a roof! We don't know a whole lot about the disease, but it comes on without much warning except for a sharp pain, as you described. Then the skin on one side of your body breaks out into pustules that look like chickenpox, except there are more of them, and they are closer together. They spread into a rash and then scab over. But unlike chickenpox, a second and third layer of the pustules can break out under the first scabs, and eventually, you have layers of scabs that look, actually, something like the shingles on a roof."

"But I've had chickenpox and nursed children with chickenpox. People don't get it a second time."

"No, they get shingles instead. You're in for a rough time of it, I'm afraid. Your first scabs are now beginning to form. You may have the lesions for several weeks before they all heal. And the pain may last much longer than that."

"I can't stay here. I have no money, no way to pay you. There's supposed to be a train ticket waiting for me at the station so I can go back to Pittsburgh. I think I should probably do that." Nellie struggled to sit up and then cried out as some of her newly-formed scabs tore loose.

"Lie still, my child." The soothingly cool hand smoothed her forehead again and brushed away her tears. "We ask nothing from you. We want to see you regain your health. When that day comes, if you want to repay us in some way, we'll talk about it, but even that is not necessary. I'm going to have one of the novices bring you a cup of beef tea, and I want you to sip it slowly until you have finished every drop. Do you understand?"

"But . . . but. . . ."

"But nothing. You don't ever argue with a nun. We always get our way. We have a powerful Force on our side, you see."

In a few minutes, another knock came at the door, followed by a young girl in a simple gray dress. "Miss Chase? I've brought your beef tea."

Nellie was not interested in the contents of the steaming mug the girl held. Instead, she focused on the girl herself. She was wearing the same high white collar as the older nun, and the same string of beads and cross dangled from her belt. But her hair, although smoothed back and twisted into a knot, was not covered by wimple or veil. "Hello. Please come in. Are you a nun or—what was the term the other nun used—a novice? Forgive me, but all of this is new to me."

"Oh, I understand. I didn't know what was going on when I first came here, either. I'm Sister Anne, and yes, I'm a novice."

"What exactly does that mean?"

"It means I'm still in training. I haven't taken my final vows yet, but I will as soon as the sisters feel I am ready," she answered with a grin. "I'm anxious to get my full habit."

"Habit?"

"That's what we call the gown and headdress we wear. This simple dress is temporary."

"And how will they know when you are ready?" Nellie asked.

"I have to work my way through a series of chores and prove I can do them well and cheerfully, for one thing. Like this," she said, gesturing with the mug she still held. "My job for the next two weeks is to feed you so you can regain your strength. I'm to bring you six small meals a day, making sure they are all nourishing and designed to encourage your appetite. Sister Mary Xavier said to start with beef tea and work from there."

"I've never heard of beef tea, and I'm sure I don't want to know how you turn a cow into tea. But I'll drink it if that's your job."

Sister Anne giggled, revealing how young she still was. "At home, Ma would call it beef soup, but Sister thinks 'tea' makes it sound healthier."

Nellie took a sip and found it surprisingly tasty. "Unmmm. It does taste good. Thank you, Sister Anne. I'm sorry you're going to be so busy on my account. Six meals a day may be excessive. I could do with less."

"No, you couldn't. Sister Mary Xavier would have me scrubbing floors again if she thought I had slacked off on my assignment."

"So you'll be cooking for the next two weeks?"

"Yes, that, and singing the Hours seven times a day." Sister Anne still smiled brightly.

"Singing the . . . what?"

"The Hours. Oh, I keep forgetting you're not a Catholic. The Hours are short worship services in the chapel. We read the Psalms, sing a hymn, and share in the prayers of the day. There isn't a full mass or anything except once a day. The Hours come about every three hours, marking the passage of the day from dawn till dark. In a way, it's how we keep track of our time."

"So—seven Hours, six meals—you'll be feeding me between each service. Is that right?" Sister Anne nodded happily. "But what if I'm not hungry? That shouldn't reflect on you."

"Oh, you'll be hungry. Sister Mary Xavier says so. Besides, the food is really good here. We are pretty self-sufficient. We raise our own cows and chickens, so the milk and eggs are always fresh. We grow our own fruits and vegetables and put up our own produce for the winter. We bake our own bread, churn our own butter, and make our own cheese."

Nellie held up her hands to stop the flow of words. "I get the idea. I'll try to be hungry."

"I'll be really grateful," Sister Anne confided. "I've had some problems learning to obey orders, and I want to fulfill this job perfectly. Oh, no! What did I say?" she gasped as Nellie's tears erupted once again. "I'm not supposed to make you cry."

Nellie gulped and sniffed to regain control. "It wasn't your fault. You just reminded me I've had some trouble with obeying orders, too. In fact, disobedience is what landed me in this predicament."

"Well, the Sisters of Charity will take care of that, I promise. They 'have their ways' as Sister Mary Xavier keeps reminding me. Now, I have to be off to Compline, while you finish your beef tea. Then I'll be bringing you something else—oh, I know! We had a nice custard for supper tonight. How does that sound?"

"It sounds wonderful, Sister Anne."

"Then I'll be back in a bit. Mustn't be late for Hours." She called over her shoulder as she scampered out the door.

Nellie watched her go, shaking her head at the girl's energy—so unlike her own exhaustion as she lay back in her bed. She's about my age, she thought, but what a difference between us. I wonder if that's what I would have been like if I hadn't lost my innocence so early.

The next morning another nun joined the team taking care of Nellie. "This is Sister Verona," announced Sister Anne, nodding back over her shoulder. "She's going to care for your rash. But first, I've brought you a nice soft-boiled egg and a piece of dry toast. Eat every bit of it, mind you, along with your tea—real tea, this time, not that beef stuff," she said. And she was gone, bouncing out of the room as if she could not wait to see what the new day would bring.

"She's really charming. But she makes me tired just to watch her."

"I know what you mean," Sister Verona agreed. "Ah, the resilience of youth!" Sister Verona was elderly. A wisp or two of wiry gray hair escaped her wimple, and the skin around her eyes puckered into deep crevices when she smiled. Still, she seemed lovely to Nellie. There was something serene and comforting about her.

"I've been chosen to take over your medical care because I'm the only one of the working sisters who has actually had shingles."

"Am I that contagious?" Nellie asked in alarm.

"Oh. No. Well, maybe to small children. They sometimes get chicken-pox after being around a shingles patient. We're not sure why. But you won't see any children for a while. No. I'm here because I can understand what you are going through. There's no pain like it, is there? When I had the Belt, I was sure I was going to die, and then afraid I wouldn't."

"What did you call it?"

"The Belt. It's sometimes called that because it wraps itself around your waist like a belt, although only on one side, for some reason. Anyway, that's why it hurts so much, you see. The pain is not just in front, or just in back, but all the way through your body. And even when the rash goes away, you'll feel the pain deep inside for a long time."

"So I'm not being weak and silly?" Nellie's eyes overflowed again. "I can't stop crying, and it makes me feel even more helpless to lie here blub-bering like a baby."

"Tears can be healing, my child. Don't try to stop them. You have good reason to cry, and you'll be doing a great deal more of it before we're through. You're going to feel helpless and full of despair. For the next couple of weeks, you may be so engulfed in a dark cloud of misery that you won't be able to see your way out. It will pass, I promise, and I'll be here to help you along."

Nellie reached out and clutched her hand in gratitude.

"Now, then," said Sister Verona, suddenly all business. "Push down that sheet and open your gown. I've brought some warm compresses soaked in baking soda water to ease the itching of your rash, and I don't want them growing cold." She opened the covered pan she had been carrying and began to work. Nellie winced the first time she was touched. Then she relaxed as the warmth soothed her.

The routine lasted for days. Nellie slept a great deal, waking when Sister Anne appeared with her small meals. The food was indeed delicious, and Sister Anne procured one tasty dish after another to tempt Nellie's appetite: garden vegetable soups, melted cheese on toast, porridge full of little surprises of raisins or dates, eggs shirred in cups or scrambled lightly, casseroles of baked root vegetables, rice pudding. As promised, the food was fresh and delicious, and, although Nellie would have sworn she would never be hungry again, she found herself beginning to look forward to each small tray.

The rash, too, improved. Sister Verona kept up a running report. The inflamed edges were starting to shrink, no fresh pustules, the scabs drying up nicely. "You're going to be lucky," she said. "Youth has its advantages. In your case, you are a quick healer, and that will shorten the time you have to deal with the pain."

"The dark cloud you described is still there, however. How long is it going to take for me to feel happy again?"

"Happy? I don't know. We don't think much about being happy here. But I'm hopeful you will soon start to feel more contented."

"Contented? I don't even want that. I want to feel useful again. I want to feel like I belong somewhere. I want people to need me," Nellie tried to explain.

"In time," was the only comfort Sister Verona had to offer.

Several weeks later, Sister Verona rinsed away the last of the crusty patches and spread a soothing lotion over the newly healed skin. "There!" she announced, "I think we can say your shingles attack is officially over. The skin will be a bit tender for a while, but it will soon toughen up."

"I'm truly grateful," Nellie said, reaching out to squeeze the gentle hand. "You've been kind. But I'm ready to get back to work."

"You still have a ways to go," Sister Verona cautioned. "Don't be planning to pack up and head out the door just yet. You've been in bed a long time. Sister Mary Xavier sent this dressing gown for you. She wants you to practice sitting up in the chair by the window for a while. Then she'll be in for a little chat."

"I'll be fine," Nellie assured her as she sat up and swung her legs over the edge of the bed. Then she clutched frantically at the bed clothes to steady herself as the room spun madly away from her for a moment. "Oh, dear," she said, pressing her eyelids together to keep from seeing the tilting walls.

""You're just a bit dizzy, Nellie. Your body has to readjust to being vertical. It will pass in a moment."

When Nellie could breathe again, Sister Verona helped her to make her slow way across the room to the waiting chair. Nellie was shocked at how unsteady her legs were. "You don't have to worry about me running away just yet." But by the time Sister Mary Xavier arrived for her visit, Nellie was feeling much stronger.

"How nice to see you up," she said. "How are you feeling?"

"I'm better," Nellie assured her. "There's still some pain, but I can handle that."

"As far as your physical health goes, I'm sure you can, but you're still sad, aren't you?"

"No, no. I'm really fine," Nellie responded. Then she was horrified to feel the smile on her lips wobble as the ever-present tears began to flow again. "I'm sure I'm just tired from the day's exertion," she said.

"You may lie to others all you please, Nellie, but don't lie to yourself. Come, let's move out onto the airing porch. It's a lovely warm day, and I think you could use some fresh air."

Nellie moved gingerly toward the door, but her steps quickened as she caught sight of the autumn foliage on the hill outside. "Summer's over, already. The trees have all turned. I've been here a long time, haven't I?"

"How long you've been here is not a problem. But let's talk a bit, and let's be honest. When you came to us, you said something about being a great sinner. In the convent, we believe that it is necessary to confess all sins in order to have them forgiven."

Nellie felt an unexpected flush of anger. "I'm not a member of your convent; I'm just a patient. And, if you remember, I also told you I am not a Catholic. I don't believe in going to confession." She was defiant and astonished at the same time that she had found the strength to defy this powerful figure.

"I'm not about to send you to the confessional, Nellie. I'm simply talking about admitting to yourself, and perhaps to someone else who cares about you, that you have made mistakes. If you can't do that—if you deny the guilt you are obviously feeling— you won't be able to get past it."

"Is it guilt I'm feeling? I thought it was shingles." Nellie glared at her.

"You are desperately unhappy, whether you admit it or not. Something terrible has happened to you. It may have even precipitated the shingles attack. We often find shingles patients are undergoing some other great crisis in their lives. Then the physical pain combines with the emotional misery to compound the depth of both."

Nellie sat with her head bowed for several minutes, trying to absorb what she had been told. Finally she looked up apologetically. "I'm sorry. I shouldn't have snapped at you. I know you are trying to help."

"I can only help if you let me."

'Well, my sin was one of disobedience and ingratitude. I seem to be compounding that."

Sister Mary Xavier simply waited.

"All right. You know, I suppose, that I am . . . was . . . the regimental nurse for the Pennsylvania Roundheads. They are a kindly and godly regiment. Colonel Leasure took me in when I desperately needed a place to go. They have been nothing but good to me. I grew angry with the colonel when he thwarted a new plan I had hatched. I wanted to stay behind when the regiment left, so that I could establish a school for the slave children I had met in South Carolina. He wouldn't let me do it, and then he wouldn't let me take my kitten with me when we broke camp. Cotton is still young, and she's deaf. Her mother cat never taught her to do things like feed herself, and I couldn't leave her.

"So, I smuggled her aboard our ocean transport. I thought I could hide her in my cabin, and nobody would have to be the wiser. I guess I forgot she was a kitten. She got out and went streaking through the ship. She scared the general into making a fool of himself, and then, of course, he took his embarrassment out on the colonel. The colonel scolded me for disobeying him. He fired me and took the kitten away." Nellie sniffled despite herself.

"You did disobey him."

"Yes, and I apologized. But he wouldn't accept the apology. He as much as said I had ruined his entire military career. He said he—and the general, too—would never again be able to command the strict obedience of their troops, and in a battle, men might die because of it. And that would be my fault."

"What? That's absurd."

"Not in his eyes. So, yes, I feel guilty. I lost his respect. I lost my job. I lost my cat. I may have caused the deaths of soldiers in our regiment. I lost everything!"

"Surely the men in your regiment knew you well enough to know you didn't mean any harm by what you did."

"Well, but that's not the whole problem. You see, our chaplain, the Presbyterian minister I told you about, had it in for me from the time he met me. He suspected me of being an actress, or a prostitute, or worse. And when the colonel did not agree with him, he made terrible accusations that the colonel and I were . . . involved . . . in some way."

Sister Mary Xavier frowned and cocked an eyebrow at Nellie.

"We weren't, I swear! I adored Colonel Leasure, and I thought he was a wonderful leader, but that was as far as it went. I never thought of him in a romantic way. He was as old as my father, and that comparison was enough to . . . to . . . well, never mind. There was no involvement, but everyone, even the general, believed the chaplain's accusations. I did ruin the colonel's reputation, and my own." Nellie said.

"Did you mean to do all that when you disobeyed his orders?"

"No, of course not. I just wanted to take care of my kitten."

"I don't know what the Presbyterians say about personal responsibility, but I know what we Catholics would say to all of this. We believe—I believe—God cares more about our intentions than our actions. If I injure someone because I dislike him, I'm guilty of a sin. But if I injure that person while trying to save his life, that's a good intention that far outweighs the result."

"I think I understand, but. . . ."

"All I'm trying to say, Nellie, is someone has blown this incident out of all proportion. You are guilty of nothing more than a momentary weakness brought on by your love for one of God's own creatures. You are not responsible for what the colonel and the general and the suspicious chaplain happen to think about you because of it."

"But I'm the one who lost everything."

"That's true only if you let it be true. You can't control what others do, but you can control your own actions. This incident will ruin your own life only if you allow it."

They let the matter rest for several days. Nellie continued to regain her strength, although she had no idea where to turn next. The sisters went on caring for her well-being, and no one mentioned the details she had revealed to Sister Mary Xavier. It was a peaceful interlude. Then one morning, Nellie received a letter addressed in care of the convent. "We were asked to give this to you when you were fully recovered," Sister Mary Xavier told her. Nellie opened it slowly, not knowing what to expect.

Dear Miss Chase,

Colonel Leasure said I could find you at this address. I want you to know your cat, Cotton, is safe and well here aboard the Merrimac. *The colonel brought her down to the crew deck and offered her services as a ship's cat when the Roundhead Regiment disembarked. She has become a good little mouser and is busily ridding all our storerooms of the vermin that might get into our foodstuffs. She's getting fat, too, because everyone aboard the ship loves her and keeps sneaking her tasty tidbits from our meals. She seems happy with her job and sleeps contentedly at the end of her shift. If you should ever happen to be in the same port as we are, Cotton and the ship's crew would welcome a visit from you, so you could see for yourself what a fine cat that little kitten is becoming.*

Sincerely yours,
Charles Ledbetter, First Mate

Nellie could not stop crying, but for the first time in weeks, these were happy tears. "He didn't kill her!" she exclaimed with shining eyes.

"No, I didn't think he would. You've been so busy believing Colonel Leasure hates you that you have forgotten what a good and decent man he is. Remember, he was the one who brought you to us when it looked like you were dying. I saw the caring and concern in his eyes that night when he knocked on our door."

"Why didn't you remind me?"

"It's better you make that discovery for yourself, as you have. Now you can move on."

"Are you telling me it is time for me to leave?"

"No. On the contrary. I was about to ask if you would like to stay on with us, not as a patient, but. . . ."

"As a nun? No, thank you. I told you before, I'm not even Catholic."

"I understand that, but hear me out. We have lay sisters who are connected with the convent. They perform various duties. We have a woman who keeps our business accounts, another who manages the guest house, and several teachers in our orphanage. They are not nuns. They take no religious orders, and are simply paid a small salary for their services."

"Wait. Your orphanage? I've seen no children here."

"That was by design. You may remember Sister Verona telling you a shingles patient could spread chickenpox to children. We've deliberately kept you segregated so that didn't happen. But now that you are recovered, would you like to tour our orphanage and meet our children? I could arrange a visit for tomorrow morning."

Hesitating, Nellie wondered if this were not a ploy to keep her at the convent. Finally, she agreed, hoping she would not fall hopelessly in love with the children as she had done back in the slave quarters of Beaufort.

To her own surprise, Nellie found the children unappealing. She was taken from classroom to classroom, where the pupils sat primly at their wooden desks, their reed pens and inkwells arranged neatly in front of them, their hands clasped in their laps, and their eyes looking at the floor until someone addressed them by name. They wore uniforms, the boys in long-sleeved shirts and overalls, the girls in simple long dresses with white collars. They were serious, obedient, polite, and deadly dull. Not a single eye caught Nellie's attention, not a single twinkle or grin to show a lively child was there. The orphanage living quarters gave the same impression—beds neatly made up in rows, a long dining table set with utilitarian utensils, a small recreation area that sported not a single childish game. Nellie felt sorry for the children, but she realized she was not the one to rescue them.

"We would welcome you on the staff of our school," Sister Mary Xavier told her.

Nellie shook her head. "Sister, you have been unfailingly kind, and I shall never be able to repay you. But I cannot stay here. I am an army nurse, and there is a war going on out there on the other side of these walls. I don't belong here, and you have no real need of me. I have to go back to the front."

"But you said yourself the Roundheads fired you, and they are long departed from Newport News. I don't think you'll be able to find them."

"If not the Roundheads, then some other unit will need me. I have nursed men through epidemics that plague military camps. I have treated wounds and illnesses that most young women have never seen. I've even helped with amputations after a major battle. Someone needs me out there, and I intend to find them. Will you help me?"

"Of course. I know there are military build-ups going on north of here. I can ask a few questions of people in town. They may know of a military hospital in need of staffing."

"Thank you, Sister. Another wise woman once told me that I should stop running away from things and start looking for something to run to. If I stayed here, it would be another way of running away from my responsibilities. I must run toward them, instead."

23

MOVING FORWARD

Thanks to her many friends in town, Sister Mary Xavier soon had the necessary information. She called Nellie to her office and outlined a proposal. "From what I understand, the Army of the Potomac is planning a massive assault on Richmond after the first of the year. Between now and then, they will be taking control of the Virginia cities north of Richmond in order to clear their path. The forces gearing up now are coming out of Maryland, so my best advice is this. There is a steamer leaving Hampton Roads on its way to Annapolis in a few days. You can take passage on it and report straight to Army Headquarters in Annapolis for assignment to a medical unit."

"Two problems I see," Nellie said. "First, I have no money to book steamer passage. And even if I did, won't the Sanitary Commission reject me out of hand? I mean, I hardly fit the description Dorothea Dix issued for those seeking employment with them. I'm too young, too vain, too. . . ."

"Just stop," Sister Mary Xavier ordered. "You're throwing up road blocks where there need be none. Your passage is not a problem. The ship is the *Saratoga*, and the captain is offering free passage to anyone who wants to volunteer to become a nurse. The need is great, you see. And the same thing is true of Army Headquarters. Miss Dix may fulminate all she likes about the need for nurses who are plain and have high moral standards. But that doesn't fill out a nursing staff. You walk in there and tell them you served with the 100th Pennsylvania for a year before falling ill, and you will be welcomed with open arms. I guarantee it."

By the middle of October, Nellie found herself bound for Annapolis. Nothing like moving forward by retracing my steps, she told herself. But at least I've been in Annapolis before. I'll know where to go and what to do this time. I'm not the same ignorant little girl who arrived there the first time.

She boarded the *Saratoga* on October 13th and immediately felt at home. The ship's routines were familiar, the excitement on deck contagious, and the fresh sea air invigorating. After stowing her small bag in the ladies' cabin, she returned to the deck, unwilling to be closed in after spending so much time in a hospital bed. She stood on the afterdeck, letting the wind ruffle her hair and taking deep breaths. She was so enjoying the sensation of being set free that she hardly noticed when a man in Union blues came to stand by her side.

"I beg your pardon, Miss. Don't I know you from somewhere?"

"No, I don't think so," she replied without ever really looking at the owner of the voice.

"I'm sorry. I don't want to seem forward, but I really think. . . ."

She turned in annoyance, and then her eyes widened as she saw the uniform of the Seventy-Ninth New York Volunteer Regiment. "You're a Highlander?"

"I knew there was something familiar about you! But I still can't place you. How did you know about my regiment's nickname?"

"Because we were. . . ." She stopped in confusion.

"Please. What were you going to say?"

"I don't know you, Sir, but I was in South Carolina when your regiment was there."

"In what capacity?" he asked. "You're not a Southern belle. I can tell by your New England accent."

"No. I was with the . . . with another regiment . . . as a nurse."

"Well, there's the connection, then. Allow me to introduce myself. I am Doctor John McDonald, the surgeon assigned to the Highlander regiment. And you are. . . ?"

"Nurse Nellie Chase, formerly with the Roundhead Regiment." Now that she had admitted her identity, she held her breath, waiting for the inevitable reaction.

"Of course! I remember now. You are that amazing young woman who worked with Colonel Leasure after the Battle of Secessionville. I remember coming into the Rivers House looking for our wounded, and there you were, covered in blood and helping with amputations as if you had been doing it all your life."

"Actually, I was shaking in my shoes," she admitted, "but yes, I was helping to administer the chloroform."

"But why aren't you with the Roundheads now? Or are you heading out to join them?"

"I've been ill. They moved on without me." There was nothing false in either of those statements, but Nellie could feel her heart hammering as if she had told a huge lie. She turned away from Doctor McDonald while a debate conducted itself in her head. If she did not explain what had happened, he might continue to probe at her explanations. But if she did admit she had been fired, he would walk away in disgust. I'm tired of living this melodrama, she told herself.

Straightening her shoulders, she looked the officer in the eye. "I have been ill, but actually, I was fired," she stated, "at the order of your own General Stevens. And I really don't want to talk about it."

"I'm sorry. It must be a painful subject for you. All the same, it seems like a gross miscarriage of justice. The Union forces are in such dire need of competent nursing staff. In fact, that's partially why I've been traveling around the countryside. I've been sent to see if I can't recruit more medical staff. Are you looking for a job?"

Nellie caught her breath. "Yes, but . . . no, you couldn't possibly hire me. General Stevens would never allow it."

"General Stevens is dead, Miss Chase. He was killed in action at Chantilly on the first of September. You hadn't heard?"

"No." She shook her head, unable to reconcile her own mixed feelings of relief and sadness.

"He died bravely, actually. He was galloping across the battlefield to rescue our colors as our flag-bearer fell. He was shot in the head by a bullet, just as he grasped the flagpole."

"A good death, the kind every soldier wishes for, I understand," Nellie said. "I haven't heard anything about the war since I fell ill in Virginia. I was taken to a convent and nursed back to health by wonderful nuns who did their best to keep all unpleasant news from me. I don't even know where the Roundheads are. When I announced I wanted to go back to being an army nurse, the nuns suggested that there might be a need for my skills if I went back to Annapolis, so that's where I'm heading. Could you fill me in on what's been going on?"

"That would be a long story, I'm afraid. When did you leave your regiment?"

"Around the end of July, I think. I wasn't really conscious enough to know the date."

"Well, I'll tell you what. When we reach Annapolis, I'll escort you to the Navy Yard Hospital and introduce you to the medical staff there. That's where the Ninth Army Corps doctors are preparing for our next big campaign to take the city of Richmond. When I tell them of your combat experience, I know they'll want you to join their efforts. And if they choose to assign you to the Seventy-Ninth New York, I will welcome your help. The details of what has happened during the last few weeks will fill themselves in with time."

When Nellie stopped to ponder the course her life had taken, she was amazed to realize how effortlessly she had fitted back into military life. The doctors at the Navy Yard had asked only a few generalized questions:

Did she know how to recognize the most common contagious diseases?

What would she do if a patient came down with malaria and there was no quinine available?

What is the best remedy to soothe a bronchial cough?

What would she serve a convalescent whose appetite had disappeared?

Had she ever seen a combat injury?

Her answers had come so quickly and easily that they soon abandoned any attempt to find the holes in her medical knowledge. Nellie was a prime addition at the hospital, and they welcomed her. Soon she had her own ward of patients and younger staff members to do her bidding. The supply sergeants consulted her about the needs of a field hospital, and the cooks sought advice on hospital menus.

Now and then Nellie thought about the Roundhead Regiment, but she didn't want to ask too many questions, for fear of making her new colleagues question her loyalty to them. She waited and listened. It soon became evident the fortunes of her old regiment had not taken a turn for the better. They had fought bravely at the Second Battle of Bull Run but suffered massive casualties—27 dead and 117 wounded. At Chantilly, they lost another seven men, although their actions had helped save the northern army from suffering a severe defeat at the hands of Robert E. Lee. At South Mountain, they drove the rebels from the field but were not allowed to follow up their victory. And at Antietam, they were positioned on the hill above Burnside Bridge, which protected them from the kind of massive loss suffered by other Union forces but cast them once again in the role of bystanders.

To Nellie, it was an all-too-familiar story. The Roundheads had been on the sidelines at the Battle of Port Royal, the Coosaw Ferry assault, and the taking of Fort Pulaski. When they finally reached the battlefield for the first time, some ten months after their organization, they had been ambushed and driven from the field at Secessionville. On each of those occasions, she had seen the events as sheer bad luck, or someone else's fault, but at this distance from the regiment to which she had felt such great loyalty, the message was clearer. The Roundheads were amateurs, farm boys from the hills of western Pennsylvania, fighting a war with trained military experts. As such, they and all who accompanied them were at a distinct disadvantage.

After the intense fighting in September, the Roundheads had been allowed to take a much-needed break from the action. Rumor had it, however, they would soon be joining the Ninth Army Corps for its march on Richmond. John McDonald confirmed that rumor for her the next time she saw him. "Your old regiment will be with us by the time we march toward Fredericksburg," he told her. "Will you want to rejoin them?"

"No! I can't imagine doing that. There were many rumors about me before they fired me. I would never be able to live down that reputation, no matter how false it is."

"Well, the Highlanders will welcome you as part of our medical corps, if you would like that."

"I would. I've been hearing about plans to set up a field hospital outside of Fredericksburg in anticipation of a great battle. Is that where we would be working?"

"Yes, there's a fine old house across the river from the city. It's called Chatham Manor, and it has plenty of room to stockpile medical supplies and set up wards. It appears to be out of range of the rebel guns, so our group will be moving out there almost immediately."

"And will it serve just your regiment, or a whole brigade, or everyone?"

"We're talking about a centralized medical unit that will serve all three brigades in our Corps. And yes, Nellie, that means you may well end up caring for soldiers from the Roundhead Regiment. Can you handle that?"

"Of course. I don't hold a grudge against the Roundheads. But I do worry about them. They are good men, although many of them are not suited for combat. They have this innocent view of war—that it should be something glorious. Then they see it means blood and pain and death, and they don't know how to deal with it."

"But Colonel Leasure is a talented leader, surely."

"Yes, he is, but he can't completely overcome some of the bizarre notions these men bring with them."

"Such as?"

"They're nearly all Presbyterians, for one thing, and they've been brought up to believe in the doctrine of predestination. I've heard the chaplain tell them nothing they can do will change the plan God has for their lives. If they are meant to survive a battle, they will, and if not, then there's nothing to be done about it."

"Not the best attitude for a soldier, I agree."

"It's deadly. One soldier asked the chaplain why he didn't take cover when someone shot at him. His answer was that, if he ran, it would mean he didn't trust God to protect him. And furthermore, if he ran, he might get in the way of a bullet God meant for someone else."

"So they think they should stand still and dare the enemy to shoot them?"

"They stand up to see where the bullets are coming from, and they get themselves killed." Nellie sighed at the implications of what she was saying. "I loved being a Roundhead while I was with them, but then I'd never seen a trained army for comparison. When I see the drills and preparations that are going on here in Annapolis, it forces me to face the truth about their own weak preparation."

Nellie had felt a pang of guilt when she thus criticized the boys from Pennsylvania, but she was also surprised to discover how liberated she felt for having done so. They don't have a hold on me anymore, she mused. When Reverend Browne told me a war was no place for a lady, I believed him and berated myself for my youth and inexperience. Now I realize a war is no place for a man like him. He was preaching sermons for the folks back home, not for the soldiers who needed real spiritual guidance from him. And when Colonel Leasure tried to make life more comfortable for his regiment by housing them in well-stocked plantation houses, throwing Christmas parties, inviting visits from wives and children, he was really weakening their ability to withstand hardship.

The city of Fredericksburg stood as guardian over the northern approach to Richmond. The Army of the Potomac, under the leadership of General McClellan, had failed to move fast enough to prevent General Lee from establishing a strong Confederate line between Fredericksburg and Richmond. Angry with the Union Army's failure to block Lee, President Lincoln fired McClellan and turned the army over to General Burnside in early November. His assignment: Open the way to Richmond.

The Ninth Army Corps was a key ingredient in Burnside's plans. The medical corps Doctor McDonald had described was in the forefront of what was an amazingly rapid movement of troops. 110,000 men assembled near the small town of Falmouth, located directly across the Rappahanock River from Fredericksburg.

Burnside planned to use a series of pontoon bridges to allow his men to cross the river rapidly and carry the attack straight to the Confederate line. Unfortunately, there were enough delays in the construction of the bridges to allow Lee to position his Confederate line in a nearly impregnable position. Burnside had chosen a location for the bridges that took full advantage of a deep spot in the river where the water currents slowed. But once across the river, the Union troops would find themselves on open fields and headed straight toward a ridge of high ground known as Marye's Heights. There, a half-mile long stone wall provided additional protection for the rebel guns.

By the time the Union attack began, on the morning of December 13th, Lee had amassed such a volume of firepower behind that stretch of wall that the sharpshooters were able to keep up a constant barrage of bullets and cannon balls. Fourteen Union regiments hurled themselves across the Rappahanock and straight into the gunsights of the Confederate line. Wave after wave struggled to reach the base of the stone wall only to be cut down as they advanced.

At Chatham Manor Hospital, Nellie and the rest of the medical staff waited to learn the fate of the Union troops. They could hear the guns, but a tall stand of trees blocked their line of sight. All day long the firing continued. They had anticipated a stream of walking wounded, but not a single soldier appeared to seek their help.

"A quiet day in a hospital is a good day," observed one of the orderlies.

"Perhaps," Doctor McDonald replied, "but it can also mean there are no survivors to need our help."

Swallowing hard, Nellie knew he was right.

By the time darkness fell, putting an end to the attack, some 13,000 Union soldiers lay dead or wounded in front of that stone wall. And now came the parade of stretcher-bearers, carrying grievously injured soldiers to the hospital. Nellie and Doctor McDonald established an initial screening area outside the house. The wounded men were dropped there so the bearers could return to seek other survivors amid the carpet of dead bodies and body parts that littered the ground near the wall.

Nellie and the medics moved through the wounded men, trying by lantern light to separate the most seriously wounded from those who had no further need for medical care. Nellie's practiced eye located those who needed amputations, and those whose abdominal injuries required immediate attention. She paused thoughtfully and knelt beside a young soldier whose face was entirely obscured by blood. Gently she tried to wipe way enough blood to allow her to find the point of injury.

"Let that one go, Miss Nellie. He's nearly lost an arm, and he won't survive a head wound like that." The doctor's voice was kindly, but he was in a hurry to move on.

"No, Sir, I don't agree." She was remembering the operating table at Secessionville, and the lesson Colonel Leasure had given her about Hugh Wilson's injury. "The head wound is a minor one. It's bleeding a lot, but head wounds do that."

"When you compound that with the blood loss from his arm. . . . Look, he's already turning blue." The doctor turned to his next patient.

"He's unconscious and cold, but he's breathing regularly," Nellie said. She called to an orderly. "Bring that flask over here, will you, please?" She offered a lid full of brandy to the man's lips, but he simply jerked away. "Hold still, will you. I'm trying to help." When he tightened his closed lips against her ministrations, she reached out and held his nose closed. In an instant, his mouth flew open as he gasped for air. That was chance Nellie needed. She dribbled a few drops of brandy into his mouth and smiled as she saw the warmth begin to penetrate his consciousness. Slowly she offered him sips until he seemed to relax.

"Now he needs some beef tea," she instructed the orderly. When he looked at her in complete confusion, she almost laughed at herself. "Bring me a small cup of the soup over there on the porch," she explained. Now, she realized, it was Sister Mary Xavier who seemed to be whispering in her ear. I have learned so much from those who have been kind to me, she marveled to herself as she began to spoon up the nourishing broth.

The wounded soldier swallowed eagerly, and at last his eyes opened. "Are you an angel?" he asked. "I thought I was dead. I was dreaming I was dead, and now here I am being fed something warm and delicious by a beautiful young woman. You must be an angel," he insisted, "although I never heard of one covered in blood."

"I'm afraid I can't make that claim." Nelliehe smiled back at him. "I'm a nurse, and you are in safe hands now at Chatham Manor Hospital. You have some serious injuries, but you will be fine. I'm going to have the orderlies move you into the house out of the cold. I think they can find you some blankets, too, to warm you."

"Please. Don't leave me." He attempted to reach for her hand, but the damaged arm refused to obey. Nellie took his other hand and pressed it re-assuringly. "I need to look at another patient, soldier. But I'll be back soon to check on you."

"Once he's a bit warmer, get him some laudenum for the pain," she whispered to the orderly. Then let Doctor McDonald know there is an am-putation waiting for him."

"He's going to lose his arm?"

"Yes, I'm afraid so, but he's not going to lose his life. Now go."

The work continued far into the night. Nellie moved from pallet to pallet, soothing, treating, staunching blood flow, and evaluating injuries. When the last patient had been dealt with, she sank onto the porch steps. The pre-dawn air was bitterly cold, and frost was forming everywhere she looked. Doctor McDonald found her there, clasping her arms around her knees to keep from shivering.

"Come inside, Nellie. You need proper rest if you are to be of any help to the soldiers we have taken in."

"I don't think I can sleep," she responded. "When I close my eyes, all I see is blood, and all I hear are the cries of the wounded."

"Come inside," he insisted, lifting her to her feet. "What you should be hearing is the gratitude of the lives you have saved this night."

"That's a bit strong, I think. I haven't done all that much except hold hands and dish out soup."

"There's at least one young man who would disagree with that assess-ment. His name's Johnny McDermitt, and he's a member of my own regi-ment. He came out of his arm amputation asking for the angel who saved his life. The orderlies tell me that was you."

"Did they also tell you he was disoriented and delusional?"

"Don't make light of his gratitude. If it had not been for you, the staff doctors would have let him die. You have a unique gift, and you use it well. I'm proud of you."

"Thank you," Nellie murmured. She was both touched and embarrassed by his words. To change the subject, she asked, "What happens now? Will they renew this awful carnage as soon as the sun comes up?"

"Not even General Burnside could be so foolish. We have our dead to bury, and that alone will be a horrific task. A flag of truce will give our men time to dig the graves. The troops will withdraw across the river by tomorrow night. There will be no drive onward to Richmond. Burnside will take the brunt of the blame for this disaster, but Lincoln will get his share, too. I'm guessing the whole focus of the war will turn to some other area for a while."

"And the men? What happens to all of those who will need hospital care for a long time to come? And what about the regiments who are here?"

"Rumors have already sprung up. My guess is the Ninth Army Corps will be sent to Mississippi or western Tennessee. There's a new fight brewing there over control of the Mississippi River, and General Grant will be happy to have his forces augmented by ours."

"And the Roundheads? Despite myself, I could not help watching last night for familiar faces among our patients, but I did not see a single one."

"That's because they were not in the fight, Nellie. Your analysis of the regiment may be shared by others. The Roundheads were held in reserve across the river all through the battle. They were ordered not to advance until summoned, and that summons never came. They were tucked safely out of the way. Not a scratch on them, I assure you."

"They'll go west with the rest of the Ninth Army?"

"I would assume so."

"And our patients? Surely they can't be expected to travel."

"They certainly can't stay here for long, especially after the main army departs. This wonderful old house is still considered a prize by the Confederates, and they will reclaim it as soon as possible. Arrangements are already in the works for a massive removal of our wounded to a permanent military hospital. They will be transported right after the first of the year."

"The first of the year!" Nellie shook her head in bemusement. "I keep forgetting the holiday season is coming. Last year at this time, I was planning Yuletide celebrations for a plantation full of slaves and a party for a regiment of bored and homesick soldiers."

"Well, it wouldn't be a bad idea to arrange a bit of festivity for our men here, before they have to head to Philadelphia."

"Philadelphia! Why there? Surely there are hospitals that are closer?"

"Of course there are, but most of them are already overflowing with patients from Manassas, Chantilly, and Antietam. Besides, the new Chestnut Hill Hospital set to open in Philadelphia is supposed to be a model of military efficiency. It should be a wonderful place to live and work. They've even chosen a location where patients can be transported by train right to the door of the hospital.

"So what will you do, Nellie?" he asked. "You are in the enviable position of being able to choose. You can travel with the Ninth Army and see what kind of trouble we get ourselves into next. You can quit and go home, knowing you have contributed your bit to the effort. Or, you can help escort our wounded to Philadelphia. Your services, as I keep reminding you, will be welcome anywhere."

"I'll stay with our patients until they are well settled in the new hospital," Nellie answered. "The men will need someone they know to ease the transition. But after that? I'd rather be back in the field, I think. It doesn't seem right, somehow, to think about settling down in comfort when so many are still suffering."

Nellie was busy during the next couple of weeks. Besides doing what she could to provide a holiday atmosphere, there were many decisions to make about which men could be sent home and which ones needed further hospitalization and treatment. Johnny McDermitt, the young man whose life Nellie had saved at Fredericksburg, was one of those who was almost ready to go home. His amputation was healing without any sign of infection, and he had become skilled at performing most personal tasks with just one hand. "Look," he told Nellie one morning. "I've buttoned my jacket and tied my boots as neatly as ever. Outside of playing my fiddle, I can't think of much I can't do."

"You're going to be fine in civilian life, Johnny. I'm really proud of you for the way you have adapted to your handicap."

"But it's not a handicap, you see. Now if I'd died out there in the cold, that would have been a handicap. But this? This is a minor inconvenience. Except for getting girls, maybe. Do you think they'll mind I only have one arm?"

"A girl who loves you will never notice it," Nellie said.

"What about you? Do you notice it?" he asked.

"Me? Uh, well, I know about it. I . . . I even helped make the decision to amputate. I do see it when I look at you. But what I'm really seeing is how well you have recovered."

"But could you love a one-armed man?"

Nellie suddenly realized the conversation was moving into dangerous territory. "If I loved you," she said carefully, "the missing arm wouldn't make any difference."

"But could you love me?" he repeated. "Could you forget I had been your patient? Could you love me, just for me? Without checking my scar?"

"It's not going to happen, Johnny. You are going back to New York. You are going to receive a hero's welcome when you get home. Your friends and family will be there to greet you, and maybe a special young lady in the crowd will notice only your eyes and your quirky smile."

"What if that's not what I want?" he demanded. "You're the one I dream about. You're my angel of mercy. I don't have to go home to find someone new. I could stay here with you."

Nellie looked away from the unbearable longing on his face and knew there was only one way to shut this discussion down without making him feel ugly and repulsive. What she was about to say would be a lie, but it would put an end to the discussion.

"I'm married, Johnny."

"No!"

"I'm sorry. My husband is in one of the Ohio regiments, and I haven't seen him in over a year. But we're still married, and I'm not free to have this kind of conversation with you."

"You never told me!"

"I just did. I've been your nurse, doing for you what I would do for any of my patients. I didn't realize until now you might be seeing the situation differently. I'm sorry," she repeated. And then, lest he spot the tears that were beginning to form behind her lids, she reached out, briskly shook his one good hand, and walked away.

24

CHANGING SCENERY

At the new Chestnut Hill Hospital in northeast Philadelphia, the central yard housed the administrative offices, along with a parade ground, a chapel, a library, the kitchen and dining hall, and barracks and quarters for the hospital staff. A wide corridor, with tracks for an innovative tram system, encircled the central area. And off that corridor, forty-seven wards branched out like the spokes of a wheel. Each ward had its own running water, flushable toilets, and anywhere from fifty to one hundred beds. The entire hospital could accommodate nearly four thousand patients, but none were far removed from the central service areas. The tram delivered meals, fresh linens, and medical supplies to each ward in a few minutes, and the staff was never far from assistance, should it be needed.

Large windows admitted sunlight during the day, and gas lights illuminated the wards in bad weather and at night. The surrounding yards provided a peaceful and invigorating exercise area for those men who were ambulatory. The air was fresh, the accommodations clean and well-furnished, and the rations plentiful. The women of Philadelphia worked tirelessly as volunteers, providing assistance to the staff of some two hundred doctors and nurses. It was the best possible destination for Nellie's patients, and she was happy she had agreed to accompany them. Clean sheets, nourishing meals, comfortable mattresses, and smiling faces kept the patients happy. And when they were content in their surroundings, their recovery periods were shorter.

Nellie threw herself into her new job. Nursing was a way to reach out to another human being. She pressed a cool hand against a fevered brow or offered a word of encouragement to someone who was feeling down. She was there with a cheerful smile to celebrate each small triumph. She made an extra cup of tea for a patient in need of comfort. She listened to endless stories of family and friends back home, always suggesting by her interest and enthusiasm that the patient would be going home soon. She let sunshine and fresh air into the wards whenever possible and encouraged the ambulatory patients to join her in walks around the gardens.

Not surprisingly, her wards saw quick turnovers, as patients developed the confidence to help with their own recoveries. Nellie inaugurated a small ritual farewell party for each man who was headed home, and those who remained discovered in the custom a renewed hope for their own farewells. Nellie herself was content. She took pleasure in her successes, while trying not to think too far ahead. The end of the war might mean the end of her career, but for the moment, she was where she needed to be, and that was enough.

The restful interlude into which she settled was interrupted in a way she never expected. It was an ordinary day in early February, and she was sitting at her desk, trying to finish her record-keeping. The young man who approached her was an ordinary young man, too, or so she thought.

"Excuse me, Miss. Can you tell me where I might find Doctor Andrew Hopkins?"

Nellie looked up, thinking it odd a private was asking for the Surgeon General of the hospital. "Perhaps I could help you," she suggested.

"No, thank you," the man said. "I don't mean to be rude, but my orders are to speak to Doctor Hopkins directly. I should have introduced myself. I'm Private George W. Earnest, of the Anderson Troop Cavalry. I'm carrying special orders from General William S. Rosecrans."

"I see. Well, then, if you'll follow me, I'll take you to the administration building. I'd send you on your own, but our layout here can be a bit confusing to first-time visitors."

"Thank you. I really didn't know where to start."

"While we walk, why don't you tell me a bit more about who you are and what you need, so I can be sure you get to the right office. You said you were with a cavalry unit?" Nellie was still regarding him with a hint of suspicion.

"Yes. We are now attached to the Hundred Sixtieth Pennsylvania Volunteers, but the old name sticks. The Anderson Troop Cavalry was organized as a special unit assigned to General Anderson's Headquarters in Kentucky. Now we serve with General Buell, and some of us are attached to General Rosecrans's staff. We are escorts, bodyguards, dispatch carriers—whatever the general needs. I'm part of an investigative unit, sent to learn as much as we can about the existing medical facilities here in the eastern theater."

"So you're on some sort of inspection to see if we're operating efficiently?"

"No. I'm not here to judge, I'm here to learn. The major war effort is shifting toward the Mississippi River, and the Union has no adequate medical facilities in the west. General Rosecrans has made the establishment of new military hospitals one of his priorities. Our unit is gathering ideas from established hospitals to guide his efforts. I've been assigned to the hospitals of Philadelphia because my family lives in the area. Actually, I'd have volunteered sooner if I had known the nursing staff was this attractive."

Nellie opened her mouth but no words came out. He was a hopeless flatterer, but a charmer. Another nurse might have been tempted to flirt with him, but Nellie just wanted him off her hands.

"Well, here's Doctor Hopkins's office. Perhaps if you explain your needs to his aide, he'll be able to help more than I."

Nellie almost stumbled in her haste to withdraw. Whatever is wrong with me? she wondered as she returned to her own ward, where several of the younger nurses were clustered in the doorway, heads together. "What's going on here?" she said. "Why aren't you about your duties?"

"Who was that handsome soldier you had in tow?" Maggie Johnson asked, giggling.

"An official visitor. Why?" Nellie was unreasonably irritated at their questions.

"Well, we don't often see someone that healthy-looking around here," Maggie replied. "Is he staying?"

"I have no idea, and it's none of our business. Now get back to work, all of you. If you are looking for men, there's a whole ward full, just waiting for you."

Nellie hoped that would be the end of the incident, but within the hour the young nurse sought her out again. "He's back!"

"Who's back?" Nellie asked, although her heart was already beating a bit faster.

"That handsome young private, of course! He's got Doctor Hopkins with him, and they are asking for you."

"Thank you, Maggie. Now please, quit hovering. I'm sure it's a small business matter. I don't need you drooling at him over my shoulder."

Pouting a bit, Maggie returned to the ward while Nellie made her way to the hall where the two men were waiting.

"Nellie, I'd like you to meet Private George W. Earnest, here on a special assignment. Private, this is Miss Nellie Chase, the nurse you were asking about."

"We've met," Nellie and George said, both of them looking startled at hearing their voices in unison.

"Really?" The doctor cocked his head at them. "When was that?"

"Just now," they both answered, and Nellie was horrified to hear herself giggle.

"Miss Nellie was the first person I met when I arrived, but I didn't think to ask her name. She kindly showed me to your office and then disappeared."

"You said you were looking for Doctor Hopkins. You didn't say you were. . . ."

Doctor Hopkins made an attempt to explain. "Private Earnest had orders to report to me with his papers. General Rosecrans has asked our hospital's full cooperation during his visit. On a personal note, someone in Annapolis recommended you as an ideal guide during his stay here."

Nellie tried to clear her thoughts. "Someone in Annapolis?"

"Doctor John McDonald, of the Highlander Regiment. You'll remember him, I think?"

"Oh, of course. He's the one who sent me here." Nellie and George were smiling at each other. Somehow, identifying a mutual acquaintance had made both of them relax a bit. "How is he?" Nellie asked.

"He was there to reorganize his regiment's medical staff for their move into Mississippi, so he was a bit harassed. But he couldn't have been more enthusiastic about your talents. He fairly insisted I look you up so I could profit from your knowledge of how a hospital functions."

Sensing the conversation was slipping out of his control, Doctor Hopkins made one final attempt to regain their attention. "Miss Chase, can you spare the time to show Private Earnest around for the next several days? He needs to understand how we operate, how our wards are arranged, what measures we take to ensure a clean and healthy environment for the patients, things of that nature."

"I'd be happy to," she said, hoping she was not sounding too enthusiastic—which, of course, she was.

"Well, then, I'll leave the two of you to work out the details," the doctor said as he walked away. Nellie and George did not notice his departure.

"It's fairly late in the day," Nellie said, "but we can start wherever you like."

"How about we start first thing in the morning? I'd like to spend an entire day following you around and seeing how the hospital operates. After that, I'll have a better idea of what I need to look at in detail."

"Certainly. I didn't mean you had to start right this minute. I'm sure you have other business to take care of." Nellie was flustered again.

"I'd really like us to be friends before I get started. Please. Have dinner with me tonight. I'm staying at the railroad hotel. They appear to have an elegant dining room, but I'd feel awkward eating there all by myself."

"Oh! I couldn't. I live here at the hospital and take my meals in the dining hall. That way I'm always available if someone needs me. I can't leave for the evening."

"You make this job sound like a prison sentence. All the more reason why you should let me take you to dinner. You need to get away once in a while."

"But, what would everyone think?" Nellie was grasping at straws.

"I assure you, my intentions are honorable."

"I didn't think you were trying to . . . uh. . . ."

"We'll have a lovely meal, and I'll escort you back here before it's time for 'lights out'. No more excuses. I'll be waiting when you get off duty—at six, is it?"

They did indeed have a lovely dinner. George wisely kept the conversation light, exploring Nellie's likes and dislikes. "Are you a dog person or a cat person?" he asked.

"Oh, cats, definitely! It's hard to have a pet at all when you work in a hospital, but once in a while, a stray kitten comes my way, and I can never resist."

"Why would you prefer a cat over a dog?" he asked, teasing her. "Dogs obey your commands, they are loyal, they'll follow you anywhere. Cats ignore you."

"Cats are loyal and obedient, too, but you have to earn their trust. They don't blindly leap up and lick the face of anyone who pats them on the head."

"Rather like yourself," he said. "I keep having the feeling I'm on some sort of probation here. How does one go about earning a cat's trust?"

"By not being too forward. By letting the cat come to you. By respecting her wishes. By trying to understand her language."

"Oh, come on," he said. "Cats meow. They don't have a language."

"Oh, but they do, once you get to know them. A cat who trusts you will ask for attention by making this strange sound in the back of her throat. It's sort of like a purr, but vocalized. And it means, 'I like you and I trust you enough to tell you what I need.' They greet you in the morning with a cute little chirp, and sometimes you can carry on a long conversation with a cat who is making understanding little comments." Nellie laughed at herself. "You must think I have an over-active imagination."

"I think you've had some lucky cats."

Nellie looked pensive for a moment, and then shook her head decisively. "I've vowed not to adopt another cat until I can be sure I can spend the rest of its life taking care of it."

George realized she might be speaking of a man as well as a cat, but he did not pursue the question.

Nellie also had a bit of probing to do. "Why are you staying in a hotel during your visit? Didn't you say you were from Philadelphia?"

George drew a deep breath before answering. "My parents do, indeed, live in Philadelphia, but we have a problem at the moment. They would be embarrassed to have me staying there."

"Why?"

"They are Quakers."

"Oh." Nellie was not sure what to say.

"And the answer to your unspoken question is, no, I'm not a Quaker any longer."

"I didn't mean to pry."

"Don't misunderstand. I love my parents and I respect their religious beliefs. I just can't share their principles when it comes to a matter of civil war. I tried to stay out of the war for a while because I knew they wanted me to, but it felt wrong to keep on working as a bookkeeper while all my friends were fighting for their county."

"So you enlisted?"

"I thought I could find a middle ground by joining the Anderson Cavalry Troop. Our regiment has special responsibilities that do not include fighting. As a matter of fact, I haven't received much military training of any kind. Certainly no drilling or marching, or artillery firing. But I wear a uniform, and I carry a gun. That makes me an anomaly in a pacifist household. If I get a leave, I go home in civilian dress, and we don't talk about the war. When I'm on duty, I stay away. It's not an ideal situation, but it's one we've managed to live with."

"I can see it must be difficult for you, but it sounds like a good solution. You could have allowed the disagreement to cause a permanent break in your family. Instead, you've all refused to let anger overshadow your family ties. I admire that."

During the next few days, Nellie and George became friends. He was often busy with the general's business, and she frequently had nursing cases that required her attention. But when both were free, they enjoyed sharing a meal or going for a long walk in the nearby park. They were simply friends. Nellie found she could tell George anything without fear he would judge her. Whatever she found the courage to reveal to him he accepted with understanding and compassion. It was an idyllic time for both of them. Despite a war that seemed as if it might never end, Nellie and George shared an outlook that welcomed the future, unafraid of whatever might be coming their way. They were enjoying their lives, their jobs, and each other.

One morning, Nellie was waiting for George's arrival with more than her usual excitement. "I have wonderful news," she told him. "John McArthur, the architect who designed this hospital, will be here next week to see how our buildings are working. He's under government contract to build a number of other new medical facilities, and he wants to re-examine Chestnut Hill to see what improvements could be made."

"Nellie, I. . . ." George looked apprehensive, but couldn't seem to finish his sentence.

"Don't you see? It's the perfect opportunity for you to meet him and discuss his plans."

"It would be that, if I were going to be here." His voice was flat.

"What? What do you mean?"

"I mean I won't be here. Our investigative unit is scheduled to re-assemble in Annapolis on Friday, and then we return to Nashville to submit our reports."

"But I thought . . . I assumed you would be here for as long as you needed to be. Couldn't you tell them you're not finished?"

"Nellie. You know the Army doesn't work that way. I have written orders and train passage. And General Rosecrans doesn't like his soldiers to go about making their own plans. I'm sorry you didn't realize we were almost finished with our mission."

"No, no, it's my mistake. I should have paid closer attention to your schedule." Despite herself, she felt her eyes flooding. "It's been a pleasure to work with you."

"You sound like you're saying good-bye."

"That's what this is, isn't it? You leave tomorrow and head back to Tennessee. We're finished. That's fine. Now I can get back to my own work."

"What on earth do you mean? No! Please don't say *we're* finished. I have to go to Nashville. That's where my duty lies at the moment. But you know I have ties to Philadelphia. And I value your friendship, far above our professional relationship. I'll be back, I promise. As often as I can." George's voice was rising, and he fought to control it. The devastation on Nellie's face was overwhelming his own deepest emotions. "We'll talk more about all of this tonight. We'll have dinner and hash it out."

By dinnertime, both Nellie and George had given themselves some strong lectures, and they each came prepared to deliver a much-rehearsed concession speech. After a couple of strained moments when both started to speak at once, George dipped his head in graceful defeat, and gestured for Nellie to go first.

"I'm sorry. My reaction was selfish and short-sighted. Of course you will return to Nashville. You need to go as quickly as possible. The general needs your information on how to establish medical facilities. I want you to go." She swallowed hard. Those words had come out with difficulty.

George started to answer, but she held up her hand to show she was not through. "When you said you would be going to Nashville, I think my first reaction was jealousy. You will get to be a part of this new endeavor in the west, and I will miss it."

"You don't have to. . . ."

"No, let me finish. It finally occurred to me I might be able to be of some help from here. If the general has questions we have not covered, you can write to me, and I'll respond immediately. If there is equipment you need or supplies you can't get through military channels, you can let me know, and I can contact the Ladies' Aide Society here to see if they can help. If you need additional staff, I can send recommendations your way. If you happen to come home on leave, we can have a visit. It will all work out for the best."

"In this best of all possible worlds?" George rolled his eyes at her and grinned. "Are you through playing the role of Voltaire's Pangloss?"

Nellie sputtered a bit. She couldn't decide whether to be impressed with his literary knowledge or insulted that he thought her an overly-optimistic old fool. "I only meant that. . . ."

"Nellie, hush. All your suggestions are wonderful. I'm delighted and grateful you want to help. But I have come up with a plan of my own. Will you hear me out?"

Taking his words as rejection, Nellie slumped back in her chair and dipped her chin. "Of course," she said.

"All right. I've gained a great deal of knowledge since I've been here, thanks entirely to your efforts. I'll be organizing my notes during the long train ride between here and Nashville, and I'll have a plan ready to submit to General Rosecrans as soon as I can gain an audience with him. I'll be prepared to implement my recommendations—with the possible exception of one. That one will depend on the general himself, and on your help."

He paused and regarded her speculatively. When she responded only with a cocked eyebrow, he hurried on. "I'm going to advise the general that what he needs most is a strong woman to take on the position of matron in his main hospital. I intend to suggest your name."

Nellie shut her eyes and swallowed again. "You want me to come to Nashville?" she said, not sure she had understood him correctly.

"Correction. I want General Rosecrans to invite you to come to Nashville. I want him to look at your qualifications and recognize you as by far the best person for the job. I want you there, of course, but I don't want anyone to think I have an ulterior motive in all of this. I want to see my plans succeed because they are in the hands of a capable and experienced administrator."

He paused and grinned at her. "If it happens that the capable and experienced administrator is also an attractive and delightful young woman, all the better for me."

By now, Nellie's eyes were wide with excitement. "Oh, George. What a wonderful opportunity that would be. Do you really think the general will find me qualified enough?"

"I'll see to it personally."

The next three weeks were some of the longest Nellie had ever experienced. George's investigations had taken up more of her time than she had realized. Without him there, she had little to do, except for minor duties in the wards. She found herself wandering about the hospital grounds, grumbling to herself about her own lack of enthusiasm. Most of her Highlander patients were gone—on their way home or back to active duty. Newcomers to her wards were there to finish a convalescence and didn't need much personal attention from her. The younger nurses twittered over every new man who came in, but Nellie saw each one only as three more meals and an additional set of linens to be added to her daily requisition sheet. With each passing day, she became more convinced she would never hear anything more about a move to Nashville. She quit anticipating the day's mail delivery, sure it would bring only more disappointment.

"Nurse Chase?" Her supervising doctor interrupted her thoughts. "Doctor Hopkins would like to see you in his office. Right away, please."

He's probably going to chastise me for having a bad attitude, she guessed. Maybe he's going to fire me and I can go home. If I had a home, that is.

With unwelcome memories of a similar interview with Colonel Leasure swirling in her head, she had to stop for a moment outside the commander's closed door. Then, straightening her back and assuming her best expression of respectful interest, she knocked and entered.

"Sit down, please." Doctor Hopkins regarded her with a wrinkled brow. "Miss Chase, are you unhappy here?"

"Well, maybe feeling a bit under-utilized at the moment, but, no. Why do you ask?"

He picked up a sheet of paper and scrutinized it. "I have received a letter from General Rosecrans asking that you be released from your position here to take a job in Nashville. You know about this, I assume?"

Nellie caught her breath. "I knew there was a possibility I would be offered a position, but I did not know you would receive the request before I did."

"It's the doing of that young Private Earnest, I suppose. The one who was smitten with you."

"Private Earnest and I became friends while he was here, and he asked if I would be interested in moving to Nashville. He offered to recommend me for a job under General Rosecrans, but that's all there was to our discussion. I have heard nothing from Private Earnest since he left here."

"Well, he's obviously been acting on your behalf. Are you really interested in this new job, or is this an excuse for the two of you to be together?"

"Sir! I beg your pardon, but I think you are making a great many assumptions on the basis of small evidence. There's no such thing as 'the two of us' and further, even if I go to Nashville, Private Earnest won't be there. He told me before he left that his regiment would be moving almost immediately into southern and eastern Tennessee."

"So you are really interested in a position in a Nashville hospital—one that is apparently being cobbled together from existing buildings—rather than working here in a institution that represents all the latest and best medical advantages? Somehow I find that hard to believe."

Nellie floundered for a way to make herself understood. She didn't know much about this man, but it was obvious he was going to regard her departure as a personal insult. Anger bubbled up from somewhere deep inside, but she pushed it back. Lashing out at him was not going to help. That was one lesson she had learned from her year with the Roundheads. She opted for honesty.

"Chestnut Hill is, indeed, a marvel of efficiency and convenience," she began. "I could not ask for better working conditions. But for me, it's too comfortable, too safe. I signed on with my first regiment, the Twelfth Pennsylvania, because I needed to do something good with my life. I didn't exactly crave danger, but I came in with a desire to give my life, if necessary, for the sake of my country. I still pursue that goal.

"Here at Chestnut Hill, I feel like things are being done for me, not by me. I don't want to be comfortable. I want to spend my time doing things to make others comfortable. Surely you can understand that.

"I've lived in a tent, survived a hurricane aboard ship, managed a household of abandoned slaves. I've watched men die, treated hopeless cases of deadly disease, helped with amputations after one battle, and dressed wounds in the dark on another battlefield. I have skills that deserve to be used, not avoided. I want my life to have meaning. When I'm not working, I feel useless. So, yes, I want to go to Nashville and help cobble together a hospital for people whose lives are in imminent danger. And I'm not expecting to get anything out of the experience other than the knowledge than I have given of myself to people who really need me."

The train ride from Philadelphia to Nashville took four days, and included stops and train transfers in Philadelphia, Pittsburgh, Alliance, Crestline, Bellefontaine, Indianapolis, and Louisville. Nellie was nervous about the stop in Pittsburgh, but she saw nothing except the depot and the railroad hotel. She suspected not many of the people she once knew there were still around, although the smoke and soot hadn't changed much.

She ventured a small complaint, asking a conductor why they were heading west when their destination was south. Her fellow passengers were quick to point out that if she wanted to risk her life by taking a train through Confederate territory she might do so. As for them, they preferred a roundabout journey during which they did not have to worry about somebody blowing up a trestle under their train. Nellie took their point.

From what she saw on the last leg of their journey, much of Tennessee was still a wilderness. The mountains came up without warning, and the valleys between them were deep and unbroken by traces of civilization. The railroad track disappeared quickly behind them, and the way ahead was usually invisible until they were actually on it. But, oh, how green this state was!

Nellie hoped George would be waiting on the platform to welcome her, but he wasn't there. Instead, a pimply-face recruit of barely eighteen years waited, holding up a badly-lettered sign that was supposed to say "Miss Chase." Nellie let him know he had found his target, and he rushed her through the process of gathering her valise and small trunk.

He had a rickety wagon waiting, and without comment he pushed her up onto the board that served for a seat, clucked to the old mule, and set off down a muddy street heading into the heart of the city. Nellie caught only a glimpse of the magnificent Capitol Building sitting high on a hill overlooking the river. Then they were passing though what seemed to be residential streets. "Is the hospital located in one of these homes?" she asked her young escort.

"No, M'am. We ain't headed to no hospital. This here's the Cunningham House. The gen'rel said to bring you straight to him."

"General Rosecrans?"

"Yes'm."

They stopped in front of an elegant Renaissance-Revival style mansion. Several soldiers were milling around outside the wrought-iron fence. "I'll wait here with your things 'til he's through with you," the young man said, not offering to help her down. She clambered down by herself, feeling terribly awkward, and approached the entranceway. A soldier with a rifle slung across his chest stepped in front of the door and demanded to know who she was.

"I'm Nurse Nellie Chase, here at the order of General Rosecrans," she said, trying to sound official and businesslike.

"You are, huh? I'll check."

When he finally returned, he led her though a central vestibule to a book-lined study. General Rosecrans was an intimidating figure. Heavy brows shaded his dark eyes, and he stared at her down an incredibly long Roman nose. His neatly trimmed beard could not hide the fact that his face bore several nasty scars, one of which twisted the corner of his mouth into a perpetual smirk. He chewed on a large unlit cigar and looked her up and down until Nellie felt she was shrinking into the ground.

"So you're Nellie Chase," he finally commented. "Been readin' 'bout you." He gestured toward a folded newspaper on his desk.

"Reading about me?" she asked, puzzled.

"Don't you know 'bout the letter from a one-armed man that's been circulating all over the northern papers?" He waved a much-folded sheet of newsprint at her and then squinted at it, hunting his place. "Seems the gentleman, whoever, he is, thinks you are, to quote him, 'a noble girl . . . an angel of mercy . . . a woman with the soul to dare danger; the heart to sympathize with the battle-stricken; sense, skill, and experience to make her a treasure beyond all price.' Guess we're lucky to get you here."

Nellie was still at a loss for words, although the mention of a one-armed man told her immediately the writer must be Johnny McDermitt. Perhaps this was his way of working through his feelings for her, but it made her uncomfortable to know he was publishing them in this fashion. Unable to think of a suitable comment, she simply waited to see what else the general might have to offer.

"So! Private Earnest tells me you are the only one capable of organizing the kind of centralized hospital system I am planning. Daniel Leasure and John McDonald both praise your work for them. My good friend, Salmon P. Chase, says you may be a distant cousin, and if so, you'll have the strong Chase character to recommend you. And now an anonymous one-armed man calls you a 'treasure beyond all price.' That's a lot to live up to, young lady. Are you prepared for it?"

"You've been checking up on me," she said. "You even contacted the Secretary of the Treasury?"

"Why not? Salmon and I have known each other all our lives. Of course I asked him if he knew you, since you share a surname. He said to ask you if you knew which of your Chase ancestors was the first to arrive in America."

"My father drilled that information into all of us from the time we were children. His name was Aquila Chase. I didn't forget it because I thought it sounded silly."

"That's the one. Ah, but its Latin meaning makes it a noble name, does it not?"

"Aquila? Oh! The eagle!" Nellie was surprised to realize she had never made that connection. The general, for his part, gave a bit of a nod, as if she had passed his literacy test.

303

"And that particular eagle seems to have given rise to many outstanding descendants. We'll see how well you live up to your noble family. Now, have young Clyde and his wagon deliver you to the Ensley Building in downtown Nashville. That will be the center of the hospital complex I am planning to set up with your help. There are a few patients there already, and a skeleton staff. They'll have your room ready, and you can start in the morning to learn your way around. Welcome to Nashville, Miss Chase."

25

OCCUPIED NASHVILLE

Nellie met Doctor Jacob R. Ludlow, director of Hospital #3, the next morning at breakfast. He, too, was new to Nashville, but he fairly bubbled with enthusiasm for the plans General Rosecrans had laid out.

"I'm happy to have you here, Miss Chase. Your reputation precedes you."

Nellie cringed. "I'd prefer to let my work speak for me, Sir."

"I'm sure it will. But first, you need to get yourself oriented."

"I didn't see much of my surroundings last night," she said. "Is this whole building part of the hospital?"

"Ah, yes, the renowned Ensley Building. Nashville considers it the finest architectural jewel in the city—all five floors of it."

"It's five stories tall? And we're using all five floors? That sounds difficult." Nellie realized she was being prematurely critical and bit her tongue.

"It's a problem, yes. How to utilize it properly is one of our first priorities. But this is not our only property. We're also meant to use the Jones Hotel, catty-cornered across the street to our right, as well as a four-segmented commercial building over on Broad Street. And finally, we have the use of a couple of private homes and an elegant mansion next door to the commercial building."

Nellie shook her head. "You are right. I need to get my bearings. At the moment I can't imagine how that all fits together."

"Well, if you don't object, I've taken the liberty of arranging a tour for you. A young soldier from the Anderson Troop cavalry stopped in a couple of days ago to inquire about your arrival."

Nellie's heart started to beat a little faster and then plummeted at his next words.

"His name is Bill Currin. He said he was a friend of a friend of yours. Seems your young man, George Earnest, is down in Murfreesboro on the general's business, so he asked Private Currin if he would help you get settled."

"I see. Forgive me if this sounds rude, but I don' t have a young man, as you put it. I know George Earnest, it's true, but he has no reason to feel responsible for me or to arrange for a substitute on his behalf. I'll be perfectly fine looking around on my own, thank you."

"I'm sorry. I didn't mean to offend. But young Mr. Currin seems like a capable fellow, and he's already agreed to bring a carriage around this afternoon and show you the sights of Nashville. It would save me embarrassment if you would accept his offer."

Nellie certainly did not want to start her new job with a quarrel, so she nodded her head in tight-jawed agreement. "In the meantime, I'll prowl around the Ensley Building, if that is all right."

"Certainly. Explore wherever you wish."

By the time Bill Currin arrived to take her on her introductory tour, Nellie had grown upset and impatient with her situation. The Ensley Building might well have been the most beautiful architectural structure in all of downtown Nashville, but that was only from the outside. Inside, its stairways were narrow and dark, too steep to allow someone to carry a stretcher to one of the upper floors. The bath facilities on each floor were centrally located, which might be fine for travelers but highly inconvenient for hospital patients. Worse, the rooms had only one window apiece, and the windows themselves were sealed shut. The hallways, too, were unventilated, and already the air was hot and stuffy. What must this be like in summer? Nellie thought. The place makes me want to punch a hole in the wall.

"What would you like to see first?" Bill asked as he helped her into the carriage. "How're your accommodations, by the way? Are you comfortable? Got everything you need?"

"That building's a tomb!" Nellie said before she thought to temper her words. "I need fresh air."

"Well, then, we'll take a ride out to the state capitol first, to let you breathe a bit."

Despite her brewing anger, Nellie was impressed by the Capitol Building. From its hill overlooking the Cumberland River, its towering bell chamber dominated the skyline. Each of its four sides had its own portico, supported by heavy Ionic columns. Around the base of the building, earthworks and palisades protected the entrances, and parrot guns trained their sights on the city below. Military tents lined the surrounding hillsides.

Nellie found the contrasts disorienting. "I can't decide where the power lies," she said. "That huge Greek temple up there speaks of an invincible state government, but the military trappings around it seem to hold it captive."

"As indeed they do," Bill agreed. "Ever since Andrew Johnson was appointed military governor at the beginning of 1862, wags have referred to this as 'Fort Johnson'. Those cannons have never been fired on the city, but the threat is enough. This capital city of a Confederate state has become a Union stronghold, and the citizens of Nashville are not allowed to forget it."

"What was Nashville like before the war? How did this all happen?" Nellie asked.

"When Nashville became the permanent capital of Tennessee, it developed into a cultural, educational and medical center. At the start of the war, the population was around thirty thousand, with maybe twenty percent of that number slaves and free blacks. The city had theaters, a fresh water system, and gaslights. The University of Nashville had the finest medical college south of Philadelphia, and the city's female academies drew students from all over the South. People called Nashville 'The Athens of the South'."

"It sounds lovely."

"Yes, but unfortunately for Tennessee, its capital had little in the way of defenses. There are two navigable rivers that run through the state. One is the Cumberland, which you see in front of you; the other is the Tennessee, seventy-five miles west of here. Both of them flow north into the Ohio River. At the northern border, Fort Henry guarded the Tennessee River, and Fort Donelson, a few miles further east, protected the Cumberland. In early 1862, Grant led attack against those two forts, and they fell within a day or two of the attack. With both rivers open to Union boats, the citizens of Nashville evacuated the city in panic, and Confederate troops only hesitated long enough to burn a few facilities and a bridge before they, too, fled ahead of the arrival of the Federal armies."

"So our armies simply marched in?"

"Some did. Others came across the Cumberland by boat. But by the time they arrived, most of the citizens of Nashville were gone. Not much glory in walking into a deserted city, I'm afraid."

"Still, I can see that occupying the capital city of a Confederate state was a major coup."

"The first task of the Union was to turn the city into a war materials storage depot for potential attacks on the interior southern states. Since most of the city was empty, we took over warehouses and turned homes and stores into military barracks. Schools, hotels, and churches became hospitals both for the sick and for the wounded. We've converted the railroads and wharves to exclusive military use, and we've added two new bridges across the Cumberland to facilitate the movements of troops and supplies. But we have neither the time nor the resources to improve the city itself. Thus you'll see the contrasts—unpaved streets and rough sidewalks leading to luxurious mansions. The wealthy citizens left behind some comfortable lodgings for our commanders. The common people who couldn't afford to leave are the ones who have to deal with poor sanitation, high death rates, and poverty."

Heading back toward the center of the city, Private Currin pointed out the buildings surrounding the Public Square—the huge City Hall and Market, the Central Courthouse, whose architecture echoed that of the State Capitol, and the Southern Methodist Publishing House, where the Union was now printing army forms. Most of the other fine buildings around the Square had been confiscated as storage facilities, some for ordnance and others for medical supplies.

After taking her back past the Ensley Building to allow her to regain her bearings, Currin took her on a tour of the other buildings that would make up Hospital #3. Nellie was particularly interested in the Jones Hotel, which boasted a huge dining hall and kitchen, along with a laundry facility that extended down to the river. "This will work," she said. "We can consolidate facilities here and serve all the other buildings. And the smaller buildings will do well as separate wards for the sick."

Private Currin couldn't contribute much to her musings, but he was happy to see her mood had improved. "I know the people you need to meet to make all that work," he said. "As it happens, we have a supper invitation."

"Oh, no, I couldn't possibly. . . ."

"You're anxious to get back to horrid hospital food?" he asked.

"No, but whoever you are talking about—they're strangers, and they won't want to be bothered with me."

"On the contrary, the Camerons won't be strangers for more than five seconds, and they are anxious to meet you."

"Why? Who are they?"

"James Cameron is the sutler General Rosecrans relies upon, so if there's anything—absolutely anything—you need for your hospital, he's the man who can find it for you. And Matilda, his wife? She mothers everyone she meets. She's heard all about you from George, I'm afraid, and she practically demanded I bring you straight to their house for supper tonight. As a matter of fact, that's their house right across the street, and Mrs. C. has already spotted us. You can't possibly refuse now."

"I don't like being manipulated, Private Currin." Nellie frowned at him. "You've been most helpful this afternoon, so I'll go for supper, if you insist, but then I want to be taken back to the Ensley House as soon as possible."

"You must be Nellie," Matilda Cameron exclaimed as she came down the front steps to meet her guests. "Goodness, child, your hands are cold. You must have caught a chill riding around in that open carriage. Come inside now. There's a fire burning and we'll get you warmed up in a jiffy. Have you had an interesting afternoon? I hope Bill, here, was a satisfactory guide. I know George gave him some pretty strict orders about what he was to show you."

Nellie couldn't help but smile as the older woman hustled her into the parlor. Matilda took her shawl, settled her into a comfortably padded rocking chair by the fire, and then scurried off to find a cup of tea, all before Nellie could open her mouth to answer one of the questions that flew past her. As much as she usually hated to be fussed over, it was lovely not to have to make polite conversation. Moreover, the house was full of delightful cooking aromas. Nellie identified fresh-baked bread and chicken, along with a faint whiff of onion. She was surprised to discover she was hungry.

"Thank you, Mrs. Cameron," she managed to say before the next volley of questions hit her.

"Oh, you're welcome, dear. We're delighted to meet such a close friend of George's. He's told us all about how you met in Philadelphia, and how you're going to make over General Rosecrans's hospital system. Have you decided how you're going to handle that monstrosity of a building? Is there anything we can do to help?"

Nellie held up her hands, whether to stop the questioning or to surrender, she wasn't sure. "I've only arrived," she reminded them. "It will take a while to determine how to make the best use of our facilities."

"Oh, but George says. . . ."

"Mrs. Cameron. . . ."

"Call me Matilda, won't you? I want us to be such good friends."

"All right. Matilda. But please understand. I don't know what George has told you, but we're not all that close. And he really knows little about me."

"Ah! He knows enough to be head over heels in love with you."

Nellie sighed. "I'm an Army nurse. Soldiers tend to fall in love easily when they are lonely, and we nurses seem much more available than we really are. I'm here in a professional capacity only, and we'll have to wait and see if I can make any noticeable difference in the hospital. I don't expect to make any difference in George Earnest's life at all."

"That's where you're wrong, dear. I'll lay you odds on it."

"Matilda, quit berating George's young woman," James Cameron spoke for the first time. "Maybe she doesn't want to discuss her love life with you yet."

Nellie clenched her teeth to keep from shouting at him. I'm not George's young woman, she thought furiously.

"Come along to the supper table, then. I've cooked us up a pot of chicken and dumplings. Nothing's better for making you feel at home. And there's a lovely apple cobbler for dessert. We'll talk about George later."

Not if I can help it, Nellie muttered under her breath as she let herself be led to a warm and steamy kitchen table. Once they were settled, Matilda turned the conversation toward Nellie's professional responsibilities.

"Have you had a chance to think about how you will organize Hospital #3? It's such a hodge-podge of structures."

"Actually, that works in our favor," Nellie said. "One of the lessons I learned while I was at the Chestnut Hill hospital in Philadelphia was that the wounded and the ill need to be kept separate."

"Why's that?" Matilda asked.

"In the field, where we don't have a choice, a broken leg may be in one bed and a measles case in the next. And if the broken leg case hasn't had measles before he arrives at the hospital tent, he'll have them before he leaves. Here, all those separate buildings on Broad Street can serve as disease wards, and we can lessen the chances of diseases spreading among healthy young men recovering from war wounds."

"That makes good sense, dear, but do all those buildings have the necessary facilities to house the sick?" Mrs. Cameron looked skeptical.

"No, they don't. But that's the other lesson from Chestnut Hill. It's vital we be able to centralize our meal preparation and laundry areas. The Jones Hotel has everything we'll need to do that, if I can figure out the transportation problem. In Philadelphia, we had a cog tram to carry supplies from one ward to another, and clearly we can't do that here."

"No, not with our streets as muddy and rutted as they are. But there's a way to handle it," said James Cameron. "Nellie, I can get you all the push carts you'll need, and you can use the sidewalks to move your linens and meals. There's a surplus of labor among the free blacks and former slaves here. They'll jump at the chance to serve as runners."

Nellie was suddenly excited about her job again. "Wonderful, but how do I go about arranging all of that?"

"Draw up a list of what you'll need, submit it to General Rosecrans, and he'll pass it on to his favorite sutler," James grinned. "I'll have your centralized system up and running in short order. Now, what else do you need?"

"Well, then, since you're solving all of my problems, what can you do about the Ensley Building?" she asked. Nellie was holding her fork in mid-air but had forgotten to eat.

"What's the major problem?"

"More transportation, but vertical this time," Nellie said. "I think we'll use the beds at the Jones Hotel for our most serious cases, and keep the Ensley Building for our convalescent wards. The exercise of climbing all those stairs will help our patients regain their strength, and if they have to come down to the main dining hall for their meals, it will get them all up and moving. One problem will arise when our nurses have to carry linens and other supplies up those same flights of stairs. The more serious issue, however, is ventilation. Fresh air is vital, and those sealed windows are of no earthly use. If we could get them opened, with some sort of protection to prevent falls, it would help. My big wish, however, is to open some of the walls for dumb waiters and ventilation shafts. How's that for a dream?" Nellie laughed at herself.

James wasn't laughing because he was busy calculating. "We can do it. Opening the windows only takes a small pry bar to break the seals. Then I'll find you some railings to use as protection. As for the shafts, I suspect the building is honeycombed with hidden shafts that were used during construction. We'll have to find them and open them up again."

"Really? It can be done?"

"In the Army, labor is never a problem. What's usually missing are fresh ideas. But since you already have those, I promise you the workers and materials to make them a reality. George certainly knew what he was doing when he recommended you for this job." Then James bit his tongue.

He hadn't meant to mention George and he waited, half expecting another denial from Nellie.

Instead, she grinned back at him. "That's what I've been trying to tell everyone."

The next several weeks were so busy Nellie seldom had time to think about anything except the formidable list of tasks awaiting her attention. As Bill Currin had promised, the Camerons proved to be an invaluable resource. James had quickly hired a crew to open the windows of the Ensley Building. Then he went off to the Courthouse and managed to find the original plans for the building's construction. Just as he had predicted, the shafts Nellie needed for dumb waiters and ventilation were already in place. Now the task was to break through the walls to reach them, a process that involved a great deal of noise and even more dust and debris.

Meanwhile, Matilda was busy locating employees for the new hospitals. There weren't many Union sympathizers in Nashville, but the ones she knew were eager to be doing something to help with the war effort. Soon, Nellie had a class of nursing recruits to train, as well as a kitchen staff to improve the quality of the hospital's menus.

George's name seldom came up. Everyone around Nellie had learned it was not wise to suggest Nellie was interested in him. No one asked if she had heard from him, and no one told her when he might be coming back to Nashville. Thus Nellie was caught off guard one June morning when an orderly told her a young man was asking for her at the front door. Brushing construction dust from her hands, she hurried down the stairs, only to be brought up short by the sight of a familiar face in the doorway.

"George!"

"Nellie, my dear," he reached out to greet her. "I'm sorry I've been away from Nashville so long. I didn't even know for sure you would be coming— or when. I should have been here to welcome you."

"Why?" She glared at him. "You're not responsible for me, although you seem to have led several people around here to believe otherwise."

"What? You seem angry and I don't understand why. What have I done? You knew I would be tied up with official regimental duties, didn't you?"

"I'm upset—and have been for some time—that you led the people I was going to be working with to believe we were an item. I'm not thrilled to see you now because it has taken me weeks to get people to quit referring to me as 'George's young woman'. Now here you are on my doorstep again, acting as if we are the best of friends."

"But we are, aren't we? Back in Philadelphia, you certainly gave me the impression we could be friends—maybe even more than friends."

"Yes, I suppose I did. But I was being foolish. I tend to do that when I act before I have time to think. This job sounded wonderful then—and it's wonderful now. For that I am grateful to you. But I've come to realize I can't have a personal life and a professional life at the same time."

"Nonsense! You can't mean that."

"I certainly do. Look, George. I'm a woman trying to function in a man's world. Ever since I joined my first regiment, well-meaning folks have been telling me a war is no place for a woman. I make people uncomfortable because I am somehow out of place. I have to work constantly to show I am good at what I do and I am serious about my work. Any hint of a relationship with a man throws a shadow of doubt on my intentions. If I'm to be the head matron of Nashville's Hospital #3, I can't also be 'George's young woman'. Do you understand?"

"I understand what you are saying, but I can't believe you're right. Surely we can be friends without raising suspicion."

"No, I'm afraid not. You took care of that possibility by whatever it was you told all your friends about me. Mr. and Mrs. Cameron were convinced we were a couple long before they met me. I've needed their help in many ways, and you made that more difficult. You even had General Rosecrans leering at me as he asked whether I was really up to the responsibilities of this job."

"I . . . I'm sorry, Nellie. I never meant to cast doubt on your capabilities. I was excited about bringing you here so we could have more time together."

"Exactly, and you let all your feelings show—to my detriment. You need to go away, George. I don't want to be seen with you. You need to let all your friends know you have no interest in me. Go on about your duties and forget about me."

"Nellie. . . ."

"No. Enough. Good-bye, George."

Nashville's summer was unbearably hot, and Nellie blamed the weather for her own misery. To avoid the heat, she worked longer hours, starting earlier in the morning and continuing until late at night. She was a demanding and exacting supervisor. She checked on every project several times a day, and no small omission escaped her notice. No one complained that she was unreasonable or unfair, but neither did she encourage any familiarity from those who worked with her. If asked, they would have said no one disliked her. But no one liked her much, either. She was unfailingly polite, but cold and distant to her employees. Even the Camerons gave up asking her to the house for a meal or a social event. Only with the patients themselves did she allow herself to relax. The sicker the man, the kinder she became.

Her hard work paid dividends, of course, as she knew it would. General Rosecrans returned to Nashville after the Tullahoma Campaign had run its course, and on July 16th, he began a tour of all the hospitals and defenses in the city. Work was still going on in many of the hospitals, but he pronounced himself well-pleased by the improvements he saw. Nellie's influence had encouraged an emphasis on cleanliness and fresh air. Most medical facilities were running smoothly, their staffs well-trained and well-organized. Hospital #3 itself was a model of efficiency. Nellie's plans to designate the Broad Street units as disease wards had resulted in a dramatic drop in the death rate. And her plan to keep the convalescents exercising themselves on the stairs worked to send men home or back to their units sooner than expected.

At the end of his review, Rosecrans called Nellie in to praise her accomplishments. "Is there anything you lack?" he asked.

"Yes, but I don't know how to solve the problem."

"Name it."

"Well, our patients are comfortable enough. They have fresh linens, good food, knowledgeable care, a chance to exercise in the sunshine and fresh air of this beautiful climate. What they lack is mental and social stimulation. We have staff enough to do what is necessary, but not to spend time with the patients. They need visitors, books, music, things to do with their hands, religious services, games, social hours. . . ." She stopped, having run out of breath.

The general cocked his head at her. "Sounds delightful, but maybe impractical for a hospital, don't you think?"

"No, I don't. In many of the northern cities, there are Ladies' Aid Societies to provide such activities. I'm not talking about the services of the Sanitary Commission, but about groups of women whose husbands and sons have gone off to war. They find their own comfort by caring for the soldiers in hospitals. They come in with cookies, books, fresh flowers, Bibles, whatever they can think of to make life cheerier for the patients. I've seen women set up painting classes, chess tournaments, musical entertainment. They write letters for those who need help, they share pictures of families, and sometimes they just listen."

"And we have nothing of the sort going on in Nashville."

"No, Sir. As you know, there aren't many women in Nashville anymore. Those citizens who chose to take a loyalty oath to the Union and keep their businesses open to serve our needs—even they sent their wives and daughters off somewhere for safety. Matilda Cameron was able to find a few women with Union sympathies to fill out our hospital staffs, and they are doing a fine job. But we need women with leisure time on their hands, and we just can't find them."

"I wish I could help, but even I can't create a supply of such lovely ladies for you."

"I didn't expect you to," Nellie said, "but I thought I'd mention it just in case you hear of a bored housewife or two. . . ."

"I'll be sure to let you know."

Nellie thought no more about her impossible suggestion. She knew the general had no time for such a flippant request, and she was a bit ashamed she had even asked. Then, almost a month later, she received another summons to Rosecrans's headquarters. As an aide showed her into his office, the general waved a newspaper at her. "Been reading about you again. You certainly have a way of getting yourself into the papers."

"I can't imagine what. . . ."

"Another fellow falling in love with his nurse, I suspect. Listen to this."

A Western soldier, at Nashville, writes of Miss Nellie M. Chase, the Florence Nightingale of the Western army: "As a Western soldier boy, I take pride in acknowledging—and I speak of the Western boys in the army—that we have the real Florence Nightingale of the United States army with us, and, were it within their power, every soldier who had in any way been thrown under her care, or within the range of her influence, would procure a picture of Miss Nellie M. Chase, and preserve it as memorial of the chief deliverer of the suffering soldier in this war, wherever she operates. I seek not the opportunity to speak of her noble deeds, but, as a patient of her hospital, and a witness of her unparalleled kindness and services, I wish to add the testimony of one, not of her adopted state, that by her deeds of kindness, her superior skill and judgment, her coolness and powers of endurance, both of body and mind, she has already gained a name that will be handed down to succeeding generations, by hundreds of sick and wounded soldiers who may have been the recipients of her care.

"That little article appeared in the *Philadelphia Press* on August 19th. Tell me, Florence Nightingale, what exactly is it you do to these young men?"

"I have no idea, Sir. It's really embarrassing."

"No need to be embarrassed. It suggests to me you are doing something right—and you are probably right about the need to have more women working in the hospitals. How would you like to take a trip for me?"

"A trip to. . . .?"

"Philadelphia. To talk to one of the founders of the Ladies Aid Society there."

"Oh, no, Sir. I couldn't possibly get away for something like that."

Rosecrans lifted one of his famous eyebrows at her. "Miss Chase. When a general of the army asks if you would like to do something, your only choice is to say yes. It's an order, couched in polite terms. Got that?"

"Yes, Sir, I understand, but. . . ."

"Miss Chase. Kindly quit talking and start listening. You leave on Monday. Your train fare will be covered by official orders. You will go to Philadelphia and meet with Mrs. John Harris. She is expecting you. If she likes you—and I do mean if—she will arrange for us to receive some personnel to start a Ladies' Aid Society here in Nashville. Further, she will keep you supplied with the kinds of things their ladies take to the hospitals—Bibles, books, writing materials, games, all the things you mentioned. You asked for this, and I have arranged it. Now go and start getting ready to leave."

"Yes, Sir."

"Oh, and while you're at it, in Philadelphia there's a fellow named Gutekunst. Takes good photographs. Go to his studio and have some *cartes de visites* printed up. If our patients want pictures of you, they shall have them." The general held up his hand. "And don't protest that, either. I figure it's best to encourage all these young blades to fall in love with you. The more suitors you have, the less chance you'll take off with any one of them."

26

THE POWER OF WORDS

By the time Nellie returned from Philadelphia, General Rosecrans and his army had departed for Chattanooga, where they were preparing for the push into Georgia. To many observers, it appeared the Confederacy was suffering its death throes. The fall of Vicksburg and the Union victory at Gettysburg suggested the Federal forces were carrying the war away from Nashville. Despite a few guerilla attacks on Middle Tennessee, the clearest evidence of declining Confederate strength came from an influx of rebel prisoners sent back from southern Tennessee.

Then, in the Battle of Chickamauga on September 19th and 20th, Confederate General Braxton Bragg drove Rosecrans and his army back to Chattanooga. The losses from those two days of battle were staggering on both sides. In a three-day period, over 12,000 rebel prisoners were paraded through the streets of Nashville on the way to their detention barracks. The news that many soldiers from Nashville's most prominent families had died in the battle caused further grief among longtime residents of the city. Union sympathizers mourned their own losses, as on one day alone over 900 seriously wounded Union soldiers arrived for treatment in Nashville's military hospitals. Bragg, although ultimately victorious, had lost some 20,000 men, Rosecrans's losses numbered 17,000.

For Nellie, one day blurred into the next. She moved from bed to bed, offering what little comfort she could to men who had suffered amputations and other crushing injuries. By September 28th, every available bed was full, and it seemed there could not possibly be any further disasters. But that morning, a blast rocked the city. A steam locomotive had exploded minutes after leaving the Nashville station. Although there were no deaths, the flying shards of metal had caused innumerable injuries to both soldiers and civilians. When another rumbling explosion occurred the next day, even the usually nerveless Nellie leaped to her feet in alarm.

"What was that?"

"Cannon fire?"

"No, it lasted too long."

By now, people were rushing by in the streets, and Nellie hurried to the doorway.

"Is this a hospital?" one passer-by asked. "Can you come? The convalescent barracks at the Maxwell House Hotel has collapsed."

Grabbing her medical bag, Nellie rushed toward a cloud of dust rising some four blocks away. Near the site of the disaster, a cordon of soldiers blocked access to the shattered building that had housed Confederate prisoners.

"Let me through," Nellie demanded, but a strong hand grabbed her arm and turned her away.

"This here's a dangerous place, M'am. The rest of them walls could come a tumblin' down most any time. It ain't no place for a lady such as yourself."

Nellie's struggles only resulted in the soldier gripping her arm even tighter. Then someone clasped his shoulder and pulled him back. "Let go. Take your hands off of her, Private. This woman is a trained nurse. She is needed inside."

"But, Lieutenant, they said. . . ."

"Never mind. Come on, Nellie. I'll help you through."

"George?" Out of breath and terrified, Nellie looked at him in complete puzzlement. "Where did you come from? What are you doing here?"

"Later. We'll talk later." He helped her to climb over a pile of rubble and led her to a semi-open area, where rescuers were depositing the victims of the disaster.

"You can do the most good here. Can you do a quick assessment of the men's condition as they come out? You'll know better than we will whether a case is serious or a minor injury."

"Of course." Nellie snapped into a battlefield role she thought she had left behind after Fredericksburg. She fell to her knees beside a young and frightened prisoner whose head was bleeding profusely. Reaching into her bag for a handful of lint, she pressed it against his wound.

"Look at me, Son. I need to see your eyes. Ah, you're going to be fine, I think. Head wounds like yours bleed a lot, but they're not serious. You'll have an impressive black eye for a while, but you can probably get up and navigate your own way out of here. Want to try it?" She stood and held out a supportive hand. "There. I knew you could do it. Keep pressing that lint against your forehead, and check in with one of the doctors outside."

"Over here, please," someone called. "This fellow's got hisself trapped under some boards."

Nellie quickly looked for blood and then moved to see if she could reach the trapped man's foot. Putting a hand gently on his ankle, she pushed his stocking down and ran a fingernail over his leg. "Can you feel that?"

"Feel what, M'am? I don't hurt at all, but I can't seem to move."

She pinched him hard. "Now?"

"No, M'am."

"All right. Just lie still for a moment while we figure out how to get you out from under that beam. Can someone find me a wide plank we can slip under his back?"

"Why don't we pull him out first and then worry about finding a way to carry him?"

"Because he has a serious spinal injury. If you pull him out, you'll kill him."

And so the day went. Nellie examined victim after victim, offering reassurance to those with minor injuries and directing the more serious cases to the waiting ambulance wagons outside. It was late afternoon before the captain of the rescue squad came in to thank her for her efforts.

"That's all of them," he said. "Everyone has been accounted for. We've lost six men and sent ninety-one to Hospital #19 for treatment. But we're lucky there weren't more casualties."

"It seems silly to ask now, but does anyone know what happened?"

"Apparently the prisoners were headed down from the fifth floor to go to breakfast. The stairway tore away from the wall under their weight, and then the other floors collapsed under the weight of the falling debris. The lucky ones were those who had the furthest to fall but ended up on top of the heap. Our deaths occurred among those at the bottom. We're glad you were here, M'am. Good thing Lieutenant Earnest found you."

"Lieutenant? George?" Nellie looked around to find him standing behind her. "What's going on? Since when are you a lieutenant? And what were you doing here?"

"It's a long story, Nellie. I was going to suggest I tell you all about it over dinner. But if I'm as dirty and blood-streaked as you are, we probably shouldn't be seen in public."

Nellie laughed. "I think you're right, but I'm starving. We've been at this all day. Why don't you come back to my hospital with me. We can get washed up, and I'll ask the cook to find something for us to make up for today's missed meals."

Nellie was too exhausted to notice the raised eyebrows and knowing smiles that greeted her as she and George stopped in the dining room. "Bertha, we're back from helping with the casualties over at Maxwell House, and neither of us has eaten in hours. Is there anything left over from lunch, or ready in advance of dinner?"

"Yes, M'am. I've got a nice Brunswick stew that's simmering away on a back burner, and fresh bread's about to pop out of the oven. Will that do?"

"Perfect. If you'll show Lieutenant Earnest where the men's cloakroom is, I'll stop by my quarters, and then we'll be ready to eat. Can you tuck us away somewhere quiet? It's been nerve-wrackingly noisy all day over there."

Bertha smiled behind her hand and then nodded solemnly. "Yes'm. I'll set you up some plates in that small meeting room across the way."

George and Nellie began eating immediately when Bertha served their dinner. Both were too famished to make polite conversation. After a few bites, George looked up at Nellie apprehensively. "I know you asked me to stay away, Nellie, and I've tried to do that, but it's good to see you again."

"And you, George. But how did you manage to drop from the sky at the moment when I needed you?"

"Perhaps I'm really your guardian angel," he suggested.

"I doubt that. Seriously, what were you doing there? I thought you were in Chattanooga with the general."

"I was part of the unit that delivered the prisoners from Chickamauga. As a matter of fact, I was in the Maxwell House barracks moments before it collapsed."

"Oh, no! You might have been killed."

"That fact has not escaped my notice, believe me. I had just left when I heard the rumble behind me. When I turned to see what was going on, the floors were coming down." He shuddered at the memory. "And then you were there, being pushed away by that young private, and my only thought was to get you to the men who needed you."

"Well, the rescue was most welcome. Now, what about this lieutenant business?"

"My promotion's new. General Rosecrans has asked me to become commander of a company of the Thirteenth U. S. Colored Infantry."

"Really? I've never even heard of them."

"That's because they don't exist yet. We're about to start recruiting efforts here in Nashville among the free blacks and emancipated slaves. They'll be put through some basic training, and then they—we—are to be employed as guards and laborers while a railroad line is extended from Nashville to the Tennessee River."

"I like the idea of giving the freed blacks a way to serve their country. It should provide much needed employment, as well as giving them some self-pride. When I was in South Carolina with the Roundheads, I learned the slaves there were capable of much more than anyone gave them credit for."

"I've been hoping to have a chance to talk to you about that. Not to-night—we're both too exhausted. But you've had experience dealing with newly-freed slaves, and I'd value your suggestions on how I can best do my job."

That set the stage for a renewed friendship. Nellie and George were both swamped with responsibilities, but now and then they found time to share a couple of hours. Perhaps unwittingly, George had found one of the keys to Nellie's affection. She tended to resist any attempt to instruct her or assist her, but she could not resist reaching out when someone needed her. They met now and then to discuss George's new command. Nellie had several suggestions to make, most of them emphasizing the need to respect the cultural differences the colored troops brought to the army experience. George, for his part, had much to learn, and since his lessons made Nellie smile, he was her eager pupil.

Nellie continued to face the demands of overflowing hospital wards, assisted now by several recruits from the Ladies Aid Society of Philadelphia. True to her promise, Mrs. John Harris came to Nashville at the beginning of November with several assistants in tow. Other help arrived, too, including a group of volunteer surgeons from Indiana and nurses sent from the Sisters of Charity in Cincinnati. General Rosecrans provided Nellie with papers that authorized her to requisition whatever she needed for her patients. With Nellie directing their efforts, the newcomers soon had the hospitals of Nashville running smoothly. Nellie even managed to send Mrs. Harris to Louisville for turkeys and all the accompaniments to provide Thanksgiving dinner for every hospital patient.

Meanwhile, George and his troops helped to lay seventy-five miles of railroad track. When the line was finished, it proved to be a key factor in breaking the remaining strength of the Confederate forces. This rail link allowed supplies to be transported via the Tennessee River, conveyed directly to Nashville, and then distributed to General Sherman's army as he marched through Georgia.

By May, 1864, George's role in that success brought him once again to the attention of his superiors. He returned to Nashville to serve in the Headquarters of the Army of the Cumberland. He also had a pending job offer from the Louisville and Nashville Railroad. His first act, naturally, was to call upon Nellie at Hospital #3.

"Come have dinner with me. I have all sorts of things to discuss with you." He reached for her hand and pulled her from her chair.

"Oh, I can't possibly leave right this minute, George. I have paperwork to complete, and doctors' rounds to observe. And there's no one to supervise the night duty nurses in the wards."

"Nonsense. This place runs so well they probably won't even notice you're gone."

"But. . . ."

"Come on, Nellie. We've had this conversation before. I don't make many demands on your time, but right now I need you."

Once they were settled at a quiet table at the City Hotel, George took a deep breath and began. "The war is winding down, Nellie. Sherman's march on Atlanta is about to begin, and that will surely spell the end of Confederate strongholds in Georgia and South Carolina. It's only a matter of time. Have you thought about what you intend to do after the war?"

"I suppose I'll keep right on doing what I'm doing now," she answered. "The end of the war will not mean a miraculous end to the suffering it has engendered. Our wounded soldiers will need medical attention for a long time."

"Yes, but they'll be making the transition to civilian hospitals. Ever since General Rousseau took over Nashville Headquarters from General Rosecrans, he's been making contingency plans to close the hospitals here. The citizens of Nashville are going to want their homes and businesses back."

Nellie's eyes widened in alarm for a moment before she straightened her shoulders. "I suppose I hadn't thought about that. Well, then, I shall do what I have done in the past. If someone moves my patients, I'll accompany them and keep on treating them wherever they go."

"Don't you think it's about time you start worrying about Nellie Chase instead of the anonymous soldiers who pass through your wards?"

George held up his hands to stem her coming protests. "All right. I won't argue with you. But let me tell you about my own dilemma concerning the end of the war. My enlistment was for a three-year period. It will be over in December. I could sign on again, but I've been given a tempting offer. Mr. Guthrie, who runs the Louisville and Nashville Railroad, came out to observe our new rail line. He seems to have been particularly impressed with the records I'd been keeping. Called them the 'most meticulous example of good book keeping he had ever seen.' The upshot is, he's offered me a job with the L&N as their chief bookkeeper. He's willing to wait till December, but no later."

"So you'd be moving to Louisville?"

"No. He says I can remain in Nashville if I want. It doesn't matter which end of the railroad I choose to make my headquarters."

Nellie was trying to conceal her relief. "I think it's a wonderful chance, George. Jobs are going to be scarce when all the soldiers return home at once after the war. You'll be lucky to have secured your own position ahead of time. But don't you want to return to your family in Philadelphia?"

"You know the situation there. I love my family, but we get along better from a distance. I can't say the same about you and me, however. I want to be wherever you are. If you'll allow me to be underfoot all the time, that is."

"Well, I'd be delighted to have you here, but I don't want you making that kind of decision for my sake."

"Why shouldn't I? I want you to marry me, Nellie. We can get married here in Nashville now, before the end of the war. I will have a steady job with the L&N railroad, and later we'll go wherever the duties of that job take us."

"No!" Nellie started to stand, and then sank back into her chair as she realized tears were welling. "I'd be afraid to marry you, George." Nellie was shocked she could actually say those words, but this was George, after all, the friend to whom she had been able to confess all of her darkest secrets. "I've never been 'in love' and I've almost never witnessed a truly loving marriage. I don't know what it is I feel for you, and I can't guarantee I will always feel the way I do now. How can I make promises when I can't be sure I can keep them?"

"You've lived your life one day at a time, haven't you? That's what you indicated you would do about your own job."

"Well, I've learned to do that at work, yes, but. . . ."

"So that's how people get through a marriage, too—one day at a time. We're good friends, Nellie, and beyond that, I happen to be tail over teacups in love with you. I want to wake up each morning knowing you are there beside me, that no matter what troubles the world has to offer us, we will be strong enough to overcome them, as long as we face those troubles together.

I trust you with my life, and I would lay down my life for yours. That's what love is all about, even if you don't recognize it—yet!"

It was destined to be a happy marriage. The Camerons pitched in to offer their home for the ceremony, and members of George's old cavalry regiment turned out to give the affair a formal military touch. On June 8, 1864, Nellie Chase became Mrs. George W. Earnest.

The year of separation had given both Nellie and George the time to hash out their areas of disagreement and to fill in their appreciation of each other as individuals. Nellie's last lingering fear that she would be unable to love her new husband evaporated when she walked into her new house for the first time. There, warming herself in a spot of sunlight, was a small calico cat. Her fur was long, and her marking were so distinctly irregular that she looked like a fluffy little clown.

"Oh, George," Nellie cried. She fell to her knees and held out her hand. The kitten looked at her and yawned. Then she stretched, one leg after another, before approaching Nellie. She sniffed curiously, and then rubbed the side of her head against Nellie's outstretched hand.

"I think she's saying, 'Welcome home, Momma'," George said.

Nellie scooped up the kitten, who purred contentedly under Nellie's chin. Struggling to her feet, Nellie threw her free arm around George's neck. "I don't know what to say. I have never received a gift of love like this one."

"Are you talking about the kitten's love?" George grinned at her.

"No, yours. You always know exactly what I need. I can't believe you actually had a cat waiting for me! Oh, she's adorable. Does she have a name?" Nellie's excitement was bubbling over.

"I've been calling her Patches, but you are free to change that. She's your cat."

"Patches is perfect. That's where I found her—in a patch of sunlight—and her fur is in patches, too. Oh, George," she cried as the happy tears flowed. The kitten, who was being crushed between them, struggled free and jumped to the floor, where she set about the important task of grooming the fur Nellie's enthusiasm had ruffled. Nellie laughed through her tears. "The perfect cat. She even knows when to leave us alone!"

The Civil War that had dominated Nellie Chase's entire adult life ended when General Lee and the Army of Northern Virginia surrendered on April 9, 1865. As George had predicted, the first closures included military hospitals. The existing patient load at each hospital had to be evaluated. The staff could submit the names of those who would continue to need hospitalization and extensive care in the years to come. Serious cases were assigned to regional or state medical centers. The remaining patients were sent home.

Nellie struggled with the paperwork involved with the transfer of both groups. Finding beds for the long-term care patients was a more difficult task than it sounded, and the patients themselves were feeling great anxiety about what was to become of them. Nellie tried to be as reassuring as possible, but she could answer few of their questions. They wanted to know where they would be sent, but until she received an acceptance letter from the hospital in their state, she could tell them nothing. "They look at me with such fear in their eyes," she complained to George. "I've always been the one to reassure them, but I have no reassurances now, and it breaks my heart."

Nashville recovered quickly, once again functioning as the capital of Tennessee instead of an occupied city under military control. For Nellie and George, however, it grew more and more inhospitable. Although the new legislature seemed to be, at least temporarily, in control of men who were loyal to the United States, there was an undercurrent of bitterness and barely suppressed anger. Yankees were unwelcome and assumed to be nothing more than opportunists bent on profiting from Reconstruction. When Mr. Guthrie suggested George might be better off in Louisville, he jumped at the chance to start afresh.

Nellie had worried she would find nothing to do in Louisville, but she soon discovered the end of the war had given rise to a series of philanthropic ventures. A new Home for Aged Women provided shelter and care for the widowed wives and mothers of Civil War soldiers. One of Nellie's neighbors was a champion of women's suffrage and ran the local branch of the Women's Educational and Industrial Union. Another neighbor left half his estate to charity shortly after Nellie arrived in Louisville. His bequests were designated for the creation of a public park, a public high school, and an orphanage.

Each of these institutions offered Nellie an outlet for her organizational talents. She shared her medical knowledge with the staffs of both the home for women and the orphanage. She became a familiar visitor, bringing dishes to tempt the appetites of the women and stories to expand the knowledge of the children. She filled her spare time with such activities, worked hard to make a comfortable home for George, and tried not to remember the time when she had had a career of her own.

One evening in the fall of 1868, George came home carrying a hefty book. "Have you seen this?" he asked.

"I don't think so. What is it?" She read the title: *Women of the War: Their Heroism and Self-Sacrifice*, by Frank Moore. "What has that to do with me?" But she was afraid she already knew.

"Turn to page 536."

"Nellie M. Chase," she read. "Oh, no. How on earth. . .?"

"This Frank Moore is the son of an army nurse. To honor his mother, he wrote letters to soldiers asking them to tell him about their own favorite nurses on the battlefield. Apparently one of his contacts sent him a copy of an anonymous newspaper article. The author could not resist the story of a nurse who saved a man's life at Fredericksburg. The book is in our local shop, and our friends and neighbors are sure to see it. I suspect you are about to become famous."

"Maybe no one will recognize my maiden name."

"I don't know. Some surely will. In fact, that's how I learned abut the book myself. Mack Sweeney, who owns the stationers' shop, came into my office this morning, all excited, to ask me if this 'angel of mercy' was my wife."

"What did you say?"

"I told him I hadn't read it, so I didn't know."

"How bad is it?"

"It's not bad. It's a wonderful tribute to your virtue, but the author says he has not been able to find out anything more about you than appears in the story sent to him from a one-armed volunteer."

"Johnny McDermitt!"

"Yes, I suspect so. You'll be more certain when you read the entire story."

There it all was—the story of his wounding in front of the stone wall, his regaining consciousness in the dark, the kind voice that corrected the doctor who thought this victim was too far gone to be helped. He described the liquor she had given him to stimulate him, and the warm soup that followed. In the words of the wounded man, she was "a noble girl . . . an angel of mercy . . . a woman with the soul to dare danger; the heart to sympathize with the battle-stricken; sense, skill, and experience to make her a treasure beyond all price." He even disclosed her attachment to the Roundhead Regiment and the fact she was an unpaid volunteer, one whose only reward was "the unbounded admiration and gratitude of the private soldiers, who almost worship her."

"It's a wonderful story, Nellie. You should be proud of your contribution. We'll not call attention to this, if you wish, but I don't think you should deny it, if the question arises."

"But, George, words are always a two-edged blade. They can be used as praise or turned to do infinite damage. I don't want to be praised for what I did in the heat of battle. Some are sure to misunderstand or expect me to be someone I'm not. What if a member of the Roundhead Regiment reads this and decides to track down the woman who was suspected of having an affair with the colonel? Or what if someone recognizes the name of the runaway Nellie? I should never have involved you in my life!"

"You don't mean that. Nellie, you are my wife, and we have a bountiful life together. Don't wish it away because of a few pages in a book."

"I don't wish to change a moment of it. I only fear something or someone may attack us from outside, and we won't be able to stop the damage. I would never forgive myself if you became the focus of gossip or ridicule because of something I did in my foolish past."

"That's not going to happen, my dear. I won't let it."

"But you may not be able to stop it."

"I can encircle you with the protection of my love. I have told you before, but I'll remind you again. No matter what the world throws at us, we will be able to survive it as long as we have each other."

Once again, George seemed to know best. Some of their friends did ask whether she was the woman in the book. They knew, of course, that she had been an army nurse throughout the war, so they turned to this popular account to see if she was included. Since there was only one 'Nellie' in the roster of nurses, connecting Nellie Earnest with Nellie Chase was a natural thought. Nellie never denied the question, although she was always reluctant to talk about her days as Nellie Chase. Most of her friends respected that and did not pursue the question. Nor did it strike them as unusual.

"It's not surprising to me, my dear," George told her. "I've been telling you there was no need to worry. Nellie, the woman you are does not resemble the young girl you were in 1861. No one, looking at you now, would see anything but a sophisticated and capable woman. Today's Nellie is loved by wrinkled old shrews who complain bitterly about the treatment they receive at the hands of every one, with the exception of lovely young Mrs. Earnest, who always has time for them. And she is equally loved by the small children in the orphanage, who climb into her lap and beg for another one of her wonderful stories.

"That's what you need to accept for yourself, Nellie. Put Nellie Chase Leath to rest. She is long gone. Then welcome your grown up Nellie and enjoy the full flowering of your personality. When you give up the load of youthful guilt you are carrying around, you'll find that all those other grown up burdens are easier to bear."

And that might have been the end of the story, except that one person—Nellie never did know who—wrote to the publishers of Moore's book, telling them who Nellie Chase was and where she could be found. This bearer of tales, the Earnests decided, did not mean any harm. He—or she—was trying to be helpful. But it did open the door for one last meeting of the old Nellie and the new one.

One day a letter arrived from Frank Moore, addressed to Mrs. George Earnest. The writer wasted no time in asking if she was the real Nellie Chase. He plunged into the reason for his contact. He had received an anonymous letter concerning Nellie, and he wanted her to know that a question had been raised about her reputation. He was offering her a chance to respond to the implied accusations in the anonymous letter. He had included a hand-written copy:

Dear Friend,
I do not like to write anything that I am not willing to put my name to, but you will excuse me when you know it—only to give you a hint—that if you intend issuing another edition of the Women of the War, that you had better make some enquiries about Miss Chase's character before you put her along with true-hearted girls like Georgy Willets, Mary Shelton, or Miss Maria Hall. Most any one of our old Roundhead Reg't, except the Colonel can give you a great deal of information.

Nellie sighed as she read the letter for the second or third time. Who would do such a thing? she asked herself. And why? What purpose does this vague threat serve? She handed it to George, and he read it aloud.

"Who does it sound like, Nellie? Obviously it comes from one of your sainted Roundheads because he speaks of 'our regiment.' Who would do such a thing, throw such a slur at you and your colonel?"

And then she knew. Absolute certainty almost took her breath away. "It's Reverend Browne. It has to be that sanctimonious Robert Audley Browne. He's the only one who openly questioned my character. But why? Why would he do this now? It's been years since I saw him last. He won the fight. He drove me out of the regiment. What more could he possibly get out of doing something like this, something so cowardly that he is ashamed to put his name to it?"

"It's probably guilt, Nellie. When did he actually see you last?"

"When I was being carried off to the convent, I suppose. I remember he had been in to see me the night before. He came to see if I needed consolation in my last moments, since he had heard I was near death. He may not even have known I survived until he read this book. My devoted one-armed soldier made the comment that I always considered myself a member of the Roundhead Regiment. I suppose Browne could not stand to think of that—to know I survived—and that I am now being praised for being 'an angel of mercy'. What a bitter man he must be."

"Why does he hate you so?"

"I've never known the answer to that. He did hate me from the moment he first laid eyes on me. He saw me running into a soldier's tent and assumed I was a prostitute. No matter how many times Colonel Leasure explained I was a nurse doing my best for the men, he could not see beyond that initial impression. He also idolized Daniel Leasure, but when the colonel took my side in each of our many clashes, he must have felt betrayed by the man he considered his hero. In some ways he came to hate Colonel Leasure, too. He was willing to tarnish the Leasure name to make his accusations against me sound more valid."

George shook his head sadly. "A man of the cloth, too. He must have known with a part of his mind that what he was doing to you was wrong. How guilty he must feel, that he is still trying to prove he was right."

"It is sad," Nellie agreed. "For a long time, I hated him, too, but I've moved beyond that. Now I simply pity him."

"So what are you going to do about this letter? Will you answer it?"

"No, I don't think so. You know, our friends know, and I know, there is no basis for his accusations. Frank Moore is not going to change his book on the account of some anonymous letter-writer, and there is nothing I could say to correct an accusation that is only hinted at, never expressed. The war is over, George, and that phase of my life is behind me, too. I have no reason to look backwards. You have taught me—and taught me well—to leave the past behind and concentrate on making the future better. That's what I am going to do."

She looked at the letter one more time, and deliberately tossed it into the fireplace. They watched it glow, turn to white, and then crumble into dust.

Epilogue
SEPTEMBER, 1878

Nellie came out onto the porch of the Railroad Hotel in Paris, Tennessee, plucking her damp collar away from the back of her neck. Then, after checking to be sure that no one else was around, she pulled the neckline of her dress away from her body and blew several cooling breaths between her breasts. She usually loved her Sunday afternoons. Once their guests finished the main meal of the day, she had no duties until supper time. George was busy over the week's books, and the usual influx of railroad officials looking for inexpensive lodgings was not due until the next day. It was a time to relax, reflect, and recharge her energy.

Today, however, the late summer heat hung oppressively over the hotel and its grounds. Even Gingersnap, Nellie's big orange tomcat, lay sprawled on his stomach, paws extended front and back, chin planted on the floor, eyes squeezed shut against the glare of the sun. "That's a pretty undignified pose for a cat," Nellie told him. "I've seen dogs assume that 'full-frog' position, but cats are supposed to curl up in fluffy balls."

Gingersnap merely flicked the tip of his tail at her.

"Never mind. I'm jealous that I can't join you."

Nellie stood at the railing and gazed at her favorite views—first the yard, bursting with late summer blooms. The hydrangeas were beginning to look a bit papery, but the magnolia and crepe myrtle trees still filled the yard with their blooms. Nellie bent over and plucked a hollyhock. Using the fully opened flower as a skirt and a barely breaking bud as a head, she recreated the hollyhock doll of her childhood. Then with a shake of her head at her own foolishness, she tossed the flower at the cat. He opened one baleful eye at her and went back to sleep.

Next, she looked up and to her right, where the crenellated towers and widow's walks of the town's antebellum mansions still encircled the downtown area at the top of the next hill. Paris was a small town, if one compared it to Nashville or Louisville, but it was energetic, friendly, and beautiful. When Mr. Standiford, the new president of the L&N, first told George that he was being transferred to Paris to run the railroad hotel in 1874, the young accountant had been disappointed. Nellie, however, was happy to leave Louisville and return to Tennessee. They had been sharing a triple house with two other couples, both of whom had small children. The racket and laughter of the children was a constant reminder to Nellie of her own childlessness. Then, too, the philanthropic efforts she had been using to fill her time were simply not satisfying enough to give her a useful purpose in life. "Most of these women," she complained to George, "only want to take on a project if there's a chance of getting their names in the newspaper. I want to do something important with my time."

Here in Paris, Nellie was a part of every day's activity. The hotel was not large by most standards. It had six rooms upstairs and three downstairs, along with the "chain gang" room where train crews who were passing through could grab a quick nap. The dining room, however, was large enough to feed not only the hotel guests, but anyone who was employed by the railroad. Nellie and George had their own apartment on the ground floor, so they could always be on call.

Since Paris was a major crew transfer point on the line that ran from Memphis to Bowling Green, Kentucky, a steady stream of soot-covered trainmen made their way in and out of the hotel. For every one of them, Nellie provided a hot meal, a clean bed, and a kind word. While George kept the accounts, both at the hotel and at the depot, Nellie supervised the hotel staff. She had the help of a wonderful cook named Emma Williams and a man of all trades, Chester Price, to do the repairs and heavy lifting. In many ways, the hotel reminded her of her days in Beaufort, and she reveled in her responsibilities.

"I don't know about you," she told the cat, who had awakened enough to stretch out even further, "but I think I could be content to spend the rest of my life here. Except maybe in early September! I'd certainly be grateful for a cooling shower."

Restless because of the heat and stillness in the air, she walked to the other side of the porch to look down at the train depot. It was usually deserted on Sunday afternoons, so she was first surprised, and then alarmed, to see a crowd of men milling about on the platform and front sidewalk. "George! Can you come out here? There's something happening at the depot."

"The damned fools!" he exclaimed as he joined her on the porch. "Sorry for the language, Nellie, but I've been afraid it would come to this."

"What would come to what? What's this all about?"

"What you're seeing is fear in action. Surely you've heard some of the talk about the yellow fever epidemic that's been spreading up the Mississippi River from New Orleans."

"Yes, of course, but it's seemed pretty far removed from here."

"Well, we've actually had two cases in Paris, and it's getting really bad in Memphis. The most recent news from there says—wait, I'll get it." He returned bearing a folded newspaper and waved it at her.

"You won't believe these numbers."

"Whew! What's that smell?"

"Every paper that comes in from Memphis has been sprayed with carbolic acid before it's allowed on the train. That's supposed to kill the germs, or something."

"Ridiculous!"

"Yes, of course it is, but that's not my point. Here's the reason for the fear. The paper says 596 people have died there from yellow fever in the month of August, and the numbers are multiplying. On Friday alone, over two hundred people sought treatment from the Howard Society and the YMCA. The paper's full of horror stories, too, like an old woman whose husband died at home. The servants fled in terror, and no one will come to pick up the body. She reports he is about to burst open and soon won't be fit to pour into a coffin. She's sitting there by herself while he rots."

"That's horrific."

"Yes, and that's what people fear will happen here if the fever gets a foothold. Everyone seems to have a different way method of protection.

The citizens of Memphis are abandoning the city if they are healthy enough, and wealthy enough, to get out. Many of them are headed here, hoping to visit Sulphur Well, where the fumes, they think, will keep the germs away."

"That sounds positively medieval—like carrying around a clove-studded orange to ward off the plague."

"Exactly, and about as useless. Governor Porter is recommending that each Tennessee city pull out their left-over Civil War cannons and fire them off to keep up a protective cloud of smoke. And I know what you're going to say, Nellie," he said with a smile. "If the smoke of gunpowder warded off disease, there wouldn't have been so many deaths during the war. But that's the point, you see. When people feel helpless, any action is better than no action. So, someone started the rumor that yellow fever is being spread by the railroad, and there was some talk yesterday of stopping anyone who tries to get off the trains here. Looks like somebody decided to do exactly that. I've got to get down there."

"Wait, George. Take me with you."

"No. You'll be safer up here."

"I don't need to be safe. Most people know I'm a nurse. Maybe I can help answer their questions and talk some sense into them."

The crowd outside the depot was not in a mood to listen. A man with a shotgun barred the door when George and Nellie approached. "You cain't go in there, Mr. Earnest. There's Yellow Jack in there!"

"Stuff and nonsense. I was there this morning. Nobody's sick."

"There is now, since the noon train pulled in from Memphis. That there mechanic of yours and his two hostlers were aboard one of the freight cars. They got off puking their socks up, right there on the tracks. We've got 'em corralled in here, and they ain't gettin' out to spread the sickness."

"You have Pete Henderson locked in there? Let me see him."

"No, Sir, you cain't go in there."

Suddenly, George's whole demeanor changed. Instead of the mild-mannered accountant, the former Union army officer strode toward the door. "I can, and I will! Moreover, I'm taking my wife, who's a trained nurse, with me. This is my depot. Now clear off, the lot of you, because I'm opening this door."

The blustering men drew back as George flung the door open and took Nellie's arm. It was stuffy inside, and the air smelled of sweat and stale tobacco juice. Huddled on the wooden benches lay three miserable men. Pete Henderson raised himself on one elbow in acknowledgement of his boss's arrival.

"I'm sorry to have made trouble, Mr. E. We can't have yellow fever, 'cause we wasn't near anybody sick in Memphis. We went down there to deliver a spare part and fix a locomotive that was stuck with a broken flywheel. Then we jumped right back on the train and headed home."

"The men outside said you were throwing up. Is that so?" Nellie asked.

"Yes, M'am, and you would have, too, if you'd had to ride all that way from Memphis in a boxcar stinking from sulphur powder, creosote, and carbolic acid."

"No doubt. However, I'd like to examine you for myself, if you don't mind."

"Nellie, it may not be wise to get too close to them."

"And how else are we going to determine whether they are infected, George? Let me do my job." She bent over each man in turn, checking pulses, listening to their breathing, and noting the goose bumps on their arms despite the heat of the day.

"Do you have a headache, Mr. Henderson?"

"Yes, M'am, from all those fumes."

"I see. Can I bring you something to eat?"

He grimaced at the thought of food. "No, thank you kindly. My appetite's kind of puny these days."

Nellie drew George to one side. "It's a bilious fever of some kind, certainly. Their heartbeats are like little bubbles under the skin. They're pale, chilled, and dehydrated. I can't say it's yellow fever without the evidence of black vomit, but I suspect that will come soon enough. We've got to get them to a place where they can get proper care."

"There's no place to take them, Nellie. When Thankful Caroline Terry and her husband had the yellow fever in town a couple of weeks ago, not a single doctor would attend them. People locked them in their house and stayed away. They died at home, alone, and there was trouble enough finding somebody willing to bury them. If we have yellow fever here, all we can do is quarantine the victims where they are, put up a sign to warn folks off, and then burn the place after they are gone."

"You realize that would sentence them to death, don't you? I can't allow that. Go bring the wagon down from the hill and we'll take them to the hotel."

"You can't do that. You'd be exposing every railroad employee to the fever."

"To quote you, George, I can and I will. That's my hotel, too."

"But. . . ."

"The second floor is unoccupied. We'll put them, and whatever other patients turn up, in those rooms, close off the stairs, and keep everyone else away. With proper care, many people who get this disease develop only mild cases and survive without ill effects. We've got to give them that chance. You, Emma, and Chester can run the hotel downstairs, and I'll handle the nursing upstairs."

"Nellie! Think what you're saying. I can't let you sentence yourself to death."

Nellie shook her head impatiently. "I'm not going to catch it, George. I've already had the fever, down in Hilton Head, and I survived. Nobody gets it twice."

"Are you positive that's what you had?"

"Sure enough. Same symptoms, and it was connected with swarms of mosquitoes, like this outbreak in Memphis. Now go get the wagon. I'll help the men out, so you don't have to get too close to them."

"But the folks outside aren't going to. . . ."

"Believe me. Nothing's going to break up a mob quicker than the approach of a yellow fever victim."

Paris was in a panic. During the following week, four more deaths occurred in town, two of them young children. Newspaper reports confirmed that every town along the track of the Memphis line had cases of yellow fever. Some forty families packed up all their belongings and moved far away, while innumerable others went to the countryside, hoping to escape the pernicious effects of the railroad. The streets of town were white with disinfectant. On Sept. 9th, a body was discovered along the tracks about four miles outside of town. Despite a doctor's declaration that the man had died from the effects of alcohol, it took two more days before anyone could be found to bury the body.

The disease wiped out one entire family who shared a household. The Tedros and Mrs. Tedro's parents, Mr. And Mrs. Foley, were new Irish immigrants to Paris. Mrs. Foley was the first to die, followed by the Tedros and their children, and then last, Mr. Pat Foley. E. E. Milam, the only doctor who had been willing to help Nellie with her patients, collapsed and died of yellow fever. More railroad employees joined the ranks of the sick—the station agent, a freight agent, a conductor, and several members of passing train crews. The train dispatcher walked off the job, announcing he would return in two months, if there was still anything to return to by then. Nellie's case load doubled, and then tripled, although reports from the hotel announced all patients were doing well and were expected to recover.

On the morning of September 18th, George Earnest noticed Nellie had not collected the morning breakfast supplies. He opened the door and called up the stairs, thinking she might need help. Then he stared harder at something lying at the top of the stairs. Nellie lay crumpled where she had fallen. He rushed to her, lifting her into his arms. To his relief, her eyes fluttered open and she smiled weakly. "Don't make a fuss, dear, There's nothing I need." Then she lapsed back into unconsciousness.

George bounded back down the stairs, cradling her in his arms. "Emma! Chester!"

"Oh, Lordy, What's happened to Miss Nellie?" Emma Williams stood wringing her hands.

"I'm taking her to the Yellow Fever hospital in Louisville. You and Chester will have to close up the hotel."

"But there's patients upstairs. You can't just close the door and let them die up there," Chester protested.

"Send them back to the depot. Do whatever you have to do. Don't wait for orders from me."

At the depot, he faced another argument. "There's no tickets available to Louisville until next week, Sir. The trains are booked full out of Memphis, and the locals won't let any passengers disembark here," the new station master told him. "I can't make room just because you ask for it, even if you are the boss."

"This woman is my wife, Mr. Steed, and she is in danger of losing her own life because of her efforts on behalf of this railroad. We're getting on the next train. Do you understand me?"

"Yes, Sir. I'll do what I can, but you may have to ride in the coal tender."

"Where we sit doesn't matter. What does matter is time. Every minute we waste here takes her that much closer to death."

George rode on a makeshift bench with Nellie in his arms. Shortly before they arrived at their destination, Nellie revived again, and once again she tried to smile. "Don't look so stricken, George. I'm not afraid to die."

"I won't let you die."

"Oh, yes, you will. In this case, you will not have a choice. But it's all right. During the war, I learned the meaning of a good death. I've always believed I was meant to give my life for some great cause. I thought it would be the war. Since it wasn't, I've been waiting to learn what else I was meant to do."

"Nellie. My love, I can't. . . ."

"Hush, George. Let me finish. I would have disliked growing into a cranky and idle old age. I can't imagine that. I hate leaving without you, but I don't mind the going."

Nellie Chase Earnest died in Louisville's Yellow Fever Hospital on the morning of September 20, 1878. The nursing staff gently led George from her bedside. Their worried looks indicated concern for more than his grief. He was pale, clammy, and debilitated. Two days later, he, too, died of yellow fever.

Back in Paris, the deaths continued as well. J M. Wells fell ill on the 18th and was dead on the 23rd. Mr. Thomas Lewis and his son, W. J., contracted the disease at the depot and died on the 24th. Others, who had been patients in Nellie's makeshift hospital, continued to improve. Later, the records would show that of twenty-seven cases treated by Nellie, the majority survived. Railroad employees, however, continued to fall victim to yellow fever in disproportionate numbers. Deaths in late September and early October included Mr. Beler, another freight agent, John Kayton, an engineer, and Ed Carroll, a conductor. Two brakemen and another conductor had only mild cases, but the new depot agent, W. H. Steed, succumbed, as did both Emma Williams and Chester Price. Two more doctors died, along with several nurses. Finally, on October 20, 1878, a killing frost put an end to the mosquito infestation, and along with it, any further outbreak of yellow fever.

The president of the railroad, E. D. Standiford, examined his books at the end of the epidemic. As nearly as he could tell, the L&R Railroad had 145 employees stricken with yellow fever, nearly half of whom survived. He also estimated that the company had lost over $350,000 from failed revenues. He was, however, particularly saddened by the deaths of George and Nellie Earnest, whom he had sent to the jobs that had cost them their lives.

"Do we know where the Earnests were buried?" he asked his clerk.

"Yes, we received a letter from the hospital, telling us they had a contract to bury all yellow fever patients in the Cave Hill Cemetery."

"Were their graves marked?"

"Only with simple name plaques, I believe. But we do know that they were buried side by side."

"That's not good enough. I want a monument erected to them—something dignified, but large enough to attract the attention of visitors—a stone arch, perhaps, spanning the space between them to recognize their joint efforts. It should be suitably inscribed, and dedicated with some ceremony. George Earnest and Nellie Chase gave their lives, first to the service of their country, and then to the good of this company. Their deaths were meaningful, and I will not allow them to be forgotten."

Photo courtesy of Cave Hill Cemetery, Louisville, Kentucky

AUTHOR'S NOTE

History is not the facts, not the truth, not the story of what happened. History books only record what we think we know about what happened at any given moment. The challenge for a writer of historical fiction is to take that incomplete historical record and fill in the blank spots with a plausible story—one that explains and adds to what we think we know about an event, without violating established facts.

Nellie Chase was an intensely private individual. She left behind no children, no diary, no letters. Only a few official records of her life exist: a problematic 1850 Maine Census record that may or may not refer to her family and an 1870 Kentucky Census record in her married name. The notice of her marriage has disappeared from the archives of Davidson County, Tennessee. Her badly-spelled and inaccurate obituary appeared in a Reading, Pennsylvania newspaper. A monument to her and her husband still stands in the Cave Hill Cemetery in Louisville, Kentucky. All else is hearsay.

Everything I think I know about Nellie comes from her friends, her patients, and her co-workers. The officers and men of the Hundredth Pennsylvania Regiment knew her best. Colonel Daniel Leasure often referred to her and praised her nursing care in his correspondence. His letters, and those of the other officers, are accessible in the M. Gyla McDowell Collection (Historical Records and Labor Archives, Pattee Library, Pennsylvania State University, University Park, PA). Most of the italicized quotes in this book come from that major collection.

Rev. Robert Audley Browne also wrote about her in his daily letters to his family. His opinion, however, stands in sharp contrast to the high regard in which others held her. His original letters, housed in the Browne Collection (U. S. Military History Institute, U. S. Army Heritage and Education Center, Carlyle, PA), reveal his intense dislike of the lady and his ongoing suspicions that she was a loose woman with nefarious intentions.

Many Union soldiers Nellie nursed during the Civil War wrote home about her. A one-armed man composed a lengthy tribute to her for saving his life at the Battle of Fredericksburg. That article first appeared in the New Orleans *Daily True Delta*, on Friday, January 16, 1863. Frank Moore later incorporated the story into his book, *Women of the War: Their Heroism and Self-Sacrifice* (Hartford, CT: S. S. Scranton, 1866). Moore's papers, including the anonymous letter that hounded Nellie years after the war, reside in the Moore Collection (Manuscript Department, Perkins Library, Duke University, Durham, NC).

A wonderful miscellany of information about the Hundredth Pennsylvania Regiment appears on the official Roundhead Regiment website (http://www.100thpenn.com/). Descendants of the Roundheads have opened their private family collections to make available copies of the memorials they cherish—photos, artifacts, letters, and diaries. The webmaster, David Welch, himself a Roundhead family member, has provided me with invaluable research assistance.

Then there are the stray bits: the sole extant picture of Nellie with the staff at regimental headquarters; a newspaper clipping announcing that a famous Philadelphia photographer had just issued a *carte de visite* for Miss Nellie Chase; an interview with members of the Ladies Aid Society in Philadelphia, showing that one of their agents is a Miss Chase of Nashville; a comment from a soldier that she worked in Nashville under special orders from General Rosecrans; an Army roster of the military hospitals in Nashville that lists her as head matron of General Hospital #3. From those bits and pieces, I have tried to reconstruct Nellie's life and personality.

Readers may want to know which parts of this story are factual, and which are the products of the author's imagination. Here are a few guidelines. Nellie's early years are obscure, except for Colonel Leasure's recounting of what she had revealed to him. I have used his version, although, of course, what she told him may, or may not, have been the truth. The year she spent with the Roundheads is extensively documented. We know exactly where she was and what she was doing. The reader can trace the events in William G. Gavin's *Campaigning with the Roundheads: The History of the Hundredth Pennsylvania Veteran Volunteer Infantry Regiment in the American Civil War 1861-1865* (Dayton, OH: Morningside House, Inc., 1989) or in my own historical monograph, *A Scratch with the Rebels: A Pennsylvania Roundhead and a South Carolina Cavalier* (Chicora, PA: Mechling Bookbindery, 2007). After that year, however, large gaps appear in the records. I have had to create the events that explain her departure from the Roundheads, her short tour with the New York Highlanders, and her move to Nashville. Those fictional events are, I hope, plausible in the light of what was going on during the period.

Except for the census of 1870, which shows her living in Louisville with her husband George, there is not a single mention of Nellie Chase's life between 1865 and 1878. The same gap, therefore, necessarily exists in *Beyond All Price*. The end of Nellie's life is fairly well-documented in the records of the yellow fever epidemic of 1878. That story takes its details from several historical accounts of the epidemic in Tennessee, most of which can be found in the Memphis Room of the Benjamin L. Hooks Central Library, Memphis, TN, or the Genealogy Room of the Paris Public Library.

Wherever possible, I have used the names of actual people with whom Nellie associated. Every soldier's name and service record can be found in the regimental rosters of the Civil War. The medical doctors for whom she worked, and the neighbors who shared her fate in Paris, Tennessee, are real people. The only completely fictitious characters in the novel are some of the civilians—Mrs. McMurphrey, the tavern-keeper's wife; the slave women, Bessie, Maudy, Maybelle, and little Glory; and the Sisters of Charity in Newport News.

Similarly, the locations are as accurate as I've been able to make them. The Pointe in Pittsburgh looks quite different today, and Joel Barlow's home has disappeared to make way for the elegant embassies that now occupy Kalorama Heights in Washington, DC. My descriptions of those spots take their details from photographs taken in the 1860s. Hilton Head Island's gated communities conceal much of the evidence of the old Union camp, but just off the main thoroughfare, the cemetery is still accessible and large sections of the encircling ditch and wall remain. The foliage has not changed, and it is possible almost anywhere to step a few feet off the road and find oneself in a setting Nellie might have recognized. On James Island, the pluff mud keeps waging a battle with those who would pave it over. The site of the Battle of Secessionville as been partially restored, but the mosquito squadrons guard it as ferociously as ever. Paul Hedden of J&G Tours in Charleston guided me on a tour of James Island that helped me understand the logistics of the battle.

At Beaufort, all the mentioned houses are intact. Verdier House, which served as Gen. Wright's headquarters, is now a museum, while the others remain private residences. The current owners of the Leverett House allowed me to explore their home. The interior has been remodeled to add bathrooms and a kitchen, but the original flooring and the general layout remain unchanged. The slave yard is long gone, of course, but the owners showed me where they had found remains of the cookhouse and the cistern. I based my description of the slave yard on a similar, but unrestored, antebellum property, the Aiken-Rhett House in Charleston.

The Chestnut Hill Hospital in Philadelphia became known as Mower Hospital. Despite its modern innovations, it was torn down after the war. Only the sketches and plans remain. In Nashville, the Capitol Building still overlooks the city, and the Ensley Building, central structure of Hospital #3, remains the architectural masterpiece of Courthouse Square. James A. Hoobler's *Cities under the Gun: Images of Occupied Nashville and Chattanooga* (Nashville, TN: Rutledge Hill Press, 1986) provides detailed pictures of the Nashville Nellie knew.

In Paris, Tennessee, however, nearly every trace of Nellie's life has disappeared. All possessions of yellow fever victims were burned to prevent the spread of the disease. The Railroad Hotel at 905 Depot Street remained closed until the turn of the century. It reopened during the early 1900s and then fell into disrepair after the 1940s. According to the Paris *Post-Intelligencer*, (May 4, 1974, and June 2, 2006), the city auctioned off its contents and razed the building after a series of small fires. Even the hill on which it stood was bulldozed. All that remains are the same dip in the road where stage coaches used to bog down after a rain and the train station, rebuilt but still operating in its same location across the street.

As a professional historian, I am well aware of history's tendency to ignore the contributions of women, and I hope this imaginative re-telling of Nellie's story can at last give her the credit she deserves. I am not sure, however, that Nellie herself would appreciate it. She was very much a woman of her own time, and she went out of her way to avoid drawing undue attention to herself. She wanted her life to count for something, but the only recognition she really wanted was her own. After Nellie's bout with coastal malaria at Hilton Head, Daniel Leasure wrote, "I believe she expects and wishes to die at her post, sooner or later, to the end that she may lay down a life in the service of her country that has been a burden to her." Nellie Chase was content to die when she could believe that she had contributed something worthwhile, something that bettered the lives of others. She did not find that assurance on a Civil War battlefield or in the praise of those who called her the "Florence Nightingale of the West." Nellie Chase found the cause for which to lay down her life in a railroad hotel in a small Tennessee town.

Carolyn Poling Schriber received her Ph.D. in Medieval History from the University of Colorado. After she retired from her position as a history professor at Rhodes College in Memphis, Tennessee, she focused her research on the history of America's Civil War. In 2007 she published *A Scratch with the Rebels: A Pennsylvania Roundhead and a South Carolina Cavalier,* which documented the experiences of the 100th Pennsylvania Volunteer Regiment during the first year of the war. *Beyond All Price* is a historical novel based on the people in that regiment.